Taken with a Dark Desire:

The Underworlds.

A Novel By: Dennis Scheel©.

Thanks to the inspiration by Stella, the aid by Devon and the awesome editing by Alex.

Dedicated to my treasure Yoshi, the sweet dog who helped save me

Also written by Dennis Scheel
NO WAY BACK- THE UNDERWORLDS

Prologue

Screams of terror sounded in all directions, but Claus was not concerned, as he had his own terror to deal with. Time in Hell felt eternal for each soul. Claus might have been suffering torment for decades as time passed differently here than in the Underworld, as it did between the Underworld and Earth.

Claus held onto his sanity by nursing his hatred for Denida who'd handed him over to Lucifer.

"Enjoying yourself?" Lucifer appeared and gave a devious grin.

Lucifer never paid the slightest attention to the torture surrounding him, somehow making the suffering worse, Claus had noticed.

Fear and anger warring in Claus' soul, he glared at Lucifer.

"What do you expect? I'm in hell, not on vacation," Claus spat out discontent.

Lucifer just smiled back at him. "What would you say, if I had a way for you to buy back your freedom, a way to get back at Denida?"

The same damn smug look on Lucifer's face he remembered from the Underworld, but painful hope blossomed in Claus.

"How?"

Lucifer's smile broadened and suddenly they were inside his throne room.

I know this place. The lack of torment made Claus dizzy. *Denida was here, this is Lucifer's throne, where the Gate is!*

"Denida has two weaknesses. Nina and Daniel," Lucifer said. "Nina is too headstrong... Daniel on the other hand..." Lucifer chuckled.

Am I hearing right? "You want me to kidnap Daniel? Why?"

Lucifer chuckled. "Denida with his ring is too strong even for me. Bring me the ring, you have your freedom!"

Claus' mouth twisted into a smile. *My freedom!* And a way to make Denida suffer too. Anything was bound to be better than being tortured in hell, after all.

Claus' hatred and hope burned in his soul. "I like that idea."

"We have a deal then?" Lucifer held out his hand.

Claus had a small glint of red within his eyes as he grabbed Lucifer's hand and shook it. "We do!"

Chapter 1: Kidnapped

Daniel was playing with his friends, the ball got thrown across the field. As Daniel ran to fetch the ball, his two guards moved to follow him, never letting him out of sight. Three months before, Daniel would have complained, but after the journey he'd been through with his Dad, he'd actually argued against only having two. He'd had enough adventure for a lifetime, and planned to never get within sight range of a gate again. Waving at the guards, Daniel ran back to his game. This was more fun than following his dad around, and safer too.

Daniel passed the ball off to his friend, who kicked it back. A kid on the other team intercepted the pass and everyone chased him, yelling and laughing. Though the smoldering heat had them dripping with sweat, this was exactly what Daniel wanted to do.

He kicked the ball wrong and it flew over the fence. He laughed and shook his head and ran to get it while the rest grabbed cold drinks from their bags.

Around three o'clock, one of his guards cleared his throat. Daniel ignored it and grabbed a sandwich. The same guard cleared his throat again, this time more heavily. Daniel glanced in his direction, before turning to his friends again. The other guard started walking impatiently towards Daniel.

Daniel noticed from the corner of his eye. He sighed and stood up. "I've got to go."

The two bodyguards escorted Daniel to the car. It was a walk which took a few minutes. The closest bodyguard next to Daniel gave him his jacket. "Had fun with your friends?"

Daniel nodded, these last few months had really helped in putting him at ease, though he'd never forget what happened. When they'd talked about guards, his father had shown Daniel his ring. *If Dad feels we should, it must be true.*

A car slammed into their car. Another set of vehicles surrounded them, men in battle gear rushed out of the trucks, they kneeled and readied their guns. The guard in the passenger's seat ducked. The strangers started shooting the car's front seat.

The guard raised his head as the bullets were zinging. He pushed Daniel to the floor as the other guard was shot full of holes. The guard shouted for help into his radio, then as the shooting paused he jumped out and started returning fire.

First man reloading went down, second too, the third reached for his sidearm, he returned fire, the guard dropped, his gun clattering on the road.

The men rushed to a shocked Daniel and dragged him out of the car.

Daniel glanced at the guards, lying lifeless. His eyes went wide with shock. He didn't even know their names, but in seconds they'd died for him. He glanced over at the men taking him. Though they were armed to the teeth, Daniel yanked free and ran back, but men circled around him. He sent a gust of wind at them with his hands and several fell over, but rough hands grabbed him from behind and hauled him to a car.

Dad should have taught me something stronger. Daniel tried to scream, but they had picked a good spot to ambush them, and nobody was around to hear him.

4

One guard put his gun to Daniel's head.

"Shut up, kid."

They drove away, as fast as they had ambushed them. One of the guards zip tied Daniel, tight.

They positioned their guns at Daniel's face.

"Don't try anything," one of them said with an intense look. "No magic, either!"

"What do you want with me," Daniel asked, while the car swerved around corners. "My Dad's the President of the Underworld, he'll give you whatever you desire!"

One of the men with the guns chuckled a little. "We know who you are, Daniel."

This is not good... Daniel looked around the van, which had no windows, he tried to focus to hear if they passed anything he would know; nothing stood out.

Where are they taking me?

***

The remaining car, which had been shot full of holes, was not left alone for long, as the distress call had a team dispatched.

The Colonel arrived with the backup team.

Crap. The Colonel didn't like the sight which met him. This was way too professional for his taste. Daniel was Denida's son, there'd be no keeping him away.

The Colonel kneeled to the guard next to the car. *He must've fought, what about the other?* He glanced inside of the car.

"He died on impact," a medic said.

The Colonel sighed. *Why were they parked in this remote place?* "Nobody heard or saw anything?"

The medic shook his head. "It was too far away from the others..."

Professional... doesn't bode well- damn them, not being more careful!

Denida arrived, just as the Colonel finished that very thought. He wore gloves everywhere now.

He wanted to hide the magic ring. He also had an eye patch over his right eye to cover his dark side. The Colonel imagined the red rising in his friend's eye.

Denny's more determined nowadays since the Gate, yet this still happened...

Denida examined the guard, who laid covered in blood next to the car, full of bullet holes. He walked over to the car. He walked around and glanced at the back seat. "No bullets," he muttered. He squinted his eyes, sniffed at an open place, a little away from the car. He walked over. "Magic," he mumbled.

The Colonel wrinkled his forehead.

Denida took off his glove and rubbed his ring. An image appeared of Daniel sending off a gust of wind, but getting overpowered from behind. He put the glove back on and shook his head. "They overpowered him, they haven't used magic..."

He came over to the Colonel. "Do tell me you have something- anything!"

The Colonel wished he could say something, he tried to reassure him. "They took Daniel, he seems to be unhurt at least. Don't know who, they were professionals though, knowing when and where to hit." The Colonel scratched his forehead. "Why did they park here though, so far away from the others?"

Denida glanced towards the car and around the surroundings. "Daniel felt secure here, somewhere where nobody was." He raised his eyebrow. "-but whoever it was, were prepared." Denida sighed. "Find out who, find me Daniel!"

Denida went back towards his car.

The Colonel knew Denida would ask for a search, that's why he had already ordered it, throughout all the Underworld, to hopefully find Denida's son. He glanced at the bodies again. *I doubt it'll be that easy though, I better not worry Denida- he could have been wrong, after all.* He rubbed his forehead.

***

Denida fretted. He'd made a mistake easing off security for Daniel. Now he had to tell Nina their son had been taken because of his choice. *Not looking forward to that conversation.*

"Dynasty," he told his driver when he returned to his car.

He glanced out the window on his way to Dynasty. The drive felt endless. The beauty of the scenery usually lifted his spirits, but he didn't care today. They finally reached Dynasty and Nina.

The car stopped, but Denida just sat there, trying to gather the courage to go see Nina. He stroked his ring, hoping it would calm him. As he sat there he realized something; he would never get the courage, procrastinating only made it worse. He sighed and climbed out of the car.

Denida hailed the butler over. "Where's Nina at?"

The Butler titled his head towards the stables. "Angel."

Nina was out riding her horse Angel, with Daniel being more mature now, she had the time to enjoy her hobby. She loved all her animals, but especially Angel. Denida hoped it meant she'd be in good spirits.

Denida walked towards the stables and stood for a moment watching her brush Angel. Nina never failed to take his breath away. She was in the middle of brushing the favorite of her horses. He smiled as he walked up to her, still trying to gather the courage to tell her.

Nina put the brush down and wrapped him in a hug, kissing him hello.

Denida gave her a half hug.

"What's the matter, you're blocking your thoughts, why?" Nina's hands tightened on his shirt.

Denida took a deep breath. "It's Daniel…"

7

Nina's eyes got wide. "What?"

"His escort was attacked… his two guards were killed… he disappeared," Denida stuttered.

"Disappeared," Nina yelled. "Not again, I just got him back from the Gates!"

Denida sighed, he was too embarrassed to look her in the eyes.

Nina's face tightened. "Wait, two? I thought he had more protecting him?"

Denida ground his teeth and looked down at his feet. "I changed it. Nobody wanted to get me after Claus was beaten, I wanted to give him some peace…" Denida awaited her outburst, but nothing came. All that came was silence. "Daniel and I talked-"

"You told *my* son, a child, and not me?" Nina pushed Denida.

Nina turned away from Denida and stroked her horse.

"The Colonel is trying to find him," Denida wanted to ease her anger, but she gave him no answer.

Denida felt uneasy, an outburst was better. *Anything other than her silence!* He sighed. "I regret it deeply, but-"

"Denida." The butler walked into the stable and handed Denida an envelope. The man's hand shook, and Denida would swear he'd been running.

"I was cleaning-"

Denida waved his hand dismissably. "Not now, just put it in my office."

The butler tried to smile at Nina. "- this appeared in the air in front of me; it said Daniel's name."

Denida and Nina focused on the envelope. She reached out towards it, but stopped. Denida glanced over at her before he opened it.

Inside it was a letter that turned by magic into a hologram of Daniel sitting in a cell. He heaved a sigh as they watched.

"Daniel," Nina screamed, but there was no response, so she yelled repeatedly.

"It must be one way." Denida pointed at the wall behind Daniel. "The time- it must be live!"

Nina grabbed at Denida's arm. "But Daniel!"

A voice Denida didn't know said; "Want your son back, give us the ring!"

"Ring?" Nina muttered, clearly confused at what the voice meant, but Denida knew exactly what he meant.

'Our magic has been shielded with a cloaking Spell, so don't bother trying!' The feed abruptly cut off.

Nina frantically stared at Denida. "Can't you?"

"I'll try!" Denida ripped off his glove and squeezed his fist as tight as he could, sweat dripping, Denida ground his teeth and grabbed his hand tight with his other hand. *Nothing…* He shook his head and put his glove back on.

Nina patted Denida on the shoulder.

"I'll take it to the Colonel."

Before Nina could say anything, Denida had run out of the stable. He headed back to the car. His security detail jogged out of the house to meet him, but he was in too much of a rush. He jumped into his car and with squealing tires sped off.

Chapter 2: Daniel's Idea

At the Underworld Headquarters everyone ran frantically around. This chaos was the first thing Denida noticed. *Panicky around here.* He walked to the elevator and clicked to the floor, which held the Colonel's office.

The Colonel lifted his head as he heard the elevator sound and Denida coming out. "Something's up," he muttered.

The soldier he stood with raised his eyebrows at the Colonel. "Sir? Something the matter?"

"It's nothing." The Colonel smiled. "What did you want to show me?"

"Oh yes-"

Denida slammed the envelope down on top of the other papers the Colonel held. "The ones who took Daniel contacted me- they used magic-" He glanced at the soldier next to the Colonel. "they want the *ring!*"

"Really?" The Colonel was surprised at what he just heard, only a few knew about the ring. "Lucifer, again?"

Denida shook his head. "Guess it's possible, but I don't think so."

The Colonel glanced back at the letter. He turned it around and felt the paper, even sniffed at it if he could find out anything from it, there didn't seem to be any obvious signs. "Can you tell, who put the spell on it- or if it was Dark Magic?"

Denida nodded intrigued. "Daniel used magic, there was an imprint of it. They didn't!" He stared into the Colonel's eyes. "-yet the letter has magic, but if it were Dark..." Denida shook his head. "I don't know who, nor if it was Light or Dark magic..."

The Colonel handed the letter over to the soldier. "Get it examined, find me something!"

The soldier nodded and ran off with the letter.

The Colonel walked with Denida towards the elevator. "Doesn't Dan oversee the Gates; wouldn't he know how to contact the other Underworlds?"

"He does," Denida nodded. *Dan has connections in the Underworlds, up to World 8.* "I see what you're saying, I'll go see Dan!" He jumped into the elevator.

Denida ground his teeth and hurried out when the elevator reached the bottom. He went towards the lab, which held the Gate within.

Dan had made progress with the Gates and staying in touch in between the worlds, so he would know if anyone had any information. If not, Dan could contact the Warlock, who might.

Inside the lab, Dan was busy talking to the Colonel from world 3, the next world to theirs.

"It's always nice-" the Colonel in the other world froze and got a look of resentment on his face.

Dan turned to look behind him, his eyes widened.

Denida smiled as their eyes met, he and this Colonel were still not on the best terms. "Hello, Colonel."

"We should continue later," the Colonel said, a chill clear in his voice.

Dan nodded with a smile. "Hi, Denny, something wrong? Thought you wanted to avoid the Gates personally?"

Denida nodded. "Daniel has been taken, Dark Magic seems to be involved. I can't avoid it now- heard anything from the other worlds?"

"What!" Dan gasped. "How-" He shook his head regretfully. "Really? Want me to send a feed to the Warlock? It won't take long..."

Denida nodded. He suspected from the moment he felt the magic on the letter he'd have to talk to the Warlock. She was the best in her world, maybe in all the Underworlds.

They just needed to get the Warlock to come to the robot in her world, which shouldn't take long. Denida paced about in the lab, while he waited impatiently. He glanced at the big Gate, which stood in the center of the lab, he sighed and rubbed his ring with his thumb.

"Denida," the Warlock ecstatically said with a smile. "How nice to see you again!"

"Not a social call." Denida ground his teeth. "Daniel has been kidnapped, they used Dark Magic on a letter to show a video feed of him. Any guess on who it could be?"

The Warlock kneeled, she gasped and reached as if to touch the robot, then her face hardened. "You do know, Lucifer still has demons in your world- and that spell requires very strong Dark Magic."

"More? Who?" Was my mistake bigger, lowering his security? There are still demons here?

"When your Dark Angels fell, were there any left, other than *Danyel*, the Dark Angel, who escaped?"

Left? Denida pondered the question. There were several who escaped when Danyel had, they had been on the most wanted list since. "Only low-level ones..."

"The Scientist! The one who helped Claus!" Dan shrugged.

Denida sighed. *Claus...*

"Very bland name," the Warlock said, "but who was he in Hell?"

Denida shrugged. "I don't know- maybe-" He glanced over at Dan. "We should ask Lucifer…"

"Might be a good idea," the Warlock replied. "but remember to take anything the Devil says with a grain of salt…"

Denida turned to Dan, their eyes interlocked, he didn't want to ever have any contact with Hell or Lucifer again, but it seemed he had to if he wanted to find out who this Scientist was, and he *did want to find out.*

***

Daniel had been taken to a remote location. The room he was in had a sensation he'd hoped he would never have to feel again. *This is Dark Magic, I'm sure of it!* A magic barrier sealed the room. The men had thrown him in and left him. Daniel took stock of his cell. *Am I ever gonna get out? Can I even?* It was big enough but held nothing but a bed, a sink and a toilet; it was not a place he would enjoy staying in.

Whoever took me, planned it for a while. What can they possibly want? That one guy from the van, said he knew exactly who I am, they have a clear intention, maybe for Dad?

The door burst open, startling Daniel. Several men stinking of Dark magic entered.

"I don't think you realize what my Dad is!" Daniel crossed his arms defiantly.

One of his guards smiled at him. "We do realize, that's why we took you!"

Not going to get anywhere that way. "Why are you all here now? Want to let me out?" Daniel smiled with as dear puppy eyes, as he could at them.

"We're just setting up a camera." The guard laughed and peered back at the other guards, who were setting it up.

"You want to watch me," Daniel glanced over at the big mirror on the wall. "but you already have one, don't you?"

"We're keeping watch," the guard replied and walked out with the rest.

Daniel glimpsed suspiciously at the camera. They had one set up, wonder why they didn't just set both up before they brought me here? Everything else has been prepared for me...

Daniel sat staring into the camera, which had a red blinking as if it was recording.

If only I can find a way to convince them, then maybe I can persuade them to let me go.

Another guard came in, bringing Daniel food.

And there's a shield here, I can't do anything- or can I? Daniel stared at the guard. I'm too small to try force on him.

Daniel smiled at the guard, making sure to get eye contact. "Do you really know *what* my Dad is?"

The guard wrinkled his forehead puzzled at Daniel's question. "We know he's the President." He put Daniel's food down.

"But do you not know *WHAT* he is?" Daniel insisted.

The guard stopped on his way to the door. He turned back to Daniel. "You want to tell me I should fear him, perhaps?" He chuckled.

Daniel shook his head. "So, you really have no idea what he is."

"I know who he is," the guard asserted.

Daniel shrugged. "Not whom, *what!*"

"All right, I'll bite," the guard replied. "You know something I don't? Do tell me, *WHAT* is he then," the guard smirked at the camera.

This could work, I'm halfway there... Daniel smiled. "My Dad told me, long ago when he was born, of how everything changed..."

14

"He told a child?" The guard grinned scornfully.

Daniel glared at the guard but smiled. "You may remember the Gates, after my Dad and I came out of it, my Dad told me his story the first time to anyone since he remembered…"

The guard wrinkled his forehead. "Remembered?"

"After he got the ring, he remembered everything…"

Chapter 3: Daniel's Story

It was a cold winter month, the blizzard had been raging throughout the entire month, it was a coincidence, so no one thought of it. The gods of Norse Mythology, who were left in the wild, all overthrown by God, no one thought of them anymore.

When the raging of the weather came, as a hint of something approaching, there was one person who did notice; the last President of all the Underworlds. The President decided that the one thing he could do was to go see Odin and his fellow gods, as they might know what was up. Even though pushed away to the fringe, Odin could see what was happening in the world.

As the President entered Valhalla, he could feel very clearly, by the looks he got, something was up. He weaved through the permanent party which is Valhalla, straight to see Odin, who was sitting next to his sparrow on his throne when the President came in.

"You know my answer," Odin said as soon as he entered, not turning around to look at him, but dropped more grain in his palm and held it up for his sparrow to peck at.

"I feel it in the air, something *IS* up," the President said, but Odin didn't move a muscle. The President examined around him, something he realized; *there was no sign of Thor there!* "The weather has been raging on Earth, where's Thor?"

This made Odin turn towards the President. "You're meddling in stuff which doesn't concern you! We'll tell you nothing."

The President met Odin's gaze for a moment before he turned and stalked out of Valhalla. He needed to take precautions; whatever it was would be big.

As the winter days went by, the days got shorter. On the night of the shortest day of the year, the President got a visit by his old friend Archangel Gabriel.

The President's gut twinged, this couldn't be a coincidence.

"Gabriel? Why are you here?"

Gabriel tried to smile, but it only looked like a twitch. "Both God and Lucifer are starting to act worried. You've met with Odin, do you know why?"

Gabriel couldn't ask Odin himself since God had taken Earth from them, this the President knew. *True, Valhalla doesn't like God...* The President shook his head. "Odin wouldn't tell me, but something's up!"

Gabriel nodded.

The day before Jesus' birthday, the 24th of December, everything went bad. All of Heaven and Hell, even all the magical world could feel it was coming.

A blizzard raged on Earth. But as bad as it was on Earth, it was nothing in comparison to Heaven. Gabriel had been summoned to God, and only him. Gabriel sighed, he didn't like being the archangel who needed to deal with God's misdeeds.

God came down from his throne to greet Gabriel.

Gabriel glanced curiously at his Lord. He had not seen him like this, since the day he had thrown Lucifer from Heaven. "What do you need?"

God peered around him, he turned back to Gabriel. "I need you to do something a little special for me!"

Gabriel lifted his eyebrows.

"When we left our old world, our Lord prophesied something only Lucifer and I heard." God beheld around himself once more. "Our Lord was mad we destroyed her world and wanted vengeance, so it was a prophecy *against* Lucifer and me…"

Gabriel's eyes widened. He gasped. "A prophecy?"

"She would get her justice! Someday a child with a power unlike any other would be born." God beheld an intense glare at Gabriel. "This child will set all the injustices right, *in* its childhood years…"

"You think that time is now?"

"You feel it too, the change in magic, I know you do!" God insisted. "The child has to die, it can't be allowed to live."

Gabriel sighed.

"I already weakened the child, it'll be born early, sick and ready for you."

"Me? But won't Lucifer want it dead too?" Gabriel objected.

"I don't care if *your* friend kills it- or you do, just make sure it dies tonight."

"This is what the President meant," Gabriel muttered.

God wrinkled his forehead.

Gabriel shook his head. "Just someone I gotta see…"

He hurried to see the President, as he needed to be fast, so he would be able to prepare in a way that seemed he was doing God's bidding.

The President examined for a clue on Gabriel's face, which clearly showed concern.

"It's time," Gabriel just said.

The President nodded in agreement.

The child was being born in Europe on Earth, under the overweighing cloud of a blizzard at Christmas, the day before Jesus' birthday, but God didn't care, he wanted him to be born as soon as possible, so he could die, at last.

There's only one place I can go get help...

The people of Valhalla all had eyes at him with suspicion, just like the last time, he was here. And just like last time, he had no time to deal with them. He weaved his way through the crowds into Odin's chamber. Thor was here this time.

"Not you again," Odin remarked when he saw the President entering.

"You may want to listen to me this time!"

Everyone in the room turned towards Odin when the President said that.

"God wants to kill a chosen child!"

"We know- if he succeeds, he succeeds." Odin stroked his bird.

The President was surprised, he couldn't believe what he just heard. "Am I hearing you right?" he asked. "Did you not hear me?"

"We can't help you!" Odin stood up and stomped his staff onto the ground. "You best leave if you know what's good for you."

The old gods stood and walked toward the President, loosening their axes and swords. He took a deep breath and backed away. He sighed. *I'll have to do it myself.* He glanced down at the ring he rarely used, but maybe this was the time. He was sure after this morning, *everything* would change.

He arrived at the Hospital, where the destined child was to be born, but he was met by a face he knew, the leader of one of the Underworlds.

I wonder why he's here? Can it be something to do with the dimensional rifts? He went over to him.

19

"Why are you here? I sent messages, that the gates were to be disassembled!"

"I wanted to know, why you wanted this now?"

The President sighed. "A legend has come to fruition, which is crucial to the Underworld, we need it to protect it, at whatever the cost."

The man nodded and walked away.

The President continued to the maternity ward, he stopped; his eyes fixed on a man. *A demon!* He stormed over towards the demon.

While the President went after the demon, Gabriel arrived at the Hospital to do what God had told him to do. Gabriel, as an Archangel, knew exactly where the child was. It was weak. The observation room it lay in was empty of nurses, but someone was in there with the child, hovering over him, Gabriel knew this person very well. It was the prince of Darkness.

"Lucifer?" Gabriel asked cautiously.

He slowly walked up to Lucifer looking down at the boy in the crib. "You're here to kill him like God wanted?"

Lucifer smiled at Gabriel. "How wrong his mindset is! This little boy has all the power our old Lord did, why kill him, when you can harvest it?"

"You want to devour his soul?" Gabriel threw up his arms.

"No, train it in Hell, to be a master of Darkness!" Lucifer smiled deviously. "His power can be used in the service of Darkness!"

Lucifer lifted the soul from the baby in the crib. He smiled back at Gabriel at what he had in his grip. And with a look of joy in his eyes, he and the soul of the child vanished. Behind Gabriel, the President ran in gasping for breath, after a battle with the demon, he had met. He had a wound, which was bleeding over his right eye.

"It is too late," Gabriel said with a sorrowful tone.

The President walked up to him. He saw the child in the crib without a soul.

"There's no choice then," the President said and turned to Gabriel. "We must go to Hell, to get him back!"

Gabriel appeared in Hell in a flash of light, he found Lucifer within his throne room, with the baby laying on the floor, which had a giant pentagram around it. There were several demons around the baby, who seemed more interested in the baby than Lucifer himself.

"Lucifer? What do you plan to do with the child?" Gabriel asked.

"Nurture him and train him in the Dark Arts!"

"But God wants him dead! He will not just let you have him." Gabriel peered at him in disbelief.

"Simple," Lucifer smirked. "Tell God, I killed his soul, he won't be able to feel the child's lifeforce."

Gabriel nodded solemnly.

"The child is now destined to grow up in hell, or his soul anyway. And his human form to be barren without a soul to protect him forever more."

Gabriel glanced at the child that now had demon eyes all around him.

Lucifer went over to Gabriel and patted him. "Don't worry, my friend- this is a new beginning."

The President appeared next to the Gate, which lead into Hell from world 8, thanks to his ring.

He had been to Hell a few times before, but unlike Gabriel, he didn't know it that well, and the demons there, didn't know him. But, what he did know, was that he needed to find the child's soul before it got the mark of Dark Magic.

The President forced the demons to bring him to Lucifer's mansion. Whoever tried to stop him, he killed. The demons fled as Lucifer came out to meet him.

"An intruder," Lucifer chuckled. He never had that, so he was curious. "President! What a surprise."

"Lucifer," the President said, covered with demon's blood. "I'm here for the child!"

Lucifer smiled even more at that. "You and what army?"

"This!" The President raised his hand in a swift motion and sent a force of energy towards him.

A gust of wind blew towards Lucifer, it increased in force as it got closer, sending the other demons into the sky. Though Lucifer stood as it was nothing, his mansion got torn up and flew into the wind. As the force increased, Lucifer started to get hit with debris. He flickered his fingers, ending the wind. The mess was annoying Lucifer. "Is this all you got? Cause I can do so much more."

Lucifer smiled back at him, raised his hand, repairing the damage in seconds, then sauntered towards his mansion, tons of demons swarmed the grounds.

"But why should I deal with little you?" Lucifer lowered his hand and smiled back at him. "I think you have enough, to keep you busy."

The President swung his hand over his head sending demons flying in all directions. He ran into the mansion.

The mansion was a labyrinth of hallways and doors. He rubbed the ring.

Where?

'That way.'

The President pushed through the door the ring indicated.

Lucifer turned to look at the President from where he stood leering at the child. "You don't give up easily, I see," Lucifer said with a smile. "You won't get the child, he's here to stay."

Lucifer and the President were suddenly outside again, away from the child.

"I'll get the child; you won't stop me!" The President put his hands together and started to form a ball of energy.

Lucifer chuckled. "Why don't we have some fun then!"

He disappeared into the air and surrounded the President with a Cloud of Darkness.

The President tried to shoot balls of energy after Lucifer, but it did nothing to harm him.

As the air around the President got darker and darker, the maliciousness in the air grew heavier.

He realized now, he wasn't going to get the child, he wasn't even going to make it out alive, as the ring on his finger was nowhere powerful enough to overcome the Devil.

There's only one choice. He touched the ring one last time.

It dissolved from his finger, appearing in the place he'd prepared.

For Denny to find when the day is ripe!

The Darkness grew so thick the President could hardly see his hands in front of him.

Lucifer resurfaced in front of him, grinning with the change. "Ready to die, Mr. President?"

The President did want to say something, but he'd used his last energy sending the ring away.

"What?" Lucifer's grin faded, as he could see something was not right on his face. "No smart-ass remarks? So disappointing. In that case..."

Fires appeared around Lucifer, as to prevent any force of magic hitting him.

He must still think the ring's here.

Lucifer moved towards the President, who knew what was coming, he had no way to fight it now. The fire in Lucifer's eyes was glowing, as he approached him.

"Why do you even want this child?"

Lucifer stopped. "A child which has more power than me and God put together! Kill that, as God wants? Never,

23

much better to use it." Lucifer had an evil, devious look on his face. "But you won't experience it!" He pulled his hand, with the fire surrounding it, into the President's body, and ripped out his heart.

The President fell in front of Lucifer's feet, who now dropped the heart and kneeled to take the ring from the corpse's hand.

But there was no ring, not on his hand, not on the other one either.

Lucifer searched frantically through the President's pockets.

"You won't find anything." Gabriel came up to him. "He was prepared, he always was!"

Lucifer stood with a face as black as the darkness around him.

"We need to talk…"

"What?" Lucifer stared at him angrily.

"God wants the child dead, if he dies, he'll know where the soul is…"

Lucifer chuckled to himself. "Simple! He won't cause of the demons watching him."

"What demons?"

"The ones I am sending to Earth!" Lucifer walked away, out through the Darkness, which now dissipated.

Gabriel glanced down at his friend, lying dead on the ground. "Sorry, old friend."

***

"… and that is how my Dad was chosen!" Daniel smirked at the guard.

"I already knew he was in Hell." The guard left him there and locked the cell behind him.

Daniel ogled the mirror. "You won't be able to keep me here, my Dad will come looking for me," Daniel yelled, but there was no response. He sat down, buried his head between his legs. "How long will they keep me here?" he muttered.

On the other side of the screen Claus stood, watching Daniel, he never had heard this story of Denida's birth.

"He told you a very interesting tale, I see..." Claus glanced over at the guard. "If he wants to continue it, let him."

The guard nodded.

"It will be a benefit to know, what Denida has told him..." Claus left the room. He knew what he had to do- or wanted to do.

He went into his private room. This room was Dark, Claus set fire to candles throughout the room, and turned to face the pentagram in the middle of the room. He sat down on top of it, with his eyes closed, humming chants.

Darkness fell over the room and surrounded him.

Claus continued with his chant until a Dark being appeared in a cloud in front of him.

"Master!" Claus opened his eyes and smiled.

"Claus. What do you want? Have you gotten the ring yet?"

Claus shook his head. "Soon, but-"

"No buts, we're done then..." The Dark presence started fading.

"Daniel, his son mentioned Denida's birth," Claus spoke quickly.

The Dark Presence reappeared. "Yes?"

Claus smiled. "He said God wanted him dead, but you took his soul? By the help of Archangel Gabriel."

"This concerns you?" The Dark Presence asked.

"... And you killed the former President of the Underworlds?"

The Dark Presence had a flicker of red, it got heavier in the room. "You have a question?"

"But he shafted you with the ring of the Underworlds?"

25

"The ring was lost for thirty years, yes. That's all you need to know."

As soon as it said that, the spirit vanished again, leaving Claus alone in the dark room.

I do need to know more about Daniel's story.

Chapter 4: Tales From Hell

So much to do. Denida wanted everything ready. He had gone to the forest next to Dynasty, for what he needed; *to be alone, where no one can see.*

"Reficul, Reficul, Reficul," he chanted, after scoping the surroundings.

As the times before, Lucifer appeared right in front of him in his human form.

"Denny!" Lucifer smiled at him.

"Lucifer," Denida wasn't happy about it, but he had to see him. "You still have demons in *my world*?"

"A few." Lucifer chuckled. "Why do you ask?"

"The Scientist!"

Lucifer made a face, to show he clearly knew who he meant. "Jack."

"So, you do know him. Do you have any control of this *demon*?"

Lucifer shook his head.

Denida ground his teeth. "Do you have any involvement with my son's kidnapping?"

"Of course not! I want you to come back to Hell willingly."

Lucifer and Denida stared deep into each other's eyes. Is he serious? Can Lucifer really be trusted?

"Fine, but I never will!" Denida started to walk away.

"You will," Lucifer yelled at him with a chuckle.

Denida went back to see the Colonel.

"The Scientist, Jack, is a demon of Lucifer's. He's our prime suspect!"

"Lucifer took Daniel?" The Colonel gazed confused at Denida, who shook his head.

"I don't think so, but the Scientist, I think he's responsible…"

"I'll find him!" The Colonel ran over to one of his soldiers.

"Denny!" Nina stormed in and ran up to Denida. "There are still demons here? Why didn't you tell me?" Nina jabbed at Denida's chest accusingly.

"I don't-"

"No! Don't even bother. Dan told me of your conversation with your Warlock."

"There's just one. We're looking for *the Scientist*. He had a big role with the Dark Angels."

"You first thought of it now?" Nina got a menacing look, her eyes got cold.

Denida shrugged. "I didn't know he was a demon before."

Nina peeked around the room at all the eyes watching them.

"Don't worry Nina, we'll find him." The Colonel came back over to where Nina was.

***

Daniel peered up at the guard, who brought him food. He didn't say anything though.

The guard slid the tray onto the table. "Want to tell me the rest of your story, if you have more?"

28

I've got him curious, I so can do this! "I do, what can I call you?"

The Guard glanced at the mirror, he licked his lips and nodded. "Edward."

Daniel snickered, of course they'd have a recorder. "OK, Edward." Daniel nodded happily. "My Dad was in Hell for a long time. Time passes slower in Hell, even slower than in the Underworld."

"I know…" Edward sat down opposite Daniel.

"As a soul, he was showered with Dark Magic, Lucifer set his demons to train him as a regular demon."

***

A scream echoed throughout Hell.

"Den, you're gonna make the other demons jealous."

"Why would I?" Den sarcastically smirked at his friend.

"Because you seem to be incredibly good…"

"So?" Denida grinned. "the harder they are to break, the better!"

"You mean the worse they scream."

Denida raised his eyebrows with a leer.

A scream echoed through Hell, and Gabriel winced but stayed invisible to the boys.

The boy sure has grown… Gabriel grumbled. *If only Lucifer had listened.* He was watching him, at every chance he got, Den, as he was known as, seemed to be really good at wielding the Dark Arts.

"Hello…" Gabriel appeared where the boys could see him.

"Who are you? Do I know you?"

"Yes, I am Lucifer's friend, my name's Gabriel."

"I see, the *Master's*!"

Gabriel twitched a little at that remark. "Yes, you like being a demon?"

"Of course, I serve the Master by helping with the new arrivals!" Den's eyes glowed red, as he said that.

"Maybe it's too late," Gabriel muttered.

Den raised an eyebrow.

"Nothing important," Gabriel said.

**

"No!" Claus stormed in. "Not possible, he's not a demon."

"My... hello Claus. You're here." Daniel's eyes widened. "Does that mean Lucifer sent you here?"

Claus motioned Edward to leave. "Lock it from the other side!"

This can't be good. "What can I help with?"

"You're right, Lucifer *did* send me. But that's all you're right about."

"You really think I'm wrong? Why else does Lucifer want him back, so badly," Daniel gloated. "That's why you're here, no?"

Claus shook his head. "He doesn't! He wants his ring."

Interesting. "You mean the ring no one but Dad can use?"

Claus' face turned cold.

I've got him!

"Watch him," Claus yelled at Edward as he stormed out.

Edward inspected confused at Daniel. "Shall we continue?"

Claus must be watching too, perfect. "Of course," Daniel smirked.

**

The fiery days of Hell, what a break. 'You are to go to Earth to gather souls first hand.' What a joy!

Den went to Earth, accompanied by other demons.

So many to play with. Den had a glee in the eyes. There's a familiarity to this world, why's this?

"Don't you worry about that."

Den turned around to see a man standing there. "You're a demon?"

The man nodded. "I'm Luci, I hear you're good at capturing the hardest souls?"

Den nodded. I'll show him!

He went out into the street and turned back to Luci.

"Just tell me who you want, I'll deliver them." A glow appeared in Den's eyes as he said it.

"Alright, I'll bite," Luci chuckled with a glee in his voice and went over to Den.

He spectated the surrounding and turned back to Den. "The kid, deliver me his soul."

"You don't want to make it harder?" Den grinned. "Fine, I'll be back."

Den chuckled, as he walked towards the kid, who was playing in the sand. "Wanna play?"

The boy nodded at Den and they started to play. Luci watched curiously.

"Hey, I know of a way to have more fun, a way to have so many times more, no one would ever stop the fun," Den said after a while playing with the boy.

"How?" the boy scrutinized him curiously.

"If you walk up to that man behind me, say you give him your soul, he'll grant your every wish."

The boy glanced at Luci and back at Den. "Really?"

Den nodded. The boy stood up and went over to Luci.

Den smirked, as he leered at Luci with the boy approaching Luci.

"Hello, Mister. You'll give me anything I want for my soul?"

Den went back to training in Hell, amongst his demon friends. He and his friend, Danyel enjoyed messing around with the new arrival of souls.

"Den," their teacher yelled, interrupting the time of enjoying their fun with the new souls.

Den went over to his teacher disappointed. "Yes?"

"The Master wants you, come with me."

The master? Den was led to a mansion on the darkest side in Hell, that no demons even dared to approach; Lucifer's mansion, it often changed the location to ward off intruders. Den was brought here for a *purpose.*

A demon guided him into a room with a throne. On the throne, was the man he saw on Earth, allegedly the Master of Darkness, Lucifer.

"Master," Den and his teacher said and kneeled.

"Leave us!"

Den was left alone with Lucifer.

"What can I do for you, my Master?"

"Rise. You've got a talent for the Dark Arts. You got the soul *easy*! What do you say to I train you in advanced Dark Arts?"

What did I just hear? "You want to teach me?"

"Yes, you have a gift."

Den's mouth gawked. "But Master Lucifer."

"Call me Luci. Your friends call you Denny, no?"

"Or Den." Denny nodded. "Yes, Luci…"

Denny came out of Lucifer's mansion, feeling weird. *Everything will change now.* Outside he ran into that Gabriel guy, he seemed different than all the other demons. *Why's this?* Gabriel smiled kindly at him, as he passed him by.

***

"That's how my father learned Lucifer's nickname." Daniel smiled at Edward.

"Your Dad sounds bad…"

Daniel raised an eyebrow. "He was, but this was only where he started, you have no idea."

"Your Dad really trusted you with this?"

"My Dad told me after our travels in the Underworlds. Stuff no one else, not even my Mom knows."

Edward peeked towards the screen. "I should return before Claus throws a fit." He walked out, leaving Daniel alone in the cell.

***

Claus was watching a broadcast on TV of Daniel's abduction. Denida was asked about it.

I'll get you, you'll feel my pain!

"Not possible." Lucifer surfaced next to him, looking at the same screen.

"Why the hell not! He's why I got taken."

Lucifer smiled. "Why don't you listen to Daniel's story, you might learn something."

"Like why you want him," Claus smirked.

Lucifer chuckled. "I'll have him if you treasure your freedom. You can learn who he truly is." He dissipated into the air.

Claus turned and walked over to the screen, which showed Daniel, who was sitting in silence.

Lucifer surfaced in front of Daniel. He smiled back at the screen, startling Claus.

"Daniel, long time no see."

"What do you want?" Daniel said annoyed.

Lucifer grinned. "I want to give a different perspective for you all."

Daniel raised an eyebrow. "You... what?"

"Tell you about your Dad, when he was in Hell..."

***

Home, sweet home! And finally, he's starting to excel in Dark Arts, life's good.

Gabriel walked into Lucifer's chamber.

"Gabriel." Lucifer jumped up to greet him.

"I see, you had Den here?"

Lucifer nodded gleefully. "He'll be my apprentice- at last!"

Gabriel shook his head. "You need to see this." Gabriel went over to Lucifer's *'well of memory'*.

An image appeared in the well. Lucifer smiled intrigued.

A boy with bandages over his one eye appeared in a street. He turned his head before crossing the road, where he yelled to someone who waved back. He ran across the road, as a car sped around the corner, and ran into the little boy.

"Yikes-"

"It's not the first time..." Gabriel gave Lucifer a stern glare.

"God?"

"Yes, he fell down stairs as a newly born twice. God will keep trying, he still wants him dead- your demons protecting him isn't enough..."

Lucifer's eyes flickered. "We need to protect him before it's too late!"

He walked into the air and resurfaced in another place within Hell.

A female arch-demon was teaching Dark Arts to young demons. She peeked up as Lucifer came.

"Lucifer?" The demon's eyes flared as she gave a disrespectful stare.

"Medusa, I have something for you; a new task!"

Medusa smiled gleefully.

"I have a boy who needs protection from God and other dangers- on Earth."

"That's all? I can have fun with the Angels at least?" Medusa chuckled hopefully.

Lucifer grinned and nodded. "Anyone who comes to Earth that's a danger to him, I expect you to do as you wish to. But you're not to be seen by anyone!"

Lucifer turned and disappeared into the air, he resurfaced back where Gabriel was.

"He'll be safe now, I've set one of my best demons on it."

"It won't stop God."

Lucifer smirked. "She'll stop God, trust me! Anyone God sends will meet her fury."

Gabriel scoffed. "You have too much faith in one demon..."

Lucifer raised an eyebrow. "As a child, she painted Diabolique images with her own feces!"

"That impresses you?"

"When she got older she did the same with her family pet's blood; *that* impresses me!"

"I should get back to Heaven." Gabriel unfolded his wings and set off in a flash of light.

***

Lucifer chuckled, looking Daniel in the eyes. "So, you see, he belongs in Hell. I always took care of Denida." Lucifer smiled and gaped around the room smirking.

"Aren't you forgetting one thing?" Daniel insisted.

Lucifer shrugged curiously.

"He's blind in one eye, thanks to his Dark side; meaning you!"

Lucifer's eyes grew red. Claus rushed through the door and grabbed hold of Lucifer.

"Edward, watch Daniel!" Claus led Lucifer out.

"You shouldn't enrage the Devil." Edward turned to Daniel.

Lucifer turned back towards the door.

Claus stood in front of the door, blocking Lucifer. "What's the point of your story? It serves no purpose."

Lucifer sighed. "It does! It shows where Denida belongs."

"Because you had a demon watch over him and kill off any competition?"

"Not why." Lucifer studied Claus' face. "Just let me know when you get the ring!" Lucifer turned and walked away into the air.

Chapter 5: Jack

This is nice! Jack lay back on a beach and sipped his cocktail. A newspaper landed on his lap

"Hey!" Jack got up and looked at the newspaper.

'The hunt after the Scientist is on after Denida's son got taken!'

"They're looking for you," the man who threw the paper said.

"Only one person can have taken his son; it means my vacation is over." Jack got up and handed him the paper and his drink. "I'm leaving!"

He stopped in the middle of nowhere after he'd been driving a few hours.

Jack got out and walked into a tall cornfield, he stopped when he was sure he was far from the road.

I hope I'm wrong... "Reficul – Reficul – Reficul."

Lucifer appeared in front of Jack. He smiled at Lucifer when Lucifer noticed Jack.

"What can I do for you? I presume you brought me to this wasteland for a reason?"

"Daniel! You took him, didn't you?"

Lucifer grinned. "That doesn't concern you."

"I'm the one, they're looking for!" Jack threw his arms out.

"It doesn't concern me, goodbye." Lucifer dissipated into the air in front of Jack.

This is not good. I need a backup plan before they find me.

***

Denida observed his private file of the 'Scientist'. *Something feels wrong.* He put the file back down and rubbed his ring. *What am I missing?*

Nina came into his office. "Denny! It's a ring, they want?"

Denida wanted to object, but he nodded with a sigh.

"We're looking for the Scientist who worked with Lucifer and Claus."

"Why would I care, give them the ring!"

Denida sighed. "This ring is more powerful than anything, the President died to protect it from Lucifer."

Nina shook her head, she thought. *'Lucifer!'*

No. "I talked to Lucifer, I don't think he has anything to do with this. The Scientist- Jack is out of his control."

Nina sighed and dropped down into a chair. "Do you think Daniel's ok?"

"Can you not feel him?" Denida's stomach knotted.

"I-" *'I didn't think of that!'* "I can!" Nina smiled ecstatically and ran back out to her car.

For now... Denida shrugged.

***

The Colonel had called for both Nina and Denida. He wanted to introduce them to the person who seemed the only choice for finding the Scientist.

"You called? Have you found the Scientist?" Nina leaned on the desk, her eyes hopeful.

The Colonel shook his head.

"Then why the hell are we here?" Nina turned to storm back out.

"I may have an idea…"

Denida raised an eyebrow. "What idea?"

The Colonel smiled and went to the door. "Michelle," he called. "Don't be alarmed, she looks masculine, but that's a benefit."

Michelle came in through the door. "Howdy, you called?"

The Colonel nodded and gestured towards Nina and Denida. "Yes. Michelle is an expert on the former Dark Angels and their associates. She knows everything about the Scientist."

Denida got up, and Michelle turned to face him. She smiled at him.

"Hello, Denida. His real name's Jack, by the way, I'll find him for you."

"What was he for the Angels?" Nina interrupted.

"He conducted their research, but more importantly he helped Claus with Susan's kidnapping."

Nina's eyes widened and she took a big exhale.

Michelle saluted them and walked back out of the Colonel's office.

"There's something off about her…" Nina scratched her arms.

The Colonel patted Nina on the shoulder. "Don't worry, I trust her. She has proven her worth."

"How?" Nina crossed her arms.

"She has caught several of the former associates of the Dark Angels."

"OK! Just find this *Jack*." Nina walked out without waiting for Denida.

The Colonel sat back down behind his desk, he tried to smile.

After knocking on his door, Michelle came back in.

"What's wrong?" The Colonel wrinkled his forehead in worry.

She glanced over at Denida, who'd remained in his chair. "I didn't want to say this when Lady Nina was here-allegedly Jack has gotten part of a secret stash Claus stole from Denida. So, he might not be easy to find, not even for me."

The Colonel nodded. "Good thing you didn't say that, try your best. No resource you need is too much."

Michelle saluted and left again.

The Colonel glared over at Denida. He might be better off giving Lucifer the ring back.

Denida grunted at the Colonel, he got up. "Never!" He followed after Nina.

***

Edward brought Daniel supper. Daniel sat down and started eating, not giving Edward so much as a glance.

Daniel didn't lift his head even when Edward cleared his plate.

Why isn't he saying anything? "Daniel?"

Daniel glanced up from his supper. "What? I thought Lucifer ended it with his tale?"

"No, of course not, I want to hear it, truly I do!"

"Good to know. Allow me to continue then." Daniel leaned back in his chair with a glee in his eyes. "Dad continued hanging with the other demons he had gotten close to despite being taught special things, especially his *best* friend Danyel..."

***

"Does the Devil teach you anything good?"

"No, Danyel, nothing useful." Denida turned away. *Yet.*

"But he's teaching you more advanced arts?"

Denny smiled. "Yes, mind reading and blocking others from doing it, is the best one so far."

40

"The Instructor wouldn't teach us that yet." Danyel stared annoyed. "meaning they wouldn't think we would know it! You can block others from reading us, including controlling *what* they can read?"

"Yes, we can have fun." Denny giggled back.

Denny ran outside with Danyel. *Now we're gonna have some fun.*

They stopped as they noticed the Instructor who taught them before Denny went to train with Lucifer.

Danyel looked at Denny.

"He thinks we're all weak and should be honored to be taught by him," Denny whispered.

"Master!" Danyel rushed over to him. "Denny has something he wants to tell you." Danyel turned back to Denny.

"Yes." Denny shrugged. "Lucifer wasn't happy with you; he thinks you're beneath your students."

The Instructor gave Denny an intense stare.

Denny could feel him reading his thoughts. It's sad Lucifer thinks he's so worthless.

"I see…" The Instructor hurried away, forgetting his fellow demons.

Denny and Danyel giggled.

It's so easy!

They went on to mess with some of the young demons until another Instructor came and dragged them both with him.

"Where are we going?" Danyel demanded to know.

"The Master wants you both!" He projected them into Lucifer's throne room.

Danyel peered with big eyes around him, full of anticipation.

"Not smart, Danyel and Denny. Your messing with your Instructor ended up with him coming to see me." Lucifer stood up and got close to Denny. "how I hated it, never *ever*

41

try more of your boyish antics with your powers, you *will* be punished. Same goes for your friend!" Lucifer glanced over at Danyel.

Both Denny and Danyel nodded.

"I don't think we should call you Denny anymore either, everyone should know you're *special*; *Denida* you'll be known as. Leave me!" Lucifer flickered his fingers, and they were back outside of Lucifer's mansion.

Danyel sighed. "I guess I need to call you Denida when we're amongst others. But I'm still calling you *Denny* when we're alone!"

Denida turned back towards the mansion. "Someday, I'll be stronger than him. Until then, we must be careful not to get caught."

In the following time, the other demons started to pay attention to Denida, or as he was referred to

amongst the demons; 'Little Evil'. The need to get stronger with the fellow demons was clear.

"Why are we here?" Danyel examined cautiously around the old and barren place, where five other of Denida's friends stood, all demons in training.

"I called you all! Danyel, meet Ignacio, Pedro, Nicklas, Mia, and Jan."

Danyel nodded to them. They glared suspiciously at each other.

Denida came and stood in the middle of them. "We need a place, Lucifer, or anyone else for that matter, can't watch us."

"The seven of us?" Danyel ogled at the others.

"You're all my best friends, so we should all be a part of it if you're interested?"

"Like the idea, Denida," Ignacio said.

"Call me Denny when we're just us."

Pedro nodded and walked into the place, the rest followed him.

"Might not be enough to shield us from Lucifer," Danyel said after the others went inside, away from a hearing distance.

"We'll make it be enough!"

Denida and Danyel walked inside.

Inside, the hideout was dark and empty.

"We need to make it ours!" Danyel kicked at an old chair. "We can get stuff throughout Hell, and you, Denny, can pilfer some from Lucifer's mansion."

Denida, as well as the others started to collect stuff for the hideout.

I'll have to be extra careful, it's a higher risk with me. I'm stealing from the Devil, after all.

"Thank you for the lesson, Master Lucifer." Denida smiled.

"I told you, when we're alone you can call me Luci, no master needed." Lucifer patted Denida on the shoulder.

This room is too dangerous to take anything from, one of the other rooms perhaps.

Denida left Lucifer's throne room and went around the mansion. It was covered with a Darker Presence than anywhere else in Hell. Almost all the doors were locked with strong Dark Magic. *What can it be hiding?* Denida tried one of the doors, but the magic he knew was nowhere near a match to that of the spell on the door. He wanted in, now more than before, but there was no way, even he had to accept that. He turned around and went back to the hideout.

Ignacio lifted his head from putting up the stuff he and Nicklas found. "Hey, Denny."

"Weren't you able to get any?" Danyel asked.

They can't know I'm too weak with Lucifer's spells. "There's a Dark Presence watching the place at all times. I need to be careful. At least you got some I see."

"Of course! I did what you couldn't." Danyel smirked.

"It's fine," Ignacio argued. "He has to be careful, it is next to the Master himself."

Wish I could have gotten something, anything.

***

"I'm done." Daniel got up from his table with his food.

"*Danyel*, why does that name sound familiar?" Edward stared at the wall deep in thought.

A small flicker of enjoyment appeared in Daniel's eyes.

"Because it's close to my name, Daniel. Also, you may remember him as the leader of the Dark Angels, Danyel in our world." Daniel winked at the screen.

Edward's eyes widened.

"You might want to go see Claus." Daniel chuckled.

Edward grabbed Daniel's tray and hurried out and went straight to Claus, who was, as he expected, waiting for him in his office.

Claus peered at Edward coming. "You're doing exactly as Daniel wants."

"I don't think he's smart enough for that. Was Danyel a Dark Angel?"

Claus nodded at the screen at Daniel, who sat making faces at the screen.

"I wonder how much he's like his father…" Claus mumbled.

"Danyel?" Edward went in front of Claus to get his attention.

"Yes, he was the Dark Angel who led them, he escaped here, he got killed in Hell by Denida."

Claus moved closer to the monitor. "I made the mistake last time of underestimating Susan, I lost due to it."

Claus turned to Edward. "Be careful you don't make my mistake."

"I won't, it's only a story told by a child, nothing to worry about."

"…Which is Denida's son, and Daniel's not done yet!" Claus turned back to watch Daniel.

***

Lucifer's sacrificing me. Jack needed an assurance, he knew who was left of those who worked with the Dark Angels.

So back to the Capitol he went, even if it was risky being so close to where those who hunted him were. He needed to meet those he once knew.

Jack kept his head down, even wearing shades and a wig to hide his appearance.

I'm not taking any chances. He couldn't help but be nervous, someone would recognize him.

He reached the rendezvous without incident. He was met by a flash of light which blinded him.

"You're quite wanted, 'Scientist'. Why do you want to meet?"

"I didn't kidnap the child. I'm being set up! I hope you can help me figure out who it is?"

The silence in the room lengthened.

"I can pay," Jack tried.

Chatter could be heard behind the strong white light.

"Come back tomorrow, the same time," the same voice yelled. "Leave!"

Jack backed cautiously from the building.

He slowly found a place he could stay until the next day, when he hopefully could find out who was setting him up.

Morning came and he used a spell on his face instead of the wig. The night before he'd seen his face on a newscast as wanted.

Why not be extra careful, a new face, no way a spell can fall off like a wig can.

He camped out next to where he was going to meet them. Nothing else to do with my time, and I need to be sure I'm not walking into a trap. But there was no movement throughout the day. They must use magic to appear here...

Jack watched the clock. When the time of the meet finally came, he jogged towards the building.

The same clear light blinded him when he came into the building with his bag of money. He lifted the bag, where they could see it.

"I brought you the money. Who set me up then?"

"Show us the money," a voice echoed behind the light.

Jack opened the bag and tilted it, so it could be seen.

"Alright," the voice said. "Claus set you up. But other than that, we can't help. Michelle, the Sergeant, who caught many of us is hunting you."

The bag got pulled across the room by magic. "Good luck."

The light got even brighter, before it disappeared, leaving Jack standing in an empty, barren warehouse.

Claus again, it must mean Lucifer has a direct hand in it too. Lucifer always saw Claus as a pawn...

Jack wrinkled his head, as he walked back out of the warehouse. A police car drove past him, making him stop up. *Wait, I have my disguise on. I know what I must do!*

Jack was a demon, so he could feel where Dark Magic was concentrated. I wonder why Denida hasn't thought of it? Maybe Darkness won't... Lucifer, the Dark Master would when he sees Claus leave an imprint...

Jack squinted his eyes and put on his shades since Darkness filled his eyes. He hailed a taxi.

"Hello, where to," the driver asked.

"Military Headquarters."

The taxi stopped in front of the building with the Colonel and the rest within.

Jack paid the driver and got out, the big building was still intimidating.

The receptionist welcomed Jack in his disguise, he smiled back as he passed.

He took the staircase and went to the basement, which now held the cells.

Soldiers walked down the hall towards him, Jack closed the door quietly till they passed.

He walked out afterward down the hall, looking around to be sure no one saw him before he slid in through a hidden door. Dust covered every surface of the room.

At least I know no one has been here since the fall of the Dark Angels. Claus went into the back room, which had an active chart with all usage of magic in this Underworld. *It still works!* Jack chuckled, as he examined the chart. It didn't take long for him to find a clear mark.

"Got you!"

Jack left HQ and found a car. It wasn't a long drive to where Claus had hidden out.

He kneeled, Claus was ordering others around. *Isn't that funny, little teeny Claus.*

A man walked up to Claus.

"What do you want? I told you to get Daniel talking!" Claus threw a small ball of magic at the man.

The man spun around, he ran back into the building.

Jack went down and faced Claus in his disguise.

"I used to be a Dark Angel henchman, are you Claus?"

"Yes and your name?" Claus spectated, ready to draw his knife.

"Just Jack." He almost smiled, but he held it back just before he did. "You can use some help to finally overcome that bastard Denida?"

Claus examined Jack's face a little extra, he calmed down, he let go of his knife.

"Something wrong?" Jack inquired.

"No, I just knew someone by that name once. We can always need help, Denida's no easy task." Claus led Jack into the building he stood in front of and into his office.

Jack peered towards the screen.

"Go ahead." Claus chuckled and pointed towards the screen. "I know you want to."

Jack turned and stared at Daniel.

"It was so easy getting to him, but I have a strong feeling he needs to be watched, he's as conniving as his Dad!"

"What can I help you with?" Jack turned to Claus.

"You'll just be set to patrolling with the other guards."

Not good enough, I'll need to find a way to get closer to Claus or Daniel. "Glad to be of service with Denida's end!" Jack smiled and was about to walk back outside when he stopped. "Why do *you* want him, by the way? You don't seem like a demon?"

"Perceptive!" Claus winked. "I need to bring his ring to Lucifer in exchange for my freedom. After all, he sent me to Hell, he needs to pay!" Claus' anger flared up.

"OK, I just wondered!" He rushed out, before Claus took his anger out on him, not wanting to get on his bad side. *Interesting. I can see Lucifer still wants Denida, this is going to be fun!*

Chapter 6: The Darkness

Michelle set up a perimeter and put a prize on Jack's head *alive*.

A former employee of a resort a lot of criminals used stepped forward hoping to claim the reward.

"He left shortly after the boy got taken."

Michelle turned to the soldier next to her. "You don't mean before?"

The man shook his head. "I remember showing the manager the paper, he rushed out to see Jack, who said his vacation was over!"

Michelle rubbed her face. "Did he have any contact with anyone outside?"

"Yes, we presumed it was over the money he stole from Claus."

Michelle jotted down a note. "Did he give any hints of where he went after he left? Or if he was coming back?"

The man shook his head. "We don't let fugitives stay- he wasn't coming back."

"Thanks." Michelle shook the man's hand and led him out. "I'll let you know if I have any more questions, or if this leads to us finding the Scientist." *I better update Denida.*

Michelle drove towards Dynasty. The huge building and grounds were daunting.

Claus met his end here, on these very grounds, scary.

As she drove up to the main house, she was met by the house Butler.

"Hi, I've got an update on the kidnapping." Michelle tried to smile, but it wasn't that big news.

The butler nodded. "Follow me, I'll lead you to Denida. Lady Nina is out with her horse."

"With her horse?" Michelle raised her eyebrows.

The Butler nodded. "It soothes her nerves." He led Michelle through the house. It was not any less intimidating on the inside.

Denida hurried to his feet when they came into his office.

"Yes? Good news?" Denida met her with anticipation in his eye.

"News, not necessarily good or bad." Michelle let her eyes sweep the room. "Since Claus' demise, we know Jack has been living in luxury. But he left there after Daniel got taken. Seems as if he might be working with someone."

Denida bit his lip. "How, what money?"

"Some he took from Claus. From a secret hideout or something?"

Denida walked back to his table, rubbing his face. "Is that all? Where's he now?"

"He left there, he said his vacation's over."

"That's all you came to tell me?" Denida sat back down. "It's wasting precious time. The Colonel could inform me of this. If you have nothing more valuable..."

Michelle saluted. "Sorry if I upset you."

Denida ran his hand through his hair. "It's fine." Denida sighed, he waved his hand at the door. "Close the door."

Michelle wrinkled her forehead but did as she was asked.

50

"Between us only, if it can help find Daniel."

What's he getting at? Michelle rubbed her cheek intrigued.

"I may know the money you're talking about. In the north, I had hidden a backup from the days before the Dark Angels- Claus took it." Denida ran his hand over his face. "It was a different time, you need to understand."

"Of course." Michelle sat down.

"We all did *things* we don't want to remember. I trust you can keep this between us."

Michelle smiled, as their eyes met. "You can trust me."

The door banged open and Nina came running in. "You found Daniel?"

***

Jack did well at his guard duties, but he didn't like it. I'll need to find a way further up the command chain. Claus has been bad news, since the day I took his call…

A smile came to Jack. He couldn't help but smile, so wide that the other demons peered suspiciously at him. He ran into the building to Claus' office.

"The hell? Haven't you heard of knocking?" Claus stood up furious Jack just busting in.

"*Michelle*," Jack said.

Claus' fury got softened by his confusion. "What are you talking about?"

"'The Scientist' called a meeting to find out info about who's hunting him. Michelle is. She's hunted a lot of the former Dark Angels' associates successfully. She's a part of the hunt for Daniel!" Jack glanced over at the screen to Daniel. "My former comrades told me; I think we should move, it's not safe here!"

"Because of this Michelle girl?"

Jack hunched over the table. "Sergeant Michelle's not to be trifled with."

Claus stared into Jack's eyes, he held the eyes locked for what felt like forever.

He suddenly broke the connection. "Fine, prepare the move. Hope you have a safer place in mind."

"I do." Jack chuckled to himself. "We can no longer use magic."

"What? Why not?" Claus' eyes widened.

"Magic leaves an imprint. It's only a matter of time before they think about it."

But a small imprint won't matter, to hide my face.

Jack followed Claus, who gathered the demons to inform everyone of what was going to happen, including everyone from now on, was forbidden from using any sort of Dark Magic.

A benefit no one will use it, only me.

"Jack's lead on the relocation!" Claus pointed towards him.

Finally, I'm where I belong. Jack went to the front. "We need to relocate as soon as possible before Michelle gets wind of our whereabouts, so gather everything, we're leaving at dawn, the place better be clean of any evidence!"

Jack nodded at Claus and walked over to him. "I'll need to go see my family," he whispered.

Claus gestured for him to go ahead.

Jack went out to his car and drove off. *Time for the last step of the plan.*

He drove three hours from the hideout, then bought a disposable cell at a convenience store. Back in the car he headed for the bad side of town.

Outside a house filled with junkies he stopped the car and let the spell lift from his face, so he would appear as the real 'Scientist'. He went through the building, passing by countless junkies, he continued until he reached the basement, where there was a lab producing drugs. He went over to the man, who sat behind a desk.

"Hello Oliver, want to make some money?"

"Jack, and how so?" Oliver smirked.

"I need you to make a call tonight, to a specific number with a specific message. I have a burner phone with me." Jack opened a bag, which had a phone on top a pile of money.

Oliver grinned and took the bag. "Of course."

Jack smiled and handed him a paper with instructions.

He grinned all the way back to the hideout.

***

Daniel watched confused, as the guards took everything of surveillance away, but left him.

Edward stayed and watched over him, as the others emptied everything.

"What's going on?" Daniel's heart lifted. *Has the Colonel found me?*

"We're leaving before anyone discovers us," Edward said.

Before! Could they be close? "I see, want me to tell you more of my Dad, while we wait?"

"Definitely." Edward sat at a chair left behind.

He's already into it, this can work if I can get him scared enough. "My father, Denida continued being taught by Lucifer…"

***

Lucifer had Denida sit and meditate in a room, filled to the brim with a heavy spirit of Darkness, so heavy it was hard to breathe. *What's the purpose?*

The air got darker until it felt like there was a presence there watching him.

"Nice work! You're done." Lucifer knelt and patted him.

53

Denida opened his eyes and saw Lucifer next to him. "What's the purpose of this?"

"It strengthens your spirit power." Lucifer smiled, and a small flicker appeared in his eyes.

Denida got up. "Alright, see you tomorrow, Luci." He went towards the exit.

Lucifer nodded.

Denida went back to his hideout, where Ignacio was practicing his Dark Arts with Jan, which he had taught him and the rest of his friends advanced versions of. He stopped at the door, just looking at him, not going in.

"Have you ever sensed a Dark Presence in Hell, other than with the Master?"

Ignacio's eyes widened in surprise. "I doubt-"

"What?" Denida asked curiously.

"I have actually. There's a presence sometimes, I presumed it was just Lucifer watching us, but it has been there when the Master was there too."

Denida sighed. Maybe I'm right.

"Playing hooky, Denny?" Danyel came over and jabbed at Denida and giggled.

"Of course not, just asking Ignacio something."

"Boring. Let's go make some trouble." Danyel dropped down on a couch. He lay shooting Balls of Darkness into the ceiling. "I'm bored, isn't there something interesting we can do?"

Denida and Ignacio's eyes met.

"The Darkness," they both said in unison.

Danyel shrugged. "What about the Darkness?"

"It's watching us, as if it has a presence of its own, why not see if it does?" Denida winked.

Danyel got up. "That does sound like fun, but how?"

"Come on." Denida, Ignacio and Danyel ran out. "Lucifer's mansion is filled with doors sealed with strong magic." Denida squinted his eyes.

"So?" Danyel's face was full of confusion.

"You lure Lucifer away. Ignacio and I will try one of the doors."

"You want me to lure *the devil*, and miss out on the fun?" Danyel raised his voice.

"It has to be you. Lucifer remembers you from when we last got in trouble. Besides, to get his attention, can be fun too." Denida's eye flickered red, as he winked.

"Yea, I see it, let's do it!" Danyel jumped up.

The three boys went out towards Lucifer's mansion and stopped halfway there.

Denida turned to Danyel. "Know how you'll get his attention?"

Danyel grinned. "Of course, I'll get *all* their attention. Leave it to me!"

Denida nodded, he went further towards Lucifer's mansion with Ignacio.

It was not long after they arrived till Lucifer walked out followed by several other demons. *Whatever Danyel did, must've worked.* Lucifer and the others appeared mad.

They waited for a little before Denida and Ignacio went into the mansion.

"This feels very dark."

Denida nodded to Ignacio's comment.

Denida went around the hall, feeling the Darkness in the air, he was feeling the spells on the doors. He stopped abruptly in front of one. "This is the one!"

Ignacio went over to him. "Sure, you're strong enough to break the seal?"

"Lucifer has taught me well, there's only one way to find out…"

Denida lifted his hands, while he started to chant.

Ignacio backed away from him, a magic beam started to form out of Denida's hands, around the door.

Ignacio peered around the hall, as the Darkness seemed to grow behind him and Denida. It started to approach them, but the door blew open before it reached them.

"Told you," Denida said with a smile. "Come."

Ignacio followed Denida while looking behind them, he hurried into the room.

Inside the room, Denida turned to Ignacio. "It's the Presence. You need to leave before Lucifer returns!" He grabbed Ignacio and pushed him towards a wall, but Ignacio disappeared into the air before he reached the wall.

Denida took a deep breath and walked further into the room. *Lucifer...*

"Reficul, Reficul, Reficul," Denida muttered, as he had been instructed to if he ever needed to call his Master's presence.

Lucifer appeared behind him.

Lucifer was startled to see Denida. "You're not supposed to be in here."

"You knew I would come here someday." Denida turned to Lucifer. "What's this room? It seems important to *you.*"

Lucifer walked around the room. "It holds relics of my time from Heaven."

"Heaven? You really were in Heaven?"

"Yes, but God-" Lucifer's eyes flared red. "wanted me dead, after he found out about me and Heavani."

"*Heavani?*" Denida's eyes glanced across the room and back to Lucifer, whose eyes instead of red, turned warm.

"Yes, my sweet Heavani, God's treasure, and my true love."

"Why isn't she here then?"

Lucifer's eyes flared again, the Darkness within the room grew heavy.

"Because God has her! My only way of knowing how she is, is through Gabriel, my old friend, who helped me escape."

The Darkness in the room slowly dissipated.

"All of this is a reminder, why God needs to pay!" Lucifer tightened his fists.

Denida peered around the room. "I should get back…"

He went back to the hideout, to find Ignacio with Jan, Ignacio ran up to him when he came.

"How did you send me back here so fast? What was all the weird stuff in the room?"

Denida sat down on the couch, he buried his head in his hands.

"Don't ask. Where's Danyel, hasn't he come back?"

Ignacio shook his head and sat down next to Denida, to accompany him in waiting.

Hours went, several of their friends came and went, but no Danyel.

At morning, Danyel finally walked through the door, they turned.

Danyel seems different somehow. "What happened?" Denida ran up to him followed by Ignacio.

"Nothing," Danyel said and pushed further into the room and fell onto the same couch, they'd just got up from.

Denida and Ignacio's eyes met in disbelief, but neither of them said anything.

***

Edward couldn't believe it, he was a little shocked at what he just heard.

The door sprung open and several men came in.

"Jack, it's time?" Edward asked.

"Yes. Sorry to break up your *story time*," Jack smirked at Daniel.

The demons approached a scared Daniel.

Daniel's eyes wandered to Edward, who gave him a reassuring smile.

The demons chained and gagged him and put a hood on him.

Claus led Daniel out with the other henchmen.

A man came running out towards them when Claus came out of the building, almost stumbling over his own feet.

"The Military's coming, maybe that Michelle detected the magic use?"

Jack shook his head. "We stopped using it, *before*."

Claus grabbed Daniel and ran to a car with him. "We need to get out of here, but how?" His eyes widened. "Reficul, Reficul, Reficul," he yelled, as he could see the cars approaching in the distance.

Lucifer observed the surroundings. "Why am I here?"

"We've been discovered! We need to get away if you still want to get the ring, that is?"

Lucifer smiled and raised his hand towards the cars approaching, the cars approaching stopped, as frozen in time. "Go ahead and leave."

Claus and Jack stormed out towards the cars. They all ran to their cars and set them into motion and sped away.

The cars went off its freeze in time, as soon as Claus and the others were gone in the distance.

Claus peeked back at the cars, speeding in the other direction, towards their hideout.

Chapter 7: Medusa and the First Escape

Michelle and the others came out of their cars with their guns drawn. Lucifer was about to return to Hell when he saw this. *Interesting, this looks fun.* Michelle made gestures to instruct them on who was to go, she led the charge into the hideout. Lucifer raised his eyebrows and followed them, continuing where only demons would see him.

Michelle swept through until she came to the room Daniel had been in.

"This is where Daniel was, why did they move him?" She turned to her soldiers and holstered her sidearm. "They're gone, they must have known we were coming, inform the Colonel."

Michelle walked around the chair Daniel sat in.

Lucifer chuckled.

Michelle stared towards Lucifer, stopping him in his tracks.

Does she hear me? Only demons can.

Michelle walked over to the wall, almost next to where Lucifer was standing.

"This is *my world!*"

The Colonel came into the room, Michelle turned back around and sighed.

"This is the room from the video of Daniel, but there doesn't seem to be any other trace left."

This is no longer interesting, just some girl talking to herself.

Lucifer turned and faded into the air.

***

It worked! Jack smiled, as he sat in between Daniel and Claus but said nothing.

"That was Lucifer helping you?" Jack broke the silence.

Claus nodded. "He wants Denida for some reason."

Daniel tried to speak through the gag, so Jack elbowed him.

"Just be careful. From my understanding, it was not just Denida, but also Lucifer who sent you to Hell."

Claus leered at Jack and nodded. "He'll give me freedom, if I give him Denida, we both win."

So, you think.

"Where exactly are we going?" Claus wrinkled his forehead.

Jack grinned. "A place that has remained hidden since the time of the Dark Angels."

The cars drove through the night until morning came when they arrived at a place surrounded by barb wire and cameras.

Claus turned towards Jack in surprise. "What exactly is this place?"

"The Dark Angels used it as a research fortress," Jack said and smirked.

Claus got out of the car and inspected the surroundings. Jack instructed the others to set up command.

"The problem remains though-" Claus suddenly said. "If it wasn't our magic, someone betrayed us!"

Jack turned from the other guards to Claus, who was glaring at him.

"I know, but I've no guess at who it could be."

"Me neither." Claus sighed. "I think you should handle security here, you know this place. We need to be careful it won't happen again."

"Follow me." Jack led them inside to a room where Daniel was chained.

Daniel checked out the new room, it was a bigger room, but clearly more like a cell.

"Nice place," Lucifer chuckled, as he appeared next to Daniel.

"Lucifer? Why are you here?" Claus stepped forward.

Lucifer turned back to Claus. "I'm here to tell you more of my story."

"Your story? Of your demon, Medusa?" Daniel raised his eyebrows.

"They'll understand it better, with *your story*, Daniel."

Daniel took a deep breath.

Jack deliberately stayed in the background, as blended in as he could.

"Medusa went to Earth to watch over Denny. No one monitored her, as long as nothing went wrong. She could do whatever she wished, and she did."

***

Medusa sat sipping coffee while keeping an eye on the little boy, who was now eight.

"You're watching him?" Gabriel sat down opposite her.

Medusa peered over at him, before looking back towards Denny.

"Are you here, because you want to kill him? I'll kill you then, a friend of the Master's, or not!"

"No," Gabriel said. "I just wanted to see if he was OK."

Interesting. "I'll see to it, he'll be protected, don't you worry." Medusa turned with a red fiery flicker in her eyes. "Wherever, however, I need to." She swallowed the rest of the coffee and followed after the boy, Denny.

Denny went through a dumpster with his friends.

Kids will be kids. Medusa glanced around to be sure no one was following them, still concerned with her meet with Gabriel. *He might be a friend of Lucifer's, but he's an archangel after all.*

"Look what I found!" Denny crawled back out of the dumpster, with a dead bird.

He finds that interesting, shows his soul's in Hell. Medusa giggled.

Denny put the dead bird in his pocket and jumped back inside the dumpster. He leaned out of it to look at his friends when an angel appeared, who shot a beam towards him.

Medusa gestured her hand towards the dumpster, the lid fell on top of Denny, deflecting the spell, but the lid hit with a mighty bang on Denny's thumb.

The boys rushed to Denny.

Medusa went in between the angel and the boys.

"Oops," the angel said with a smile. "Didn't go as you thought. did it?"

"My job is to protect him, not baby him!"

Medusa shot a dark cloud towards the angel, but the angel flew through it, his beam of light overcoming the darkness.

The angel locked on Medusa's shoulders, she couldn't move as the Angel tried to pierce the Darkness with Light.

She reached into the depth of Darkness within her and sent the Angel banging into a wall.

Medusa gasped at how the Light had weakened her. She frantically searched around, but the angel was nowhere to be seen. *Where is he?* She spun around to look at Denny, sweat dripping from her face from the worry, but also from the warmth of light.

Suddenly, a Light Spear appeared behind her. She took hold of the Angel's grip, stopping him from piercing her.

He pushed with all his might, but Medusa sent out a wave of energy, sending the angel flying, the spear rolled far off. The clouds turned dark, blocking out the light, as she strolled towards the angel casually grinning.

"I don't fail, *ever*!" Medusa gave a mockingly stare at the angel, who was trying to crawl away. Dark energy surrounded the angel and pushed him back towards her. She squeezed her left hand, which now was forming a Darkness around it. Medusa stared into the Angel's now, fearful face, and jabbed her hand through the Angel's body.

"How God will suffer, he shouldn't have tried again." Medusa ripped out the still beating heart and took a bite of it. The clouds above her dissipated again.

"We should go back, it might be rain. That weather looks bad," one of Denny's friends said after looking upwards towards the quick change in weather. Denny crawled out of the Dumpster and ran with his friends.

"Reficul, Reficul, Reficul," Medusa said when they had left.

The Dark cloud that had almost gone, returned above her head.

"Yes," a Dark Presence asked, which formed above her head in clouds.

"God sent an angel after the boy. I took care of it."

"Good, keep up the good work." The Dark clouds disappeared.

I thought this was stupid, but with God continuing sending others to kill this boy and Gabriel coming, there might be some validity to this.

***

"So, your Dad would not be alive if not for us," Lucifer smirked at Daniel.

"That's why you told us? To show us that you're best for him? Maybe you should wait for me to finish my tale first." Daniel crossed his arms.

"I know what you're going to say," Lucifer put his hand on his chest, pretending to be offended.

"Do you? My story is told from my Dad's side; did you ever hear it from him?"

Lucifer's eyes grew black, as that was the one area, he always wondered; *how Denny got out of Hell.*

"Doubt it's interesting!" Lucifer dragged out Claus from the room, he spun around when they got out. "When Daniel tells you how Denida escaped Hell, I want to know!"

"It's important?" Claus wrinkled his brow.

"Yes, it's the one thing I never could understand." Lucifer turned to look at the door. On the other side, Daniel sat smiling on his bunk, the infuriating child. "I see some of Denny in Daniel."

"That's nice," Claus said.

Lucifer faced Claus and stared deep into his eyes until the man wilted. "No, it's not, what I see of Denny, is the defiance, be careful!"

***

Edward watched as Daniel lay back in his bed. He turned to leave.

"Don't you want to know more of my story? I'm sure Lucifer does," Daniel said, while still staring at the ceiling.

Edward went back to the other side of the bars, where a desk watching Daniel was.

"Haven't you told me everything? He went demonic and found out the Presence of the Darkness, what else is there to say; it's done."

Daniel smirked. "You think. Want to know how he escaped Hell, or not?" He peered over towards Edward, who stood up. "No one knows how, don't you want to know?"

Daniel could see the thoughts churning in Edwards' head.

He looked around the room unsure.

"If you need to see Claus and find out if you're allowed, go ahead." Daniel turned back, looking at the ceiling.

Edward rushed out, he grabbed hold of a guard he met in the hall. "Where's Claus?"

As he did, he saw Claus coming out towards him from the corner of his eye.

Edward yanked the guard to the side and ran towards Claus, who held up his hand to stop him.

"I know what you want to ask, the cell has cameras. Yes, you can find out how Denida escaped."

Edward sighed out a relief and nodded.

"Actually, anything Daniel tells you about Denida, you're allowed to find out!"

Why's he so curious? "OK," Edward said, frowning.

"Lucifer wants Denida, finding out as much as we can about him is a benefit." Claus patted Edward on the shoulder and left.

Edward went back to the cell.

Daniel stood next to the bars, waiting for him to return. "I take it you're allowed?"

Edward nodded.

Daniel chuckled. "Then story time; Dad realized the Presence of the Darkness. He learned of Heavani, so he felt a little sorry for Lucifer. But his attention was on the Darkness, which he discovered was there."

***

Denida walked around Lucifer's mansion. *I can feel it watching me.*

65

"Denny!" Lucifer came to greet Denida.

Lucky, he's taught me how to shield thoughts. If I had discovered before...

"I think it's time for you to meet someone." Lucifer led Denida towards his throne room, where a man stood waiting.

"Who's this?" Denida's stomach clenched. *I've seen him somewhere.*

"My old friend, Archangel Gabriel."

Gabriel turned and smiled at Denida. "Hello, Denny."

Why's he so smiley? "Yeah sure, I wanted to ask you something, Luci!"

Lucifer turned to Denida. "Yes?"

"The Darkness has a Presence of its own, doesn't it?"

Lucifer's eyes flickered red for a second, he glanced at Gabriel. "That's some question, you have."

"And what's the answer?" Denida didn't look away from Lucifer.

Lucifer sat down on his throne and took a deep breath.

"I survived after Heaven cause the Darkness took me in. I'm who I am thanks to it!"

"You owe everything to the Darkness, it controls everything?"

"That's right," Lucifer said. "It's everywhere, Darkness is within every living thing."

Gabriel cleared his throat. "Denida, why don't you show me around Hell?"

If you're Lucifer's old friend, why doesn't Lucifer? Lucifer still seemed on edge, red flickering in his eyes. "As you wish, Gabriel."

Denida led Gabriel around Hell. *Doesn't he know it already?*

Gabriel followed Denida, listening to his every word.

Denida stopped and spun around.

"You're the Master's friend, have you not seen all this already? Haven't you been coming to Hell for millennia?"

Gabriel smiled. "I have, but I wanted you away from Luci. The Darkness not only controls everything, it has a lock on Lucifer, it feeds on his hatred, you were asking a hard thing."

Denida turned back around.

"Wait," Gabriel stood in front of Denida. "If you have any questions, just ask me instead."

Is he serious? Denida's gut twisted but Gabriel's warm look gave him a feeling the archangel could be relied on. "I will."

Denida took Gabriel back to Lucifer's mansion.

Denida went back to the hideout, where he found Ignacio with several of his other demon friends.

"Hey, Denny." Ignacio came over to him. "Danyel's still acting strange," he whispered.

"We can't stop it, there's only one way," Denida met Ignacio's gaze. "You know what I mean!"

Denida and Ignacio both went into the hideout, where Danyel was laying.

"Why are you acting strange? We both noticed it," Denida asked.

Danyel lay on the couch playing shooting with balls of magic. He stopped, sighed and sat up.

"Things changed, Lucifer warned me, if I got in trouble again, it'd be the end."

They sat down on the couch next to him.

"Don't worry, we'll keep Lucifer in the dark, if we're caught, we'll take the fall." Denida lifted his eyebrow.

"We'll watch your back, man," Ignacio said.

"The others might-"

"No," Denida said. "We'll keep it from the others."

"Great!" Danyel rushed to his feet. "Let's go make some trouble."

Denida smirked at Ignacio. "Why not," he grinned.

They went towards where the new arrivals were being tortured.

Danyel hurried to it, as they arrived.

Denida stopped, looking at the faces of the new arrivals.

"Aren't you going, you're the best at it?" Ignacio scratched his head.

Denida sighed and turned to Ignacio. "The Dark Presence, it doesn't feel right, the look on the faces- and Lucifer…"

Ignacio wrinkled his forehead. "But don't we like the terror in their eyes?"

"Do we?" Denida peered back on the faces. "or have we just been indoctrinated into it. This was *us* once, wasn't it?"

Ignacio pulled Denida away, and back to the hideout. "You need to get away from prying ears."

Denida sat down, still looking lost. *We can't do this…* "I just don't feel it anymore. Lucifer was turned to the Darkness after he got thrown out of Heaven. The Dark Presence seems to be using us all, should we really help more to become like us?"

Ignacio sat down next to Denida almost whispering.

"Well, what can we do, we're demons in training. No one has even ever escaped Hell."

Denida buried his head in his hands. "I know this, but, I'm not going to like it."

Danyel came in. "Where'd you go, the fun was just starting."

"I need to go train with Lucifer." Denida trudged out, leaving Danyel staring after him.

Denida walked towards Lucifer's mansion, *My Master, or is the Darkness my Master?*

He walked into Lucifer's throne room, to find him standing next to some big device.

"Luci?" What's he doing?

Lucifer spun around and smiled, he embraced Denida.

"This is just a gate, you can travel between dimensions, it's made of an old material."

"Dimensions? Out of Hell?"

"Yes, another place of the soul realm."

Interesting, just in time!

"But enough of that, have you tried eating a soul to gather its soul energy? Crush the heart to completely kill it off. There's one other way you need to watch; for the soul to escape, shoot a person in the eye, the soul shall be set free, so be careful with that!"

Free? Denida ground his teeth. "I see, you want to teach me something about that?"

"I'll show you a spell, which will make your hand like a dagger, which can rip out the still beating heart with the power of the Darkness."

Ignacio and Danyel were dueling with strong magic Denida had taught them when Denida came back.

Danyel seemed very into it when he got the upper hand over Ignacio.

"I surrender," Ignacio yelled, but Danyel continued pounding spells towards him.

Denida's right eye flickered. "Stop!" Time froze for Danyel only.

Ignacio turned gasping for breath towards Denida, he went over to him.

Denida shook his hand and Danyel's time freeze vanished.

Danyel studied confused around him until he noticed Denida, then his eyes turned red.

"Ignacio and I have an idea," Denida said.

Danyel spat on the ground next to him. "What for?"

"There's enough of us here, we need to make sure no one else will become like us; I found a way to get any demons out of Hell."

"How?" Ignacio's eyes wandered.

"The Gate in Lucifer's mansion leads to another dimension, out of Hell."

"You want to help someone escape," Danyel asked mockingly.

"I want to try it, not sure if it'll work." Denida rubbed his face.

"Why? It sounds crazy-" Danyel shook his head. "Let's continue, Ignacio."

"He's coming with me," Denida said. "We need to try to see if a new arrival can escape or would he face the fury of the Master!"

Danyel chuckled and he ran after them. "I think I want to help then, to cause more trouble sounds fun!"

Denida and his two friends went back to see the new arrivals.

He stopped, as he approached the place.

"Why are we stopping?" Danyel asked impatiently.

"We need to find the most scared new arrival, and get him to ourselves." Denida scouted the surroundings.

"Boring, let me just go get one!" Danyel ran forward, Ignacio's eyes widened.

"Stop." Denida raised his hand, like last time, Danyel froze in his tracks, but not in time, he could see this time, so he glanced back towards Denida, as he couldn't move his body.

"What the hell?" Danyel gawked down at his body, which was frozen in spot.

"We need to be careful, especially *you*." Denida shook his hand and Danyel fell to his knees from being in the same position for too long.

"Found him." Denida walked towards a man, who stood screaming and crying hysterically.

Ignacio went over and helped Danyel to his feet.

"I'll take him." Denida smiled to the Instructor.

"Anything for Little Evil," the Instructor smirked.

Denida led the man back to their hideout.

"No, no, no, no…" Danyel objected and came rushing over towards Denida. "You brought a new arrival here, he's too wimpy, he'll tell others about the place!"

"He won't be here long, it'll be OK."

Danyel shook his head rapidly. "You better hope it works now, he has to *die* if not!"

The man sweated, he was even more scared than before.

'Don't worry.' Denida glanced the man into his eyes. "We have an idea we want to try, to maybe get you to escape from Hell."

The man shook his head in disbelief at the three of them. "That's possible?"

"Yes," Ignacio said, reassuring him. "Why we brought you here."

"Aren't we going yet, time's wasting." Danyel stood beside the door.

"Not yet, I know when Lucifer's gone, that's when we try." Denida turned to Danyel. "Don't make me freeze you again!"

"I'm just saying it's dangerous to keep him here." Danyel slammed the door.

"That boy feels like bad news," the man said.

"I agree," Ignacio muttered.

"You're both wrong. We should go to Lucifer's mansion." Denida got up.

Denida called Danyel over when they got outside, he led them to Lucifer's mansion.

71

They hid where he had hidden with Ignacio before, waiting. *Guess we'll see now…*

It was not long before Lucifer came walking out to a meeting Denida had known about. He smiled, feeling smug. "Told you."

Denida casually walked towards the mansion.

"Shouldn't we wait, until he's been gone for a while," Ignacio objected while running after him.

"I know Lucifer, he won't be back." Denida continued towards the mansion, followed by the others.

Inside the mansion, Denida went straight to Lucifer's throne room, Ignacio, and the man cautiously examined it was safe. Denida shook his head and went to the gate standing on the side, it was big, old and dusty.

"Showtime!" Danyel came running in towards the gate. "If it doesn't work, I'll show him *real* fear," he smirked at the man with glee in his eyes.

Denida turned to the man, and Ignacio brought him to the Gate.

"Bummer!" Danyel watched the Gate. "How do we get it to work though?"

Denida giggled. "Let me handle that." He shot a black beam out of his hand, the Gate suddenly fired up.

"Guess it's time to try," Ignacio said and pushed the man forward.

"Try?" The man turned panicked to Ignacio. "Didn't you do this before?"

"You'll be the first…" Ignacio raised his eyebrows.

The man set into motion, running back towards them and away from the gate, but he was grabbed by Danyel.

"No, you don't!" Danyel threw him into the Gate, the man vanished through the Gate. It buzzed and powered down instantly. "Aw, he didn't catch on fire, I'm disappointed."

Denida went over and examined the Gate in disbelief. He licked his lip. "It actually worked."

"We should get out of here before anyone finds us," Ignacio said worriedly.

They went back to their hideout, acting as nothing had happened. Their friends, Nicklas and Pedro stared suspiciously at them.

Denida saw Ignacio and Danyel in the corner of his eye. *I need to find out where this gate leads.* "I need to go see Lucifer." Denida got up before anyone could say anything to that.

"Lucifer," Denida asked, as he came to his throne room, where he saw Lucifer examing the Gate. *Have we been discovered?*

"Someone was in here, where the Gate is." Lucifer continued to examine it.

"Why does it matter, where does it lead to, anyway?"

"Out of the Underworlds, it's a shortcut away, if something were to happen."

Fascinating. "You said it leads to another dimension?"

"They usually do, this leads into Heaven..."

Denida raised his eyebrows. "Why don't you lock it into the back room, where no one but us can enter? How do you even know it's been used?"

Lucifer spun around. "Because of this!" Lucifer held out a shoe.

Must have fallen off when Danyel pushed the man into the Gate.

"But you're right, we need to protect it, from outsiders." Lucifer took a deep breath. "Even the Darkness doesn't know; it's the one room where it's never allowed into…"

"A place for you only." Denida nodded.

"Exactly, I'll keep it here, just locked by a spell, only those who can enter know. Those that have proven their trust; *like you*." Lucifer grabbed Denida's shoulder and smiled.

***

"This is how they helped the first one to escape Hell." Daniel looked Edward in the eyes.

"He *betrayed* Lucifer?" Edward's eyes glanced at Daniel. "I thought you said, you would tell me how he escaped?"

"I am." Daniel gave a fake smile. "This was only the beginning of the end for Dad's time in Hell."

Edward tilted his head up towards the camera, he ran his hand through his hair. "I see, you should go on then."

"Be aware, from now on what I tell you, Lucifer does *not* want it to get out, Dad didn't either."

Edward fiddled with his hand nervously. "I don't care, go on!"

"As you wish," Daniel said. "Lucifer set a strong, powerful spell sealing the door to his throne. They had no idea who, or what had been in there. Denida, Danyel, and Ignacio were careful no suspicion would fall on them, so they continued being the '*good demons*.'"

Chapter 8: The Seven Dark Angels

Denida lifted his hand to open the door. "See you tomorrow, Luci."

He went outside but was met by Gabriel.

"Hello Denny, how've you been?" Gabriel smiled with those warm eyes of his and kept standing in front of Denida as if he expected an answer.

"I'm fine." Denida pushed by him. He went to the hideout, even with the tension between him, Danyel and Ignacio making it a less than a joyful place. *But what can you do?*

Denida stopped outside the hideout. *We really need to fix this*. He grabbed the handle and went in.

"Denny," Ignacio said and lifted his head.

Danyel just let out a grunt.

"This can't go on, Lucifer never found out, stop the whining!"

"Fine. We'll stop, but if we got away with it, shouldn't we try again?" Danyel smirked.

"No!" Ignacio abruptly interrupted. "They'll catch us if we try so soon."

"Actually no- but we should bring in the others in if we do it again, we have to be united." Denida stared straight into Ignacio's eyes. "All seven of us."

"Sounds like we could make some serious trouble, I'll get the rest!" Danyel dashed out.

"You do realize, Danyel only wants to do this cause it inflicts more trouble, right?"

Denida nodded. "For now…"

He was teaching Ignacio some advanced arts when Danyel returned with the rest.

"We're back," Danyel grinned. "Time to tell them."

Everyone's faces turned confused at Danyel.

"Tell us what?" Pedro, one of their other friends wrinkled his forehead.

"Yes." Denida took a deep breath. "Danyel, Ignacio and I tried to help a new arrival out of Hell, through the Gate Lucifer has in his throne room - we succeeded."

"Get a soul out of Hell?" Pedro asked.

"But that's betraying the Master!" Nicklas shook his head.

"If we do it again, I think we should all agree," Denida yelled.

The chatter died down.

"Why would you let someone escape Hell?" Pedro yelled and stared at the faces of his other friends.

"You really want someone to become *us*? Wouldn't you have wanted to have someone give you a chance to escape when you first came?" Denida raised an eyebrow and scoped around at their faces.

Everyone in the room lowered their heads.

Jan and Mia stared into each other's eyes before they nodded.

"Why not?" Danyel grinned.

"Let's do it," Nicklas jabbed Pedro.

Pedro nodded.

"You all agree?" Denida examined the room, where all his friends nodded.

"Great!" Danyel puffed at Denida. "Let's go find the next one."

"Not yet, we need to find a way to do it, where we all play a role." Denida peered annoyed at the inpatient Danyel.

"We need to be careful, there's a Dark Presence watching everything in Hell. It can't know what we're up to..." Denida laid out the plan to use Danyel, Ignacio, Pedro, and the rest of his friend's strengths, so they wouldn't be detected when they did it.

Danyel ran up to his Instructor with the new arrivals.

Denida grabbed Danyel and pushed him to the side. "No, you don't, remember what Lucifer said; cause trouble, it'll be the end of you!"

Danyel grinned. "But, it's so fun."

While Danyel distracted the Instructor, the others snuck the most scared of the new arrivals away.

They led the souls to the hideout, where Ignacio waited with them until the time was ripe.

Ignacio then took them to the mansion, were Denida was waiting inside, Pedro and Nicklas kept watch outside the mansion, Jan and Mia watched the inside. Denida snuck into the throne room. He knew the strong spell to unlock the door to Lucifer's chamber.

Inside he let out Dark Energy to ignite the Gate. He made the new arrivals walk through together, as it would power off instantly after.

"Wait," one of them stopped the others and turned to Denida. "You seven really are truly *angels* to risk saving us from damnation, thanks!"

Denida chuckled. "Yea, I guess we're the Seven Dark Angels."

They went through the Gate and it buzzed off right away. Denida went over to make sure, nothing was left behind.

"Seven Dark Angels, huh?" Ignacio grinned.

"Heaven had some, so why not Hell," Denida smirked.

Ignacio and he went back out, Jan and Mia joined them, Pedro and Nicklas ran to them as they came out of the mansion, they hurried back to the hideout in joyful spirits, where Danyel waited.

"The Dark Angels are back," Denida grinned.

"Dark Angels…" Danyel muttered. "I like that! We should use that, bring fear into Hell, by the mere talk of us."

"I was just…"

"No," Danyel interrupted Denida. "We need a name, it's a good one, we're the Seven Dark Angels."

Denida licked his lips. "It could work."

"Definitely," Danyel smirked.

The rumors of seven Dark Angels spread like wildfire throughout Hell. Vanishing new arrivals, and old tormented souls, completely disappearing from Hell. It could not be ignored. Lucifer and the other Arch-Demons were pissed, they called to a meeting, where Denida was invited, as the high apprentice of Lucifer, one of highest users of the Dark Arts.

"We need to stop these 'Dark Angels.' The story of escapes is spreading. They used the Gate once, but there are no signs of them anymore. They must have found another way!" Lucifer's eyes flashed with red.

"There's no sign indicating who it might be," an arch-demon said. "It's like they know we and the Darkness are watching."

Lucifer's face tightened with fury. "I want them, whatever the cost, this has to stop!" He glanced around the room. "How can it be *none* of you are able to!"

"We need to find them first," one of the arch-demons said.

"Then do that, *find them now.*" Lucifer slammed the table and stormed out.

Denida couldn't help but chuckle within. *They've got absolutely no idea.* He followed Lucifer, who went into his throne room.

Inside he found Lucifer talking to Gabriel.

That guy again. "Hello, Gabriel." Denida smiled. "What brings you here?"

"I was bringing an update on Heavani…"

"Thanks, Gabriel." Lucifer slowly walked out with his head down.

"Not good news, I take it?" Denida turned back to Gabriel.

"There's no good news these days, you should know."

Does he know? Denida stared into Gabriel's eyes. *He can't!*

Denida spun around, about to leave.

"You still enjoy it here," Gabriel asked.

What a strange thing to ask. Denida squinted his eye. "Still?"

"You likely wouldn't remember, but I was here when you first came. I wished you wouldn't need to be demonic…"

"When I came? From where, Earth?"

Gabriel nodded and put his hand on Denida's shoulder. "If you ever need help, I'm here."

The arch-angel's hand felt uncomfortable, it felt warm to Denida, but after a second he walked out.

Am I from Earth?

Denida went back towards the hideout, but outside of the mansion, he was greeted by Ignacio.

"Ignacio, why are you here?" Denida had a bad feeling about this.

"I need to talk to you- alone."

"We can talk when we get to the hideout."

Ignacio, the always welcoming demon, was being forceful. "No, now!" Ignacio stormed to the front of Denida. "- I don't want the others to hear…"

"All right, all right." Denida held up his hands. "What's so important?"

"Danyel."

Not this again. "You're being worried for no reason; he just enjoys having fun."

"You're wrong, he's our weak link." Ignacio stared determined. "You've got to have noticed."

Denida sighed. "I've known Danyel longer than any of you, just take my word, trust me."

He tried to give Ignacio the reassuring eyes Lucifer taught him. Eyes that could persuade anyone. "None of the others feel what you do, he'll be fine!"

Ignacio sighed and nodded.

***

"Jesus, he created the original Dark Angels and betrayed the Devil?" Edward shook his head in disbelief. *Really?*

Daniel took a deep breath and raised his eyebrows. "Yes, you're surprised?"

"That can't be possible! Is this how he escaped? Through the Gate?"

Daniel shook his head. "I'm not done yet."

Jack came rushing through the door. "Edward, you want to see this."

"But," Edward insisted.

"Now!" Jack sounded determined.

Edward sighed and rushed after him.

Jack led him to the common area, where a lot of demons were surrounded around a big screen.

What is it? Jack just rushed through, Edward took the chance to get through the same way Jack cleared.

On the big screen in the center of the room was an image of their old hideout.

"Have they found something?" Edward turned curiously to the others.

"No," Claus said. "But you're all here for another reason, too."

Another reason?

"Someone- one of you told this Michelle where we were, Jack oversees our security now. He'll find out which one of you did. When we find out, you'll face my wrath!" Claus' eyes wandered across the room. You could see a red flicker in his eye, even though he was no real demon, still he had endured torture in Hell.

"Denida created the Dark Angels, he led them in Hell," Edward said without thinking.

All eyes focused on Edward, their expressions ranged from disbelief to shock.

"Dark... Angels?" Claus muttered. He leered at Jack and around the room.

"Yes, the ones who helped the souls escape the Devil?"

Jack hurried and pulled Edward out of the room.

"He must have misunderstood, get back to your stations!" Claus sped after Jack.

Jack let go of Edward in Claus' chamber.

"What did you mean?" Claus stared with fire in his eyes.

"Denida formed the seven Dark Angels."

"You mean the original ones?"

Edward nodded. "In Hell."

Claus ran his hand across his face. "I have to tell Lucifer, did he know?"

"I don't know, he was about to tell me the rest, including how he escaped Hell himself."

Claus took a deep breath. "Go." He waved his hand. "Let him tell you the rest, inform me as soon as he does!"

Claus gave Edward stern gaze. "If he formed them, and Lucifer doesn't know- I hope how he escaped is a good thing..."

Edward nodded and ran out.

When Edward returned to the dungeon, Daniel sat waiting.

"Welcome back, something up?"

"Just trouble about who betrayed us, when we left the old place."

Daniel wrinkled his face. "Really? Someone betrayed you?"

"Don't get your hope up, it won't happen again. You wanted to tell me the rest?"

"Yes, you want to know the rest of Dad's time in Hell."

Edward nodded and sat down.

"A lot happened in Hell. As much as Lucifer tried, he couldn't find out who the Dark Angels were. It bugged the Devil, but things continued as normally as they could. The seven demons were changing, they enjoyed helping the souls more than serving the Darkness."

"I guess," Edward muttered.

"But not everyone. Danyel still got even more vicious…"

***

Hell is more dangerous now than ever before. Denida knew the danger he was in with his Dark Angels, but he didn't care, they got a feeling like no other, every time they helped a soul. It was like the danger was worth it, but Lucifer had set all he had into finding them. *Will he punish me, his precious student, as hard as everyone else?*

Security around Lucifer's mansion had been tightened, as Lucifer took more precautions. This meant Denida had to be extra careful, the hatred for 'the seven Dark Angels' couldn't be understated.

Danyel grew more distant again; it didn't seem like he wanted to work together with the rest. Denida knew the doubts Ignacio had, Nicklas was starting to sense it too, so he went to see Danyel by himself.

He found him in a remote part of Hell, where no one else was, it had a heavy Presence of Darkness in the air. He was practicing his Dark Arts, arts that were strong, but Denida didn't remember teaching him it. *I must've forgotten.*

"Danyel," he yelled and waved his hands.

Danyel scuffed, and threw a magic beam with a force Denida hadn't seen in anyone but an advanced user.

"I came to see you alone; you've been distant again. Worried they'll catch us?"

Danyel stopped and spun around. "You wouldn't need to worry, would you? Being 'Little Evil', the precious apprentice of the Master."

"Lucifer will make *me* suffer too if caught. I betrayed him- something not even an arch-demon could get away with."

"But you made us!" Danyel smirked. "The question isn't if, but when. Eventually, we'll be caught."

"That's why you're practicing Advanced Arts?" Denida wrinkled his face in worry.

"I'm just taking precautions, you needn't worry about me." Danyel turned back and started shooting

his dark beams out.

Maybe, maybe not… Denida glanced nervously at him for a few minutes, then turned to walk away.

When he came back to the hideout, he walked over to Ignacio.

"I talked with Danyel, you shouldn't worry, he's just wanting to take precautions to be safe if we get detected."

"That's why I'm worried, all the rest of us, think the danger is worth it, but Danyel *waivers*. Like the danger matters more- that he matters more than those we help to freedom!"

Denida sighed.

"I know you agree, why else talk with him?" Ignacio stared at Denida with a piercing look.

"Just relax on the suspicion, Nicklas is starting to share it. I need to go see to my lesson with Lucifer for today."

Denida went back out towards the mansion, he stopped as his eye focused on a demon getting tortured and questioned about the Dark Angels. *I need to remember, we save souls!*

The Arch-Demon chuckled. "*Little Evil*, want to join?"

Denida shook his head and sped off towards Lucifer's mansion who now had several demons walking around it. He noticed Gabriel sitting next to the building. *Why's he not inside?* "Gabriel?"

Gabriel smiled at Denida. "I'm just relaxing, the Darkness seems to be very on edge within. These 'Angels' of yours are causing quite an uproar."

Denida tried to give him a smile.

Gabriel stood up. "Just remember, I'm here if you need anything, just call my name from your heart." He pointed to Denida's chest.

"I'm a demon, I don't have a heart," Denida smirked.

"Of course, you do, Denida. The Dark Angels do too, why else would they help save all these souls." Gabriel locked into Denida's eyes and smiled.

This made Denida feel uncomfortable.

Gabriel broke off the look. "I need to return to Heaven." He unfolded his wings and set off in a spectacular light.

What a fascinating light. Denida broke out of concentration, hearing the demons watching the mansion walk by, he continued inside to see Lucifer.

Lucifer appeared right in front of him as he entered the mansion, even before he got to his chamber. Denida stopped, startled.

"Denny, the lesson for today's canceled."

"But it's never canceled. Why?" *I don't like this.*

"Don't you worry, I'll see you later." Lucifer smiled with the smile he taught Denida to use when he tried to persuade someone.

Something doesn't feel right. "Alright, I'll-"

Denida found himself suddenly standing outside. He had a bad feeling in his gut.

They couldn't have discovered us? He rushed towards where Danyel was, he needed to be sure, so he wouldn't panic.

But Danyel was not at his secret spot, no one was there. *Maybe at the new arrivals?*

Denida trudged as fast as he could to the grounds.

But it was empty, no new arrivals, not even any Instructors or Arch-Demons were there.

Something's definitely up. Denida rushed back to the hideout.

A Dark aroma filled it, it had for once a heavy Presence of the Dark Presence.

No, no, no... Denida ran inside, to find the room covered in blood. Nicklas was laying in a bloody pool, he rushed to his side, but he was already gone. Denida's eye opened wide as he saw the next room spattered with blood and Mia, Jan and Pedro's bodies with holes where their hearts had been ripped out.

Denida knelt next to Pedro's. The heart's gone, has Lucifer-

'Bang.'

Denida rushed up and ran to the room he heard the noise from.

Danyel stood hovering over Ignacio's body, in a swift move, he ripped out his heart with a Darkness filled hand.

"No," Denida yelled.

Ignacio's body fell limp to the ground in front of Danyel.

Denida threw a spell to send the heart flying towards Denida, he grabbed it and ran to Ignacio.

He knelt beside him, with the heart in his hand, he tried to put it back, but it was too late, he was already long gone. Denida's eye flared a bloody red, he turned to Danyel. "What… have… you… done?"

"What was needed. I made a deal with Lucifer, to end them all, except you, his precious pupil. He wanted you to feel the consequences of what you've done!"

"You did all this- to save your own ass? You told Lucifer who we were?"

Danyel chuckled. "It was only a matter of time before they would find us. Precautions, I already told you!"

Denida's red was now in both his eyes, even his good eye, which never turned red.

"I was told not to harm you," Danyel grinned.

"You already did!" Denida sent a Dark Spear towards Danyel.

Danyel waved his hand, and the spear flew out through the wall.

"You'll need to remember, I have the soul energy of four of our friends." Danyel grinned. He sent forth Advanced magic while he was chuckling.

Denida had trouble keeping up with all the spells thrown at him. It was truly the force of five demons, fighting him.

"Gabriel," he muttered before he completely lost out.

A bright light appeared in the Darkness, blinding both Denida and Danyel.

Danyel scurried away as soon as the light appeared.

When the light lifted Gabriel stood in the hideout.

Denida rushed after Danyel.

Gabriel blocked the door. "If you follow him, you can never come back."

"He killed my friends, I saw him kill Ignacio!" Denida's eyes started to glow red again.

"The Dark Angels, I presume?"

"I should have listened to Ignacio- even Nicklas felt something off..." Denida breathed hard. "If you're going to tell me it was just a matter of time, I... don't... care!"

"No, only it's not who you are, you and the Angels let others escape, why not yourself?"

"Lucifer has it watched, especially now! I can't use the Gate to leave, so what I want is *him*." Denida pushed Gabriel aside.

"Or you could leave with me; into Heaven."

Denida's eyes went back to normal, he stopped, looking at the door in front of him. "And let Danyel get away with it- I could've..."

"Lucifer will tend to him."

He made a deal with Lucifer.

"You know the Devil can never be trusted." Gabriel smiled reassuringly.

Denida's eyes wandered around the room where his friends lay dead. "Lucifer wanted all this to teach me a lesson- I no longer belong in Hell, I'll go with you..."

Gabriel unfolded his wings, the light reappeared around him. He reached out his hands towards Denida.

"It's safe?"

"Trust me." Gabriel winked.

Denida went slowly over towards him, Gabriel put his arms around him, and the wings folded around them. In a split second, the light of Gabriel flew upwards towards Heaven, and away from Hell.

Chapter 9: Afterwards

Denida wrinkled his forehead with worry at the sight which met him when he arrived with the Colonel. *This is where they had Daniel?* Michelle came over and greeted them, she saluted the Colonel.

The Colonel gave a salute back. "Sergeant. What do we have?"

"Nothing, it seems like they cleared all the traces, but we did find the room from the video, where they held Daniel." Michelle led them towards the room.

Denida let out a deep breath when he came to the room. He turned around the room, examining it from every corner and spun to the Colonel. *Back then, can it be?* He wrinkled his face. "I know this place, this was a place I used with Claus, back when he worked for me..."

"Claus?" Michelle said.

The Colonel and Michelle shared a glance.

"Why would Jack use a place Claus knew about?" Michelle wrinkled. "Wasn't he sent to Hell? Jack's a demon, right?"

The Colonel nodded. "Claus tried to scheme for power when Denida was locked within the Gates." He peered towards Denida. "Denida gave him to Lucifer..."

Denida stroked his forehead. "It can't be!"

"Is Claus who he worked with?" Michelle pondered.

"Don't search for Claus. Keep it between us for now, I need to check on something." Denida ran towards the car. He demanded the keys from the driver, then drove off, heading toward the lab where Dan worked on the Gate.

"We might have a problem."

Dan stopped fiddling with the Gate and turned to Denida. "With?"

"Claus, he might be working with Jack."

Dan gasped.

"I need you to find out through the other worlds, how likely that is," Denida stared into Dan's eyes.

"You mean check his other version?"

"I 've got a bad feeling. Before I check with Lucifer, I need a just cause." Denida rubbed his eye patch. "Lucifer might not have given up. If that's the case, we're all a lot worse off."

***

Such a beautiful gem, he's always there. Nina groomed her horse, Angel. Caring for him relaxed her, so she came out here every day.

"Hey Nina, this is where you're hiding?" Susan stood in the corner of her eye. "Where's Denida?"

"Denny is out inspecting the place they found, where they held Daniel."

"You're not?"

"They won't find anything." Nina led Angel back into the stables and came back out.

"The Colonel wanted you to watch over me?"

Susan sighed. "How- Oh, you can read minds! I forgot, but how are you?"

"You expect me to say; I'm fine? Denny has a ring, but won't give it up to save our son!" Nina sighed.

"He hasn't told everyone about the ring, he keeps it hidden as if there's something special about it…"

Nina grunted and walked out of the stables, annoyed.

Susan hurried after Nina. "He would if he could, but it's a powerful ring, you know that."

Nina groaned. *So, what!*

"You two were soul mates, always connected, feeling each other. When he was gone, *you* doubted Claus, as the only one! Denida went to Hell to keep Daniel safe- literally, remember?"

Nina stopped and spun to Susan. "I just worry it isn't enough."

"Daniel proved he was smart, it surprised even Denida. He outsmarted Claus in one of the worlds, have faith in him."

Nina chuckled. "I guess the Colonel was right sending you to watch me."

"A chance to enjoy the beautiful scenery, I wouldn't miss that for the world."

Nina and Susan both laughed.

Daniel, my sweet boy… Nina paced through the halls of Dynasty. *He must be scared,*

all alone.

She walked into his room, untouched since he got taken.

She scanned through the room, her tears dripping down her face. *This is worse than when he was lost in the gates, at least I knew Denny was with him.* She fell on the bed sobbing and buried her face in her arms.

Susan walked in, she stopped in the doorway. "I'm sorry Nina."

"There's nothing which can be done," Nina muttered with her head still buried, she sat back up. "But it pisses me off!"

Susan's eyes widened. "What does?"

"Denny won't give up that bloody ring! Powerful or not, he should want to do anything he can to save Daniel."

Susan straightened herself up. The uncomfortable look on her face was clear.

"He says it's valuable, but is it worth more than Daniel?" Nina tightened her face, she felt sure she had to do something herself, but what?

"I don't know what to tell you," Susan shrugged.

"But you work with the Colonel, you should know stuff I don't." Nina got up and walked over.

"I guess?" Susan shrugged.

"I need to do something to help, you can tell me what they know, but might not focus on!"

"I don't know about that…" Susan started to act jittery, she was clearly not liking the idea.

"You don't want to help me?" Nina smiled with her puppy eyes.

"I… of course I do," Susan stuttered and took out her cell phone. She clicked on the Colonel's contact number and looked at Nina as she brought the phone up to her ear. "I'm going to regret this," she muttered.

"Thanks," Nina said in a low voice.

Nina watched as Susan inquired about the latest updates. Susan ended the call after asking a few questions and turned to face Nina. "If you want this info, know Denida will not be happy."

"I don't care! What did they find?"

"Apparently, the hideout was Claus'. Denida told them to keep it secret for now."

Not him! The anger within Nina had no end against the one who schemed towards Denny and Daniel. She remembered how she had tried to convince everyone what he had been up to, even Susan always felt something was wrong about Claus.

"They don't know for sure, Denida left himself to check something."

Nina lit up like a switch got turned on. "I know where he went; *Dan*."

She walked out to her car followed by Susan.

"Think Dan will tell you anything?" Susan got in on the passenger side.

"He better!" Nina set the car in motion and sped off towards the lab.

"Dan," she yelled as soon as she entered the lab.

Dan came running out as if he wanted her to not go further in. "Nina, Susan, what brings you two here?"

Nina smiled just as sarcastically as Dan. "You know why!"

Dan shook his head and turned to Susan. He sighed. "We don't know if Claus is back, Denida asked me to just check."

Nina pushed past him, towards the Gate.

Dan hurried after her. "There's no reason to be here!" Dan tried to stop her.

Nina turned to him. "You know me, Dan, did you forget I can read minds?"

'Crap.' Dan sighed. "Please understand; I'm only checking the other Claus as a precaution, we don't think Claus actually has anything to do with it."

"The world, where the young Claus ruled the adults."

Dan nodded. "That's who we need to see."

"I never saw that. Claus had me locked up back then." Susan sighed.

They went over to the monitor, which was affixed to the wall.

"We should get a feed from the robot we have in that world soon." Dan pointed up towards it.

Nina sat down. "We'll wait."

'Not what I was hoping.' Nina peered over at Dan after she read his mind. If eyes could kill, hers would've. "We're staying, live with it!"

Dan fell into a chair too. "Fine," he muttered.

All three of them were bored out of their minds.

Dan was tapping his fingers on the table when the feed finally came.

"Ahem." The General appeared on the monitor. They all came to attention and stood up to salute him.

"You wanted to see me?" The General examined the monitor.

"Yes." Dan moved closer to the screen. "I wanted to ask you about Claus. You left him imprisoned, right?"

The General cleared his throat, he was clearly uncomfortable with something.

"What's wrong? I know that face from the Colonel, something happened, didn't it?" Susan wrinkled her forehead.

The General took a deep breath. "What happened is not our fault."

"You don't need an excuse, just tell us." Susan glanced at Nina.

"We had him under guard, but under the cloak of night, a Darkness surrounded us, he and all his guards were killed, their hearts ripped from their very bodies. Even Claus'. We're still investigating, but..." The General lowered his head in shame. "I can't tell you why it happened."

Nina sighed. "In other words, the only Claus who remains is our Claus?"

The General nodded.

"He's in Hell," Susan cut in. "Denida gave him to Lucifer in exchange for leaving our world."

"I have a bad feeling." Nina shook her head.

"Denida did too," Dan muttered.

Nina nodded at Dan.

"We're done then." Susan smiled towards Nina.

Nina's eyes turned back to eyes which could kill. "No, but thank you, General!" She unplugged the feed and turned to Dan. "Make me another robot."

Dan spun startled at her. "A robot? Why? What for?"

"I'm sending it somewhere."

Dan turned to the Gate. "Through the Gate? Where to?"

Nina smiled straight at Dan. "Hell!"

***

Edward stared, his mouth hung open. "I don't know what to say to that."

Daniel smiled. "This is how he left, now you know." Daniel shook his head. "Must have been hard for Dad," he muttered.

"By Gabriel? Denida was in Heaven?" Edward was almost afraid to say the very word.

"Yes, you want me to tell you how that went?" Daniel glared with hopeful eyes.

Edward shook his head violently. "I need to go!" He stumbled on the chair as he got up, and rushed out of the cell to go see Claus.

He walked so fast he almost ran, he pushed through anyone he encountered. When he reached Claus' door, he stopped and knocked, while taking a deep breath to gather himself.

"Enter," Claus yelled from within.

Edward turned the knob and went in.

Claus put down his pen. "Found out anything yet?"

Edward nodded. "Lucifer did know Denida led the Dark Angels, Danyel sold them out and killed everyone but Denida." He took a deep breath. "Gabriel helped him escape-to Heaven."

Claus stood up in shock, he dropped his pen on the desk. "What!" He glanced at the monitor behind him, Daniel was looking straight at the monitor. "Denida was in Heaven too?"

"Yes, Daniel will tell me about that time next, but I thought you wanted to know as soon as I did!"

Claus nodded and waved his hand for him to leave.

"You want to know about Heaven too, right?" Edward stayed at the door, looking back waiting for an answer.

"Yes, we have to know! But I have to call Lucifer…"

Ah, I get it. Edward nodded and backed out of Claus' office.

Outside, Edward stumbled into Jack.

"Why are you here?" Jack peered with suspicion at Edward.

"I needed to tell Claus how Denida escaped Hell. He apparently-"

Jack nodded. "He knows of Danyel's betrayal, get out of my way." Jack pushed by him into Claus' office.

Guess Claus will tell him, he must be in a hurry.

Edward set off back to the dungeon.

Claus rushed out of his office. "Edward, get back in here!"

"Why?" Edward was confused but followed Claus back in.

"We need to tell Lucifer, someone who heard Daniel say it, is best." Claus closed the door behind them.

Claus poured a drink and swallowed it. "Reficul, Reficul, Reficul."

Lucifer appeared in the middle of the room. He leered across the three of them.

"Interesting," Lucifer chuckled. His eyes went from Jack, completely past Edward and unto Claus. "Why have you called me, this time?"

"You asked me to," Claus swallowed another drink.

Lucifer raised his eyebrows.

"When we knew how Denida escaped Hell," Claus said.

Lucifer wrinkled his face.

"Gabriel took him to Heaven when Danyel killed his friends," Edward interrupted.

Lucifer's eyes turned red, just as Daniel had described.

The three of them took a step back from Lucifer.

"He was under God's control, and he got away?" Lucifer turned with anger towards Edward.

Edward shrugged as he kept backing into a wall. "Daniel didn't tell me yet."

"Didn't he? Why don't you go find out then!"

Edward nodded hysterically and ran towards the door.

"Why don't I go help." Jack turned, but the door slammed before he reached it.

"No, you don't. This explains a lot."

"A lot?" Claus asked.

"The mysterious last report I received from Medusa."

Edward's eyes wandered unsure where to focus, unsure if he should leave since Lucifer slammed the door, he just stood frozen in spot.

***

I'm getting bored. It had been awhile since any angels had been trying to kill Denida.

It meant there was little for Medusa to do but watch Denida. She had no direct contact, except when God almost had him killed in a car accident. Then she had appeared as a nurse and watched over him while he recovered; watching in case any more angels came- no one did.

But why hasn't God tried anything lately? She ground her teeth while looking towards Denida.

As night fell, she went to a barren field and summoned the Darkness, to inquire of Denida's souls' well-being.

The Darkness surrounded her. It wasn't Lucifer who appeared, but the Darkness itself.

"He's well and in the Darkness possession *for now*," the Darkness assured her, it left in an instant.

Medusa sat there for a second. Something doesn't feel right. Wait, did it say; 'for now'?

That feeling didn't leave her, it stayed with her the next day, where she watched Denida.

As soon as he turned in, she hurried back to the barren field, this time she couldn't wait for the long chants, she was too impatient.

"Reficul, Reficul, Reficul," she said so fast the words almost blended.

Lucifer appeared above her head in a thick cloud, as he couldn't physically appear on Earth without a lot of magic used.

"Yes, Medusa?"

"I talked to the Darkness yesterday. It said; Denida's in the Darkness' possession *for now*. Why did it say that?" She raised her head towards the Dark cloud.

"You worry too much," the Presence in the Dark cloud said.

"No angels have tried to attack him for a while, still think there's no need to worry?"

"Just a bad coincidence, God must be busy. Concern yourself with your task, anything else doesn't concern you! Don't call me unless you have something important."

The Cloud above her dissipated. Her eyes flickered red. *As you wish, but I know something's up.*

The following day Denida moved from his father to his mother's home, a huge change for a young boy.

This has to be a sign, my service is to the Darkness, not Lucifer; For the task of protecting Denida, he won't need protection here on Earth anymore.

98

Medusa turned, with both her eyes red and peered once more at Denida. *I'll protect you wherever you are.*

***

Lucifer watched back at the three puzzled men standing in front of him.

"The puzzlement you feel is what I felt; this was the last anyone saw of Medusa. One of my best arch-demons ever..."

Claus smiled. "She betrayed you too, like Denida!"

Lucifer stormed towards Claus and pushed him up against the wall, with fiery eyes.

"No one betrays the Devil!"

"OK, OK!" Claus lifted his hands in terror.

Lucifer let go of him. "Just remember, inform me of Heaven!" He flicked his hand and vanished

into the air in front of them.

Chapter 10: Heaven

Claus came into Daniel's cell with dark eyes, Edward was following behind.

Daniel sat up worried in his call. "Claus? You're here…"

"I decided I need to hear the rest of your story myself."

Edward sat down behind Claus at the desk watching the cell.

Daniel let out a sigh of relief. "Edward is here to protect you?" he smirked.

"Smart ass!" Claus sat down on the other side of the bars. "Do you have more, or were you just blowing air?"

Daniel giggled. "I do have more." *This'll make this trickier.*

'Am I ruining your plan?' Claus smirked and stared at Daniel.

"I… um… will tell you," Daniel stuttered.

"Gabriel flew Dad all the way into Heaven…"

***

Gabriel appeared next to a giant pearly gate. He sat down and unfolded his wings.

Denida stepped out cautiously, it was a strange sight. All this pure light felt unreal to him. It seemed like they were standing on a cloud. He looked around in disbelief.

"Who's the kid?" a man at the gate asked Gabriel.

Gabriel took a deep breath. "Someone I need you to watch while I go talk to God." He walked past him through the gate.

"You're a guard?" Denida squinted his eye.

"I'm the Archangel watching the gates of Heaven. Who may enter or not is up to me."

Denida grinned. "In other words, you're a security guard."

"I'm Saint Peter," he abruptly said, with a frown.

If this is the worst of his anger, even Ignacio has him beaten- had him. Denida sighed.

"Gabriel knows you from where?"

Denida took a deep breath. "I'm from-"

"I'm back. God wants to see him." Gabriel dragged Denida with him within Heaven.

Wow. It's not any less impressive on the inside. Gabriel led Denida past several angels, but no one paid them any attention. Are we going to the leader? In Hell, everyone would watch.

Denida was led into a gorgeous building, the most extravagant he had ever seen. Must be this God who resided here. *This is a throne room, no doubt! I can tell a throne room when I see one.*

"Welcome, you're Denida?" a voice from high above them asked.

"Yes, my friends call me *Denny*. Gabriel said you could help." Denida tried to fake smile, but he stopped midway. "I can't go back to Hell, you've got to help me!"

The man on the throne shrank to Denida's size. He stood up. "Denny." He smiled, with an even warmer gaze than Gabriel had.

Must be where Gabriel got it from.

"You can relax, you'll remain safe here. Peter won't let anyone in who's not welcome." He sat back down in his chair. "but don't tell anyone you were in Hell."

Denida returned a real smile and nodded.

Gabriel led Denida back out.

"You'll see Lucifer soon?" Denida glared with a dark eye.

"You want to know how he is?"

Not that! Denida's eye started flickering red. "How Danyel was punished!"

Gabriel grabbed him, he tied a ribbon around his head, covering his right eye. "You'll need not to let the Darkness out here if you want to stay."

That's right, I'm not in Hell anymore... Denida nodded.

"I can't always be here with you, you must be careful."

Denida adjusted the bandana over his eye as Gabriel left.

Time to go out into this strange world of light.

Denida paced around Heaven. *It's so unreal, no one's watching me, so different than Hell.* He saw a man sitting next to a tree meditating. *Like back home...*

"Strengthening your soul power." Denida chuckled.

The man opened his eyes. "It nurtures the soul, does make it stronger. The soul needs attention too, as everything else." The man waved his hand. "Why don't you join me. I'm Michael."

Why not. Denida sat down next to him. They both started to meditate 'for their souls'. *This feels different.* He felt a surge of light filling his soul.

'Having fun with Archangel Michael?' The thought Denida heard made him open his eyes to see Gabriel standing there, smiling.

Denida started to get up.

'Don't, I just wanted to make sure you were okay, but it seems you'll be OK here.' Gabriel smiled and spun.

Wait!

'Lucifer's still searching for you, Danyel will be assigned out of Hell,' Gabriel said in his thoughts.

"You need to focus," Michael whispered.

Denida sighed and went back to his meditating. After a while, they both stood up.

"What were you doing?" A little boy peeked curiously at them.

"We're just nurturing our souls." Michael turned to Denida. "This boy is Jesus. You- what's your name, I forgot to ask."

"Denida- Denny among friends…"

"We're all friends here in Heaven, Denny it is."

Jesus approached Denida. "Hey, want me to show you around Heaven?"

Denida nodded. The two boys sped off.

***

Claus stared with intent dark eyes t at Daniel

Daniel leaned back into his bunk bed.

"That's where he went. He became close to several angels, it was a new start for Dad."

Angels? Claus got up and peered towards Edward.

"Cat got your tongue?" Daniel glanced intently at Claus.

Claus rubbed his face, his glance got more vicious. "Watch him." He stormed out.

Outside the door, Claus stood, breathing heavily, almost panicky.

Jack, who stood opposite him came over to him. "Something wrong, Claus?"

Claus shrugged. "Denida was in Heaven. This is the last thing I need to tell Lucifer, I must wait. He might- I hope good news will come…"

"Don't worry," Jack said. "Denida left Heaven too."

Claus lit up, as a light switch flickered on.

"You're right! He did." Claus laughed. "Must be good news then."

Claus patted Jack, turned around and went back into the dungeon.

He smiled broadly, as he came back. "Daniel, why don't you continue your story. Why did Denida leave Heaven, as he did Hell?"

Daniel wrinkled his forehead. "Too soon, I haven't gotten to that yet."

"Then do," Claus demanded.

Claus and Daniel's eyes met for a second, the darkness in Claus' eyes flared.

Daniel nodded. "Your wish, I shall continue. Dad became quite close to Michael, who taught him Light magic. Dad found it interesting, it was so different from Dark Arts."

"Light and Dark," Claus chuckled.

"Yes, Jesus and he were often together playing, everything was good, so good Dad almost forgot about Hell…"

***

Denida and Jesus played outside to Peter's dislike.

Peter kept looking over at them with concern written across his face.

Denida and Jesus ran around throwing clouds at each other, giggling.

Suddenly Jesus stopped in his tracks, Denida took the chance to send a row of clouds after him.

Jesus didn't move, he just stood still and raised his hand and pointed. "What's that?"

Denida squinted his eye and examined what he pointed at.

An old Gate stood buried within clouds, so deep it was hard to tell it was even there.

I know what this is. "It's a Gate, there was one in Luci-" Denida stopped himself. "I have seen one before, it leads to another world…"

Denida carefully approached it. *How this brings back memories.* He examined the Gate, it was made of the same material as the one in Lucifer's chamber. *Why would a good place as Heaven have one, which Hell also has?*

Denida spun to Jesus. "How do we even get back?"

Jesus giggled. "I know how, you can easily get lost out here." He led Denida back towards the Pearly Gates to Heaven. Peter gave an unhappy glance at them, as they walked through the gates.

Denida walked aimlessly through Heaven, he could not get the Gate out of his mind.

"Hey, Denny!" Gabriel smiled at him, as he came out of the big tower.

"Gabriel," Denida muttered. "Why's there a gate here? It's identical to-"

Gabriel hushed Denida and pulled him aside.

"That's a name you don't want to say here. The Gates are throughout many dimensions, it's not connected to *him.*"

"Why is it not within Heaven? Why is it so well hidden in the clouds?"

Gabriel ran his hands over his face.

"God doesn't want it within Heaven, out of fear that *you know who* could use it to get in."

That makes sense.

Gabriel smiled and walked off.

Why does it feel like he's relieved? Denida noticed the tower, Gabriel had come out of. *That's a big tower.* Denida stretched his neck, but couldn't see the top of it, he went over trying to grab the door, but he was pushed back by a strong magic shield. He couldn't even approach it. *The hell? But everything in Heaven is transparent, why can't I enter here? What a strange day, this is.*

Denida met with Michael to learn more Light magic.

"What's inside that tower? It has a really strong spell on it?"

Michael nodded. "God sealed it, it has Darkness within!"

Darkness? Denida's eyes widened, he felt something he hadn't in a long time in his gut, was there a piece of home here?

As soon as Michael finished the lesson of the day, Denida ran off to find Gabriel. It didn't take long.

"Gabriel," Denida said ecstatically.

Gabriel gave his warm, but worried smile. "How're you, Denny?"

"The tower?"

Gabriel's smile faded. "It's sealed, to protect-"

"From Darkness!" Denida winked and nudged him. "There's Darkness here, is it like back home? I saw you came out of it!" He smiled and lifted his eyebrows.

Gabriel glanced nervously around him. "No. Only God can allow people in."

"Fine, I'll ask God." Denida ran off, not giving Gabriel a chance to object.

Denida burst into God's throne room.

"What a pleasure." God opened his arms in an embrace.

"Your tower, it's sealed by magic! How do I get in?" Denida stared with a dark glow.

God gave a smile, though not as broad as before.

"Not possible, Darkness lies within."

"Have you forgotten who I am? Where I'm from? I can handle Darkness," Denida smirked.

106

"You've got no idea who you are! You were in Hell once, but not anymore."

"But-"

"No, that's final." God lifted his throne high above, ignoring Denida completely.

Denida stumbled out, not sure what to think.

Is this tower a lost cause? Denida arched his neck all the way back to look up at the tower. Why would Darkness be within a tower overseeing all of Heaven? I must see my old Darkness!

Denida went back towards the tower, he examined it from every angle, but he could not enter, he had no ideas on how to break the seal.

My light magic's too weak... "Of course," Denida muttered.

He went over to the front of the tower, the seal still prevented his entry. He checked around to be sure no one was watching and waited a little for some angels to pass out of sight.

When he was alone, he turned back to the tower, his eyes, even the one not hidden away, glowed red. His hand gathered Darkness around it, as he reached for the door.

This time, the barrier didn't stop him.

Darkness is the way to go. God, the steps. Denida prepared himself as they looked daunting.

He started to climb the stairs, but shortly after he started, he reached the top.

Wait, I'm at the top already? Denida peeked back in disbelief. Must be a spell.

Denida smiled, finally he would see the Darkness he so missed.

He grabbed the door and went in.

He stopped abruptly, *this isn't Darkness.*

Denida stood in shock. *But-*

A boy played next to a woman, who was sipping tea.

"Denny, I take it?" The woman smiled. "Come in, I'm Heavani and this is Daniel."

Denida scratched his head and frowned.

"There's no Darkness here," he muttered.

"Afraid not," Heavani said. "That's God's excuse to keep everyone out."

Denida bit his upper lip. "But Gabriel was here…"

"God has him watch over us." Heavani poured Denida some cider.

"Why're *you* here?" *Heavani, how do I know that name?* Denida spaced out.

"Luci…" Heavani took Denida's hand. "God locked me up, after Lucifer and I fell in Love, and God tried to have him killed."

Denida got back up, he shook his head in disbelief. *This can't be.* He went to the window; he could see everything happening in Heaven below.

Denida turned towards the boy, Daniel. "Who's the boy then? Not…"

Heavani nodded. "Yes, Luci and I…"

Denida knelt beside Daniel. Lucifer's son, I can't escape him completely, can I?

"Luci knows through Gabriel, right?" Denida spun and stared at Heavani.

Heavani smiled. "Gabriel and Luci were close friends before. Gabriel does everything he can for us."

I think I'm beginning to understand why Gabriel visits Hell.

**

Daniel raised his eyebrows. "The Devil's son."

"No," Claus yelled. "You're not stopping now!"

Edward glimpsed startled at Claus' response.

"Tell me what happened, you can't stop there!" Claus moved to grab his gun.

Daniel nodded. "Dad visited Heavani and her son whenever he was sure Gabriel was away, so no one would be the wiser."

Claus loosened his grip on his gun.

Daniel smiled. "Dad learned Heavani knew everything that happened below from watching out the window and being told by Gabriel. But besides Gabriel, Dad was the only other soul she had seen since she was locked up in the tower..."

***

This is a very complicated place, at least in Hell, you knew Luci was bad. Here no one even knows who is locked up above them, or by who...

Denida turned his head as a crowd of angels passed him by.

"Denny, you're not focusing?" Michael puffed at Denida.

And you too, like Jesus, all so ignorant. "Sorry, just thought about something." Denida continued focusing on the energy of Light magic.

As their lesson concluded, Denida noticed Gabriel. *The only one in Heaven not clouded from what's going on.* He ran over to him. "Gabriel, long time no see."

"Not that long, just been busy." Gabriel wrinkled his forehead.

"With the tower?" Denida winked.

"How-" Gabriel raised his hands and nodded. "That's right! You saw me come out of it."

Denida chuckled.

"I'm just watching it for God." Gabriel smiled.

"Are you? Well, do say hi to Heavani for me."

Gabriel's eyes grew big. "You've been in there, how?"

Denida lifted his one eyebrow.

Gabriel shook his head. "Not possible, it's sealed!"

"Not for Darkness, which I can still use," Denida gloated.

Gabriel grabbed Denida and pulled him to the tower.

He checked around him to be sure no one saw them, when he was convinced, he turned to Denida.

"Show me."

Denida faced the tower and with a Darkness filled hand he opened the door to the tower and went in.

Gabriel followed as fast as he could to be sure no one would see them. "You've been here a lot? Does anyone know?"

"Whenever you're gone from Heaven, but only you, Heavani and Daniel."

Gabriel pushed him up the stairs to Heavani.

"Gabriel and Denny?" Heavani stood up, her face pale as a cloud.

"We need to be sure God doesn't know," Gabriel said in a determined voice.

"Does anyone else knows about Heavani?" Denida spun to Gabriel.

"Saint Peter." Gabriel rubbed his forehead.

"Figures." Denida shook his head.

"What?" Gabriel wrinkled his forehead.

"He's always looking at me suspiciously, even when I'm with Jesus. This explains it." Denida nodded to himself.

"How's Luci? Is he well?" Heavani went over to Gabriel looking excited, like a little schoolgirl blindly in love.

Denida watched them from the corner of his eye, he couldn't help it. *If only she knew what he's become.*

Gabriel and Heavani drank tea together until he bid them goodbye.

Denida couldn't resist. *I have to know.* He went over to the table and sat down, he met Heavani's eyes.

"You do know what Luci is now, don't you?"

She let out a big sigh. "Circumstances, he's still the same Luci deep down…"

Denida ground his teeth. He ripped off his bandana. "See this, the Darkness in the eye. I have to hide it here because of Hell!"

She shook her head. "It's not because of him, only the Darkness."

"Jesus…" Denida muttered under his breath. "Ignacio died only because Luci wanted to teach me a lesson. This *is* who you love, the one leading all astray!"

"Darkness is the one who led *him* astray."

Denida glared at her in disbelief. "How can you defend him?"

"The Darkness was there before him, it was created from the darkness in God's heart. Peter protects it from entering Heaven."

"God?" Denida put his bandana back on.

"Luci's as much a victim as me."

I'm not going to convince her.

Denida got up and went back down. He was not sure what to think. Is God worse than Lucifer? I know Lucifer's bad from experiencing it, but take the word about what God is? Maybe he was once, but has he changed?

Denida sat down at the fountain where he trained with Michael.

Several doves flew across. He peered after them. *I know who can tell me!*

Denida rushed up and ran towards the Pearly Gates leading into Heaven.

He stopped just before he reached the gate, so he wouldn't cause any suspicion.

"Hey, Peter." Denida smiled, with the same smile he learned from Lucifer.

"Hello," Peter ground his teeth.

111

This is going to take some effort. "I think we started off on a bad note. It's fascinating what you do, mind if I join you?"

"Do as you please." Peter stared out away from Heaven to see if anyone would be coming.

In the following weeks, Denida came by every day, to keep Peter company. As he was expecting, Peter mellowed a little over time.

Maybe it's time? "Gabriel mentioned some Darkness you're protecting us from," Denida suddenly asked one day.

"Yes, over the millennia a lot has changed. God had a time with darkness within his heart. When he threw out *the one who's not mentioned*, the Darkness found someone it could take advantage of!"

She was right!

"Lucifer was always a pawn," Denida muttered.

Peter's expression got stone cold. "How do you know about Lucifer?"

Not good. "Um- I um- Gabriel mentioned the name," Denida stuttered.

Peter still did not look convinced, examining Denida's face. "I need to check something; can I ask you to watch the Pearly Gate?"

Denida smiled. "Of course."

Peter ran into Heaven, leaving Denida sitting watching its entrance by himself.

He never asked me that before, should I be worried?

Peter came back followed by Gabriel. *Why's Gabriel with him?*

Gabriel sighed. "Denny, God wants to see you." He tilted his head to follow him.

Peter gave Denida a cold glare.

He followed Gabriel, who led him back to God.

"Lucifer- I told you not to mention that name!" God stared into Denida's eyes. "Peter has told you something few know, only him, me and Gabriel."

And Heavani.

God got a big stare. "Leave us, Gabriel."

Gabriel nodded and backed out while looking with nervous eyes at Denida. He closed the door from the outside.

Denida started to feel uneasy.

"You should have remembered to seal your thoughts, Denny. I can read minds too…" God approached Denida, who now felt very uncomfortable.

"I brought you in here when Lucifer killed all your friends, and this is how you repay me?" God's eyes were locked on Denida. "I'll give you another chance to prove to me I can trust you. Don't, and you will return- to Hell."

The look God had, made Denida feel like he could see through him, his gut turned more uncomfortable. Never had he felt his life threatened near Lucifer, but somehow, he felt truly in danger. *There's only one choice.* "You can trust me!"

***

Are they happy now? Daniel inspected Claus' face.

Claus just ground his teeth. "If only God had killed him there, our problems would never have happened."

"Sorry," Daniel could feel the regret in Claus, he couldn't help but feel a little bit of regret, even though he knew if Claus discovered why he was telling the story, he wouldn't live!

Claus sighed. "It's getting late." He patted Edward. "Feed him. We'll get the rest later, I need a drink!" Claus glanced over at Daniel. He sighed and walked out.

Edward brought Daniel some food. Daniel sat up to eat it as Edward relaxed behind his desk to watch him.

Daniel took a drink. "Just remember to be careful, especially if Claus is starting to watch me himself. Aren't they still searching for who sold your last place out?"

"That's ridiculous," Edward said. "They'll want the real culprit, which isn't me!"

Chapter 11: Journey to Hell

Dan felt guilty telling Denida what Nina wanted him to. He lowered his head and sighed.

Denida shook his head, he licked his lips. "No change to Claus, you say? Are you sure?"

Dan nodded. "I'm sorry Denida, but there's nothing to find…"

Denida walked about the lab, rubbing his forehead. "I was so sure; how could I be wrong?" He sighed and turned to Dan. "It's not you." He waved his hand. "Thanks!"

Denida trudged out to his car, and he sped off.

Dan watched as Denida drove off, he kept sighing. As soon as the car disappeared in the distance, he turned. "Are you happy? I *lied* to Denny for you!"

"Yes." Nina came out from behind the Gate. "The robot?"

"Why can't he just know?" Dan took a heavy exhale.

"Denny won't give up the ring; I believe he needs to. I'm going to make him see it!"

"Still," Dan insisted. "I had to lie to Denny," he muttered.

Susan came over and hugged Dan.

"Why are you aiding her, anyway?" Dan stared into Susan's eyes.

"The Colonel told me to watch her; I am!"

Dan sighed heavily, but Nina didn't waiver, she just waited impatiently.

Didn't seem like it worked on her. "It has to go through several worlds before it gets to Hell…"

Dan picked up the robot he prepared. He had attached a controller to it, this time for it to manage itself so it didn't need assistance. He set it in front of the Gate, stood up, glanced in the women's direction, and went to the controls at the robot.

Dan paused at the controls. *This brings me back, standing here with a robot.*

He turned on the Gate with the controller and set the robot in motion. It drove towards the Gate. Nina and Susan watched in silence as the robot went through the Gate, the feed died with the familiar buzz.

Nina sighed and moved anxiously in her seat. The feed came back on the monitor.

"It begins." Dan picked up the controls and drove the robot out of the dense forest.

Dan drove it towards the road with a big building opposite the road.

The soldiers there were used to seeing the robot, so paid it no attention. Dan drove it to the Colonel's other self in this world, where another version of the robot already resided.

"Dan? Why are you here with another robot?" The Colonel wrinkled his forehead.

"Don't ask." Dan shook his head and glanced at Nina. *I don't like this one bit!*

Dan drove the robot through the Gate. When the feed returned, he set it back in motion.

He drove around a hilltop, which lay next to the Gate, as it was hidden away from the rest of the world.

"It's a nice change since Danyel, the Dark Angel was beaten." Dan couldn't help but smile, as he drove through the streets to get to the Palace.

"What?" Susan glanced curiously at Dan.

"This world laid in ruins when Denida and Daniel first came to it, but now, it's starting to shine."

The Palace had become the high command of this world, but like the last world, everyone knew of the robots, so when Dan drove through it, no one paid it any attention.

"Hey Colonel," Dan said when he drove into the room with the Gate.

"Hey," the Colonel muttered.

Dan didn't stop, he just drove through the Gate to the next world.

"You sure went through a lot of worlds!" Susan pondered, looking at the monitor.

In the next world, a guard stood to watch over the gate. He stared at the robot, as it came through the gate, but he just watched it drive off.

Dan set it into motion in the direction of the castle, where the President of this world led the world.

The castle shined beautiful in the sunlight, bathing in the colors surrounding it.

Dan gazed back at Nina, Nina hasn't seen these worlds since her son had been lost within the Gate.

He had established contacts through the worlds, so he knew how it was and where to go.

Dan drove it through the castle towards the Gate in this world, it was very well guarded. The Colonel had been overseeing its security.

"Halt!" The Colonel pointed suspiciously at the robot. "We already have one of the robots here, why is there another here?"

Dan made a face. "Hello Colonel, we just need to get to another world."

"Why?" The Colonel was not convinced.

"I need to see something about Claus…" Nina stepped forward.

The Colonel nodded. "I see, Claus again. Let them through!" he yelled.

Dan set the robot back in motion and drove through the Gate.

On the other side of the Gate, they were met by several kids training magic on a field next to the Gate.

Dan scratched his forehead. *Where is it again? Oh, yea!* Dan had not been in this world that often, he set the robot on auto mode to go to 'the Holy Lands', an old famous historical site.

When he arrived, he was met by the Warlock at the Gate.

"Lady Nina." She smiled. "I see. Come with me."

Dan peeked back at Nina. Is she saying something to her mind, I wonder?

The Warlock led them to the High Sorcerer.

"Why did you lead us here? We need to go to the Gate." Nina stared with a cold gaze at the Warlock.

"The Warlock told me by telepathy, you want to see the Devil?" The High Sorcerer knelt to the robot. "You do realize, if he's behind your son being taken, you won't get him back before he has Denida again?"

Dan and Susan both held their breath.

"Maybe so, but I'll know what situation we stand in then."

The High Sorcerer made nervous ticks while looking towards the robot. He got up and led them into another room, with the Gate. "Here you go, good luck."

Nina nodded and smiled.

Dan turned on the Gate through his controller, which was built into the robot and it drove through the Gate. When it came out on the other side he stopped and turned to Nina.

"Two more worlds and we're within Hell." Dan turned back to the screen and drove up the hill, towards the town that was there.

"This was a very interesting world, Susan, Claus had control over it for seventy years. It was ruled by children! The change that happened here is surreal."

The town was nothing compared to before. People weren't locked within an age anymore, they aged now, and the children were trying to rekindle their childhood, with the adults trying to have a new start. Seventy years of no aging, being controlled by the children had left a mark. A mark the General had done everything to change together with the boy, Mark.

Mark greeted them, as the robot drove into town.

"We're going on, to check something since Claus got killed here," Dan said as soon as he noticed him.

"Violently too." Mark shrugged. "I hope you find something that can explain it, the General is very worried."

Mark waved at the robot, as it drove towards the Gate and through it.

As the robot drove out into the next world, both Nina and Dan sighed heavily.

Dan glared at Nina. "Are you sure you want to do this? When we go to the other side of this world, there'll be no going back."

"Go," Nina yelled.

Dan nodded and drove towards the Dark side of this world, where the 'Dark Gate' stood. He turned off the solar power which had been charging till now, as this side had no sunlight. He flicked the light on the robot, so they could see in the eternal darkness.

I've got an idea. Dan turned to Nina. "Can't we just see Lucifer in that house we met him at in this world from last time?"

"No!" Nina shook her head wildly. "Go see the *Gatekeeper.*"

The robot trudged through the darkness with the little light it had shining the way.

It got darker and darker, the further it drove on, more and more dark figures appeared, as they passed through. Dan made a worrisome face. *I hope we'll make it.*

Dan made it to the big dark structure, which held the Gate. A lot of demons were gathered around it.

He drove the robot to the side, dropped the controller and turned to Nina.

"We don't have Lucifer this time, how do we get in to see the Gatekeeper?"

Nina smirked. "Don't worry, I know how."

Dan rolled his eyes. "Alright." He set the robot in motion and drove towards the big crowd of demons. Dan turned off the light, it drove past the legs of the demons standing in front of the structure unnoticed. Dan could see the guards appearing in the distance. *We made it!*

The robot got lifted off the ground. "Look what I found!" The robot got turned around to reveal a demon grabbing it.

"Crap," Nina muttered.

Susan ran to Dan. "What can we do?"

Dan peered at them, Nina grabbed Susan's arm and tightened her grip.

"Don't get your panties in a bunch!" Dan pressed a button on his keyboard and the robot sent out an electric charge which shocked the demon and made him drop it like a bad habit.

He set it back in motion, it sped the rest of the way, as fast as it could go.

It stopped to a halt when it reached the guards.

The guards gazed at the robot with repulsion.

"We need to see the Gatekeeper- now! He knows me." Nina stepped forward to the monitor.

One of the guards stopped the mob of demons, running towards them with a gust of wind, which sent them all backward tumbling over each other. He turned to the robot. "I don't think so. You're not from this world!"

"You're right," Nina smirked. "I was here before with Luci, how he knows me. But if you want me to tell Lucifer you rejected my entry…"

The two guards glanced at the robot and at each other, their eyes now filled with doubt and terror.

One of the guards opened the gate to the structure, the other moved out of the way.

"Enter, please!"

Dan sped through the giant door. He peeked at Nina confused.

"Denny told me how the biggest fear of a demon is Lucifer- I used it!" Nina grinned.

"Wait!" Susan got up and ran to the monitor. "That's the Scientist!"

Nina grabbed Susan's hand. "You weren't here, this version of him took over after Claus got killed. He's not the one you know. He's the *Gatekeeper*."

The Gatekeeper chuckled from where he was sitting. "That's right, when I was made in Hell, my soul was split in two; Me and Jack, or the Scientist as you know him."

Dennis Scheel

Nina turned very intrigued to the monitor. "Both you and the Scientist *are* demons?"

The Gatekeeper nodded. "We serve the Dark Lord. Jack served the Dark Angels, me the Gate."

"You got what you wanted, we don't need to go further now." Dan sounded very optimistic.

"Wrong," Nina yelled. "Take us to the Gate, we're going to Hell."

The Gatekeeper's eyes turned stone cold. "I don't think so. Nice try getting here, but this is where your journey ends." He lifted his hand.

"Certain about that?" Nina smirked. "If I don't go see Lucifer, your other self, Jack, will be hunted like a dog! Instead of who I think needs to be; Claus!"

The Gatekeeper stood still, his hand hanging in the air, ready to send a destructive spell towards the robot. "I see why Lucifer doesn't like you- Go!" He lowered his arms and sat back down.

Dan grabbed the controller and sped in the direction of the Gate, he turned it on as soon he reached it.

Time to see if she can find out more…

The robot took the last drive through the Gate and into the point of no return; Hell. No robots had been placed any further than this world, Hell was still an unknown territory.

***

Michelle sat behind her desk. A soldier came up to her, he threw a paper on her desk.

"The hell," she muttered and picked it up.

"We found out where the call was from."

"The one who revealed their hideout?" She stared optimistic at the soldier.

"Yes, Ma'am. The drug hideout run by-"

"Oliver Favier!" Michelle threw the paper back on the desk.

122

The soldier nodded.

"Follow me, we're going to see Jack's old friend, Oliver."

Michelle led the convoy of soldiers towards the old ruckus of a place.

They stormed it, scaring the addicts in the house, who scurried away from them. The soldiers ran after them and pulled them up against the wall, before sweeping further through the house till they reached the basement where a door with armed guards stood. The troops hurried behind the walls before the guards noticed them.

"It must be where Oliver Favier is." Michelle readied her firearm. "Surrender, you're surrounded!"

The guards grabbed their weapons and started to shoot.

Michelle's soldiers started returning fire, but the guards were already behind cover.

"We don't have time for this!" Michelle stepped out, the guards shot, but the bullets repelled off her.

The soldiers turned to each other with big eyes.

"You'll drop your weapons." Michelle leered intent at them for a short moment.

The two guards let their guns slip from their arms. Michelle peeked back at her soldiers.

The soldiers hurried over to take the guards' weapons and contain them.

Michelle giggled. "You won't remember this." She lifted her finger towards her soldiers.

She continued through the door to the lab.

"Hey Oliver, you might wonder why the military is here for you, and not the cops."

Oliver's eyes watched in awe, he reached for his sidearm, but her soldiers came in with their guns, he threw it down and held up his arms and made a face.

"I… guess," Oliver muttered and examined across the room. "A lot of heavy artillery just for me."

Michelle chuckled. "That's because we're after Jack, the Scientist. You're connected to him."

Oliver stood up, waving his hands drastically. The soldiers around him cocked their weapons towards his temple.

"I only did a job for him, a call on a disposable phone for a fee. It had to be done with a specific message at a precise time!"

Michelle nodded for the soldiers to back away.

She glared doubtfully. "Jack wanted us to know where they were? - at a specific time?"

Oliver nodded with fear in his eyes.

This doesn't feel right. Michelle could feel it deep down in her guts.

She walked out, leaned up against the wall, stared into the clouds and gave out a big sigh.

Back at the Headquarters, she informed the Colonel of the latest development, she

went back to her desk.

Michelle went through the reports from Oliver's place, there was no sign of 'Jack.'

There are no further clues, he could be anywhere. She stretched her neck up and noticed the Colonel coming out of his office with some of his soldiers. *Maybe, he wouldn't mind if I checked something.*

She got up from her chair and walked casually over to his office. She peeked around to be sure, no one was watching before slipping quietly in.

She bit her lips. *Where is it, I wonder?* She turned her head around, with her eyes stopping at the Colonel's desk. She hurried over to it.

In front of her, on the desk was a folder titled; 'Claus'. Michelle examined to be sure it was still safe.

She scrolled through the pages in the folder while she kept looking up.

This is too risky. She grabbed the folder, put it under her clothes and walked back out and back to her desk. As she sat down, she saw the Colonel returned to his office. *Wonder if he'll notice.*

The Colonel came rushing out and frantically looked around. *Guess he did.* Her head lowered to look at some papers, after a short while the Colonel went back into his office.

Michelle grabbed her jacket and went out to her car. When she got into her car she took out the folder, from under her shirt. In the solitude of the parking lot scrolled through the folder. *There's nothing which stands out.* She sighed and put it aside.

Michelle turned the car on and drove aimlessly around. Her thoughts were raging, but none seemed to provide her any ideas. She stopped at the red lights. Her eyes glanced around while waiting for the light to switch, her eyes caught something in the distance, a former Dark Angel employee. *This is a chance I can't ignore.*

Michelle parked the car on the other side of the man. She got out and stayed a distance behind him, watching. When he started to move, she slowly followed. The man kept looking back and around him.

He seems cautious. Michelle stopped and took her hands to her head and ran them across. She mumbled something, whilst. When she lifted her hands, another face appeared on her. She peeked into a store window, where the new face stared back at her, she smiled. *I still got it.*

Michelle went after the man, who she now was sure would not recognize her.

The man went into a building, which had the shape of a warehouse. *It must be here.* She snuck over to where he went in and tried to put her ear to the door, but she couldn't hear anything, she grabbed the door and went inside.

There were several of those she was hunting within. *This is where the Dark Angel's associates are.* Michelle grinned.

"I think you went through the wrong door, miss." A man came over to her.

"I don't think so." Michelle smiled and made sure to show a little leg of her new body, to be sure he was still coming towards her.

The man couldn't help but gaze at her legs.

Michelle took the chance since his eyes were fixed on her legs. She flew with rocket speed in less than a second, gripping the man's neck, and holding it tight. The others grabbed their guns and directed them towards Michelle.

"I'm sorry, but I'm here for a purpose!" Michelle's eyes glinted as she said it. "I'm looking for the Scientist. I believe you know him as Jack."

The man Michelle held in a headlock tried to wrist himself loose of her grip. "We don't know-"

"Don't bother," Michelle yelled. "I know who you are, the former Dark Angels associates. So, unless you want to be reported, you better start talking." She tightened her grip.

"Fine," the man muttered. "Jack was here, he wanted to know who was behind the kidnapping of Denida's son, we told him for a price."

Michelle almost let her tight grip fall of the mere shock.

"Who then?" Michelle tightened her grip even more.

"Claus… for Lucifer," the man muttered.

Michelle took a deep breath; her eyes became red for the first time. "Not him again." She pushed the man into the room, her eyes still flaring red. *Lucifer, it's you again!*

The guns were still aimed at her head. She chuckled.

"You don't want to cross me." Michelle lifted her hand and all the guns were pulled from their hands and flew to the ceiling. She walked about the room. "Do you know where Lucifer and Claus have the boy?"

The men shook their heads.

"We wouldn't cross the Dark Master." The man got up from where Michelle threw him.

"He's just a mere pawn of the Darkness." Michelle's voice dripped with disgust. "You needn't worry about Lucifer, you should worry about me!" Michelle peered around the room. "Find me Claus, or you will all suffer *my* wrath." She spun to the door and grabbed the handle. *Oh, that's right.*

Michelle tilted her head. "Just in case you need them." She flicked her hand and the guns fell in a pile to the ground.

Her body turned back to her own as she walked out the door.

None of them will know who I truly am.

Michelle drove back to the Headquarters. *Can't risk using magic here.*

She took the file back under her clothes and set off to the Colonel's office.

Michelle took the elevator to her floor.

"Michelle!" The Colonel came running out of his office.

Crap. "Coming, sir." She smiled and followed him into his office.

"I took a look at your report on this Oliver guy. It looks like we might need to check on Claus."

Michelle's eyes got wide. "I disagree! Denida was very clear, nothing hints specifically at Claus."

"Denida could be wrong!"

Michelle shook her head. Wonder if I could leave it here, without him noticing?

"Fine." The Colonel threw his hands up in the air.

He grabbed the folder about Oliver and brought it to Michelle.

"Thank you." Michelle smiled and turned with the folder. "Crap." The folder fell to the floor, scattered throughout the floor. "I'll get it." She scrambled the papers together. "Claus? Why's that here?" She shrugged at the Colonel, who rushed over.

"It must have been under the folder, why didn't I notice that?" The Colonel grabbed the folder from her hands.

Michelle wrinkled with a puzzled gaze. "I should get back, we can't waste time from searching for Jack."

That was easy.

Chapter 12: Last of Heaven

Jack peeked through the door to Claus' office. He sat behind his desk swallowing the last of a bottle of vodka. Jack knocked on the door.

"Go away," Claus yelled.

Jack entered the office. "What's wrong?" *He looks wasted.*

"Everything's wrong." Claus waved his hands in Jack's direction.

"I see…" Jack backed towards the door.

"Lucifer's not the bad one…" Claus' head fell on the desk.

That sounds intriguing. Jack closed and locked the door behind him and walked over to Claus, who had passed out behind his desk.

He hunched over him. *What a mess.* He grabbed his temple from both sides with his hands and mumbled something, Claus' memories flew through Jack's head.

Jesus, this is bad. He dropped Claus' head and it fell like a ragdoll on the desk, Claus just kept sleeping. *I should reach out to the Master.* "Reficul, Reficul, Reficul."

Lucifer appeared in a dark shade in front of Jack.

129

"What now, Claus?"

"He didn't call you, I did," Jack smirked.

"Interesting." Lucifer walked around Claus and Jack. "And what can I do for you, *Jack*?"

"Daniel told the others something you won't like."

Lucifer lifted his eyebrows. "Has he now?"

"About the Darkness coming from God, you're being a pawn thanks to it?"

Lucifer's eyes started to turn red. "Did he now? Denny has told him this?"

"Yes, when he was in Heaven. They wanted some good news before telling you…"

"Good news, which will never come." Lucifer rushed Jack, stopping when he stood right in front of him. "You, not Claus- but you, tell me when you find out what else happens in Heaven."

The dark cloud dissipated with Lucifer.

Heh, I'm back in.

As morning came, Claus woke up with a banging headache.

"Ouch, my head. What happened?" Claus held his hand at his temple.

Jack set a glass next to him. "Drink this, it'll help. You drowned your worries about what Daniel told you."

"That's right." Claus glanced at the glass with a look of disgust. He turned to Jack, who nodded for him to drink it. Claus gave a big sigh and swallowed it.

"We'll need to get the rest of the story from Daniel."

"We?" Claus shook his head.

"I think you'll need someone with you today." Jack patted Claus.

"No, you go instead, you can tell me after!"

Perfect. "As you wish." Jack went towards the cell.

Edward stood up as soon as he entered. "Sir."

130

"Don't worry about me, I'm here in place of Claus to hear the rest of Daniel's tale."

Daniel bit his lips.

Jack walked over and kneeled at the bars. "Claus sent me, nothing special."

Daniel stared into Jack's eyes, he nodded. "It's only the rest of Heaven." Daniel scoped towards Jack, who sat down. "Peter was keeping a very suspicious eye on Dad, so he could not go see Heavani at all. He needed to stay careful. He remembered the feeling of being suspected, he had it in Hell…"

***

I can feel them watching me. Denida stretched his neck to look at the tower that soared into the heavens. *I'll see you, Heavani and Daniel soon.* Denida watched into the crowd, he could see Peter peering at him from the corner of his eye. Peter had gotten other angels to watch over the Pearly Gate. Denida smiled at Peter when their eyes met.

This can't continue, something needs to change, but how?

Denida decided the one thing he could do, which would work; learn more white magic and get closer to one of the most liked angels in Heaven, Michael.

Michael is, as most of the angels of Heaven, among the ignorant ones, just like Jesus is.

"Where exactly were you before Heaven? You were brought to Heaven by Gabriel, right?" Michael looked at Denida with those innocent eyes, like he was seeing into his very soul.

'I told you not mention Lucifer here!' God's words still rung clear in Denida's head.

"Earth," Denida said. I was there once with Lucifer, so why not.

Michael wrinkled. "But Gabriel doesn't go to Earth, only our normal angels do."

"I was a special case, why Gabriel went to get God when we arrived at the Pearly Gates."

Michael nodded like he was satisfied with that answer.

"Makes sense. Explains why you're so gifted at magic." Michael gave a tender smile.

I was, wasn't I? Lucifer selected me specifically to train me, why am I so important to him?

"I need to talk to Gabriel." Denida got up.

Peter followed him like a hawk. Denida tried to turn into the strangest places to try and lose Peter, but Peter was persistent. He walked back to his room. Outside the door, he stopped.

"Just so you know Peter, I'm just going to sleep," he yelled and grabbed the handle.

Inside Denida stood against the door, giggling to himself. *You don't know what I can do, Peter.*

Denida put his hands over his head and started a chant. The further he got with his chant, the more see-through he got until he vanished out of sight completely. He lowered his hands when his chant was done, he leered down at his body. No sign of it even being there.

Perfect. Denida crawled out of a window he had left open for this purpose.

He glanced towards Peter, still watching. Denida found it funny. *Now to Gabriel.*

Denida knew exactly where Gabriel would be at this time of day; in an audience with God.

He carefully went into God's chamber. I've got to be careful, God might see through the spell.

God was occupied with Gabriel, so neither of them saw through his 'Dark spell of Shielding'.

Come on Gabriel, be done already!

"Denida," God suddenly said. "I never should have let you convince me to let him into Heaven. I have a bad feeling…"

"He needed to escape Hell and Lucifer."

God shook his head dismissively. "He wouldn't have killed him."

"He got out of the grasp of the Dark side."

God nodded. "Very true, but if I had only gotten him killed before. I failed when he was an infant, Lucifer got his soul, *now I have it,* but it might be too late."

Gabriel sighed. "You want to kill him now?"

"I can't, Lucifer sent some demon to Earth, who's watching his human side! And his soul, I'm not sure about yet…"

"A demon? Alone?" Gabriel raised his voice.

"She's very good, I'm sure *you know.*"

"He has mentioned one; Medusa." Gabriel ground his teeth. "I better go see Heavani."

God nodded and raised his throne up, as Gabriel walked out towards the tower. Denida hurried after, but Gabriel was already halfway there when he got out.

He needed to be extra careful so God wouldn't see him.

Denida got to the tower, with Gabriel already within. He grabbed the handle and went within, he hurried up the stairs, where Gabriel was talking to Heavani.

They turned surprised around at the door, which sprung open.

Heavani grabbed tightly at Gabriel. "How did it spring open?"

Gabriel walked over and closed the door, staring into the room. In the direction Denida was. "Something's here, there's a presence! I can feel it."

Denida let his cloaking spell lift. He surfaced right where Gabriel was looking.

133

"Denny, you didn't!"

"Oh, I did!" Denida walked closer to Gabriel. "And I did too, while you and God talked of a demon- *Medusa*, I think."

Gabriel rubbed his head.

"Lucifer took me from Earth. God said he failed when I was an infant, what did he mean?"

"Tell him," Heavani interrupted the tension in the air like a bullet.

"What?" Denida turned to Heavani. "What does she know, I don't?"

Gabriel sat down and took a deep breath. "When you were born, an old legend resurfaced." Gabriel glared with piercing eyes at Denida. "-one that was prophesized at Gods Lord's deathbed. 'All the wrongs in the world shall be put right by a child, within his childhood years- This child will have powers like I'- that was the legend."

Denida sat next to Gabriel. "What exactly does this have to do with me?"

"At Christmas, the magic in the air was unlike any before. On Earth under a stormy blizzard you were born, God instructed me to kill you…"

"You- but I'm still alive?" Denida felt his insides turning.

"My friend, the President of the Underworlds, gave his life to protect you, but it didn't stop Lucifer from separating your soul from your body. He wanted to harness your gift, so Lucifer turned you to Darkness. God tried to kill you many times, but Lucifer's arch-demon, Medusa, repelled all the angels…"

Denida watched Heaven below the tower. *I don't belong here.*

"I'm on borrowed time here." Denida turned to Gabriel.

"I think so too." Heavani came over and grabbed Denida's hand.

"What do you want, he can't just leave!" Gabriel threw his hands up in the air.

"He escaped Hell," Heavani said.

"God will know if I attempt to fly him out of Heaven."

Heavani sighed and sat down next to Gabriel.

"We must go back." Gabriel pushed Denida towards the door.

"No!" Denida yanked himself free. "God will destroy my soul, I just escaped Lucifer, after I helped so many away. It can't-" Denida stopped suddenly with big eyes.

"What is it, Denny?" Heavani squinted her eyes.

"The Gate! I helped others escape through it, Heaven has one too, I saw it outside of Heaven."

"I've heard of that," Gabriel muttered. "I'll need to assure exactly where it is. Denny, be careful until I find it." Gabriel stormed out.

Denida set his cloaking spell on himself again and went back to his room, which Peter still watched.

Stubborn. He shook his head and crawled in through the window, and let the spell subside.

Denida went out normally. "I'm ready for you to follow me," he said to Peter with a smirk.

Peter scowled at Denida but set off after him.

I need to stay on God's good side, Michael and Jesus are the way to go!

Denida stayed close to Michael. Learning as much white magic as I can will be a benefit. Whenever Michael was occupied, Denida spent the time with Jesus. God would not want to hurt Jesus' friend, plus he might remember exactly where the Gate is. But to the disappointment of Denida, Jesus didn't remember.

"It's just an old relic, nobody cares about," was all that Jesus said.

Denida had to bite his tongue. *So, you think! I hope Gabriel finds it soon…* He sighed and noticed that Peter was still watching him intently.

"See Peter over there?"

Jesus turned his head. "Yeah?"

"Shouldn't he be watching our Pearly Gates?"

"I don't know, maybe he has someone else do it?"

Denida ground his teeth. "Maybe you should get your Dad to talk to him?"

Jesus shrugged. "I don't know about this…"

"God would be proud of you helping him, I'm sure." Denida smiled reassuringly.

Jesus nodded as he went towards God's chambers.

Just got to wait.

After a short while, several angels came over to Peter. Denida giggled, as he saw Peter walking off with them. He sat for a few minutes before he ventured towards the tower. He didn't bother checking if anyone was around, he just opened the door to the tower with the Darkness filled hand.

"Has Gabriel found it yet?" Denida asked as soon as he came in.

Heavani shook her head with a sad face.

Denida patted her shoulder and went over to play with Daniel for a while.

They were interrupted by Gabriel, who threw the door open, looking all distressed around the room.

He ran in and closed the door behind him. He rushed over and checked Heaven below.

"We… have a… problem," Gabriel muttered.

Denida went over and glanced what Gabriel was looking at; Peter stormed through Heaven with several angels frantically.

"What-" Denida muttered, he turned confused at Gabriel.

"It's over. An angel saw you go in here with your hand of Darkness, it was too much for God, he lost his patience…"

Heavani hugged Daniel tight and gave Denida a sad stare.

"God wants to do what he once failed at; kill your soul. You have to leave- now!"

"You know where the Gate is?" Denida turned as optimistic as he could, but Gabriel shook his head, avoiding eye contact.

"You'll have to find it yourself. Come; I'll take you. It's too dangerous to use your Dark Arts now."

"But won't God know you-"

"No, they're occupied finding you!" Gabriel opened his wings and nodded at Denida, who smiled back at Heavani before he walked into Gabriel's embrace. Gabriel folded the wings around Denida.

I'll leave how I came.

Gabriel walked past Peter and the angels, who still searched frantically. They were too busy to even pay Gabriel any concern. He continued outside of Heaven, far enough to be sure, there would be nobody from Heaven who could see him. He peeked back to be sure. When he was, he unfolded his wings to let Denida out.

Denida examined his surroundings. *Nothing but clouds.* He turned back to face Gabriel. "You're leaving me *here*?"

"I think it's your best chance if you find this gate, but if you want, I can take you back to Hell."

Denida shook his head. "My time in Heaven made me realize, I don't belong there, as I don't belong here in Heaven. I'll find the Gate, I know how to work it from Hell."

"Just be careful out there, it's a nowhere land."

"You always underestimated me, Lucifer too. Time to start my own journey." Denida gave Gabriel a smile and walked out into the clouds.

Where did Jesus stumble on that Gate? Denida had walked for what felt like forever.

'*Denny.*' A voice, Denida didn't recognize said his name with a chorus through the clouds, he spun frantically around, looking in every direction, but there was no sign of anyone or anything, there were only clouds as far as the eye could see.

Denida ignored it and ventured on.

'*Denny,*' the same voice echoed yet again.

Denida spun to look again to be sure, but there was nothing still.

"Who's there," Denida yelled annoyed. He sighed and turned, but Darkness met him, the clouds had gotten dark, and the Darkness was all around Denida.

"Lucifer?" Denida glared scared across the clouds which surrounded him.

The dark clouds had enveloped Denida.

'You know better than that.'

Denida stared into the clouds in front of him. "Lucifer's Darkness?"

'We're not his. We're here to give you a chance for us to be yours. All it'll take is your word, the vengeance you seek for Ignacio shall be yours!'

"This is how you got Lucifer, isn't it? Lured him with vengeance over God? Yet, here we are millennia after, with no change."

'You're different, Denny.'

Denida lifted his head, he gazed into the Darkness.

"You're right, I am!" Denida walked by, through the Darkness, no longer flinching at it, he didn't stop for a second to look back. He didn't regret it either, even though it took a long time to find the gate.

He stopped and smiled when he noticed it. *How I missed this old thing.*

Denida flicked his hand and threw a strong beam of magic energy towards the gate, and it powered on.

So long Heaven and Hell, time for a new beginning. Denida walked in through the Gate and for the first time he entered it on his own.

***

Jack stared at Daniel as if to be sure there was nothing more. After a few moments, he got up. "Thank you, Daniel." Jack walked out without saying anything else.

Edward gasped startled.

Daniel chuckled and walked up to the bars. "You should remember what I tell you."

"We have to tell-"

"Claus." Daniel nodded.

"Lucifer has to know!"

Daniel licked his lips. "Interesting," he muttered. He lifted his head, seeing Edward running out. "Wait!"

Edward ignored it and ran out, he caught up with Jack. "He could have more!"

Jack shook his head. "Doesn't matter, we have to tell Claus first."

He and Edward went straight into Claus' office.

They got met by Claus pacing back and forth.

"He told you?" Claus clenched his teeth.

Edward nodded with a sad face.

Chapter 13: The Wild West

Jack glanced at Claus, as he knew he had a roaring headache.

Claus put his hand up to his head. "Reficul, Reficul, Reficul."

Lucifer appeared out of the dark cloud in front of them.

"The three stooges again, I see," Lucifer smirked.

"We know what happened in Heaven now," Claus said, with sweat dripping down his forehead. "Denida was in Heaven until God decided to kill him, he escaped again through the Gate- with Gabriel's help."

"That's all that happened? Why did God decide to kill him?"

Claus nodded. "God didn't like his dark side, he lived there for a while, nothing else happened."

Lucifer stared at the three of them. He walked over to Claus and locked on his eyes. "Be aware, if you're lying to me, or keeping *anything* from me, you'll return to Hell- with no chance to ever get out!"

The sweat rolled down Claus' face, as Lucifer kept his gaze into his eyes.

"I've got... nothing else to tell you," Claus said in a low, trembling voice.

"Don't you." Lucifer spun away from them. "I guess I'm no longer needed here. You just get me his ring- and *soon!*" Lucifer vanished in a dark cloud.

"Think he bought it?" Claus turned to Jack, who nodded back. "Sure it was a good idea not to tell him?"

Jack patted him on the shoulder. "Don't you worry."

Jack walked with a purpose. *I need to go where no one can see me.* He peeked behind

him. When he was sure it was clear, he turned into an empty room, free from any outside intruders.

"Lucifer-" he started to chant.

"Yes?" Lucifer appeared behind him as if he been waiting for him.

Jack's mask fell with him being startled and scared down to his core.

"You should watch your mask, Jack," Lucifer smirked. "You've got something to tell me, I take it?"

Jack gathered his nerves and re-established his mask.

"Of course," he chuckled. "As you know, Claus didn't tell you everything."

"I'm sure, you want to correct that." Lucifer broadly smiled.

"Denida used his Darkness within him to get access to a sealed tower, which only Gabriel had access to."

"The tower in Heaven?" Lucifer leered very intrigued at Jack.

Yes, where God had Daniel, your son and Heavani locked up. Denida came there a lot, he learned something from her..." He paused, unsure if he should continue.

"Well, are you going to make me guess? Tell me now!"

Jack started to feel the sweat coming. "As you wish, Master. The Darkness came from God, it used you as a pawn-

furthermore, when Denida had to escape, it tried to lure him to Darkness; it failed." Jack raised his eyebrows towards his master.

"Everyone knows this? He escaped unscathed?"

"Yes, Claus, Daniel, and Edward does too, but the Darkness?" Jack ran his hand over his face to remove the sweat.

"However the Darkness came to be, doesn't matter, I control it now!" Lucifer turned his head towards Jack. "Unless you want them to know who you really are, you better make sure they remember that." Lucifer tilted his head. His face changed to worry. "As always let me know about any changes." Lucifer spun and walked into a cloud of darkness.

Maybe I need to see this Darkness instead, but how?

Jack stopped by the bar in the hideout. *I need a drink!*

Claus was drinking a few seats down from him, he ordered a hard shot, which he swallowed in full.

Jack went over to him with his drink.

"Claus, got some sorrow to drown?"

Claus sipped another drink and shook his head. "More like a worry, what if *we fail.* If we don't get this ring, Lucifer won't grant me my freedom, Darkness or no Darkness."

Should I pity him? He always was a weakling. "Daniel."

Claus rolled his eyes. "You want to hear the rest? Why he left Heaven."

"Might still be interesting." Jack raised his eyebrows.

Claus poured himself more of his drink. "Go find out if you want. I doubt it will be that interesting."

He needs to be somewhat in control of himself. Jack shook his head at the bartender.

The bartender nodded.

Jack went towards the dungeon.

Edward sat next to the prison bars acting cozy with Daniel. *What's he doing?* "Edward!"

Edward got startled, he rushed up. "Jack, sir. I was just checking with the boy."

Jack walked over to the cell. "If you're trying something, it won't work!" He stared into Daniel's eyes, his own eyes flickering black with Darkness.

"I'm-"

Jack held up his finger. "Don't bother trying to excuse it. I'm watching you!"

Daniel nodded and smiled before his eyes wandered to Edward, who avoided his gaze. "You wanted to hear more about what happened to Dad after he left Heaven?"

Jack got distracted from his suspicions. He turned his attention to Daniel. "Of course, it's why I'm here."

Edward went back to his guard post and Jack sat down next to the cell.

Time to hear what happens to him next.

***

Denida walked out from the Gate feeling nervous. He checked cautiously around himself, unsure what he would see. *Hell and Heaven, what's next in line for me?*

A sparrow flew off the Gate. Denida watched it as it vanished into the distance, all his eye could see was a barren field.

Denida walked to the top of the hilltop, where he saw men riding horses out in the horizon. He followed in their direction, it was a way to reach anything, here in the middle of nowhere.

It feels different here than Heaven and Hell, like the air is different.

Denida's journey took him hours, but he finally reached a settlement. It was very unlike anything he knew. Even from Earth, which he had been to in his days within Hell. The roads didn't have pavement but were dirt with tumbleweed blowing. No cars, but carriages and horses filled the street. The people wore strange clothing and carried guns.

Denida gasped. *Where have I ended up?* He wandered through the town examining his surroundings.

The people he passed spectated him with confusion, eyes following him. Denida glanced back. *They're still watching me!* He turned down an empty road, that was even more barren.

A gun fell to the front of his feet. *What's this?* He kneeled and peered where it came from; a man was hiding behind a barrel, with no way out. Another taller man was approaching him with his own gun drawn.

"Time to meet your end, Sheriff." The tall man chuckled as he neared the man behind the barrel.

"Don't do this," the Sheriff pleaded when he reached him.

The tall man smiled and raised his gun.

"Hey!" Denida tightened his grip on the gun. "You shouldn't attack an unarmed man."

The man turned annoyed. "Shut up, Kid. I'm busy."

"I'm not letting you."

"Letting me?" The tall man pointed his gun at him.

Denida aimed the gun in an instant and shot the man.

The man's eyes went lifeless as he dropped dead to the ground.

The man behind the barrel came out and examined the body, he took the dead man's revolver from the ground.

"That was fast!" He gave Denida his hand. "I'm sheriff here, you can call me Robert."

"Denny…" Denida fiddled with the gun in his hand. *I haven't taken a life since Hell…* He met Robert's eyes and gave him the gun and shook Robert's hand.

Robert shook his head. "With how you can shoot, you keep it! Come with me, I'll get you a holster and belt for it."

Robert led Denida back to a saloon, where a lot of people associated with the law hung out. Denida glanced worried around the room, everyone wore guns in their belts.

They didn't pay attention to Denida, despite him being a child. No children were allowed in, but since he was with the Sheriff, no one argued.

Robert handed him a holster. Denida put it on and sat down, Robert knelt next to him and tried to remove the bandana over Denida's eye.

Denida grabbed at Robert's hand before he could take it off.

"Trust me, Denny." Robert smiled.

Denida let go, Robert took the bandana off and attached an eye patch to his eye instead.

"Much better." Robert patted him. "How did you learn to shoot so fast? Where are your parents?"

Maybe, I can make it? Denida stared back at the exit.

"I see, you're alone, aren't you?"

Denida was about to get up. Robert held his shoulder.

"Why don't you stay with me then, as a way for me to thank you for saving my life."

***

Jack ground his teeth. "There's nothing more about Heaven or Hell?"

"That's what you're waiting for? Might want to have Edward tell you a recap."

Jack got up annoyed. "If there's no more of Lucifer, who cares!"

"I never said there wasn't, only that it won't come yet…" Daniel smirked.

There's more! "Edward, inform me and Claus if there's any interesting development!" Jack's eyes were filled with fury, he stormed towards the door.

Daniel turned to Edward with glee. "Dad went to live with Robert, he never felt as free, freedom from magic was a blessing. Robert eventually retired from being a sheriff as the years passed…"

***

Denida pulled his gun from his belt and shot the three coins Robert threw in the air.

He chuckled smugly. *As expected.*

"I'm still surprised you're so good since your eye to aim is on the side, where you're blind."

Denida giggled. "Reflexes are good from where I've been…"

Robert gazed at Denida with raised eyebrows. "You never told me where that was?"

No way I'm telling you. Denida shook his head. "It's best forgotten, I'd rather not think about it."

Robert smiled and nodded. "If you ever want to talk about it, I'm here."

Robert walked back to the house with Denida, but he suddenly stopped, as if hit in the gut.

"Stay here," Robert abruptly said with a strict glare at Denida before he continued alone towards the house.

Denida stayed back, he saw Robert clearly was not enjoying the talk with the men at the house.

Wonder if I should go near. The thoughts raged in Denida's head, but he stayed put. It was harsh, but luckily it was a short conversation Robert had. When the men got on their horse and left, Denida hurried to the house.

Denida came towards the house with a frown on his face. "You need to go, don't you?"

Robert sighed as he buckled his belt. "Yes, I do. I have to help, only I can stop them."

"No, who cares about them, you're done," Denida yelled.

Robert came over and grabbed Denida. "I am, but if we don't help, where we can, we're no better than them." He smiled and hugged Denida, he left through the door.

Denida scratched his forehead. No better than them? Them- like I was in Hell? Denida sighed. What if this ends as it did with Ignacio?

Denida walked over to a cabinet to pick up a gun, he hid it in his pants, then he spun and yanked open the door to go after Robert. *I'll find Robert, and protect him, I won't fail this time!*

Denida ripped off his eyepatch and mounted a horse. He used his magic to track Robert and set the horse into a gallop, he rode like the wind after Robert. His magic showed a clear trail of where Robert went in the evening sky. He caught up to Robert at nightfall.

Oh well, darkness in the air always makes me feel at home. He dismounted from his horse, as it ran further. He kneeled and snuck towards a locomotive and saw all the horses were stopped at the tracks.

Several armed men were walking about. This would be easy with Dark Magic, but I know Lucifer can feel where it's being used, so it would leave a too big an imprint in a world which has none, I better find another way.

Denida wrinkled his forehead as he examined his surroundings.

"Hey, you," a voice came from behind him.

Denida spun around, he grabbed the gun the man had pulled from his belt. They both tried with all their might to wrestle the gun from the other.

The man headbutted Denida, as he gained control of the weapon, which made Denida stumble to the ground and drop the gun.

The man grabbed the gun and pointed it towards Denida. He checked frantically around, pointing the gun in every direction as he turned; Denida was gone. The man ran back towards the others, but Denida appeared from a hidden spot, he grabbed the man in a headlock.

The man dropped his gun from the shock. He wrestled with Denida to get him off, but Denida was adamant, he proved too much and eventually, the man lost consciousness and fell to the ground.

Denida went over and picked up the gun and put it in his pants. *I need to wait till it's pitch black.* As the darkness fell, the wagon the armed men waited for finally came.

They started to fill it up with gold from the train. *Must be a robbery.*

Denida snuck over to where all the hostages were, including Robert.

Robert's eyes widened when he noticed Denida. "No, get away," he whispered frantically.

Denida snuck up to him to untie him. "Don't worry, I'm here to help."

"You're going to get hurt!"

One of the armed men came running. He pulled his gun as he ran towards Denida.

Denida reached for his own gun and in a blur he'd shot the man.

The rest of the outlaws came running as soon as they heard the noise. Their guns were raised, but Denida had already directed his attention to them and each of them fell to the ground with a bang from Denida's revolver.

Denida turned and smiled at Robert. "See, nothing to worry about, I'm untouchable," he smirked.

"You think, little boy!"

The gun was ripped from Denida's hand and he was kicked to the ground. He fell next to the other hostages. He stared at the man, who kicked him again just for the measure.

"Guess you forgot about me, but you killing them, saves me the trouble."

The man raised Denida's gun towards him. "Say goodbye, kid."

Denida's eye flickered red and he pulled the spare gun from his pants and emptied it into the guy. "No, it's bye for you!"

Denida got up and went back to untying the prisoners.

The man who came for Robert at the house walked up. "I'm impressed, your name was Denny, right?"

Robert rushed in between the man and Denida and shook his head. "You're not going to take him for the law, Alex, he's just a kid!"

"...who can shoot like nobody I've ever seen!" Alex defended himself.

"Take me? Where to?" Denida squinted his eye confused at them.

Alex gloated at Robert. "I've lost one of my Deputies, I think you could become a great one, would you like to help more, as you did tonight?"

Denida peered at Robert and back at Alex. *I failed in Hell, never could in Heaven. Maybe the time is now?* He nodded "I'll help."

Robert shook his head and threw up his arms.

"I'm sorry Robert, I have to do my best." Denida patted Robert and left with Alex.

***

"A lawman?" Edward couldn't imagine that.

Daniel nodded. "He wanted to really do something, he wanted to help. When he helped saving souls with Ignacio, he learned he liked it."

"But he didn't use magic?" Edward wrinkled his head.

"No, he knew Lucifer was searching and would sense the usage of Dark Magic."

Edward giggled. "So, never again!"

"I didn't say that…" Edward threw up his arms. "Then what're you saying?"

He must hear the rest; I don't have him yet… Daniel smiled. "I'm telling you what you need to hear to understand what comes next…"

Daniel and Edward's eyes met for a brief second.

"Fine," Edward grumbled.

***

Dan turned on the light, as the world the robot had arrived in was not just Hell, but a dark place too. Both Nina and Susan had come over to Dan. They seemed very intrigued.

"Where are we going?" Dan glared at Nina. *I don't know Hell.*

Nina bit her lip. "When we were here last, it didn't look like this. We got taken to Lucifer's place."

"Babies," Susan muttered and yanked the controls from Dan. "Now we're here, let's find it ourselves, who has ever had a chance to free roam within Hell before?" Susan drove it out in the distance.

"No!" the scream started, it was followed by many more agonizing screams.

Nina sighed, while Dan ran his hand through his hair. Susan on the other hand just continued as it wasn't anything she was worried about. The robot could see some light in the distance.

Maybe it has reached something?

Suddenly, it hit two legs and came to an abrupt halt. Susan rotated the camera to reveal a dark figure, looking down at it. Susan, instinctively set the robot in reverse as fast as she could.

"No, you don't!" The black figure grabbed the robot before it got out of reach.

"I'll take that." Lucifer smiled next to the dark figure, who handed it to him.

As soon as Lucifer got the robot in his hand, the image changed to that of his chamber, Dan remembered it clearly.

"Welcome to my home!" Lucifer threw out his arms.

Dan and Nina glared at each other.

"Why did you kill off the young Claus?" Nina demanded.

Lucifer's face clearly showed he was surprised at the question. "I didn't know he was even dead."

"Really?" Nina said with a sarcastic tone. "What about the Scientist, Jack. The Gatekeeper said they were both from Hell, or do you not know about that either?"

Lucifer gave a broad smile. "I know everything that happens in Hell, I know of their training." He wrinkled his forehead. "Is this why you have come with a robot, which has a controller from the alloy the ring is made of? You never can get it back, you know?"

"The ring is from the same alloy?" Dan went close to the screen.

Lucifer stared with dark eyes at Dan. "We're done!"

"Wait," Dan yelled and threw up his hands.

But it was too late, Lucifer had already thrown a beam of Darkness towards the robot and ended the feed.

"That's it, I guess." Susan sighed.

Dan shook his head. "We learned Jack wasn't just connected with the Dark Angels, but he was a demon too…"

And I learned something interesting about the ring.

Chapter 14: The Deputies and the Sheriff

Denida paced aimlessly about in the forest leading up to Dynasty. Birds darted overhead. Denida's neck stretched as he took in the sky. *So relaxing.*

"Denida?"

Dan! Denida kept looking up. "Unless you have something important, Dan, leave me alone."

"Your… ring," Dan muttered.

Denida shrugged, he squinted his eyes. "My ring?"

Dan approached Denida staring down at the ground. "I need to see it, can you come with me to the lab?"

Why?

"I may have an idea…" Dan wrinkled his head and smiled.

Denida sighed. "All right…" If his idea can save Daniel…

Denida and Dan drove towards the lab. Dan glanced down at Denida's gloves, before looking back at the road. "You have it on?"

Denida took off his one glove and held his hand up. "Always do, Lucifer wants it." He fiddled with the ring and sighed before he put the glove back on. "What's your idea?"

Dan squeezed tight on the wheel. "Um- the ring is old, maybe it's the same material as-"

"The Gate," Denida abruptly cut in. "It's the alloy the Gates are made of, yes."

Dan wrinkled his forehead, licked his lips and peeked over at Denida.

"You still have an idea?" Denida raised his eyebrows with a piercing look.

Dan nodded.

When they got to the lab, Dan went over to a spectroscope where a piece of the mysterious alloy from the gate already rested. He sat down, smiled at Denida and put out his hand. "The ring?"

Denida glared suspiciously at Dan, but he took off his glove again and pulled the ring off. A dark aura formed around him momentarily, then vanished as he handed it to Dan.

Dan put the ring down and examined it with the spectroscope, he moved the piece between it and the device next to it. He grunted a little every few minutes.

"Well?" Denida puffed Dan after a few minutes.

"Yes, of course!" Dan handed Denida the ring back.

Denida grabbed it and put it on.

"They are the same- exactly. The *alloy* is the same." Dan picked the piece of the Gate up and inspected it.

"I already know this, how's this an idea?"

"Jack might not know, but we know this."

Denida exhaled heavily. "I repeat; how does that help us?"

"We can produce a copy ring from the alloy!"

Denida suddenly lit up. *That can work*! "You can make that?"

Dan shuddered. "I think so, now we know, they're the same; I'll try."

***

153

Nina had gone back to grooming Angel.

Susan sat down on a bench at the stables, with her head buried in her lap.

"Why don't you want to tell Denida or the Colonel? We can't do anything anymore…" Susan shook her head with a big sigh.

Nina threw the brush in the bucket and came around the back of Angel. "Jack and his other self were demons, something just doesn't feel right!"

"Maybe so," Susan said. "But the Dark Angels aren't here anymore."

Nina nodded with a glow in her eyes. She brought Angel back into the stables. "Come on." Nina dragged at Susan.

"Where are we going?"

Nina ran back to Dynasty and in the main hall, she went down under the stairs, to a secret chamber few could access. *I can access all of Dynasty from here.* She scanned her eyes with the iris, voice and picture scanners.

Susan stopped as Nina went further in. "This is where Claus wanted to get in, cause he thought he could find something on a time machine and the Dark Angels."

Nina giggled. "He was half right, there's something on who worked with the Dark Angels, that's why we're here!" Nina sat down behind a big monitor.

She brought up a folder entitled; 'The Dark Angels and their Associates.'

Susan approached in awe written all over her face.

"We can access any confidential file in the Underworld servers from here." Nina turned her attention back to the screen.

She brought up a list of former associates of the Dark Angels who were still hunted as fugitives. She loaded the CCTV cameras, which were all connected to the network.

"What are you doing?" Susan walked over to Nina.

"Something nobody thought of…" Nina searched the cameras feed for the last month.

Susan shook her head. "You're not going to find anything, we already-"

'*beep.*' The screen flickered green.

Susan rushed over. "It found something? That's *not* possible!"

Nina highlighted what it found; A man who was one of the wanted ex-employees of the Dark Angels.

He went into a large warehouse.

"It was a long time ago," Susan argued looking after Nina, who got up.

"You're right, we better check the place out!" Nina rushed out.

"Wait! Us? Shouldn't we call the military?" Susan ran after her.

Nina and Susan drove into the city, where the warehouse was located. Susan checked her sidearm. "I really think we should call for backup."

"Might not be anyone there anymore." Nina smiled.

'*You wouldn't be going if you thought that.*' Nina peered over at her, as she could hear Susan's thoughts.

Nina parked the car opposite the warehouse. Nina was about to get out, but Susan grabbed her arm.

The man from the video came out of the warehouse. Nina gloated at Susan and winked.

"There's someone else." Susan tilted her head.

Nina spun around to see a woman, a very attractive one too, coming out after him. The two talked for a moment before the lady bid him farewell.

"I'm armed, I'll get the guy, you follow the woman." Susan ran across the street.

Oh man, the woman doesn't sound like she knows anything.

Nina got out and followed the woman reluctantly. The woman kept looking back.

Maybe Susan should have taken her given how panicky she seems.

But Nina stayed a little behind her, she didn't seem to recognize her. The woman stopped next to a truck. She examined thoroughly around her, so much even Nina had to duck. *Isn't that a military truck?*

When the woman had checked around she got into her car and set it into motion. Nina glared up to find another woman sitting behind the wheel as it drove off.

The hell? How- wait, I've seen that face somewhere...

Nina walked back to the warehouse. She saw Susan standing next to their car alone.

"Where's the guy?" Nina raised her eyebrows.

Susan sighed.

Something's wrong.

"I followed the man. He went into the warehouse." Susan glanced over towards the warehouse. "I readied my gun and charged in- but inside was only an empty warehouse. He had vanished!"

"Strange," Nina muttered.

Susan nodded. "We should report it. Michelle, the Sergeant who's helping with looking for Daniel handled the former associates."

Of course, Michelle! Nina's eyes lit up. A smile started to appear on her face, but it suddenly turned into a frown. *She's helping to find Daniel...*

"What is it? Why do you look so troubled?"

Nina bit her lips. "Don't think I'm crazy, when that woman drove off, her face changed, as a spell lifted; it showed her being that *Michelle*."

Susan wrinkled her forehead and shook her head. "You saw a change, as she drove off? The speed probably made it hard to-"

"No, I know what I saw!"

"I work with Michelle, she wants them *bad*. She wouldn't work with them!" Susan stared into Nina's eyes. Her eyes suddenly widened. "Why don't we go report what we found to her, you'll see there's nothing to worry about."

"Persuade me there's nothing?"

Susan nodded with a reassuring smile. Nina followed Susan into the car, they drove towards the military headquarters. Susan led the way when they got to the Headquarters. They came onto the floor where Michelle worked and saw her sitting behind her desk.

"I need to see the Colonel, wait here." Susan knocked on the Colonel's door.

Wait? I don't think so!

Nina walked slowly towards Michelle while looking intensely at her face.

Michelle smiled as she noticed her approaching. "Lady Nina, what an honor, what can I do for you?"

"Dark Angels!" Nina stared at her.

Michelle shrugged. "Yeah, I hunted their associates, what about them?"

Nina leaned over the table. "Guess where I've just been?"

"Where?" Michelle shrugged.

"The warehouse," Nina said smugly.

"Nina!" The Colonel dragged her away and into his office, where Susan stood leaning up against the desk.

"Let go of me!" Nina wrestled out of his embrace.

Susan rushed in front of the door, blocking Nina.

"She was at the warehouse, I know it!" Nina stopped with her mouth open.

"She's using the former associates to find Jack and Daniel," the Colonel said behind her.

"But why-"

The Colonel shook his head. "Nobody here can know we're working with them. Let Michelle handle it!"

Is he letting her do it alone? Nina gazed at Michelle, who lifted her head with a broad glare.

"I don't like this!" Nina shook her head.

***

Edward saw Jack, who sat in Claus' office, while Claus slept in the back.

He peered nervously at Claus. "Isn't it best we wait-"

"I handle security here, has Daniel told you anything useful?"

Edward shrugged. "Just how Denida became a Deputy."

Jack wrinkled his face. "Get him to tell you the rest ASAP. I'm busy finding out who betrayed us!"

Edward's eyes lit up. "Of course!" He turned and ran out.

He walked at a fast pace to the dungeon. Another demon stood to watch over Daniel in Edward's absence.

"I'm back," Edward said. "I'll take over."

The demon nodded and went out. Daniel sat up on his bunk bed.

Edward walked over to his cell. "Jack's busy finding out who sold us out, just as I said."

"With Claus?"

Edward shook his head. "Claus set *him* to do it."

Daniel grinned. "So, he's free to do as he wishes."

"That's-" Edward rubbed his forehead. "Why don't you worry about telling me the rest!"

Daniel nodded. "As you wish."

He smiled as Edward sat down in his chair. "Dad became a law enforcer for Alex in the years which followed, and he quickly became a force feared by the outlaws…"

***

Denida dismounted his horse and tied it to the hitching post, outside the Sherriff's office.

As he examined his surroundings, a sparrow flew across above.

He put down a big bar of gold with a big bump on Alex' desk, smiled and raised an eyebrow.

"All gone, I take it?" Alex leaned back in his chair.

"Naturally," Denida smirked and sat down behind his own desk.

"Be careful not to get too cocky!" Alex rolled his eyes.

"Sure." Denida smiled. *I was in Hell, this isn't cocky-but maybe I should be careful what I show…*

Another Deputy came over to Alex. "They got away. Our people all died."

Alex sighed and smacked his fist on the table, making everyone's eyes turn to him.

Denida, who was ready for a nap, lifted his cowboy hat at all the ruckus.

Alex never loses it. "Why are you getting so upset?"

Alex tightened his hand in a fist as he went over to Denida.

"We had these outlaws which had caused so much trouble. They were all cornered, they robbed the bank, got away and even killed the law."

Denida put his hat back on, raised his eyebrow with a smile. "You want *me* to get them?"

"You? Alone?" Alex shrugged.

"I'm cocky for a reason, allow me to show you!" Denida got up. "Just tell me where, and I'll take care of this thorn of yours."

159

Alex turned around. He ran his hand through his hair and put on his hat, before returning to Denida. "If you think you can, go ahead!"

Time to have some fun. Denida chuckled and went out to his horse and rode off. Denida used the bank they robbed as a starting point. From there he started to track them. Not with magic anymore, he knew how to track through what he had learned. Denida dismounted from his horse to examine the trail to be sure it was the right one he was following. *They've been here, I must be fast before the wind comes, it could remove their trace!* He jumped back on his horse and followed.

As he followed the trail he noticed something. A sparrow kept on his trail.

That's strange, there was one at the Sheriff's office too. It has to be a coincidence, if it was Lucifer, he would be all over me already. Not his style.

He turned his focus back on the trail.

When night fell, so did his luck. A huge storm blew up in front of him. The wind blew away all trace of the outlaws. The sand and dirt around Denida forced him to cover his face as the wind raged. His horse was uneasy, and he patted it to soothe it, but the storm was vast, they couldn't stay in the open.

He spotted a cave and led the horse to it. The cave was dark and quiet, but a torch hung on the wall. Denida grabbed it and set it alight.

"Ouch! The brightness," an old woman put her hands in front of her face.

"Sorry." Denida hurried to position it away from her.

She smiled. "Thank you kindly, that's a big storm which came all of a sudden."

Denida wiped some of the dust off his face. "Yes, it is. How long have you been here?"

She poured Denida some warm tea. "I'm always here, I live here."

Denida drank some of his hot tea. *It's nice with something warm- wait!* His eye lit up.

"You live here? You've seen any others come by here?" Denida glared a hopeful eye at the old woman.

"Many come by here," she said with a smile.

Denida sighed. "A large party- with a wagon or something to carry a stash of money, perhaps?"

The woman nodded. "Yes, I remember them; they were going back home from the robbery..."

Denida nipped at his tongue. "You know where their home is?"

"Of course, I often see them."

I got them! "Great," Denida said excitedly. "Thank you."

The woman poured Denida more tea. "Anytime. I'm happy to help the law."

They waited the rest of the storm out.

Denida dozed off as it grew late.

When Denida awoke, his eye patch was gone.

As an instinct he rushed his hands to his eye, he got up and hysterically, he glanced frantically across the cave.

His eye fell on the other side of the room, where the old woman sat with the patch in her lap. "What are you doing with my eye patch?"

The woman smiled. She walked over to Denida and went to the back of him, where she put it back. "I just cleaned your patch." She nodded with a tender smile. "I'm sorry if I wasn't supposed to."

Denida shrugged. Guess it was nothing to worry about.

Since the storm had passed, Denida continued further on his horse. He could no longer track, but the woman had luckily told him where they would be.

As he approached their settlement, Denida got off his horse and tied it to a tree. He snuck the rest of the way to be sure he wouldn't be detected.

It was an outlaw outpost, which had several guards patrolling it. *This won't be easy, but most are in the saloon.* He studied the surroundings, the saloon was located at the center of the settlement, he could not approach it undetected. He took off his hat and ran his fingers through his hair.

The old woman. He put his hat on and went back towards his horse, jumped on it and rushed to the cave.

Denida got off his horse and ran into the cave, while the horse munched on some grass.

Inside of the cave, the only light was from the outside which was more now in the sunlight, but the woman was nowhere to be seen, even all the stuff she lived with was gone, as if, she had never even been there.

Where's she? Why are all traces of her gone? Do I remember the place wrong?

Denida could not believe his eye. He was still at a loss when he came out of the cave.

He sighed heavily, and his eye caught a glimpse of something; a sparrow. *Is it back?*

It hovered around him. Denida walked over and patted his horse.

The sparrow suddenly flew away.

Maybe not, but why do I have such a bad feeling? Either way, the woman is gone! Denida jumped into the saddle and set it back into a lope. When Denida reached the settlement again, nightfall had arrived.

Might be easier with the darkness. There were fewer patrols at night, apparently. Denida still had the mind of a demon within him, so he knew to be careful, one never knew what could happen in the darkness. He sat behind a bush and watched them patrolling in the distance.

It's time to let the past be. Denida untied the eye patch, which everyone knew he wore. *If I don't wear it, they won't recognize who I am.* He put it in his shirt pocket and headed toward the saloon.

Denida walked past one of the lookouts.

"Hey kid," the guard yelled.

Oh no, did I get detected already? Denida turned his head. "Yes, Mister?"

"You needn't worry." The man flashed his pistol. "We'll keep you safe, no one dares mess with us!"

"Thanks!" Denida smiled and continued. *Lucky they're so full of themselves.*

He went into the saloon and walked up behind the counter.

The barmaid came up to him with a grin. "What can I help with, cockeye?"

Making a mockery of me? How dare she! Denida's eye flickered red for the first time in this world. He grabbed the maid and pulled her closer. "Before you want to play dead for me, pour me a drink!"

He let go of her and the maid fiddled with pouring him a drink, her hands shaking as she glanced at him.

In the back, there were several men being rowdy and drunk. Denida swallowed his drink and got up, the barmaid smiled nervously at him. He walked towards the back of the room.

One of them got up and blocked his way. "You're not welcome here, kid."

"No?" Denida glared past him. "I'm here to challenge your master to a duel. But if he's scared…"

A big man pushed through the rest and came to Denida. "A kid with a cockeye thinks he can beat *me*?"

Denida ground his teeth. "Yes, I heard you've reached your limit, you're not so fast anymore."

"Think so?" The big man giggled at his friends. "OK kid, you're on, this will only take a second!" He stormed out to the street.

"Boss, I don't think-" the guard ran after him.

The boss pushed the guard into a table he passed.

Under the starry skies, they gathered in front of the saloon. Everyone moved to the side, so there were only the two of them on the road.

"Say goodnight, cockeye!"

"I came to give death, not receive it." Denida smirked.

Denida and the man stood back to back. Denida smiled broadly. The tension coming was what he missed from Hell. He so craved it.

"1- 2- 3- 4..." a man yelled, they took steps as the numbers were yelled. At ten they both stopped, silence filled the surroundings, nothing but the night wind could be heard.

A man readied his pistol while looking at the two who had their hands at the ready, their backs still to each other. There was nothing but silence left in the air. A tumbleweed blew across the road. He held up the gun and fired it, the sound tore through the calm.

Denida and the man spun around as soon as the sound echoed in the silence. Denida's hand blurred toward his gun. Even without his magic, he moved inhumanly fast. His shot echoed through the street before the other man had fully pulled his gun. The big man toppled to the ground, shock in his already dead eyes.

Everyone turned to look at Denida, all filled with amazement. Denida put his gun back into his belt.

"Thought he would be too slow." Denida chuckled. "Oh, by the way-" He took out his badge and hung it on his shirt. "My name's Deputy Denida."

The faces got stone cold throughout the crowd.

"You robbed the bank, where are the spoils?" Denida spectated through the crowd, no one said anything or even moved a muscle.

The guard from before ran out from the saloon with his gun blazing. Denida tilted his head as the first bullet passed him by a millimeter. He jumped behind a wagon in the street and pulled his gun from his belt.

The guard ran towards him with his gun blazing.

Denida got back up from behind the wagon. He shot the guard, not in the head, but the hand that held the pistol.

The glee in Denida's dark eye was clear.

"The treasure?" Denida stopped in front of the guard, he grabbed the guard's shot hand and squeezed it and pointed his gun towards the man's other hand.

"Wait," the guard yelled and raised his shot-up hand. "You win, don't hurt me anymore."

Denida chuckled and lowered his gun.

A wagon came to a halt in front of the Sheriff's office.

"Alex, get out here," Denida yelled.

Alex came out with several of his lawmen with their guns at the ready. They stopped as they saw Denida sitting in the front of the wagon.

"The leader is dead, here's the bank's money."

Alex went to the back of the wagon, and Denida was right, it was all here.

Denida dismounted it and walked towards the Sheriff's office.

"Denny," Alex yelled. "I don't believe you actually did it."

Denida shrugged back. "It wasn't hard, but it's over now."

Alex nodded. "It is- for me." He went up to Denida and took off his golden badge and put it in Denida's hand. "But it's only beginning for you, *Sheriff.*"

Alex smiled and squeezed his hand before he turned and jumped on his horse, he rode off into the distance.

"You're the new Sherriff," another Deputy named Mick asked.

"I guess so." Denida attached the golden badge, he smiled at Mick. "Bring the wagon to the bank."

"Me?" Mick raised eyebrows.

"You're my Deputy, aren't you?"

Mick nodded. "Of course." He jumped into the wagon and rode off.

Denida glared back after Mick. He wrinkled his forehead. *A sparrow again?* He shook his head and walked back in.

In the days that followed, Denida and his Deputies stayed busy enforcing the law. Denida felt overworked, he lacked a deputy. *Maybe, being a Sheriff is like this?* He rolled his eye. "Alex sure handled it well."

Mick grinned. "He had you, too."

Robert was there before Alex, he might have an idea... Denida nodded to himself. "You keep watch, I need to go see an old friend."

It was a long ride to his old friend, Robert. Denida had not seen him in the time since he left with Alex to be a Deputy. Robert never did like him being one.

As he got off his house, Robert sat on the porch drinking.

"Denny, why are you here," Robert asked, still looking out into the distance, not even turning to look at Denida.

Denida went up to him on the porch. "A lot has changed. You helped me, but now I'm the Sherriff, Alex left..."

Robert shrugged. "Congratulations, you always had talent..."

"When you were Sheriff, how did you handle it all?"

Robert took another sip of his drink. "Delegate it."

Delegate... Denida grabbed his chest pocket, where he could feel his old Deputy badge laying.

"You're seasoned." Denida took out the badge and held it up with a smile. "Together again, at last; won't you come back as a Deputy to help me?"

Robert shook his head. "Under you? That's your argument to get me to come back, from what I purposely left?"

"We can be together again, I missed you!"

Robert swallowed the rest of his bottle. "I always liked you, Denny. You'll always be welcome- without the badge." He got up and went back into his house.

Denida breathed heavily and put the badge back in his pocket. *This isn't going to work; I need to find someone else.*

He dropped down in his old chair back in the Sherriff's office, not thinking that he now had another seat. He moved his head back and put his hat over his face.

"Didn't go well, I presume?" Mick came over.

Denida lifted his hat. "We need to find a new Deputy to take my old spot!"

"I might have an idea."

Denida sat back up with curious eyes.

"Jacob, a boy, like you were, who's really good with a gun."

Denida wrinkled his forehead. "I'm intrigued, let's go meet this kid."

Denida and Mick went to where this boy, Jacob was, he was out in a forest hunting, they rode towards the nearby forest.

At the edge of the forest, they got off and left their horses where Jacob's horse was.

They walked into the forest looking for Jacob, but soon heard a shot shortly after they started walking in. All the wildlife in the forest scattered throughout, the birds flew up into the trees. Denida and Mick drew their guns and stormed in the direction of the sound. It didn't take them long to find the source of the sound.

A young boy with a rifle sat between the trees, very well guarded against any spectators.

He spun and raised his rifle in their direction. Denida and Mick lifted their guns up.

"It's just me, Mick."

Jacob lowered his rifle. "What brings you here?"

"Big prey you've got." Denida raised his eyebrow and smiled. "I'm Denny, we're looking for someone to take up the role of Deputy, you can shoot! Interested?"

Jacob rolled his eyes. "Not funny!" He stared over at Mick and back to Denida. His eyes wandered down to Denida's badge, which completely changed his face. "You're… a Sheriff?"

Denida nodded. "Sheriff Denida."

Jacob's eyes widened. "I'm interested."

***

"A Sherriff?" Edward's eyes sped around, his face was full of confusion.

Daniel giggled. "I told you, my story would reveal stuff about my Dad, you would-"

The door to the dungeon sprung open and several demons rushed in and surrounded Edward.

Edward tried to rip loose, but they held him tight, he glanced confused and panicked around them. "What's going on?"

"Quiet traitor," the leader of the bunch yelled and slapped him across the face. The anger was clear, his hand was filled with fire, leaving a burnt mark of his hand on Edward's cheek. "Bring him!"

"Wait," Daniel yelled. He rushed to the bars and glared scared at the demons.

They grabbed the confused Edward and pulled him out of the dungeon, leaving only one demon, which Daniel had never seen before, behind. The demon threw out his arm towards Daniel, the bars got red with a glowing heat.

Daniel let go instantly, he held his hands and blew on them.

"Be quiet, boy!" The demon went over to the bars and stared at Daniel. "I won't be as easy..."

Daniel swallowed. "What happened to Edward?"

The demon gave a devious chuckle. "What happens to traitors!"

Chapter 15: Suspicions

Nina brushed Angel, trying to find the peace she usually felt with the horse. Susan leaned against a wall watching.

Denida walked in and clearly, he'd been informed by the Colonel of Nina's suspicions. She didn't like the look in Denny's eye. Nina's gut told her something was very wrong with Michelle, but he obviously disagreed with her.

'I do,' he said in her thoughts. 'And Michelle is coming here, so you can see.'

Nina continued to brush Angel, ignoring Denida.

Denida got up. "I'll go see if she's here." He passed by Susan, who cleared her throat from the entry of the stables where she was standing.

"Don't bother," Nina said, without looking at her.

Angel started to move about stomping the ground, his ears moving rapidly. Nina patted him while talking in a soothing voice.

"We're back." Denida walked in with Michelle.

Angel suddenly started screeching wildly. He reared up on his hind legs several times, then burst free and ran out of the stables into the forest.

Nina ran after Angel, followed by the others.

"Unrestful horse," Michelle muttered.

Nina spun to her with suspicion in her eyes, stronger than ever. "He never got upset before like this– ever!"

"Don't know then, I love animals and they love me." Michelle shrugged.

"Do you now?" Nina stared with angry eyes.

"Yes, I've had several." Michelle smiled reassuringly.

"Hold on." Denida went in between the two ladies. "Maybe you should go get him, Nina. We can talk to Michelle another day."

"No, I don't need to see her again, all animals have a sixth sense. If Angel doesn't like her, neither do I!" Nina glared with eyes which could kill at Michelle, then turned and walked towards the forest with Susan.

Nina examined the trees while she walked. "Angel," she yelled, hoping he hadn't run too far away since it was a giant forest.

"Maybe it was something else that-"

Nina spun to look at Susan. "No!" She wasn't going to listen to anything right now. She checked back into the trees.

Nina finally noticed Angel deep in the forest. He stood in a clearing eating fruits from a tree.

She turned to Susan, relieved to finally have found her horse.

"I'll go inform them, we found him." Susan ran back towards the stables.

Nina went over and patted him, he seemed completely calm now.

"He had a rough time."

Nina spun around to where the voice came from. She never heard that voice before.

A man sat on a giant boulder, eating an apple.

"Who are you?" Nina scouted around them.

"Don't worry!" He came over to her. "I'm an old friend of Denny's, my name's Gabriel."

Nina's face turned from a frown to confusion. "The angel? Why are you here?" Nina backed up nervously.

"You suspect someone, you ought to continue that." Gabriel stroked the horse. "A nice name he has, Angel..."

Michelle! Nina wrinkled and turned her focus back to Angel. *But how does he know?*

Gabriel smiled. "I'm an Archangel."

"Still," Nina insisted. "Why come here now, why not to Denny?" Nina rolled her eyes at Gabriel.

"You're his friend?" she scorned.

Gabriel shook his head. "You know as well as me, Denny would not believe me; you do!"

"Nina, where are you? I'm back," Susan yelled.

"In here," Nina turned to the voice and yelled.

Susan came through the trees with Denida and several others.

"Look who's here!" Nina chuckled at Denida.

Denida shrugged. "Your horse?"

"No!" Nina turned to where Gabriel had been, but he was gone with no signs of him ever being there. "Um-"

Denida glared at her, he raised his eyebrow.

"Angel, he's all calm now." Nina smiled.

Denida and Susan led Angel away.

Nina scanned around in the clearing. *Maybe, I imagined it?*

She sighed and turned to walk after them, but she stumbled on something. She kneeled to pick it up; it was an apple with a bite mark, clearly not a horse bite, either.

It did happen... Nina examined the apple. Could he be right?

***

Edward sat alone in a pitch-dark room. He had been chained to a chair, sealing magic on the shackles. *Wonder why not just the room?*

The door burst open, the light knifed into Edward's eyes, he squinted.

When his eyes adjusted to the light, he saw Claus standing in front of him.

"Claus, you have to help-"

"Traitor!" Claus slapped him across the face. "Be quiet, why'd you do it?"

"I didn't."

Claus' eyes flared red and he started punching Edward until he was covered in blood.

He grabbed a towel and rubbed off the blood from his hands.

"Don't make me repeat myself."

Edward gasped for air, he tried to speak. "Why... do... you... think... it's... me," he stuttered.

"Why the hell not!"

Edward tried to look up at Claus, but the blood was covering his eyes.

Claus shook his head. "Jack, *you* found the traitor. You find out the rest, you handle security." He left with his demons.

Jack came to the front of Edward, where he could see him.

"Why?" Edward could barely speak from the blood in his mouth.

"Someone has to take the fall and you're getting too close to Daniel. It makes *you* the prime suspect." Jack giggled. "I'm not heartless though, I'll show you what nobody else knows." He leaned over Edward and grabbed onto the chains, his real face appeared.

Terror made Edward's heart race. Now I understand how Daniel feels.

Dennis Scheel

With a devious grin, Jack jabbed his hand into Edward's body and ripped out his still beating heart. He dropped it to the ground.

Edward followed with his eyes, as he gasped for breath.

Jack giggled and glared into Edward's eyes, he stomped the heart.

Edward's sight faded, he passed into darkness.

***

Daniel turned as he heard the big door to the dungeon open. He rushed to the bars. "Edward?"

Claus came into view. "I'll have to disappoint you." He grinned. "That traitor won't be back!"

Daniel clung hard to the bars. "He's not a traitor," he screamed.

Claus sat down. "Of course you would think so!"

"What's going to happen to him?" Daniel's eyes were watering up.

"It already did, your *friend* is long gone!"

Daniel fell to the floor. *Edward, oh God.* He could not hold the tears back. He buried his head in his hands.

"When you're done sobbing; I understand, Denida became a Sheriff?"

Daniel wiped his face. "You want to know now?" He wrinkled his head. "Why would I tell *you*?"

"Cause I tell you to!" Claus smirked.

"No!" Daniel kicked the bars. "What're you going to do, kill me? You sure won't get the ring then! Your-" *His Boss Lucifer will want this story! Maybe I can twist them, like Edward...*

"What?" Claus raised his eyebrows.

"Sure you can handle hearing this? Dad went through a lot, with Darkness still..."

"Of course, I can handle it, unlike your friend, Edward," Claus grinned.

174

You think! Daniel stared at Claus with a hateful gaze, he turned and sighed. "Alright. I'll tell you. Jacob really impressed Dad. He and Jacob got close very quickly…"

***

Denida leaned back, soaking in the night sky. It was a clear night, he could see the stars.

Wonder if Danyel ever got punished?

"Ready?" Jacob yelled from the back of his horse. He sounded impatient.

"Yes, let's go get us some." Denida walked back to his horse.

They finally knew where the ones who pillaged farms across the county were.

It's about time we stopped them, and a chance to see what Jacob can do myself. He tilted his head to look at Jacob. "The one we caught sold them out. He said they would be attacking this farmhouse tonight."

"Can he be trusted?" Jacob glared back at Denida.

Denida peeked at him, he could tell Jacob was worried from the look in Jacob's eyes. "He wanted to save himself, so hopefully. Remember, alive! We must save everyone we can; that's our *first* priority."

Jacob nodded.

They set their horses into a gallop, to reach it as fast as they could. *Maybe we can reach it before it's too* late.

"No," a scream echoed throughout as soon as they arrived at the farmhouse, which made it clear they were too slow.

Jacob rushed off his horse and stormed towards the scream with his pistol raised.

"Wait," Denida tried to hiss at him, but it was already too late, Jacob ran into the building.

Denida got off his own horse. He turned around and ran towards the building as the gunfire started. *I should have been faster!*

Inside there was a dead body in front of a woman, who cowered in the corner.

Jacob was shooting at them, taking cover behind the furniture.

Jesus. Denida ducked and peered over at Jacob. He ground his teeth and jumped up and shot the others from a sideways angle.

How fast he responded to each, shocked Jacob. *'I've heard he should be good, but wow…'*

Denida glared annoyed at Jacob's thoughts. "Next time, don't go alone, you're not capable yet!" He sighed. "I'm sorry, we weren't faster, Miss." He helped the woman into a chair.

"It's fine, the other guy over there was just in time," the woman said.

Denida walked back to the horses not saying a word, not even giving Jacob a second glance.

Jacob turned to Denida as they rode on the way back to the Sheriff's office. "I-" Jacob muttered.

"Don't bother," Denida abruptly cut him off. "This was to see what you could do- you failed, miserably!" *Disappointingly…* He shook his head.

Jacob ran his hand through his hair and put his hat back on. Surprised that Denida had set his horse into a gallop to get back, he kicked his horse to chase after.

Denida was often out about chasing outlaws who had caused mayhem.

One day, as he returned. Mick got up and went over to greet him, as soon as he entered.

Jacob stared at Denida.

He tilted his head and pointed for Denida to follow him out the door.

"Jesus, just spill it. I'm exhausted." Denida pushed past him and sat down with his feet on the table.

Mick peered nervously back at Jacob. He turned back to Denida and took a heavy breath before he continued. "The crew we never thought we could get, because they vanished are back."

At last! Denida took down his feet and sat upright. "Really?"

Jacob came over. "They hate my guts." He grinned as he chewed on an apple.

"You're not coming, Jacob! Where are they at?" Denida buckled back on his belt.

Mick handed him a folded paper and turned to Jacob, who shrugged.

Denida unfolded the paper and read it. *That old saloon is far away, it'll take a while to reach.* He nodded with a smile and went back out to his horse. "Don't do something I wouldn't do," he yelled as he rode off.

Cloak of darkness can be a benefit. Denida finally arrived at nightfall, he tied his horse to the post and walked through the door. He checked throughout the room.

Are they not here? Maybe they're in a back room? Denida walked up to the counter to order a drink. "I'm searching for someone, you may know."

"Who you see, is all there is!" The barmaid poured his drink.

"I understand. Maybe, in the back…" Denida laid out some money and smiled.

"Listen, *stranger*, nobody but you and who's in this room has been here for years." He grabbed the money. "-but thanks for the donation!"

Strange, he doesn't sound like he's lying? Denida swallowed his drink and watched the room again. Maybe the intel's wrong?

He put his hat on and glared at the other side of the street, where there was a telegraph. He licked his lips and rushed over to send a message back to Mick.

He had to wait for a reply to why the saloon was empty. Denida was impatient, but it couldn't be helped.

The machine suddenly beeped, Denida rushed over to see what it said; 'I know. You need to hurry back here now- Mick.'

He knows? How? "Reply; Why do I need to return to you? What happened?"

Denida got even more impatient this time, luckily it wasn't long, before Mick replied; 'A new intel came, which made Jacob rush out after them. – Mick.'

Jacob. Denida ground his teeth and ran out to his horse. He untied it and jumped on and set it into a gallop back towards Mick with fury in his mind.

At dawn he arrived back at Mick's and jumped off his horse, not even tying the horse to the post.

Mick was fast asleep on a couch within, he pushed his legs down the couch, making him fall off, which woke him immediately.

"Where did he go?" Denida stared at Mick, the red within his eyes were strong.

"His message is on the paper on his table." Mick rubbed his eyes.

Denida rushed over to Jacob's desk, a note was laying on the table, Denida picked it up and read it; 'Jacob, try if you can to stop us having fun with your family...'

No! Denida ran out.

"Hey, where you going?" Mick ran after him, as Denida rode off into the distance.

The noon sun beat down as Denida reached the farmhouse where he had first met Jacob.

He stopped his horse before he got too close, as he had a nasty suspicion in his gut and walked quietly the rest of the way. *I hate it when I'm right!*

In front of the farmhouse, several armed men were standing around Jacob and his family all tied up.

Still the fool, he got caught.

"Remember why you dislike me?" Jacob chuckled.

"Yes, you screwed us over," the boss replied.

"How?"

"The hell-" The boss cocked his gun towards Jacob. "Don't you remember your-"

Jacob suddenly grabbed the boss' gun. The men got in each other's way trying to get the drop on him.

He shot them almost as fast as Denida, but not fast enough. He hid behind a well just before they returned fire. The duel commenced.

Maybe I should intervene?

Jacob shot the final one between the eyes as Denida thought that.

Nice.

Jacob went over to untie his family. Denida got up and went over towards them.

"You're... not... free yet," the boss stuttered. He fired while Jacob's back was turned.

No, not again. Denida's eyes flared red and he stretched his hand and formed a fist, the time slowed down, the projectiles slowed down to a halt in the air as the time froze. He clenched his fist and the bullets fell to the ground. He lowered his arm and spun around, gripping his gun and emptied it into the boss. *Never again!*

Jacob spun with his gun readied. "Don't be mad, you did tell me only do what you would do."

Denida grinned. "I said; don't do anything I wouldn't do." He put his gun back in his belt and turned back to Jacob. "I was wrong about you, why won't you be my deputy?"

Jacob chuckled. "Of course!"

***

Claus took a deep inhalation. This is the stories Edward endured, wonder what Jack did to him?

Daniel giggled. "As you can see, not that interesting, you would need someone as Edward here."

"I don't think so," Claus said. "I don't think you can be trusted alone with anyone. Which is why-" He walked to the dungeon's door, he flickered his finger and two demons came in. "You'll *never* be alone with only one again!"

Claus turned and left them with Daniel. He walked back towards the chamber where he had left Jack with Edward.

He opened the door to see Jack standing up against a wall smoking a cigarette.

Edward was lying dead in his chair with a bloody heart in a pool next to him on the floor.

"What happened?" Claus kneeled next to Edward's corpse.

Jack threw his cigarette butt. "He's gotten what he deserved, we don't need him."

"But kill his soul? Afraid he would tell Lucifer?" Claus raised his voice.

"He got what he deserved!"

Claus ground his teeth and nodded. "You're right- I made sure there'll be two demons watching Daniel at all times. I will hear the rest of his story *myself*."

Chapter 16: The Ring

Nina needs to trust me. Michelle parked the car at Dynasty and picked up a folder, she brought.

She walked towards the stables, where she noticed Susan. "Susan." She waved at her. "Where's Nina?"

"Inside the stables. She still thinks you can't be trusted."

Michelle held the folder up. "That's why I brought this!"

She walked past Susan into the stables.

Inside, where Nina groomed Angel, all the horses became restless. Angel stomped his hind legs, drumming with his hoofs.

Nina ran from further within the stables and pushed Michelle outside.

Damn horses. Can't hide my true nature from animals.

"Why are you back?" Nina clenched her fists.

Michelle lifted up the folder. "I want to show you what I've done, so you can-"

"Not interested!" Nina interrupted Michelle, with her eyes rolling. "Nothing you can do will make me believe you!"

Michelle gave a fake smile. "Susan can tell you too."

Nina stared at her. "I don't care, there's something about you that just doesn't feel right!"

Michelle started to get annoyed. "I'm helping to find your son."

"Really? I doubt that's why you met with the associates," Nina smirked.

"Susan," Michelle yelled.

Susan came running over.

Michelle handed her the folder. "I think you'll have more luck."

She smiled and walked back to her car. She could feel Nina's suspicious eyes on her back, but she had done all she could.

She got into the car. Time to see the Dark Angels' boys again.

Michelle drove back to the warehouse, she parked the car a few blocks away from it. Her body changed into the knock out they knew her as. She smiled at herself in the mirror and got out of the car.

A lot of eyes turned, several men whistled at her, as she walked towards the warehouse.

Strange feeling with so many eyes on me. Different than my other mask…

She walked straight into the warehouse. The men inside got up abruptly.

The same man she had met before came up and greeted her.

"Welcome back." He glared jittery at the others, then back to her.

"It's risky for us to meet, let's make this short; have you found anything?"

His hands fidgeted over his hair. "We checked the use of Dark Magic as you instructed, the high level of use was stopped after they left the old hideout…"

Michelle shook her head. "So, you're no use then."

"We did all we could," the man sounded panicked.

Michelle's face and body returned to her other self.

Everyone in the rest of the room chattered.

"Your mask went away," the man muttered.

Michelle gave out a devious chuckle. "On purpose." Her eyes got dark as she turned towards the rest.

The room was enveloped in a Dark Mist. All that could be seen were the bodies being torn and impaled by the dark shadows. The men all ran across the room trying to escape, the man next to Michelle tried to run towards the door, but his legs wouldn't move. The screams echoed throughout the warehouse. As the last scream echoed and subsided, the Darkness subsided from the room. All that was left breathing were him and Michelle.

Michelle sauntered towards him with a grin. She snapped her fingers, guns appeared next to the bodies. "Big duel. But you-" She grabbed him. "-are apprehended. You won't say anything other than that a gunfight occurred here." *Nina won't convince anyone else after this about her theories!*

The terror in the man's eyes was clear, he nodded terrified.

She handcuffed the terrified man. Michelle called it in and kneeled next to him when she was done.

"What-"

Michelle grabbed his head and started mumbling something, her hands started to flow with Darkness.

The man's eye grew dark until she suddenly let go of his head, making him fall back down. "What have you done to me?"

"Making sure Denny or anyone else won't see your thoughts!" she smirked.

It didn't take long for the military to show up. She informed them of what had happened, the terrified man corroborated her story.

The Colonel came not long after, followed by Denida.

They rushed over to Michelle, to check if she was OK.

Denida's eye turned to the only survivor other than her.

"We're lucky one is still alive," Michelle said.

"Wait here," Denida muttered. He trudged over to the man who was left. "Do you know who I am?"

"Denida." The man spat at him.

Denida cleared his throat. "I wanted-"

"Don't bother! I've got nothing to say to the likes of you." He turned away.

Michelle couldn't help but peer towards them. She stood so the Colonel wouldn't think twice of it. *Heh, he's coming back, must mean he's gotten nothing.*

Denida ground his teeth and shook his head. "He won't talk to me."

***

Dan had extracted as much of the alloy from the two Gates as he could, he hoped it was enough to forge a fake ring. But the problem now was how to shape it into a ring, as nothing could even scratch the material.

Dan examined it with his lab instruments. *There must be a way.* He peered towards the giant Gate, that stood in the center of his lab. He went over and checked every nook and cranny of it, there was nothing helpful, he could find. He turned to the main unit, which was the only part of the Gate that had the alloy. *So little, but still so strong. What if?*

Dan rushed back to his desk and sat down. He rolled his chair over to his computer to search for a picture of Denida. He zoomed in on the ring, he focused on it and magnified it as much as he could. *This could work!*

Dan worked throughout the night on his idea. The idea contained a lot of melting and welding. He was determined to make it look like the original ring, and feel as much like it as possible, he had an idea on how to accomplish it.

As the first morning light broke through, Dan rubbed his eyes and held up the newly created ring to the morning light.

I'm satisfied.

Dan put the ring down and picked up the phone. "Denida?" He smiled smugly. "I have something to show you, you don't want to miss it!"

Dan was drinking a hard dose of coffee when Denida arrived.

He rushed to greet Denida. The excitement was clear on his face.

"You look like you did when you got the Gate to work. I hope what you got won't end that bad again." Denida chuckled.

"Ha- ha!" Dan didn't like his comment. "The ring," he said smugly.

Denida's demeanor changed when he said that. "You got it duplicated?"

Dan led him over to his spectroscope. "I can't bend the alloy, so I got the idea to use electro-plating." He lifted the ring to where Denida could see. "It feels magical, doesn't it?"

Denida examined the ring, he put it on his other hand and held the two palms high above, so he could see the rings on the two hands. "They look identical and *feel* identical."

Dan gloated. *My perfect work.*

"Wrong, not yet! Does it have magic?" Denida glared at Dan. "It's the same material?"

"Same material, but I don't know if magic..."

Denida took off his other ring and handed it to Dan.

Dan grabbed the ring and frowned.

Denida clenched his fist with the ring and pushed it forward; nothing happened. He tried several more times.

Dan wrinkled his forehead. "What are you doing?"

"Strange," Denida muttered. "Same material, it feels the same- but it doesn't grant any magical powers..." He took his own ring back. "We need to test it on someone to see if they believe it's the real thing. Come!"

Denida and Dan drove to see the Colonel, to test if he would notice the change. Dan felt sure the Colonel would, he had given everything to make sure it would look identical, even Denida thought the rings did.

They got out of the car, Denida laid his gloves on the hood of the car, while he switched the rings out, as he always wore the ring on the left hand. Leaving the left with the fake one would help.

They continued into the building when Denida had put back on his gloves.

Dan's eye wandered around fascinated. Denida led the way up the floor where the Colonel was.

They got out of the elevator.

"This way." Denida puffed at Dan and walked towards the Colonel's office.

The Colonel stood up to greet them when they came into his office.

"We need to find an excuse," Dan whispered to Denida.

"No need," Denida whispered.

Denida took off his glove and saluted the Colonel. "Colonel, any progress?"

The Colonel saluted back. "No, sir."

Denida ran his hand across his face- "I see. Is Michelle here?"

"Yes, I'll go get her." The Colonel hurried out the door.

Dan turned to Denida. "Why-"

"Trust me." Denida smiled.

The Colonel came back, followed by Michelle.

"Did you get anything out of the last guy?"

Michelle shook her head. "I'm trying to make it as fast as I can, sir, but it takes time."

Denida nodded and raised his hand with the fake ring. "So, the only way is to give them this?"

Michelle sighed. "We're trying to avoid it."

Denida chuckled. "They bought it, the ring works!"

Michelle and the Colonel's eye met.

"Work? What do you mean," the Colonel raised his eyebrows.

Denida took off his other glove and held up both his hands.

"Two-" the Colonel muttered.

"Rings?" Michelle finished his sentence.

"It's a duplicate Dan made."

Dan chuckled proudly from the back of the room.

Denida put his gloves back on. "Contact Claus. It's time we made a trade for Daniel with the ring!"

"Wait." Michelle rushed in between the Colonel and Denida. "We can't yet, we need to interrogate the survivor-"

Denida licked his lips. "You're right, he has to be interrogated, but not by us, he knows us…" He turned to look at Dan.

Dan shook his head rapidly. "No, I'm not a soldier."

"You helped once with Claus." Denida smiled. "Which is why it could work, Michelle will be with you." Denida winked at Michelle, who nodded with a smile.

"Fine- I'll try," Dan said, still with doubt in his voice.

Dan walked with Michelle into an interrogation room. He peeked at the mirror in the room and back at Michelle. *I've got a bad feeling.*

Soldiers brought the survivor in and chained him to the chair.

Michelle sat down opposite the man and turned to Dan. "Won't you sit down, Dan?"

"Yes... yes," Dan muttered and hurried over to sit down. He glanced nervously back at the mirror and sighed.

"Are you going to ask anything?" The man raised his voice.

"Yes." Dan turned determined around. "You used to work for the Dark Angels, correct?"

The man's eyes wandered to Michelle.

"Answer," she demanded.

"Yes," the man mumbled.

Dan giggled and turned to the mirror. "Denida, get in here."

Michelle's eyes widened.

The door sprung open and Denida walked in, making the man squirm. "What is it, Dan?"

Dan got up and came over to Denida, he dragged Denida towards the table. "Did you not hear, he knew the Dark Angels Black magic, he might know if the rings feel the same?"

Denida took off his gloves and put both his hands flat on the table. "Tell me which one is the real one?"

It was clear the man felt scared and intimidated by Denida. He started to shake a little, fear started to show in his eyes too. He shook unsure.

188

"Well?" Dan yelled.

"That," the man pointed at Denida's left hand.

Denida chuckled. "You're right Dan, it *is* perfect."

"No." Michelle got up. "The associates had no connection with the Dark Magic by themselves!"

Dan raised his eyebrows at Michelle. *Why's she so against it?*

"I understand the need." She smiled reassuringly at Dan. "But I'm not against it, I just need to have a talk here, so we know, he doesn't know anything."

"The ring is what they wanted," Denida insisted.

"We might not need it." Michelle stared into Denida's eye.

Denida ran his hand across his face. "Alright try, you have ten minutes, we'll be outside."

Dan licked his lips and turned to gaze suspiciously at Michelle as he walked out with Denida. *Nina might be right in her suspicions.*

Dan watched the people walking by. *Worth a shot.* He straightened up and turned to Denida, but then Michelle came out from the interrogation room.

Dan and Michelle stood face to face, their eyes locking for a few seconds.

"Well?" Denida said.

Michelle turned to face him. "Claus is *not* the one who's in charge, Jack is."

"I already know that," Dan muttered.

"How would you know that?" Michelle gasped.

Crap. "Um, I don't know." Dan started to fidget.

"Yes, you do!" Denida pushed Dan up again the wall and took the glove off with his teeth from his left hand. He put his hand on top of Dan's temple.

189

Dan felt his memories flash through his head, he couldn't move a muscle, until suddenly Denida removed his hand and Dan fell helplessly to his knees.

"*Lucifer.*" The anger burnt a clear red in Denida's eye, even behind his eye patch.

Dan could see Denida's eye twitching red.

"This changes everything, I need to go see someone. Do nothing until I return!"

***

Denida sat looking out the window as the car rushed through the hillside towards Dynasty.

Nina knew!

The car pulled up to Dynasty. Denida ran through the door into the house and yelled for the Butler.

"Where?"

The Butler came up to him and raised his hand in the direction of the stables, but before he could speak, Denida was gone in the direction of the stables.

Nina and Susan stood watching Angel, who was running freely under the bathing sun.

Denida stopped a little away from them. "You knew too, Susan?"

They both turned with confusion written across their faces.

"I read Dan's memories!"

Their faces changed in an instant, but not to the same.

Susan turned to guilt, whereas Nina's face got cold as stone.

"I told Susan to," Nina said and stepped in front of Susan.

Denida twitched, he couldn't stay mad at Nina, however much he tried. "You saw Lucifer, what did he tell you?"

Nina's stone-cold face waivered as he asked that. "Jack along with the Gatekeeper were two brothers, demons created in Hell."

Denida stretched his neck and groaned. A sparrow flew overhead.

That takes me back. "I need to talk to Luci, I want you to be there too, Nina!"

Denida walked with Nina in hand into the forest. She watched curiously into the trees they passed.

When they got a piece into the forest, they reached the cabin sitting in a clearing.

"Don't worry." Denida glared tenderly into her eyes, he fiddled with her hair and kissed her softly.

Denida turned around. "Reficul, Reficul, Reficul."

A dark cloud appeared in front of them.

Denida pushed Nina behind him. The cloud materialized into the shape of Lucifer.

Lucifer gave a broad smile. "Caught Claus yet?"

Nina walked out from behind Denida.

Lucifer's smile faded at the sight of her.

"Cat got your tongue?" Nina chuckled.

Lucifer gave his old tender smile.

"Don't bother, I know you, it won't work." Denida took Nina by the hand and squeezed it. "Jack's one of your demons, you said you had none left here. Has it been you, who took Daniel?"

The tension in the air was so heavy it could be cut with a knife.

Denida and Lucifer stared into each other's eyes with a look they had not endured since Hell. The fury Denida felt deep within his heart was one of darkness.

"Not all demons are under my control, some have betrayed the Darkness, like you!" Lucifer's eyes got fiery red as he said those words.

"Darkness is destined to lose." Denida gave a smile.

"Look at your source," Lucifer said.

"Who, Gabriel? He's on both sides!"

Nina pulled her hand from Denida's grip, making him look confused at her.

'*I should go,*' Nina said into his thoughts and ran off.

"Trouble in paradise?" Lucifer gloated at him.

Denida stepped in front of Lucifer's face, as close as he physically could get without touching.

"If I ever find out you had a hand in this, you will get to see the old Denida!"

Chapter 17: Nina's Venture

Nina ran as fast as her legs could carry her out of the forest. She rushed by Susan at the entry into Dynasty.

Susan moved from where she waited by the door to Dynasty, waving at Nina and calling out to her.

Nina, however, ignored it and sped off. *Lucifer's in on it, I know it. Michelle's involved too, somehow. Just how I'm not sure about.*

She parked across the road from the military Headquarter, then prepared to wait.

It's time to find out what's up with this woman!

She sat a long time and saw a lot of people coming and going, but not Michelle. Not until night fell, did Michelle's car finally drive out.

Nina ducked as the car passed her by. She peered back after it to be sure it really was Michelle she saw, she had been waiting for a long time, maybe she was merely wishing it.

It's her. She set the car into motion and made a U-turn to follow her. Like the time she had followed Michelle at the warehouse, Michelle was very careful, driving randomly around, turning, speeding, everything to lose a tail, but it didn't seem Michelle had noticed Nina.

Nina carefully followed a few cars back, where Michelle wouldn't notice her.

When Michelle did her final U-turn, her eyes grew wide.

Crap.

Nina could see Michelle cursing as she hit the gas and screeched   away.
Nina tried to follow, but there was a car in her way. She honked her horn, but it was too late, Michelle was already gone.

I'll need to plan it better.

Nina sighed and drove towards Dan's lab.

"Lady Nina. Dan's not here." The guard leaned over.

"I know, he told me to check on the Gate." Nina smiled at the guard.

The guard nodded and let her on her way.

Nina went straight in, knowing exactly where she was going. She stopped in front of the huge Gate and turned to the monitor.

She scrolled through the different robots until she stopped at a specific one.

This is the one. "Warlock, are you here?" she spoke into the robot.

A face came to the screen. "Lady Nina." The Warlock walked in front of her aide and smiled. "How can I help?"

Nina rubbed her arm. "There's someone here I suspect, but no one believes me…"

The Warlock nodded. "Like you did with Claus?"

Nina sighed and nodded. "She's always detecting me, Denny mentioned a cloaking spell once-"

"No," the Warlock suddenly burst out, adamant. "That's Dark Magic."

"But Lucifer confirmed Claus is *not* the one, who has Daniel." Nina pushed away the cloud of despair which threatened her composure.

The Warlock turned to her aide. "Leave us!"

He nodded and walked out, closing the door behind him.

"Understand, no one can know I taught this to you. In my world, Dark Arts are forbidden!"

Great, she'll help. Nina nodded very ecstatically.

As night fell yet again, Nina went to Michelle's car. She peered back at the people

who walked by. She chanted an unlock spell, the door to the car slid open, she climbed into the back seat and chanted the cloaking spell the Warlock reluctantly taught her.

It didn't take long before Nina saw Michelle walking towards her car, she ducked down as a reflex.

Guess I don't need to duck; I have the cloaking spell. Nina sat up, worried Michelle might still see her.

Michelle turned towards Nina and threw a folder straight in the backseat, it landed smack dap in her lap.

She really can't see me!

Michelle backed out and drove around, still being careful in case anyone was following her.

"Guess Nina isn't following me," Michelle muttered. Afterward, she turned out of town.

She parked in the middle of nowhere, got out, and threw her jacket into the car.

What's she up to out here? Nina arched her neck to watch her as she walked. When she was out of sight Nina opened the door and stepped out of the car.

She felt an uneasiness, her body felt tired. *Must be the dark magic... The air feels thick here.* Nina grabbed at her throat and put her hand over her mouth, yet still followed after Michelle into the thick mist. A strong malicious sensation hung in the air, even Nina couldn't mistake it.

What is this feeling?

She walked in between the trees, where she saw an opening with lights burning.

Is this a so-called pentagram, that Denny talked about?

Michelle sat at the center, kneeling before a dark figure. "What do you desire, Master?"

The Dark cloud above her changed its figure to the form of a face. "We're not alone…"

Michelle tilted her head around and looked straight at Nina, who fell backward over her own feet in shock.

"Nina," Michelle giggled. "How amusing!"

Nina hurried up and ran back to where she came from, as fast as she could, she didn't look back. She almost forgot to breathe. After a few minutes, she ducked and hid behind a big rock. She took the chance to peek back. *Wonder if I got away?*

"You didn't!" Michelle appeared behind her, as if out of thin air. She grabbed Nina before she could run again. As soon as she grabbed her, they both appeared in the same spot Michelle had been in with the Dark figure.

Nina tried to get free from her grab. "I didn't see anything-"

Michelle chuckled. "You have no idea what you saw!"

What does she mean by that? Nina felt her forehead full of sweat.

Michelle turned to the Dark shade. "Meet the great Darkness!"

"Lucifer's?"

Michelle turned with fiery red eyes. "Lucifer," she said mockingly. "He's nothing but a pansy, this is *who* controls him."

"How do you know that?" Nina asked, trembling in her voice. "Are you from Hell?"

Michelle kneeled next to the terrified Nina. "I'm not just *a demon,* I'm the one protecting your Denny." Michelle smiled, her face turned from her human form to that of a demon. "The name's Medusa, I've always been here!"

Who's Medusa? "Should I know that name?"

Michelle glanced at the dark figure again, she threw her hand back towards Nina, which sent her flying across the field into a tree, which knocked her out.

Where am I? Nina tried to sit up, but it hurt when she tried.

"Are you OK?" Michelle rushed to her side.

"Sgt. Michelle? Where am I?" Nina's eyes wandered aimlessly around herself, she was apparently laying in the back of a car on the side of a road, cars were passing them by. *Must be a highway.*

"We were going back to Dynasty, you passed out." Michelle gave a worried look.

"I... don't... remember," Nina stuttered.

"That must be tough." Michelle patted her back. "I think I'll take you back to Dynasty, just to be sure."

"No," Nina objected and stumbled out of the car, she felt weak and bruised. "You need to look for Daniel, he's more important! I'll get back myself."

Michelle walked to the car but turned to look an extra time at Nina. "Are you sure?"

"Go," Nina yelled insistently.

Michelle got into her car and drove off.

I really feel strange, why's that? And sore too. She rubbed her shoulder.

She hailed a taxi and returned to Dynasty, but the strange feeling stayed with her. Something wasn't right.

Susan met her at the gates to Dynasty next to a guard.

"Nina?" Susan walked over to greet Nina, she squinted her eyes.

"What?" Nina was still stumbling a little. "I only went to see Michelle."

Susan paid the taxi. "You don't look well. Let me take you back to Dynasty." She led her to her own car. "Why are you stumbling? You saw Michelle?"

"Yeah, about if there were any change with Daniel."

Susan's eyes turned to Nina. "You asked *her*? But, you don't trust her?"

Nina turned to Susan in disbelief. "Why wouldn't I trust her? She's looking for Daniel!"

Susan stepped on the brakes, bringing the car to a complete halt, halfway down the road. She turned to Nina with annoyance written on her face. "You've got to be *kidding* me! You've been convinced something was off about her, especially since Angel didn't like her. And now-"

"Angel doesn't like her?" Nina scratched her forehead.

"Jesus…" Susan muttered, she got out of the car and walked aimlessly back and forth across the road.

Nina got out of the car too. "I'm not messing with you, Angel never met Michelle."

Susan gave the same look of disbelief. "Are you kidding me?"

What? Nina shrugged. "Take me back to Dynasty, I'm sore…"

Susan shook her head. "The Warlock," Susan insisted.

"Warlock? The one from the other world?" Nina raised her eyebrows.

"Yes." Susan rushed towards Nina and dragged her into the car and sped off. "You need to see the Warlock, something's *not right!*"

Chapter 18: A Return of Darkness

Daniel munched on his food while looking suspiciously at the two demons who stood to watch over him. "You know what happened to the last guy who watched over me?"

"Edward was a traitor," one of them stated with no emotion.

Daniel sighed. I'm never going to get out of here.

"Aw, isn't that sweet, you really thought you would." Lucifer chuckled, as he appeared out of nowhere, he glanced at the monitor. "Do come here, Claus."

Daniel grinned as the demons cowered in Lucifer's presence.

A few minutes later Claus came running through the door. "You called?"

Lucifer turned to the exhausted Claus. "Yes, you caught your traitor?"

Claus nodded nervously. "Don't worry, Edward's been taken care of!"

Lucifer gave another chuckle. "Edward, clever…"

Claus shrugged, but when Lucifer turned to him, his eyes widened.

"Time's running out Claus, you don't want me disappointed." A dark cloud appeared around Lucifer and dissipated with him.

Claus spun around to look at Daniel. "Start talking; Denida got a Deputy Sheriff, what happened next?"

Daniel stood stunned for a second, he could see Claus was not messing around.

"Dad… Dad's name did most of his job for him, He was dreaded now, as Sheriff Denida."

"But," Claus interrupted impatiently.

Daniel exhaled heavily. "But- nothing lasts forever!" He shook his head.

***

"You don't know who did it- again!" Denida face wrinkled in annoyance as he scowled at Jacob.

Jacob dropped his head in shame.

"Jesus." Denida put on his cowboy hat. "I'll handle it myself!" He stormed out, pushing past Mick. Mick stared with raised eyebrows. "You're leaving?"

Denida just mounted his horse and galloped off.

As Denida rode to the bank, he noticed the same sparrow following him, it flew and sat on a tree outside of the town. *Strange.*

He tied his horse to the post when he arrived at the bank.

Jacob, if you can't learn anything, time to let me try!

He trudged into the bank and was met by the manager. "Sheriff Denida, what an honor."

"You don't know why I'm here. The ones who robbed the place, what can you tell me about them?"

The manager walked Denida into his office. He turned and closed the door behind them, shut the shades and peeked out from them as he expected someone watching him.

"You- are acting strange," Denida said suspiciously.

"You didn't see what I did!"

Denida leaned over his desk and smiled. "... what would that be?"

"Something was wrong, they knew what we did before we even did it. And their speed, it was inhuman."

Denida took a deep breath- "Nice, but I'm more looking for *how* they look!"

"I don't know, I couldn't get their eyes out of my head."

Denida wrinkled his forehead. "Their eyes?"

"They were red, not a little, but a fiery red, almost as-as if possessed!"

Not possible, not... Denida shook his head in disbelief, it couldn't be what he feared deep down.

He rushed out of the bank and glared around the street.

It can't be, I would feel if there had been Dark Magic here!

It was midday, so a smoldering heat baked him. He took off his hat and wiped his face.

I need a drink!

Denida walked in through the doors to the saloon. He walked up the counter, sat down and ordered a cold drink. He swallowed it as if he had just come out of the desert.

"Hit the sweet spot?"

Denida put down the drink and nodded to the man who sat beside him.

"It's smoldering hot if you're not from a warm climate," the man chuckled.

What a strange remark. "I guess. I should be on my way." Denida picked up his hat, nodded and went toward the doors.

"Bye Denny!"

Denny? Denida stood holding onto the door. He took a deep breath and spun around.

"How do you know that name?"

The man got up from his chair and took as slow steps as he possibly could.

It felt to Denida like he was deliberately stalling.

"*The Dark Angel of Hell.*" The man giggled as he spoke his words.

Denida's eyes wandered worried across the room, he dropped his hand near his gun.

"Were you really always this dense?" The man smirked.

"No," Denida muttered. "It can't be."

"Say it!" the man demanded. He was now standing right next to Denida, looking straight into Denida's eye. "You know it, say the name…"

"We're done!" Denida yanked the door and rushed out of the Saloon.

The man walked out behind him. "Denny, don't leave me here, I feel *so* alone." He chuckled. "What is it you call it here? *I challenge you* to a duel, O mighty 'Little Evil'."

He must be from Hell, is this such a good idea?

Denida smiled and walked back to the man. "You must not be from here, anyone who brings a challenge knows it'll be answered- if you wish!" He raised his eyebrows to make his point clear.

The man chuckled. "I'll beat the mighty Denida."

The street was cleared from any bystanders, who watched from the windows, as they stood back to back.

"Goodnight," Denida whispered.

The two men started to take ten steps away from each other.

The bystanders got more intrigued with each passing step. But halfway through the steps, the man suddenly grabbed his gun and spun around.

Too fast for eyes to see he had drawn his gun and fired.

Denida felt a rush of air moving towards him and rolled on the ground. From reflex ingrained deep within him, he pulled his own gun and fired back, but the man had already hidden behind a barrel in the street.

The Darkness was now clear in the air.

Denida's eye turned red. *You're not getting away.* He pushed out his arm, the barrel the man hid behind rolled across the road.

The man fiddled with the gun, which fell out of his hands after the barrel rolled, but it was too late, Denida had already shot him and kept shooting until his gun had emptied.

He walked towards the man with eyes watching him, the spectators chattering in worry about what they'd just witnessed.

Denida paid it no mind, he reloaded his gun and buckled it away.

He's already dead, it's too late. If he's from Hell, I don't want Lucifer to know, he'll be back then.

Denida kneeled and muttered with his hands running across the man's face.

A piece of paper with a sketch of his face appeared. He grabbed the paper, folded it and put it in his pocket.

Denida got back up and flickered his hand. "Fire!" The body of the man lit ablaze.

He smiled and walked towards his horse.

Outside of town, the sparrow followed him again until he got back to the Sheriff's office.

He walked over to Jacob and unfolded the paper from his pocket.

"This is who robbed it. Put him on the most wanted list; wanted dead or alive!"

"How-" Jacob observed Denida walking out.

Denida went to the hitching post, the sparrow was sitting on. He smiled at it and fed it some crumbs.

You don't like the Darkness, do you? But I have to be careful, there's a small chance Lucifer may find me here...

Denida went to his house and put a bag together. He stopped halfway through and glared at the bag.

This is ridiculous, I've been here for years, he has never found me since Hell, why would he now?

He took out the stuff and threw the bag in under the bed and walked out.

Jacob came over to him when he came out to the street. "He's on the wanted posters. I talked to the bank-"

"Why?" Denida interrupted.

"What happened? They couldn't explain it themselves."

Denida pushed past Jacob.

"You escaped a bullet? Did he catch on fire? How?" Jacob yelled after Denida, who stopped in his tracks.

"Luck and matches." Denida gave a smirk.

Denida walked over to the town saloon and sat down with a big sigh of relief.

"Tough day?" a voice echoed next to him.

No, not him!

"Yes, me!" Lucifer grinned. "How long it has been, *Denny*!"

Denida scavenged through the room, no other demons could be seen or felt besides Lucifer. "How are you already-"

Lucifer chuckled. "Wouldn't you like to know."

"Why are you here?"

Lucifer smiled. "You left! But if you come back with me, all will be forgiven."

Forgiven! Denida's eyes flared red. "Go home, I'm *not* going back with you." He stood up and put back his hat while frowning at Lucifer. He turned and trudged towards the door.

"You know how this is going to end," Lucifer smirked. "You *will* come back, you had your vacation." He stared into Denida's eyes.

"How would you accomplish that?"

"Simple," Lucifer said with a confident smile. "You like shooting; *I challenge you*!"

Denida's eye turned from anger to worry, deep down to his core. *Challenged; by the devil?*

Lucifer walked out of the saloon. "Coming, or you want to return by yourself?" he yelled.

Outside, people were already gathering in the street.

Lucifer turned to Denida with a smile, when Denida came out. "Ready to die and return home?"

Mick and Jacob came out to the crowd.

"Jacob will oversee it," Denida said when he saw them. *I must- for Ignacio!*

Lucifer grabbed and buckled on a gun and nodded to the men he talked to. "Of course!"

Clearly shady, they're demons? Denida peered at them.

"What's going on?" Jacob asked, with curious eyes.

"Settling an old score, set us up." Denida walked over to Lucifer in the street and stood back to back to him. His face completely changed, in the crowd, he noticed some faces he knew, faces he had never thought he would see again. Gabriel, God, and Peter were all there watching.

Why are they here? I need to get out of here before it's too late!

"Walk, 1,2,3-" Jacob yelled, bringing Denida out of his thoughts.

All the eyes followed them by each step they took closer to the tenth, which would mean time for the fated shot to kill off either Lucifer or Denida.

"-8,9,10," Jacob yelled, the worry in his voice clear.

As the final number was yelled, the two men spun around with superhuman speed.

The first bullet came from Lucifer's end and tore through the air and hit a tree in the distance because Denida was not there, he had fallen to his knees and shot too, but his bullet hit Lucifer between his eyes, making him fall to the ground.

The silence filled the air, the demons who were there with Lucifer stood in shock, God turned to Peter and nodded, Peter rushed towards Denida, who threw his hand forward to where Peter was coming, a sandstorm formed. God lifted his hand, the sand settled to the ground, but Denida was long gone.

Inside the Saloon, Jacob was still dazed by what he just witnessed.

Denida put his hand over his mouth, preventing him from saying a word. "I need to leave, you've got to help me!"

"But we're the law," Jacob objected.

Denida tore off his badge and put it in Jacob's hand. "The law won't be able to stop those who are after me."

Jacob looked down at the badge in his hand. "You're not coming back, are you?"

Denida softly shook his head.

Jacob sighed. "OK, I'll aid my Sheriff one last time!"

Jacob went back out, where people still searched for Denida, especially Peter. Gabriel stroked Denida's horse as if he knew it.

"Gabriel," Jacob asked cautiously.

"Yes, Jacob?" Gabriel continued petting it.

"Um... I-" Jacob stuttered, clearly unsure of what to say.

Gabriel turned with a smile and embraced Jacob with his tender eyes. "Why don't we go see Denny?"

Jacob led Gabriel back to the saloon. When they came back, Denida came out of hiding.

Gabriel smiled happily at Denida when he saw him. "Nice to see you doing so well."

"I need your help again." Denida raised his eyebrow, he rubbed his face.

Gabriel opened his wings and took out his arms to embrace him. "I'll always be here for you."

Denida walked over to Gabriel, who closed his wings around him.

"You'll forget this, Jacob." Gabriel held up his hand and blew a small breath towards him.

Gabriel sauntered out while Jacob scratched his head, trying to recall what just happened.

The arch-angel strolled towards Denida's horse.

Lucifer appeared in front of him. "Gabriel! You're here for Denny too, right? Have you seen him?"

"Not since he killed you." Gabriel chuckled.

Lucifer grunted and ran back to his demons outside the Saloon.

Gabriel continued towards the horse which was still standing outside the Sheriff's office. He checked to be sure it was safe before he unfolded his wings.

Denida snuck out from within.

"You need to leave this world- now."

Denida shrugged and mounted his horse. *Not possible.*

"Wrong, Denny." Gabriel grabbed the horse's reins. "Each world has two Gates, one to enter and one to leave. Your friend Robert knows where to go." He made a sound and the horse galloped off.

As morning dawned, Denida reached Robert's farm. The thoughts raged in Denida's head. *Will he welcome me? Will he help me? Will God find me, or Lucifer too?*

Denida slowed his horse down to a halt.

Robert stood sipping under the morning sun. He peered over at Denida riding up to his porch.

"Something's wrong, isn't it?"

Denida gave him the same look Robert had seen in the young boy he'd first seen. "They found me."

***

Claus took a deep breath.

"You're not done!" Claus said, with annoyance in his voice.

Daniel wrinkled his forehead. "I'm not?"

Claus shook his head. "As I said, I'm not Edward, you can't stall with me!" He walked over to the bars. "Continue; how did he escape?"

"But..." Daniel sighed and glared at the demons behind Claus, his eyes turned to Claus. "You might turn bad, like Edward?"

Claus smirked. "Have you forgotten I'm the boss, and I know you tried *something*!"

Daniel started to act nervous. I... um," he stuttered.

"Your story," Claus yelled.

Daniel nodded. "As you wish, he told Robert his old master had found him, but a friend had told him about a Gate to leave..."

***

Denida watched out over the field, he ran out to find the sparrow which was always following him. He put out his arm and it landed on him as it was the most natural thing.

"Denny." Robert walked towards him. He had been out in the field all morning, so he was covered in dirt. "The Gate you mentioned needs power. I know how to gather it for you. I started it, but it will take a few days..."

Denida grunted as he continued stroking the sparrow. "You know where it is?"

"I do, but let's gather the power first!"

Denida threw his arm upwards and the sparrow flew off. "I'll hide out where the power's being gathered, so if they come, they won't find me."

He went out in the field but turned after a few steps. "Be careful, Luci's anger means he'll stop at nothing to get to me."

At night, Denida's worst fears proved true. Several men armed to the teeth arrived, led by Lucifer himself.

They stormed the house, Robert grabbed his shotgun but Lucifer threw his arm up, Robert was thrown against the wall by Dark Energy, dropping the shotgun.

"Hello Robert, I'm Luci, I'm searching for our old pupil Denny. You wouldn't happen to have seen him?" Lucifer leaned over and raised his hand to help him up.

"Luci?" Robert turned to the sound from the house. "*Our* pupil?"

"Not here," one of the demons came out of the house with the rest and said.

Lucifer used his comforting smile. "Yes, others are looking for him. Won't you let me help him?"

Robert gave Lucifer a fake smile. "Sorry. But even *if I had seen him*, I wouldn't tell you!"

The demons chattered amongst themselves behind Lucifer.

Lucifer spun in anger and shot off a beam of Darkness which devoured all the demons.

Robert shook in terror as the Darkness lifted and their bones fell to the ground.

Lucifer sat down in the chair next to Robert, the red glare in his eyes fading.

He ran his hand across his forehead. "They were always in line for destruction, you see. I need to be sure no one remembers what happened here."

Robert cleared his throat. "Happened?"

"Denny..." Lucifer's eyes had a small flicker of red again. "Don't bother." Lucifer smiled. "I'll leave, he's too smart to come here, anyway..." He got up and flicked his hand and a Dark Mist appeared in front of him. He walked into it and it dissipated behind him.

Robert got up, still not feeling himself, he limped a little, but he continued over to the bodies. He knelt and examined them.

"They're not human." Denida walked out of the tall grass fields.

"You were here?"

Denida walked to the end of the grass to where Robert could see him but he didn't go further. "I had to."

Robert nudged the bodies with a toe. "Some very bad people are after you."

Denida turned and walked back into the tall grass.

In the following days, Denida stayed hidden in the fields. Robert came and brought him food and watched for anyone to come the rest of the time.

Robert prepared a metal box, which contained the energy needed for the gate and attached it to the satchel hanging on Denida's horse. "I drew on this where it is."

Denida grabbed the piece of paper Robert held.

Robert wrinkled his face in worry. "You do realize, they might look for you there?"

Not Lucifer, but Peter might... Denida mounted the horse and nodded. "Thank you for everything, Robert."

"My pleasure, till next time, Denny."

Denida rode off while Robert watched him go

The sparrow circled around in front of him throughout his long ride towards the Gate. It was a long way, but the sparrow stayed by his side, but as he approached the Gate, it suddenly flew off.

Guess it doesn't want to come all the way.

He dismounted from the horse and put the satchel on his back. He kneeled and snuck towards the Gate.

Tumbleweeds flew around, but other than those it seemed barren here.

Denida still felt unsure, so he continued to be careful as he proceeded forward.

He could see the Gate in the distance. *I might actually make it.*

Denida took out the metal box Robert gave him and increased his pace as he hurried towards the Gate.

"Denny, Denny, Denny..." Peter walked out from behind Denida, clapping in a mockingly way.

No, not him.

"Yes, me!" Peter grinned. "...and how I'll so enjoy this."

The box in Denida's hand flew out of his grip and towards the Gate. He ran as fast as he could after the box.

Peter's wings appeared, he flew in front of Denida before Denida could take even a few steps.

"Going somewhere?" Peter reached into the air with his arm and the box flew into his hands.

He grinned and threw it in the distance high above them, so far they could not see it, if it weren't for the discharge of the energy which outshone the sun.

A thunderous blast shook them as the lid fell on the ground in front of Denida.

"Oh well." Peter smiled. "God set me to Protect Heaven, I failed with you; this ends now!"

No. Denida pulled his gun and emptied it at Peter.

Peter's wings folded around him, causing the bullets to bounce off him.

Denida threw down the gun and ducked out of sight before Peter unfolded his wings.

"Where are you?" Peter examined the surroundings. "I know you're here, you can't leave without the Gate."

Denida hid behind a boulder. *I need to find another way.*

"You do." Peter appeared right next to him.

Denida spun, ready to run, but Peter grabbed him by the throat before he could run.

"You forgot your dark magic, or maybe you're too afraid Lucifer would detect you then?" Peter taunted him. "Die, or go back to Hell, it must be a hard choice!"

Peter threw him to the ground.

Denida picked himself up. "I'll *never* return to Hell!"

"What a shame," Peter sneered. "I guess you leave me no choice then."

A light appeared before Denida's body that shaped into a Spear of Light.

A squeaking noise sounded over them. Peter turned to see the sparrow which flew above him in circles, forming a gust of wind.

"What?" Peter directed the spear towards it, giving Denida a chance to run.

Denida peered back as he started to run, he stumbled over his own feet in shock.

It's the sparrow which followed me, how can it do magic? Enough to fight against Peter, who has Supreme Light Magic?

Peter sent off his Spear of Light through the dark storm which formed. It cut through and flew into the distance, the sparrow had already gone.

He looked frantically for the bird, it flew at speed toward him.

Peter shot lightning towards it, but the bird flew around them. He set off into the sky with a beam of light, like what Denida remembered seeing Gabriel do in Hell.

The sparrow sat down on top of the Gate with small pipsqueaks. As if nothing special just occurred.

Denida stood up and came out from where he hid. "What *are* you?"

It tilted its head at the Gate.

"Not possible, the power is gone, there's no way to get it to work!" Denida sighed.

'Magic,' a voice echoed in Denida's head.

Denida wrinkled his forehead and studied the Gate.

Did the sparrow speak to me in my thoughts?

Denida walked closer and examined the Gate more thoroughly. He licked his lips.

The demons will come soon since the sparrow used magic, might as well try.

The sparrow set off. Denida stepped back and pulled his hand towards the Gate.

He focused and the strongest force of Dark energy flew out of his hand towards the Gate.

The Gate devoured the energy and it lit up.

Denida's eyes widened.

Horses could be heard behind him, demons approached at high speed.

Thank you, whoever you are. He ran through the Gate.

***

"Leave us," Claus yelled.

The demons stared with a dark glare at him.

"You told us, he can't-" one of the demons began.

Claus got up and ran towards him with red eyes and tore out his heart.

He turned to look at the remaining demon, who quaked in terror.

Claus dropped the heart and lifted his blood-soaked hand and the demon flew across the room to slam into the bars.

He smiled and tore out the remaining demon's heart.

The demon fell dead to the ground. Claus gazed at Daniel.

Daniel gasped at what he saw. "Something... wrong?"

"You know very well what's wrong!"

Daniel shook, he kept glancing back at the bloody pools on the floor. "Mom," he muttered and fell to his knees.

Do I tell Lucifer? Can I even? Denida beat Lucifer... Claus' face became as scared at the thought, he hadn't been so terrified since Hell. Claus rushed over to the bars. "You tell *anyone* what you told me, you'll never see your Dad again! Do we understand each other?"

Daniel nodded nervously. "But I didn't tell you anything *that* bad!"

"Oh yes, you did; Denida embarrassed the Devil." Claus stormed out of the dungeon, he went over to Jack. "I need a cleanup, the two demons in the dungeon needs to be replaced!"

"What-" Jack watched with wide eyes after Claus, who walked off.

Chapter 19: The Real World

What's going on? Jack hurried with several demons to the dungeon.

They all stopped as they saw the bloody pools on the floor.

Hearts removed? What's Claus hiding?

Jack instructed them to clean it up, while he slowly walked about the room, examining the remains. Nothing he could see would explain it, his eyes turned to the only one left who could, other than Claus himself; Daniel. "What happened here?"

"Claus," Daniel said with a tremble in his voice.

He looks terrified, he'll never say more. Jack smiled reassuringly. "How far did you get with your tale?"

"To the *real* world."

"Earth?" Jack turned curiously to Daniel. "He went to Earth?"

"When Dad left the Wild West world, he arrived as a spirit roaming Earth."

"Interesting…" Jack glanced back at the demons cleaning up. He sat down in front of the bars. "Tell me more."

***

Denida giggled. He flipped the traffic lights on and back off when the people started to walk. They stopped and checked around confused.

I thought this world would have nothing to do, but it's quite fun!

A man pulled a girl back, who was about to walk out into the street, a speeding car barely missed her.

She was a young girl about ten years old with blond hair, Denida couldn't take his eyes off her, there was something about her. Maybe those green eyes, he was not sure, but he was drawn, no doubt.

He got up to follow her. She slowed down and kept looking back, as she was unsure of something.

"Nina," a girl waved her hand and ran over to her, followed by another girl.

Cute name.

Nina sighed. "I can feel *something* again..."

"It'll disappear as it usually does." Her friend hugged her.

"Hope so, Kathrine." Nina hugged her, she buried her head in Katherine's curls, while her other friend just shook her head and left them.

Denida suddenly had wide opened eyes. *I don't believe it!*

He rushed forward, through everyone and everything he encountered until he stood inside the building and stared at what had him so shocked.

A boy with a short blonde hair hung his bag on a chair and sat down. The boy had the same spike in his hair as him, almost identical, Denida couldn't believe it. *Is it me?*

The school bell rang and several kids came running in, including Nina and Katherine, who sat at the two tables in front of the boy.

"Hey Denny, can I borrow a pen?" Nina turned and asked the boy.

Does he have the same name as me? Gabriel mentioned Lucifer took me from Earth, but...

Denida took a deep sigh as he watched the boy, apparently called *Denny*,

He sat at the boy's table as the class started.

"I see you met Denny."

Denida raised his head. This voice he remembered. "Gabriel, is this who I am?"

Gabriel nodded. "He grew up, without his soul..."

Denida gazed at the boy. "He can operate without?"

"Lucifer had Medusa, a demon to watch over him. She vanished..."

Denida stared at Gabriel's face.

"Something wrong, Denny?"

Denida's eyes locked with Gabriel as he realized something. "In the last world-"

Gabriel chuckled and nodded. "You beat Lucifer, yes..."

"Not that," Denida shook his head, "a sparrow always followed me. When I went to the Gate, Peter was waiting for me."

Gabriel wrinkled. "But, you're here?"

"The sparrow fought him; God's special Angel protecting Heaven."

"To beat Saint Peter? But that requires-"

"Exactly." Denida stood up. "Could it be this Medusa, you said the demon vanished?"

"Come, I'll take you to the next world." Gabriel held out his hand, but Denida didn't make a move.

He just shook his head. "No, I like it here. I want to stay."

Gabriel lowered his arm with a surprised look. "You can never return to your physical form; the process can't be reversed."

Denida smiled at the boy. "His soul will remain near him."

Gabriel nodded solemnly. "As you wish, at least Lucifer never can come here." He turned to walk out.

Denida rushed after Gabriel through the wall. He grabbed at Gabriel outside before he flew off. "He can't? Why not? I was on Earth with him!"

"No, God has condemned him from it, he physically can't."

Denida laughed loud and uncontrollably. "I finally got away from him!"

**

Jack bit his lips. *He never can?*

The two demons walked back in.

Jack spun back towards Daniel. "Thank you." He got up. "Watch him!"

He walked out towards Claus' office. He stopped outside the door.

I have to find out what Claus has discovered. Can it be what I found out about Lucifer?

He grabbed the door and went in.

Claus sat at his desk with another demon informing him of something.

He noticed Jack, he waved him over. "We finally got it!" He grinned loudly.

Jack wrinkled his face in puzzlement.

"Denida called. He's giving us the ring in exchange for Daniel."

That can't be possible.

Jack stepped in front of Claus, blocking him. "Did you speak with Denida?"

"The demon did, I need to go get Daniel!"

Jack held up his hand. "I'll prepare him. I'm the security, remember?" He smiled and walked out towards the dungeon.

The two demons turned at the door as Jack came in. He went over to Daniel, who stood up, with worry written across his face.

Jack smiled at him and spun around, he lifted his hand. "Sleep," he muttered.

A small black cloud fell over the two demons, making them slump down over the table in front of them. Jack spun back around to Daniel. "We won't have any interruptions now, tell me the rest!"

Daniel swallowed nervously, he nodded startled. "Sure, whatever you want. Dad was fascinated by his human counterpart. He followed his every step. But he still felt drawn to Nina, my Mom's physical being…"

***

Denida followed his human self; the boy Denny.

Denny stopped, waiting for the bus. He put his bag down and ravaged through it for his bus pass.

Nice day, really. Denida stretched his neck up to the sky and watched the burning sun above him.

He squinted his eye. A bird flew above him. *The sparrow, again?*

The bird flew around the sun, Denida tried to focus to make out what it was. Suddenly the bird flew across the road. *Just a crow…*

Denida felt a rush of warm air behind him, he glared back, Nina and Katherine were riding their bikes home.

He stared into Nina's eyes as she passed him by, drawn to her again.

Denny stood up from his bag and sighed heavily at her passing by.

He peeked over at Denny. So, we're both fascinated with that girl.

He licked his lips, he set off after Nina and Katherine. It didn't take long to catch up to them since they were chit-chatting while they biked on their way back home.

Nina and Katherine stopped their bikes and said bye. Katherine waved, her curly hair blowing in the wind as she turned towards the tall building behind her. *Must be where Katherine lives.*

Denida turned and hurried after Nina, who was already on her way. As she rode alone now, she wasn't as slow on the pedals.

Nina parked her bicycle when she arrived at an old farmhouse.

She ran into the stables, leaving her bag out on the ground next to her bicycle. Denida found her petting the mane of a big black horse.

The horse moved to give Denida a piercing look.

You can see me, can't you? Denida stepped carefully towards the horse and it didn't waver.

Nina was still petting it, with Denida standing right in front of the horse.

Are you not scared? Is the Darkness really gone?

"Nina," an elder man yelled.

"*Dad.*" Nina ran out and grabbed her bag from him.

Denida licked his lips. The horse hadn't moved its eyes from him.

It turned to the window in the back of the stables, where a crow sat on a tree.

I've got a bad feeling. He rushed through the wall.

The crow flickered its wings and flew higher, to a branch further up, before Denida could reach it.

No, you don't! Denida climbed the tree further upwards.

The crow flickered its wings and flew a branch higher, which didn't stop Denida, he went further up the tree.

When there were no further it could fly, it circled above the tree.

Denida peered back down, he was far above in the tree. *No way I'm stopping.* He threw his arm up towards the crow. The wind surrounded the bird and drew it closer.

It flapped its wings in a clear panic, but it couldn't escape. It stopped suddenly and burst into flames before it reached Denida, who suddenly lowered his arm.

The crow fell lifeless in flames to the ground beneath.

Lucifer can't be here on Earth; In a physical form, but is he the crow? Denida shook his head to his thoughts. It can't be, it must be who the sparrow was, and that wasn't Lucifer.

A ruckus could be heard from within the stables.

Denida put himself back to focus and went curiously through the wall. He saw Nina's dad helping her on the horse. Her dad waved her off.

Denida jotted off after her.

Nina rode on the dirt roads around the farm, which led into a forest.

She dismounted from the horse abruptly, when she noticed a cat. It cowered behind some bushes, Nina kneeled to the ground. She muttered out tender sounds to the cat, after a short while it walked slowly towards her. She picked it up and stroked it. The cat purred and rubbed itself up against her.

Sweet girl.

"Isn't she," a voice echoed behind Denida.

Denida spun in a surprise to see the same old woman he first met in the cave. "You?"

The old woman smiled and spectated the girl in the distance. "You know the crow is me, so I had to show myself!"

Denida wrinkled his brow. "You were the crow *and* the sparrow?"

The old woman nodded with a smile.

"Why, what do you want with me? *What* are you?"

221

"I've been watching you from a distance."

The cat gazed towards them, trying to wrist free from Nina's grasp.

Nina turned, but could see nothing, she tried to console the cat, it finally managed to jump out of her embrace.

She rushed after it, with the horse following behind her.

The woman turned back to Denida. "When you escaped Hell, I went looking and I found you in the Wild Western world."

"You were sent by Lucifer?" Denida took a few steps backward.

She shook her head. "Lucifer sent me here to Earth to watch you and I did, but I don't serve him anymore..."

The wrinkle returned to Denida's face.

"I serve the *Darkness* directly- we're here to protect you!"

"The Darkness," Denida muttered.

"Join us," she said and stretched out her hand. "Lucifer's time has come to an end!"

Denida shook his head in disbelief. *I can't believe I'm hearing this.* "You're a demon then? How can you be here? God limited access to Earth?"

She giggled. "When Lucifer was here with you, God noticed him, so he limited *him* from ever entering Earth, not the demons-" She walked closer to Denida. "Don't you worry, you can trust me. My name's Medusa."

Denida bit his lip. "How did you find me in this world then?"

"I'll always watch you, wherever you go!"

Denida turned his back to the woman, unsure of how to act. "I can never return to Lucifer."

"You won't! We'll replace him with you."

Denida spun around with fury in his eye. "You want to *kill* Lucifer?"

"Why does it matter? He took you from your place on Earth, you can't like him, can you?" She grinned.

"I'll never set foot back in Hell- in any capacity!"

"I'll need to find another way," Medusa muttered.

No, you don't! Denida spun around in circles, causing a heavy mist to form around them.

Medusa chanted a clearing spell, but Denida was already gone.

***

"Medusa?" Jack's forehead wrinkled. "That name sounds ominous!"

The doors opened behind them and Claus entered, followed by several demons.

Daniel felt his gut turning. "What's going on?"

"You're coming, your Dad is trading the ring for you!" Claus chuckled.

Daniel got even more worried. "The ring? He's giving the ring to you?"

"In exchange for you. Smile!" Claus pushed his hand out. "Bring him!"

The other demons came into Daniel's cell and grabbed him, then attached the chains they brought to him.

Jack went over to Claus. "I think this is a bad idea," Jack whispered. "Denida would never just give it up! Not even for Daniel…"

Claus rolled his eyes and turned to Jack. "This is why we're here! You can handle security, we'll be back; *with the ring.*" He led the way out with the demons escorting Daniel behind him.

This'll go wrong, I can feel it. Jack sighed and turned his gaze back to the cell. This Medusa, why do I know this name and from where?

Chapter 20: Michelle

Nina and Susan arrived at the lab and hurried inside to the Gate.

Susan went to the controls and found the robot she was looking for.

Nina shrugged. "Why are we here? Where's Dan at?"

Susan turned back at Nina when she said that but returned to what she was doing.

"Anyone present?" Susan yelled into the speaker. She rubbed her face and glared impatiently at Nina.

Nina felt uneasy. *Why is she so intrigued?* "Shouldn't we call Dan?"

Susan just continued looking at the monitor, completely ignoring her.

"Yes?" A man came on screen from the other end of the feed.

"Yes." Susan ran to the screen. "I need to talk to the Warlock!"

"She's seeing the High Sorcerer, can it wait?" he replied.

Susan glanced back at Nina and shook her head. "No, it's about Lady Nina."

The man's eyes widened. "Of course, right away!" The man ran off.

"What's with him?" Nina peeked at Susan.

Susan sighed. "Unlike you, he remembers the Warlock met with you."

Nina rolled her eyes. "I told you, I haven't met her since Denny was lost within the Gate."

Susan got up and went over to her. She held Nina's shoulder and stared intently at her.

What's with her? Nina rolled her eyes.

"Something's not right, you don't remember *a lot...*" Susan sighed. "Stuff you *should* remember from-"

"Lady Nina?" The Warlock appeared on the monitor.

Susan rushed over. "Something's very wrong!"

The Warlock raised her eyebrows and examined Susan. "You look like our Susan, you're a soldier?"

Susan nodded. "I'm watching Nina, but something is seriously wrong. She's forgotten a lot of important things. She ran over and yanked Nina to the front of the monitor. "Ask her when you last talked to her."

The Warlock scratched her head. "What a strange request. OK, if you insist; when did we last talk, Lady Nina?"

Nina tore herself free from Susan's grab. "This is ridiculous. I don't know- back when Denny was lost within the Gate."

The Warlock's face changed. "Leave us," she abruptly yelled to the aide.

The aide rushed out and closed the door behind him.

"She was very suspicious-" The Warlock looked over at Susan. "she wanted to learn how to perform a Dark Art, so she could be invisible!"

Nina shook her head abruptly. "No, I haven't seen you-"

"Wait." The Warlock raised her hand, her eyes narrowed. "Susan, do you know who she suspects?"

Susan ground her teeth and nodded. "Michelle!"

Nina scowled at the two of them. "This is insane, I'm going!" She turned towards the door.

Susan stormed after her, Nina shoved her away and drew breath to scream.

Susan drew her gun and pointed it at her, and forced Nina back to the Gate. Nina backed into the room, back to where the Gate was, with her hands up. Susan waved at a chair. Nina sat down.

"It's only events regarding Michelle, she doesn't remember, right," the Warlock asked.

Susan rubbed her eyes. "I think so. Do you know what is wrong with her?"

The Warlock nodded solemnly. "I suspect it's a seal on certain memories. It's an advanced form of Dark Arts."

Susan wrinkled her forehead. "But why? No one believes her suspicions."

"She said that," the Warlock muttered. "I need you to repeat after me, it's a chant which disables the spell if there is one."

"Susan has no magic ability." Nina glared past Susan to the Warlock. "Will it damage me?"

The Warlock shook her head. "It won't do anything if there's no spell put on you."

Nina reached out for Susan's hand. Susan readied her gun at her with both her hands.

Nina put up her hands. "I just want your hand. I'll provide the magic you lack."

Susan wrinkled, she tightened around the gun. "Why would you-"

"If I was used, I want to know it," Nina insisted.

Susan bit her lips, she lowered her gun and put it back in her belt. She sat down and took Nina's hand. "We're ready, I guess…"

Nina started to feel her palms growing sweaty. She watched Susan, who repeated the words the Warlock chanted.

What if this is really true? I feel uneasy. She tried to pull back, but she couldn't. Susan's grip was too tight. Susan tightened her grip more, her gaze pierced Nina's eyes as she continued her chant.

Uneasiness grew in Nina, darkness filling her vision, making her want to break loose again, but Susan's grip was still too tight.

Nina's heart pounded in terror as the Dark cloud enveloped her. Susan chanted as if nothing was happening. *Maybe, she can't see it, cause she doesn't have magic herself?* The Darkness above her seemed more and more menacing, the further the chant went, but all of a sudden it just disappeared.

Nina could feel like a heavy burden lifted. Her eyes grew wide. "Medusa!"

"What," the warlock yelled, clearly in shock. "How do you know that name?"

"It's who Michelle is."

The Warlock shook her head. "We're all doomed then," she said under her breath. "Michelle; I should have known it was a fake name."

Why? Nina stared with an empty gaze at the Warlock.

"It means the gift from God…"

Nina sighed. "She was with the Darkness, she claims it controls the Devil."

Susan jerked up from her chair and ran out. Nina gasped puzzled but hurried after. She caught up with her at the car.

Susan shook her head with water shot eyes. "I… was wrong, we have to stop her; before it's too late!"

Nina got into the car and Susan drove towards the Headquarters. Susan drove as fast as she could, not wasting any time, nearly causing a few car crashes. She skidded the car to a halt when they arrived. Nina jumped out before the car engine had even shut off.

She stormed into the building and went straight up to the Colonel's floor. Dan waved at her when she came out of the elevator, he ran up to her.

"Why are you here?" Nina wrinkled her forehead surprised at him.

"I had a great idea, which might help us get Daniel back."

Daniel. She checked the room where Michelle's desk was, she wasn't there. *Where is she?* She turned and stormed past Dan, straight into the Colonel's office.

Denida and the Colonel sat opposites each other at the desk talking, not noticing her entering.

"Where is Michelle?"

The Colonel and Denida turned startled to Nina. Denida got up and went over to hug her, but Nina pushed him away.

"Where," she demanded.

"Michelle left with the fake ring, to get Daniel," Dan said behind her.

Nina's heart raced painfully, her fear keeping her from speaking.

Denida hugged her. *'What is it?'*

Nina smiled at him, trying to conceal her worry, she wrinkled her forehead. *'Michelle-'*

'Not this again!' Denida rolled his eyes and went back towards his chair.

"Medusa!" Nina screamed.

Denida stumbled into his seat. "How do you know- why do you utter that name?"

"Michelle's true name, she told me before she tried to wipe my memories!"

Denida had a terror in his eyes Nina had never seen before.

The Colonel's confusion was written across his hard, old face. "Who is Medusa? Why is it so important, if she has another name?"

Denida turned with a rugged look at the Colonel. "It's not just any name! It's the name of the one the Darkness favors more than Lucifer…"

Nina leaned towards Denida. "Where is she?" She glanced at Dan, wrinkled her forehead. "And what ring?"

***

Michelle had gone to the rendezvous, between them and Claus to exchange the ring in exchange for Daniel and waited for the meet. She'd peeked at the fake ring in the box. *It truly does look real, has the time come at last?*

Several cars approached, and she stuffed the box into her pocket. "Stay sharp!"

The soldiers readied their guns. The cars parked not far from them, everyone watching the cars in anticipation.

"Maybe we should-" a soldier asked impatiently.

Dark figures came out of the cars opposites them.

"The ring," a voice yelled from behind the dark figures.

Claus came out from behind the dark figures, he walked towards Michelle.

Michelle took few steps towards him. "I have it, where's the boy?"

Claus cocked his head backward, two demons brought Daniel forward. They stopped abruptly behind Claus.

"I repeat; the ring?" Claus smiled impatiently at Michelle.

Michelle nodded and took out the box from her pocket. She opened the box and tilted it so Claus could see. "I don't come empty-handed."

Claus chuckled and grabbed Daniel and pushed him forward. Michelle closed the box and threw it.

Claus barely grabbed it, opened the box to check it once more, then ran with his demons towards their cars.

"Shouldn't we stop them?" A soldier grabbed tightly at his gun.

Michelle shook her head. "Let them go. We got what we came for!"

The cars sped off and the soldiers lowered their guns.

"Anyone there?" the soldier's earpiece beeped.

Michelle smiled at the soldiers and strolled over to Daniel to help him up from the ground, and released his restraints.

"Yes," one of the soldiers asked.

"You're alive," the voice from the earpiece said.

The soldiers grinned at the remark.

"Of course, we've got Daniel from Claus-"

"Claus is *not* the danger."

The soldier wrinkled his forehead. "Why not? Who then? Jack, the Scientist?"

"No," a loud voice yelled, making everyone's ears sore.

All soldiers grabbed their ears.

"Lord Denida?" a soldier sounded confused.

Something doesn't feel right. Michelle peeked back at her soldiers. Why is Denny calling?

"Michelle is a demon, don't let her near Daniel," Denida yelled with a trembling voice.

The soldiers all turned towards Michelle, their eyes locked.

Michelle giggled. "Guess the cat's out of the bag." She shot Spears of Fire which set soldiers ablaze before they could reach for their guns.

The few ones who did manage to reach their guns, rolled to the side, barely avoiding the spears.

They returned fire from the other side of the cars. The bullets around Michelle didn't faze her. A window behind her shattered and she fell to her knees.

The remaining soldiers stopped shooting, looking at each other in doubt, their guns still aimed at her.

Dammit! Michelle pushed herself to her feet.

The soldiers started shooting again.

Michelle lifted her hand, the bullets froze in front of her, she frowned at them before she sent Darkness towards them.

Figures appeared from the darkness. The soldiers turned their guns to them instead, but the bullets just went through the dark beings who swarmed the soldiers and tore them limb from limb. After the last soldier dropped dead to the ground, Michelle giggled again.

"Guess that's the last of them."

Michelle turned back to face Daniel, who was nowhere to be seen. "You can't hide, Daniel," she yelled. She examined the surroundings as she paced around, there was no sign of Daniel. *Where can he be?* "Oh... Daniel," she smirked. She perched her lips. "You know, I know your father very well... my name's Medusa. Has he ever told you about that name?"

Michelle checked around seeing nothing. "I know he told you. Your mother heard it too, I had to take care of her, maybe I should just go finish the job?"

"No!" Daniel came out from behind her.

She chuckled. "Sure about that? Who's gonna stop me?"

Daniel shook with nerves but stared her in the eye. "I will."

Oh, this is going to be fun.

Daniel muttered a few words and a cone appeared around him.

Michelle raised her eyebrows. "Your Dad taught you defensive spells, I see."

231

"This is not all." Daniel threw out his arm and shot fireballs, hitting her in the face.

Daniel kept shooting, not giving her a chance to fight back.

The ground around her lit up. Daniel smiled as he plummeted her with fireballs. A large explosion created a dark cloud and Daniel stopped shooting.

Out of the flames, a Dark being walked, skin ablaze. It lifted its arms and the flames subsided, a demon stood before Daniel, smirking deviously.

Daniel screamed with terror and ran the other way.

Michelle's eye flickered red and she sauntered casually after him.

Chapter 21: Medusa

Daniel put on the cloaking spell his Dad had taught him. He peeked around the corner of the car, Michelle was still walking in the distance.

"Daniel," she kept calling out.

Daniel sighed heavily, he carefully lifted the handle to the car, Michelle arrived with the soldiers in. He gazed in Michelle's direction. *She didn't notice!* He crawled in, he searched through the seats, the glove box, anywhere he could think of for the keys. *Nothing!* He glared back out, Michelle was still not near him. *What if...* He tried turning on the car, but it didn't work. He sighed, *Dad should have taught me to start a car with magic!*

Daniel crawled back out of the car and closed the door, he snuck to the other cars, but they were all locked.

Michelle started walking back towards the cars.

It's too dangerous here, I gotta find somewhere to hide! Daniel crawled about trying to quiet his breathing. He noticed an old car, which lay in a crevice with tons of garbage around it, he hurried to it, before Medusa reached him.

'Thud.' Daniel stumbled over a branch on the way there. *Crap.* He froze and looked back over his shoulder at Michelle.

Michelle turned her head abruptly in his direction. She ran forward, peering into the crevice.

She can't see me!

Michelle's eyes flickered red. She searched with her arms inside the crevice.

She's going to find me!

Michelle got hold of Daniel's throat. she squeezed Daniel till the cloaking spell subsided. "You're right, I can't see you, but I *can* hear you!"

Daniel shot off fireballs straight into Michelle's face, she fell back. He got up and ran off.

Michelle transformed into a sparrow and flew to the front of Daniel, where she transformed back into herself.

"No escape for you." She smirked and drew her hand through the air. Dark dust fell on Daniel and he fell asleep to the ground.

***

Several vehicles approached off in the distance.

Michelle turned to look at them.

We need to leave. Michelle yanked Daniel onto her shoulder, her own car was parked away from the others.

She threw Daniel in the back and got in.

She checked the rearview mirror, changing her body back into the sexy woman, she wore in the warehouse.

She drove away as the other cars came to a stop near the bodies. *They found them, which means the hunt will be on for me.*

'You need to be careful,' a voice said in her head.

Michelle nodded to herself. *Yes, Master.*

She drove far out into the countryside, there was nothing anywhere near, no one who could see anything they shouldn't. Michelle drove a little past a farmhouse and stopped. She scoped out the road with her rearview mirror. When she was convinced she was alone, she set the car in reverse and parked next to the house.

Michelle carried Daniel, still sleeping, into the house, and she threw him on a bed. She put her hand on his forehead, waking him up. "You'll stay here, or else!"

"What do you plan on doing to me?" Daniel curled up in a ball.

"I don't know yet." Michelle went back out and locked the door, leaving Daniel trembling, all alone.

I do need a way out. Michelle marched back out to the car. An old man was walking over towards her.

Her fists clenched. "What can I help you with?"

"Hello Ma'am." He smiled as tender as a cuddly bear. "I'm Arthur, I saw you driving up, just wanted to say hello."

I don't like this; this could be bad news!

She patted the man's back and led him away from the house. "It's so nice to have friendly neighbors, who care." She gave the man a warm smile and sent him on his way.

Michelle turned and went back towards the house. *Something feels strange.* She ran inside to Daniel's room, she rattled the handle, forgetting for a second it was locked. Digging the key out of her pocket she unlocked the door and jerked it open; the room was empty.

How is this possible? Where is he? She rushed throughout the room, checking under the covers, under the bed- nothing. She rushed to the closet and opened it, but there was nothing inside.

Michelle's eyes wandered from one end of the room to the other.

I don't get it. How could he have gotten out?

A dark figure appeared behind her. "Medusa, don't disappoint, Denida taught him magic."

"I'll find him," Michelle snarled in her defense.

"I hope so, you lost him before, and now yet again…" The dark being faded away behind her.

That Arthur guy! She rushed back out. Following Arthur's aura was easy. It led her to a house on the other side of the road, hidden by trees.

Michelle cast a cloaking spell and walked up to the front door. *They would hear if I open the door.*

Her arm turned dark, then her whole body became a dark see-through. She walked through the door, as if it wasn't even there.

Inside the old man sat with an elderly woman with Daniel sitting opposite them.

"She's a really bad person," Daniel said. "You must keep me hidden!"

Michelle giggled to herself, she bit her tongue and nodded. She spun around and walked back outside, where she turned into a sparrow and flew high above the house, they were in.

The sparrow circled the house and flew faster and faster, making a small cone of Darkness surround the house. She then flew back down, where she transformed back into a human form.

Now they no longer can reach the outside or use magic anymore.

Michelle walked casually in through the door. Daniel got up and ran to the garden door but couldn't get it open.

"Don't bother, look out the window." Michelle smiled.

Arthur watched out the window, his eyes widened in disbelief, the woman saw his expression and glared out the window too, she grabbed Arthur's arm.

Daniel glanced at the window, then immediately at Michelle. "Why?"

"Why not?" Michelle's eyes flickered red. "You'll be contained here, no longer any escape risk!"

Arthur spun around and rushed her, but Michelle threw up a hand and sent Arthur flying into a bookcase. The woman ran to check on him and helped him up.

"How long... will you... keep us locked up here?" Arthur staggered as his wife led him to a chair.

Michelle grinned. "As long as it takes, I'll bring more food if needed." She turned and walked out the door.

As soon as she turned, Daniel sprinted after her but bounced off the Dark barrier like it was a wall.

Daniel clenched his fists as he stared into Michelle's eyes. "You know who- or what my Dad is."

"I do. I can control him though."

Daniel shook his head. "After all this time, you still don't know him."

***

Denida watched nervously as Nina paced across the room. *Shall I try?*

He met the Colonel's eye, the Colonel slowly tilted his head, to hint that it was a bad idea.

She spun to Denida in fury. "In case you forgot; I *can* hear your thoughts!"

"Then you should know-"

"Should I?" Nina sighed heavily and shook her head. "I know, but what you're not realizing, it could be Daniel's end too!"

Denida rolled his eyes.

"It can," Nina yelled. "We know what Jack and Claus want; the ring; We have no idea about Michelle!"

The Colonel and Denida shared a look of worry.

Don't worry, Denida spoke to Nina's thoughts.

"I-" Nina sighed heavily. "Who exactly *is* Medusa?"

Denida suddenly turned back to the Colonel.

Nina jerked at Denida. "What aren't you telling me?"

Denida sighed heavily. "Lucifer sent an arch-demon to watch over me on Earth…"

"Not her? Why her?" Nina shook her head and took a few steps backward.

Denida nodded. "Her! But I don't know, I never met her in Hell."

"But didn't you hear talk of her?"

"I was more concerned with Ignacio and Danyel and the rest of the Dark Angels…"

"We need to talk to Lucifer then," Nina spoke lowly.

"Maybe, Michelle never got-" The Colonel turned white.

Nina ran past Denida, over to the Colonel. "Yes?" Her voice sounded very worried.

"We found the soldiers Michelle was with; they're all dead!" the Colonel looked uncomfortable saying it.

Now Denida pushed forward past Nina. "Daniel, Michelle?"

The Colonel lowered his head. "I'm sorry, there's no sign of them."

Denida ran a hand through his hair. "Are there any signs of them?"

The Colonel shook his head.

Denida bit his lip.

Nina and Denida shared a deep look and nodded to each other.

Denida grabbed Nina's hand. "Inform me the second you find out anything!"

"Where are you-"

"Do it!" Denida frowned. He walked out pulling Nina by the hand. The bodyguards ran after him, but Denida sped away with Nina before they reached him.

He drove as if Hell was on his tail, ignoring his security detail.

"Where are we going?" Nina's eyes turned big.

"Dynasty!" Denida licked his lips.

Why? Nina scratched her forehead.

Denida ground his teeth. "I put a shield on the use of Dark Magic there, stronger than anywhere else."

"I still don't see why. We need to find Michelle!"

"We will; Lucifer might help…"

Nina stared at Denida with eyes that could kill. She grumbled, turning away, she said nothing but staring at the passing cars. "It's a benefit now, I guess," she muttered.

Denida's eye wandered but snapped back to watch the road.

The rest of the ride to Dynasty passed in silence, not even a thought ran between the two of them.

When they arrived, Denida led her to the open ground near the stables.

"He can't know of the ring. Don't even think of it, *Medusa* only!"

"I'm not stupid," Nina yelled. "Reficul, Reficul, Reficul, get your ass here!"

The Darkness appeared in a mist in front of them, Lucifer took shape.

"My, my." Lucifer smiled. "Summoned by lady Nina, I'm honored."

Denida stepped in front of Nina as she moved to attack Lucifer.

He took Nina's hand. "Lucifer…"

"Call me Luci, remember?" Lucifer smiled.

Nina tried to wrest free of Denida's hand, with all her might.

"I'm not your friend- or your pupil!" Denida tightened his grip on Nina's hand. "I'm here for one reason; Medusa!"

Lucifer's smile faded at the mention of a name he clearly knew.

"Wonder why we ask? *She's here*." Nina snarled.

Lucifer peered distressed at them. "That's a demon you don't want-" Lucifer sat down on the grass and sighed. "You want to know who she is- Or maybe I should say *what she is*?"

Nina ripped loose from Denida and ran towards Lucifer. "She has my son!"

Lucifer chuckled. "You would have liked her, Denny." Lucifer raised his eyebrows with a smile. "She was the most devious demon, I ever met and watched over you on Earth but vanished around the time you escaped Hell. No one saw her since…"

"Until now," Nina remarked.

Lucifer nodded, not taking his eyes off Denida. "She's a loose cannon." He got up from the grass.

"Wrong," Nina acclimated. "She's with *your* Darkness!"

Lucifer froze in his steps, his eyes got cold as ice. He turned to face Nina. "That's not possible."

"I saw it myself." Nina met his gaze unflinching.

Denida walked over to Nina and put a hand on her temple. An image formed in front of them of Michelle talking to a dark figure in a forested area, Denida let go of Nina's temple.

"What I saw before she wiped my memories!"

Nina and Lucifer's eyes were locked on each other until Lucifer broke away.

Lucifer smiled broadly to them both. "I need to go."

He spun around and disappeared into a dark cloud. Before either of them could say anything.

Chapter 22: Lucifer's Realization

Claus and his demons arrived back at their hideout, under the fall of night.

"How did it go?" Jack paced around the entrance waiting for them to show up.

Claus flaunted the box with the ring. "Told you to leave it to me."

Jack gave him a fake smile. Claus ignored it and went into the building.

"We need to talk." Jack rushed after him into his office.

"Trouble in paradise?" Lucifer chuckled and spun around in Claus' chair to face them. "We have a problem, Medusa's here, she's a rogue demon!"

Jack's eyes lit up. "Medusa," he muttered.

Lucifer turned to Jack and gazed into his eyes.

"Doesn't matter anymore." Claus pushed forward and laid the box with the ring down on the desk. "We've got his ring." Claus gave a broad gloating grin.

Lucifer grunted and grabbed the box and opened it. His eyes widened. "You got this from Denida?"

Claus grinned. "One of his soldiers, yes. It worked!"

Lucifer took out the ring and tilted it around while examining it. "This ring always caused-" His face turned stone cold abruptly. He lowered his arm and fixed Claus with a glare.

"What's wrong?" Claus' grin slipped from his face.

"Again, you disappoint. Denny however, impressed yet again…"

Claus furrowed his brow.

"You wonder why I say that?" Lucifer threw the ring in the air and grabbed it. "This is a fake!" He threw it up and grabbed it again. "The real ring has a magic aura, this does *not*!"

Claus and Jack's eyes followed the ring up and down.

"That's not possible!" Claus shook his head.

Lucifer suddenly stopped and grabbed the ring and threw it directly into Claus' face, breaking his nose. "It's a fake, he tricked you." Lucifer scorned at Claus. "Like he always has…"

Jack grinned loudly in a mocking tone. "I knew it!"

Claus stared up with terrified eyes.

"Denida embarrassed you in the Western World," Claus said in a defensive tone. "Until someone helped him escape from your grasp."

Lucifer watched the both of them. "Daniel told you too much." He sneered at his own words. "After Hell, I knew I had to take steps…"

"Steps?" Jack peeked at Lucifer.

"Yes. I took care of all the demons who witnessed it." Lucifer let out a big sigh. "I went to the Gate in the Wild West where Dark Magic was used, but there was no sign of him…"

"Medusa," Jack muttered.

Lucifer smiled with a dark glare at Jack. "I knew there *was* only one way to stop Denny from *ever* embarrassing me again…"

"Really," Jack asked. "You didn't kill him…"

"Never!" Lucifer looked horrified. "I'll tell you what happened after the Wild West…"

***

Lucifer sat on his Dark Throne in his chamber, sealed away from everyone else in Hell. Gabriel appeared as a little white figure in the darkness. "Lucifer?"

Lucifer raised his head with a distraught face. "Gabriel, hello." He buried his head in his hand again. Gabriel stepped slowly forward, he peered cautiously around. "You ought to get out of here, what happened with Denida is over."

Lucifer looked up, straight into Gabriel's eyes. "But it's not! Denida could do it again, couldn't he?"

Gabriel cleared his throat. "That's-"

Lucifer rushed up from his seat. *Of course.* "You gave me an idea on how to stop it from ever happening ever again!"

Gabriel raised his eyebrows. "How?"

Lucifer chuckled deviously. "When I brought him to Hell, I made a contingency plan."

Gabriel jerked. "You did what?"

Lucifer turned and smiled. "He has a scar under his armpit."

"Yea sure," Gabriel said. "From the heart surgery."

"Exactly, caused by God *Almighty*, I assured his body didn't die. But it gave me an idea, he had a wound, an open chance!"

Gabriel shook his head slowly, concerned where this was going.

"Dark Magic was embedded into the wound on his soul, in case I ever would need it." Lucifer's eyes were filled with a red glow. "- that time has come."

"What-"

Lucifer cut him off. "I can clear his memories of me and everything, from before today- completely!"

Gabriel let out a big sigh. "He would be lost…"

Lucifer nodded with a grin. "Gone from my reach, but also from God's."

"Speaking of which, God needs me." Gabriel ran out.

That was quick, oh yeah, I need to remove Denny's memory.

Lucifer summoned the Darkness and filled the air with the strongest of the Dark spells in existence.

Time for us to hear the last from Denny. His wicked grin filled the room as a Dark Cloud lifted from the room and lowered into the *Well of Memories.*

Lucifer walked over to it, an image appeared of Denida laying on a pad of hay, the Dark Cloud surrounded his body, and focused just under his chest, where it circled, until the wound devoured it and ended with a Dark flicker under his shirt.

Never again. Lucifer chuckled and smashed his hand into the well, making the image vanish.

***

"- and that's the last I heard of Denida until he traveled into my world with Daniel." Lucifer gloated.

"How did he end up here then," Jack asked.

Lucifer shrugged his shoulder. "Who cares!"

"You should." Jack went over to Lucifer. "Someone aided him, the last Daniel told us, he was in the real world. You can see it with your *well of memory.*"

Lucifer checked around, Claus' eyes were filled with terror, but Jack, on the other hand, was determined. "You might be right, it can't hurt," he chuckled and raised his hands with a Dark glow surrounding them, an image formed in a dark hole in front of them. The Dark cloud entered Denida, he seemed to come to.

Lucifer's eyes brightened.

Denida shook his head and rubbed his eyes. "Where am I?" he muttered.

"Denida," a voice echoed.

Denida turned to the voice, Gabriel walked in and kneeled. Lucifer's eyes widened. *Gabriel, no, it can't be...* He shook his head in disbelief.

"Come with me." Gabriel lifted him up and folded his wings around him.

He flew him to a new world, a darker place, where he landed next to a Gate, which stood hidden behind some greenery. He unfolded his wings.

Denida walked out. "Who are-"

Gabriel put his finger on Denida's lips. "You'll forget me. You're in a new world, where no one will ever find you." He put his hand on his forehead, a bright light covered Denida's head.

Denida fell knocked-out into the grass.

"Sleep well, my friend." A white flash appeared, then Gabriel set off into the distance.

Gabriel. Lucifer threw out his arm in a rage and the image disappeared.

He spun around and grabbed Claus. "I told *you* not to fail me!" He peeked over at Jack. "You've got your chance!" He smiled. "fail me and you will return to Hell- as Claus does now," he smirked.

Claus shook his head frantically. "I can still-"

"No!" Lucifer pushed Claus into a black hole.

Lucifer glanced at Jack one last time with his red eyes, before he walked into the Dark Mist himself.

Claus ran frantically around trying to escape, but there was no escape. Demons approached, there was nothing but smoldering heat around him. Lucifer walked in between the demons, with his eyes flaring red.

"Medusa," Claus yelled. "She watched Denida, she beat Peter."

Lucifer grinned at his remark. "If I were you, I would forget that. You tell me what I already know and don't wish to be reminded of."

"- but I can still-"

Lucifer raised his eyebrows. "You've been replaced." He turned, and the demons continued to move towards Claus. Lucifer walked away with a smile as Claus' screams echoed behind him.

"Is this needed?" Gabriel stood waiting when Lucifer reached his mansion.

"Was it needed to *betray me*?" Lucifer stopped to look in Gabriel's direction. "You helped Denny out of Hell, then you sent him to a new world after his memory was cleared!" Lucifer turned and continued to his throne room.

Gabriel followed. "I had a reason."

Lucifer sat down on his throne. "I'm going to love this!"

"The same reason I helped you escape Heaven, the reason I still help you with Heavani."

Lucifer peered over at Gabriel, his eyes filled with fury. He got up from his throne and stormed over to Gabriel, who gave a cautious smile, which only increased Lucifer's rage.

He's just a fool, God's little pawn. Lucifer let out a deep breath. "Forget it!" He patted Gabriel with a forced smile.

"He left God behind too," Gabriel tried to assure him.

Lucifer chuckled as he sat back down.

"Heavani liked him too," Gabriel said.

A faint flicker of a smile appeared across Lucifer's face. He held up the ring and tilted it around.

"You've got *the ring of the Underworld* back?" Gabriel fidgeted with his hands.

Lucifer smiled and turned to Gabriel. "Sorry to disappoint, but it's not the real one."

"Not-"

246

"Denny had a fake made, quite well made too." Lucifer grinned.

"You're impressed? You do know, he'll never return to you."

Lucifer gave a broad fake smile. "So, you think."

Gabriel smiled and started to walk out. When he reached the door, he turned back to Lucifer. "He always has had luck for himself in his misfortune…"

Lucifer leered up from his chair.

Gabriel walked out.

Chapter 23: Again…

Daniel sighed. I got out, only to be taken yet again. He kicked the ground. When will it all end?

The old man came over and sat down beside him and handed him a Pepsi.

Daniel grabbed it. *What, he wants something?*

The man smiled, making his eyes wrinkle. "My name's Arthur, the woman over there's my wife, Dana."

Arthur peeked over towards Dana. "Your name's Daniel, right? You're the son of President Denida?"

Daniel solemnly nodded in response.

"You said you had something to tell us?"

Daniel sighed heavily. "My Dad lost all his memory when he came to this world, so he started fresh. I can tell you how my Dad became who he is now."

"OK…" Arthur smiled reassuringly. *'It should help him, get his mind off everything.'*

You're right, as it will for you too, mind reading is fun! Daniel giggled.

***

Denida woke up feeling a little puzzled. He sat up and looked around, he was in a forested area.

Something like a huge circle on edge stood behind him, he got up and walked curiously over to it.

"Halt," a soldier yelled. He ran, aiming at him with a machine gun.

The soldier directed him away from the big structure.

Crap.

The soldier picked up his radio. "I found an intruder near the Gate."

'Just finish him off,' sounded from the radio.

Denida staggered, without thinking he reached for the soldier's gun. The soldier grabbed Denida's hand and smacked him across the face. Denida fell to the ground and wiped his chin which was covered with blood.

The soldier chuckled and readied his gun, but before he could fire, Denida charged at the soldier.

He tried to wrestle the gun away from the soldier, but the man was just as determined to keep it.

As they struggled over it, the soldier jabbed at Denida, but in spite of the harsh punches, Denida kept on, as if the pain didn't matter.

Denida finally yanked the gun from the soldier only to have it kicked out of his reach yet again.

The gun rolled away. He ran towards it, but the soldier grabbed Denida's leg, he stumbled and fell to his knees.

The soldier rushed to the gun. Denida jumped on top of the soldier's back and tightened his arms around his neck.

The soldier tried to wrestle free, he rammed himself into a nearby tree, making apples fall, but Denida only tightened his grip until the soldier fell unconscious. He wiped his face and picked up the machine gun. He turned to look at the soldier before he marched off with the gun under his shirt.

He paced aimlessly down the streets, not sure what he should think, or do with himself.

Why can't I remember who I am? How come I knew how to overpower that soldier?

Several soldiers went by him in full battle gear. Denida turned as he passed them with a concerned eye. *They're dressed just like that soldier I met.*

The soldiers marched by a drug deal as it was nothing. *The hell? It's bright daylight, they don't care?*

Denida couldn't get himself to move, no one seemed to pay it any mind, they just walked by. They seemed more concerned with the soldiers. Everyone who passed them by lowered their head and strolled by nervously.

Denida ground his teeth and walked over to the dealers. The client took his drugs and strolled away, passing by Denida.

"What's your pleasure," the dealer asked as he noticed Denida.

Denida let out a chuckle. "Your boss."

The dealer let out a grunt and shook his head. "You're dealing with me, what do you wanna buy, kid?"

Denida rolled his eyes and pulled out the machine gun.

"Know who uses this type of gun? *Soldiers.* You better take me to your boss, if you know what's good for you!"

The dealer started to fidget with his drugs. "Okay, I'll take you, just put that away, before any of the soldiers sees…"

Denida put the gun back under his shirt and got into the dealer's car. The dealer set off and drove for a while. They passed a lot of soldiers, all armed to the teeth. *I'm starting to get why he fears them.* Denida glanced over at the dealer.

The dealer drove the car up to an old farmhouse next to a dirt road and parked it. Several men with guns came out to greet them. Denida raised his hands.

"I just want to talk to your boss. You can have my gun." Denida slowly moved his one hand to take out the gun, while keeping the other hand raised.

When they saw the gun, the men snapped their guns up to cover him.

"Where'd you get that?"

"A soldier." Denida wrinkled his forehead. *What's the fuss?*

One of the men yanked the gun from Denida and handed it to the one Denida pegged as the leader since he did all the talking.

He hoisted it and sighed. "You *do* need to see the boss!"

They lowered their guns and led him into the house. The leader stepped forward and knocked on the door.

"Enter," it echoed from within.

The man nodded towards the door. "You don't want to keep him waiting."

Denida pulled the handle and went inside.

The big room was dark, Denida could only see the shape of a desk at the far end.

"They tell me you had a soldier's gun?" a voice echoed throughout the dark room.

"I did." Denida slowly stepped forward. "I noticed your man, the soldiers paid him no mind."

"Your point?" the voice sounded annoyed. "It's always like that."

"You all fear them. I took a gun from one; I *don't* fear them!"

The man behind the desk got up. "You're a strong one. What is it I can do for you- what's your name?"

"My name is-" Denida stopped, a void in his mind, he rubbed his face. *What's my name?* But suddenly, as if his soul spoke to him, he muttered; "*Denida*." Where did that name come from, *why Denida?*

"Alright Denida, what do you want with me?"

"I want to work for you," Denida chuckled, he might have only just remembered his name, but something told him he could run this place.

***

Arthur and Dana glared at each other, their eyes locked, then turned back to Daniel.

"He did illegal stuff? The *President?*" Arthur turned pale at what he just heard.

Daniel giggled. "Not what you think, not drugs."

"You didn't answer," Dana said behind her husband.

Daniel nodded. "Perceptive, aren't you? He was hired, as muscle, so he went to pay off their bribe for being allowed to work- to the *Dark Angels...*"

***

Denida sat together with another henchman waiting. "Does it always take this long to do this?"

"They don't care, it's on their time," the henchman said.

Denida swung the bag he was holding and ground his teeth.

"I'll take that," a man walked out.

He looks like an errand boy.

He grabbed the bag from Denida's hands. The henchman got ready to leave.

Denida yanked the bag back from the man.

"No way, José!" Denida narrowed his eyes as he stared at the shocked man. "I'll *only* deliver this to your boss."

The henchman ran to Denida and tried to wrest the bag from his grip, Denida pushed him to the ground. He shook his head and jumped to his feet. "We're here to give it to them!"

Denida nodded. "To his boss, *not* an errand boy."

The man ran back into the room he came from.

"You've done it now," the henchman said.

From the door, the man came back followed by another one, who stopped abruptly as if he had seen a ghost. After staring for a second, he grinned deviously, and his eyes turned bright red. "Hello, I'm *Danyel*, I'm the head of the Dark Angels. Who might you be?"

The henchman squeezed Denida's shoulder, but he ignored the henchman, he handed Danyel the bag. "Your payment, then."

Denida smiled and turned to follow his henchman.

"Very interesting," Danyel muttered.

Denida and the henchman parked the car next to the farmhouse when they got back, only to be greeted by the Boss, waiting for them.

"Denida!" The Boss gave a smile making Denida wary.

"Crap," the Henchman muttered.

"Boss? What's up, we delivered the money." Denida scoped around for any signs of aggression towards them.

The Boss smiled. "I heard. Danyel called…"

I don't like where this is going.

The Boss patted him on the back. "Don't worry, nothing bad, he just wishes to see you again."

Denida wrinkled his forehead. "The leader of the Dark Angels wants to see me- and you're telling me *not* to worry?"

The Boss cleared his throat. "If they wanted you gone, soldiers would have come and killed you off already. Besides, it can be good for us!" He chuckled.

For you, you mean. Denida rubbed his head with his hand before he nodded in reply. He turned to one of the guards, grabbed a handgun from him and hid it in his sock.

He went to the car and waved before he drove back to the Dark Angels' headquarters. He ground his teeth as he strolled in, he stopped and checked the lobby in case it went sour, afterward he went up the front desk.

"I'm Denida, I'm here to see Danyel."

The receptionist smiled. "Yes, you're expected."

Two heavily armed soldiers surrounded him; they frisked him, took away his regular gun, but didn't find his concealed one. They escorted Denida deep into the building where he had the feeling not many guests were allowed and suddenly stopped at the end of a hallway, opened the big door and turned to Denida.

"He's at the end of this Hallway." The soldier smiled nervously.

Denida glared down the dark corridor. "Why are you not coming?"

"No one is allowed past this point, only Danyel- you too I guess…"

Denida took a deep breath and slowly marched down the corridor, it got darker the further he went. The air felt heavy, but somehow not intimidating to Denida. When he reached the end of the hallway, the door suddenly burst open.

No one was on the other side.

Peculiar. He stepped in cautiously.

"Denida, how nice of you to come." Danyel embraced him with a big hug.

Denida was baffled at the greeting. "You told my boss, you needed to see me?"

Danyel appeared entranced by Denida, then nodded suddenly.

"When I met you, I was in awe- I see a great potential in you." Danyel turned and handed Denida a drink.

Potential, what does he mean?

"You might wonder what I mean; I want to help you be everything you can be." Danyel smirked.

"How?" Denida followed him to the extremely decadent couch.

Danyel's eyes flickered red. "How would you like to become the Boss?"

254

Denida put down his glass on the glass table and leaned forward. "What, how?"

"As I said, I see potential in you. I'll help you fulfill it. As leader of the Dark Angels, I can do a lot."

"Because of my potential?" Denida wrinkled his forehead. "What do you gain from it?"

"I don't like your boss. I like you, *Denny*."

Denida ground his teeth. *He's a strange one, why call me Denny? If he'll help me, who am I to say no?*

Denida got up a put out his hand. "Deal!" He smiled.

Danyel got up and shook his hand while looking far too pleased with himself.

***

Denida and Nina arrived at where the exchange was. All that was left were pieces of soldiers in bloody pools.

How can she do this? Is Daniel alright? Nina could not help but be shocked by what she saw, despite what she had learned about Michelle.

"This is terrible." The Colonel shook his head.

Nina had to stop herself from not losing it with him. *You should have noticed! What can I do- what can we do? There's no sign of her...*

Denida embraced her tight. "We'll find her," he said in a comforting tone.

Nina jerked away from him. "How!" She turned and glared at him. "Are you forgetting what's here!" She pointed at the bodies.

"We're looking for her." The Colonel came over.

But you haven't found her- and you won't! She sighed and looked at the bodies on the ground. *Wait!*

She spun around and spoke to the Colonel. "Who did you search for?"

The Colonel tilted his head at Denida, clearly lost. "Michelle," he said, sounding unsure of his answer.

255

"Smartass. Did you search for her as for how she looks? She can change appearances, you know."

Denida rolled his eyes. "Yes, I know she can, but we don't know who she appears as now…"

"Then find out!" Nina pushed Denida. "Do you not want Daniel back?"

"I can't - I can't see into the past." Denida lowered his head in shame.

"Wrong," Dan interrupted. "They built a time machine in one of the worlds, you and Daniel visited…"

"Time travel?" Denida wrinkled his forehead. "No, that's so wrong!"

"Daniel's worth it," Nina insisted.

Denida turned to Nina with a faint red flicker in his eye. "Even if we did do it, it would take too long to make one…"

He's right. Nina turned away, the sorrow fresh in her heart again. *The Wizard!*

Nina grabbed Dan and pulled him with her into a car.

"Where are we going?"

'Good luck, my Angel.' Denida smiled back at her as he saw her leaving.

She sped down the road, passing cars at high speed, ignoring the honks which followed her.

Dan held onto the ceiling inside the car. "Why so fast? Where are you taking me?" His voice shaking more the faster she drove.

"You're going to help me, whether you want to or not!" Nina stepped on the brakes as they arrived at the lab.

Dan followed her in.

"We're back here, what is it you want?" Dan's eyes wandered, he scratched his forehead.

"Susan and I talked to the Wizard here, can't you do it faster?"

256

Dan shook his head vigorously. "Won't matter who does it. They have to find the Warlock either way."

She rolled her eyes. "Well, do it then!"

Dan sauntered over to the desk and proceeded to connect to the robot within the Warlock's world.

This better work. Nina didn't have good memories of this room. The same Aide she saw earlier, walked across the monitor. She rushed over.

"Again," the Aide murmured. "I'll go get the Wizard."

The Aide left before Nina could say anything. Dan stared at Nina, she giggled. "I might have been here before…"

Dan rolled his eyes and turned away. Nina licked her lips and sat down to wait.

It didn't take long for the Aide to return with the Warlock.

"What can I do for you this time, Lady Nina?" The Warlock smiled.

"No one but you know magic-"

"Denny does," the Warlock cut in.

"Yes, other than him. I need to view something in time-"

The Warlock's face became like cold stone, she shook her head. "No! I taught you a Dark spell, it went wrong. *Not again!*" She got up.

"Wait," Nina yelled. "I have to know."

The Warlock stopped for a second at the door. *'I'm sorry, Nina. To see in time requires too much Darkness…'* She proceeded out of the door and the feed disconnected.

Nina sighed. *How am I going to find out then? Sometimes reading thoughts is not a benefit…*

She took out her cigarettes and stormed outside, then lit one up with a sigh.

She took a deep huff of it. *I really needed that.*

"Do you milady?"

Nina jumped startled. "Gabriel," she snapped. "What do you want?"

Gabriel smiled with his warm eyes in such a way that Nina could not stay angry, no matter how she tried. "I want to help you." He stepped in front of her, his wings folded around her.

Nina saw a light, so bright she closed her eyes, but it was like it pierced into her, she fell unconscious.

Nina came to herself laying down on, what felt like a soft cushion.

She sat up, she saw nothing but white as far as she could see, all around her, the only thing besides her was Gabriel.

"What have you done to me?" Nina pushed away her fear, letting her anger warm her and fire her determination.

"I brought you where no one can see- outside of Heaven's Pearly Gate."

Nina raised her eyebrows. "Why?"

"Few have the power to see in time. I will help you, and here nobody else will know."

Nina got up on her feet, finding her footing on the strange cloud-like surface.

She finally reached Gabriel. He waved his hand and the cloud under him changed, an image formed of Daniel being carried into a car. Gabriel focused on the driver.

Nina held a hand over her face. "Is Daniel OK?" She felt tears running down her face but didn't care.

Gabriel nodded with his comforting eyes and handed her a paper. On it was the woman she had first seen at the warehouse. As she looked up, she was back at the lab. Gabriel and the cloud were gone, all that was left was the paper in her hand. *Thank you.*

She spun around and ran back into the lab, she ran to Dan and smacked the paper down in front of him. "Use your CCTV's and find me her!"

Dan picked up the paper. "She's hot- but why?"

"Now," Nina yelled.

'Yikes, she's angry.'

Dan scanned the document, he had the system search for an image of the woman. Nina stood impatiently behind Dan, tapping her foot. Dan peeked nervously back at her, only to have her snap at him, so he hurried as much as he could.

An image surfaced of the woman, driving a car.

"That's all there is." Dan hunched over as if expecting her to demand more.

That has to be what Gabriel showed me. "Try to zoom in."

Dan shook his head in disbelief. "It's a CCTV camera, you won't get much, it would take a lot of work. Want me to try and clean up the image?"

"Yes!"

Dan sighed but started to work on the camera's image. He zoomed in while sharpening elements of the image. The work took time, Nina sat down in a chair. Dan finally got the image zoomed in and clear enough to make out who it was.

"It's ready." Dan turned to Nina with a confident smile.

Nina jumped up and came over, where she nodded. "Backtrack it, where did she come from?"

Dan waved his hands in despair but returned to the computer and did what he was told.

The video backtracked; The woman in the car blurred to darkness, whatever happened wasn't clear as this part was not zoomed in.

The woman carried a figure out of the backseat, she walked off camera.

Nina grabbed the controls and played it back, she stopped it when her image appeared with the thing, she carried, before she put it in the car. "Do *it* to that image too!"

'Does she not realize how much work this is?'

Nina focused her anger on Dan. He spun back to his desk to continue his work. It didn't take Dan as long this time around. As he zoomed in and worked a clear picture started to form, a demon with a small boy; *Daniel.*

Nina felt Dan's distress as the image became clear, but he didn't stop.

Dan exhaled a heavy sigh. "I'm done…"

Nina swallowed hard when she saw what Dan had uncovered in the picture.

"We need… to show Denny… this," Nina stuttered.

Dan printed it, then they went back to Headquarters to see Denida. Nina tapped her fingers on the dashboard of the car.

"Can't we go any faster?" Nina suddenly asked.

Before Dan could answer, she waved her hand dismissively and turned to look out the window.

When they arrived at the Headquarters, Nina jumped out before the car had fully stopped. Her impatience didn't lessen in the elevator. "Come on already!"

As soon as she arrived at the floor, she ran straight to the Colonel's office. But to her shock, it was empty, no one was there at all.

Where are they? Nina walked back out of the office confused, then saw them bent over something at the end of the room, she charged towards them.

They were searching through Michelle's desk. *Probably hoping to find something useful.*

"You won't find anything."

They ignored Nina and continued their search.

"It's a demon," Nina said. "She's not that stupid!"

Denida glanced annoyed at her. *I know…"*

You don't know this! Nina smirked a little. "I have something."

Denida and the Colonel gave her their full attention. The elevator rang and Dan walked out. Nina hollered at Dan.

"Show them," Nina insisted.

All eyes turned to Dan. He handed Denida a folder. Denida grabbed the folder and scrolled through it as the Colonel peered over Denida's shoulder.

It didn't take Denida long before he pulled out a picture, he examined it thoroughly before he turned to Nina. "Daniel…"

Chapter 24: Change Coming

Daniel examined the dark cone around the house. *This is strong.*

"You know how to break it?" Arthur sounded hopeful.

Daniel shook his head. "Dad never taught me anything as strong as this, he never wanted me to have anything to do with the Dark Arts." He sighed. *I so wish you had, Dad...*

Arthur turned towards the house. He licked his lips nervously. "But your Dad, the Dark Angel is searching for you?"

"My Dad never was a Dark Angel." Daniel shrugged. "Maybe, I shouldn't have stopped my story where I did." He shook his head.

Arthur wrinkled his forehead. "There's more?"

Daniel found that amusing. "Of course. *A lot more.* I'll tell if you want to hear."

"Of course. We should go back in the house."

Dana clenched her fists as she saw them entering. Daniel stood up against the wall, facing them both and tapped his foot.

"Well, I should tell you more about my Dad, but it will get worse, before it gets better, so bear with me please..."

"I remember the days with the Dark Angels," Dana said. "I thought your Dad helped get rid of them, but you're telling me he worked with them?"

"Eventually- I'll continue if you'll give me time?"

"Yes," Dana said with an immense sigh. Arthur nodded more willingly.

This should have been to persuade Edward to let me go, but it's too late. Daniel forced a smile. "Dad was now in with the most powerful Dark Angel, Danyel. For some reason, he liked Dad. Dad used it to his benefit and had risen up in ranks within the Underworld…"

***

Denida still lay in bed, it was past noon already. The curtain got pulled to the side, revealing the sunshine. He put a pillow over his face and let out a groan.

"You need to get up," the man at the curtain said.

"Dan, it's *way* too early!"

Dan tore off the covers from the bed. "How long were you even up?"

"Who cares, I'm the boss!"

Dan let out a heavy sigh.

"Fine." Denida got up and got dressed.

"Day is passing us by," Dan smirked.

He's right. Denida walked out, followed by Dan. It was an old house with small corridors, so the guards tried to squeeze into the walls, as Denida and Dan passed then.

Denida stopped outside his office. "We really need a bigger place."

"You need more protection too," Dan said.

Denida rolled his eyes and sat behind his desk. It was the most extravagant room in the house.

Dan strolled over and sat down in front of Denida, looking disappointed. "Denny, we-"

The curtain moved and Denida ducked while Dan jumped behind a cabinet. Shots came through the curtain busting everything on his desk into smithereens. The guards rushed in as the attacker reloaded, he stepped out to shoot them leaving several guards lying in bloody pools. The bullets from the guards hit the shooter, but he didn't seem to care.

Denida took the gun he'd stashed beneath his desk and shot the man in the back.

Denida strolled out from behind his desk, now full of holes, over to the stranger. He pushed the machine-gun away from the man with his foot and stared into the dark, hatred filled gaze- he pointed his pistol at the man and fired one final shot into his eye.

"You're right," Denida muttered. He turned around to Dan who slowly came out from his shelter, still cowering from the violence.

"We need a new place, one with better security too…" Denida holstered his gun.

The remaining guards came rushing from behind the door.

"Why the eye?" One of them peeked at the stranger.

"To send a message, of course. Clean it up!" Denida walked past the guards.

Dan gulped and hurried after Denida.

Denida glanced back at Dan with a chuckle. "You're not built for this life."

"I'll be fine," Dan insisted.

Denida ground his teeth. "Stay here, I need to go see someone." He grabbed Dan's sidearm and replaced his own magazine before he handed it back to Dan.

He got into a car with tinted windows and drove toward Danyel, in the Headquarters of the Dark Angels. He parked and inside, was buzzed through by the receptionist. He went straight to Danyel's inner chambers. The guards stopped him.

"Sorry Denida, you need to wait. He has an audience," one of the guards said.

I don't got time for this! "Alright, let him know, I'm here when he's done, I'll be at the front desk." Denida spun back towards the front desk.

He smiled and leaned over the desk to talk to the receptionist. He winked at her with his left side, as he often did, for some reason he found smiling with the left side more comfortable than a full smile.

I need to get her to cooperate. He gave her a flirtatious look. "I have a friend, Dan. He would be really good-"

"Denny, what are you doing?"

Crap. Denida turned around to face *Danyel. Wonder if he heard it.*

Danyel's eyes gleamed red over his smirk.

I'll never get why he has that look sometimes.

"You want your friend Dan to be in ground planning; done!" Danyel giggled. "Anything else?"

Denida shook his head and headed out to his car. As he arrived, several cars stopped with a screech in front of the building. Denida got into his car as men in full battle gear ran towards the front door.

Must be those resistance guys, they'll be dead within minutes. As he turned onto the road, security was already cleaning up bodies.

Danyel should really find out who's leading them- Oh well. He drove back to Dan, who was talking to some of his guards. Dan sauntered over to Denida when he got out of his car. "It went well?"

Denida grinned. "You'll leave us here for a role in their ground planning."

Dan shook his hands. "But-"

Denida patted him on the back. "Don't worry, you're not suited for dealing with violence. I have a clear plan ahead for you."

***

Daniel giggled. This'll help put their focus from everything.

"What plan?" Dana scratched her forehead.

"You need to remember who my Dad is in the present."

Dana looked even more bewildered. "The President?"

Daniel shook his head. "Not just that, he also still has a consortium which started in the era of the Dark Angels. Dad made a name for himself, but deep down he knew it was dangerous, so he wanted to leave the illegal activities behind."

"He used the money from his time as a crime boss to build an empire?"

Daniel nodded. "Dad had a clear strategy," he grinned. "he'd amassed a lot of money, which he'd hidden away. He still does. He used Dan, so he could get construction wherever he wanted, when he wanted; businesses grew, and he became known as the businessman Denida."

"So, that's the end of your story?" Dana sighed relieved, as she might be hoping for there to be no more to it.

"*Far from.* Dad kept his persona as a crime boss hidden, as his fortune grew..."

***

Denida came with his bodyguard to see Dan who still worked with city planning. He gave Dan a broad smile.

"Why are you here? You can send me-"

Denida chuckled with a devious smile. "This is too important for that."

Dan wrinkled his forehead.

"Come, I'll show you." Denida patted him on the back.

Dan grabbed his jacket and followed him out. Denida drove Dan out of the city until he suddenly swerved the car onto a dirt road. After a few minutes he stopped the car. "We're here."

"Here?" Denida already got out, so Dan followed him. "There's nothing as far as the eye can see."

"Exactly."

"What, you want a secret stash here or something?"

"You see the emptiness within the glass, my friend. You need to look at what this can become."

Dan rubbed his head. "... and what would that be?"

Denida swirled around with his arms out. "My Dynasty. A secure estate for me, far from any danger- and a *humongous* one too."

Dan shook his head in despair. "Sure..." He grabbed the paper from Denida. "I'll process it!" He spun back to the car but turned to see Denida still standing admiring the field. "Coming?"

"You'll see my vision," Denida insisted.

Dan rolled his eyes. "Sure." He got back into the car.

Denida drove Dan back to the Dark Angels Headquarters. He walked back in with Dan, then headed further into the building to see Danyel. One of the guards got up when he saw Denida.

"He's not in his chamber, he's at the Gate."

Gate? "Where's that?"

The guard led Denida to a room Denida had never seen before, as big as a football field. In the middle of it stood the so-called Gate. *It's the same device from when I first came here!* Danyel came out of the Gate, all the lights lit it up, then it powered down as soon as he came through. His eyes turned bloody at the sight of Denida and the guard. His eyes wandered from the guard back to Denida and suddenly the red within his eyes died down again, as if by a switch.

"Denny, how nice of you to come." Danyel embraced Denida and led him out of the room at a fast pace.

Denida tried to look back, but Danyel marched so fast Denida barely got a glimpse. Outside the room, Danyel flicked his fingers, other guards suddenly appeared. "Bring Denny to my chamber." Danyel went back into the room with the guard who had led Denida there.

Denida didn't see anything else before he was led back to Danyel's chamber. The guards left him inside and closed the doors behind them. Denida let out a heavy sigh. *I arrived next to a Gate- wait.* He looked frantically around the room. *I'm alone in the private room of the Dark Angel Danyel.* Denida rubbed his face. *Is this stuff- demonic?* The door burst open behind him with a bang.

He spun around in shock, to see Danyel standing there.

"What happened to the guard?"

"Don't concern yourself with that, he's been dealt with for disobeying me!" Danyel gave a devious chuckle.

"But the Gate-"

"It's off limits for you," Danyel cut him off. "What brings you here?"

"We need to talk; you're making it hard for me to bribe my way forward…"

Danyel's face went stone cold and his eyes glowed red. "You're doing legal stuff, which doesn't interest me, so you pay what everyone else does."

A guard opened the door.

"This is my world, don't forget that! We're done here." Danyel nodded to the guard, who led Denida out of his chamber.

The other guard is still gone. Denida moseyed out of the building, still in shock at what he'd witnessed. *Something is definitely amiss here!*

"Denida!" Dan came running up to him. "I got the papers you need to build your dream estate; You wanted to call it *Dynasty*?

Denida grabbed the papers and nodded still a little out of it. His glanced back towards where he came from. "Does this include anything built underground?"

Dan's eyes widened. "Underground?"

"Dan!" Denida stomped the floor.

"Yes," Dan muttered.

Perfect. Denida lit up with a big smile. *I've got an idea, which will protect me against Danyel's interference!* Denida paced out towards his car. He bumped into a woman, who knocked his papers to the ground. He shrugged. The woman hurried to fiddle with collecting the papers together in a bundle.

Jesus-

She got up and handed the pile to him. Denida froze in place when he saw her face, it was the most beautiful face he had ever seen. *Those eyes, so beautiful, I want to gaze at them for an eternity-*

"You want these, Mister?" she said, bringing Denida back to himself.

Denida nodded and grabbed the papers. She hurried off before he could even return her sweet smile. She'd vanished as quickly as she'd appeared. Denida stood as if struck by lightning. He threw the papers into his car and ran back to Dan's office.

Dan lifted his head. "Something wrong? You look-"

"I need your help."

"A new building-"

"No," Denida yelled out. "I need you to check the surveillance video, I met a girl..." He walked over to Dan. "It's important, there was something *special* about her."

Dan giggled. "You've got a crush."

"Spare me your remarks, just find her!"

"It'll take time," Dan shrugged.

Denida nodded and grabbed his chest while he licked his lips. He sat down while Dan found the right video. He was fidgeting with his fingers in anticipation. *Why do I feel so impatient for some girl?*

"Found her," Dan suddenly yelled.

Denida jumped up and ran over to the screen, where his eyes watched her every move. "I need to find out who this girl is, print it out!"

"No need," Dan said with a grin. "Her name's Nina. She works here."

Nina...

***

"That's nice," Dana said with a tender voice. "How your parents met."

You have no idea. Daniel nodded.

"This is where your Dad started to pull away from Danyel?" Arthur frowned at Daniel.

"He always had a clear intent, Danyel wanted to make Dad bad. Dad was moving towards legit and Danyel didn't like it one bit..."

"But it didn't work?" Arthur smirked.

Why does it feel like he is questioning me?

"Well." Arthur crossed his arms.

Dana cleared her throat. "I think we all need a break," She got up.

Arthur might prove to be a problem...

***

Jack stared at the empty cell where Daniel had been.

I need a way to get Daniel back, but how? He sat down and put his head in his hands.

"What are you doing?"

Jack fell out of his chair in shock. He turned and hurried to stand up. "Lucifer."

"I hope I didn't make a mistake to put you in charge," Lucifer smirked. "We would both regret that!"

"Daniel's gone, Claus-"

270

"Claus's gone, his mistakes. You took over this mess."

But it's impossible. Jack shook his head dismissively.

Lucifer gazed into Jack's eyes. "Denida's still looking for Daniel. Medusa-" Lucifer's face changed, he narrowed his eyes. "Medusa has Daniel, not Denida. Find him!" Lucifer turned and began to walk into the Dark Cloud, which had appeared, but he stopped just before he entered it. He looked back at Jack, their eyes locked.

Jack could see a faint regret in Lucifer's eyes.

"Daniel's important, but if you kill Medusa, I'll grant your every desire. That's a priority!" Lucifer continued through the Darkness and vanished.

My every desire. Lucifer must really want her dead! Jack sprinted out to his car and set it in motion. He sped towards where the exchange with Daniel happened. There were several soldiers carrying dead bodies away. This Medusa sure had fun. I sense 'real' Darkness... He set his car to follow the trail, he drove slowly not to miss it. This is so strong, it's heavy.

After hours of following the Darkness' trail, it broke up, it seemed like it turned into a farm on the side of the road, but on the other hand, it also continued down the road. I guess I'll ignore that house for now. Jack set the car in motion after the Darkness, it led further down the road.

He suddenly stepped on the brakes hard.

Oh my god... Jack got out of the car and stood, not believing what he saw. A huge Dark Cone surrounded a house. No normal person would see the Dark Magic.

Unsure Jack stepped towards the barrier, but as he got close he hit a wall. As a demon, I still can't enter? How powerful is this? - wait! That farm I passed.

Jack turned and ran towards the house, which was not far down the road. A Dark Presence loomed behind as he entered the farm. He spun around to find a woman there.

"Hello sexy," Jack said without thinking.

She smiled seductively at him. "How can I help you?"

He smiled back. "My car broke down. I tried the house further up the road, but-"

"They're on vacation!" Her smile turned into a defensive frown all of a sudden. "I'm watching over their house, I'll help you." She gave a seductive smile and directed him into the farmhouse.

Jack's eyes wandered through the house as the woman led him to the living room. He couldn't help but let his eyes wander as they passed in the hallway, there was a room, where the Dark Magic was stronger than anywhere else. What's in there?

The woman turned and smiled. "Here's the phone."

"Phone?" Jack wrinkled.

"Your car needed to be serviced- or is there some other reason you're here- Jack?"

Jack grabbed his face with both hands. No! - wait, I have my fake face on- How does she know? "Jack, who's that?" Jack worked at looking confused.

She walked seductively closer to Jack. "Then why don't you call for assistance."

Jack nodded nervously and went over and picked up the phone, with her watching his every move. Who am I going to call- Ah yes!

Jack pressed the buttons and put the phone up to his ear, he returned the woman's gaze with a broad smile. "Yes, it's Jack. I need you to come get me!" He proceeded to inform them where he was before he hung up the phone. "Don't mind if I stay here, while I wait? I can help you water the plants. Won't be so lonely housesitting."

"I already did, we can wait here for your friend," she said.

"You lived here long?"

She watched him more and more suspiciously. "Longer than I can remember."

"But there are no pets, aren't there supposed to be animals on farms?"

Her eyes flickered, but not red, a dark black. "It's not a farm anymore- only the house."

Something's not right, even Lucifer had red, not dark...

Jack glanced over at her, his eyes wandered several times to her eyes to see if that Darkness returned, but in the time they waited, it never did.

Jack could feel his other demons approaching, and from her face, she could too. He got up, she followed behind. She mustn't want me to go anywhere, she doesn't want me to see.

Outside Jack turned back to face her. "Thank you for all your help."

"Anytime," she said with a smile.

Jack went out to his demons. Fast, but not so fast, she would notice.

"Get the other car, we're leaving," Jack yelled as soon as he got out to his guards. I got out! He jumped into the car closest, one of his demons got in behind the wheels.

"Back home?" The demon gazed at him.

"Not for long, Daniel is here!" Jack's eyes wandered into the farm with the woman. "Medusa is here too..."

The two cars drove back towards the hideout, after ten minutes Jack positioned for them to pull into the side of the road. Jack strolled back to the other car, where he told the other demon to drive back and keep an eye on the woman, without being seen. The demon turned around and drove back towards her.

Jack went back to the first car and got back in. "I'm done, let's go!"

The demon behind the wheel paused for a second before he set the car back in motion.

Chapter 25: First Date

Daniel stood peering out of the window, his eyes locked at the end of the Dark Cone.

I feel a malicious force incoming, but that girl is bad already. He sighed. If only I could see through... He glanced back to where Arthur and Dana were. Arthur's a problem too.

Daniel walked over and smiled innocently at them.

"What's wrong," Arthur insisted. "Something's wrong, isn't it?"

This might help make him doubt less, I'm trapped here too, after all. "I feel a malicious force here."

"Isn't there one already," Arthur smirked.

"It's not from her, it feels different- Dad taught me to notice the differences..."

"Speaking of which-" Dana stood between them, she smiled at Daniel and turned to hug Arthur. "Why not use this time to continue your story, we can't do anything else from here."

Daniel nodded and plopped down on the chair. "Dad continued his plans for his mansion, with the underground built with the focus on his less legal activities..."

***

Denida stood watching the work being conducted on the grounds. It was so big an estate, he couldn't hope to see everything, but he had intended this on purpose. He even had several ways of escape plotted from the start.

He ground his teeth and glared at the folder he was holding. *Nina…* He ground his teeth yet again.

"Something wrong?" Dan faced him curiously. "The project's proceeding as you planned."

Denida fiddled with the papers he was holding and kept peering back at them, again and again.

Dan glanced at the folder Denida was holding. "What's that? It can't be the plans, I have those, so what is it?"

Denida smacked Dan with his papers. "Nina; I had her investigated, I still can't approach-" He shook his head in despair. "- why isn't it as easy as making a deal? That I can do!"

Dan giggled and winked. "You're smitten by her; you were from the moment you saw her!"

"Wise ass!" Denida threw the file at Dan and strode to his car.

"Where are you going," Dan yelled after him.

"Where do you think?" Denida stared back at Dan. "To see Nina…"

But how do I approach her? Can I? What do I say? Does she even remember me? Denida could not stop the thoughts running through his head. *There's only one way…*

He drove on through Dynasty, out into the main road and onwards towards her workplace, the Dark Angels HQ where Dan also worked.

He parked and headed for her office. Something caught his attention. *Strange, is that her?*

Nina stood in the shade of a tree smoking. Someone behind the tree reached out a hand. She put an envelope in it and he vanished into the woods. As badly as Denida wanted to talk to her, he had a bad feeling and decided to follow the man instead. He hurried back to his car. The man drove around in an evasive manner though it didn't seem as he had noticed Denida. *This is weird.* Denida slowed down to lower the risk of the man spotting him.

The man finally slowed down as he approached a broken-down house, halfway buried in bushes.

A lot of security for that. Denida reached for something in the back of the car, while still scoping out the area. He picked up a gun from the dashboard and put it in his trousers.

Denida got out and strolled casually towards the house. Several men in camo stepped out of the bush and the house.

"I couldn't get help from you by any chance, could I?" Denida smiled to one of them. "I'm lost, you see…"

The guards surrounded him, faster than Denida expected.

"You don't have a map," one of the guards said. "Hey, go get a map," he instructed another one.

Another guard ran inside.

"Don't worry." The guard patted Denida's back. Suddenly he reached for his gun.

The gun.

Denida ducked to the side; the bullet barely missing him. More men poured out of the house, including the one Denida had followed here. He drew his own gun as he hid behind a parked car next to the house.

"What's going on?" a deep voice sounded.

"He had a gun," the soldier said, with a screechy voice, as if he doubted himself.

"Who are you?" the deep voice asked.

Now what do I say?

"Well?" the deep voice yelled. "You'll be smart to answer- we have you outnumbered!"

I won't make it if I run.

Denida took out a knife and put it inside his sleeve, he sighed.

"All right, I'm coming out, don't shoot!" Denida threw out the gun and came out with both his arms raised. He walked slowly while looking around, hoping to find a way out.

"Who are you, why are you here?" The man with the deep voice stepped forward.

He was dressed fully as a soldier, in battle gear.

Is he going to war? "I'm not a threat…"

"Then why are you here?

The man and Denida locked each other in the eyes, it was like for a moment the rest weren't there. This was a man to be reckoned with.

I can't get away from this. "I followed the man behind you here. He was meeting with Nina…"

"Nina?" The one in army uniform looked at the man Denida followed here with narrowed eyes.

"Yes," the man said. "Nina works near the Dark Angels, she helps us gather intel on them."

The man dressed as a soldier gave the man a really dirty look, making the man take a step back.

"Intel," Denida said without thinking. "Who are you- or what are you?"

"The question is who *you* are?"

"Denida." Denida winked, but the man in front of him didn't move a muscle.

"… and why were you there?"

How am I gonna get out of this? Denida rolled his eyes, his face got a little red. "I-"

"The girl," the man in army gear chuckled. "Lower your guns." He went over and patted him reassuringly on his shoulder. "My name's John, I'm known as the *Colonel* though."

Denida's head spun as the Colonel shifted from deadly to friendly in an instant.

"Your girl has been helping us with information on the Dark Angels."

Dark Angels? Why would- "You're the resistance!" Denida could feel his gut turning.

The Colonel nodded. "Don't worry about that."

With Danyel gone, I could run my business without problems. We would all be free; there's that too… His eyes sparkled. "I can help."

The Colonel grinned loudly. "Your girl's fine, we don't need you to sacrifice your life!"

"Who's talking about my life," Denida smirked. "I have real intel, I've got a personal relationship with *Danyel, the leader of the Dark Angels.*"

The guards and the Colonel traded looks.

"Why would you want to help us?" The Colonel's hand dropping toward his gun again.

"So you won't need Nina's help anymore- something needs to done about him…"

"Him?" The Colonel chuckled. "You mean the seven of them!"

Seven? There are that many? Seven Dark Angel's, why do I feel like I heard that somewhere before?

Denida smiled at the Colonel. "Sure, John! We've got a deal, I'll inform you and you leave Nina be, so she *won't* be in any danger."

Denida put his hand forward.

The Colonel lifted his hand, he frowned. "Only a deal, if you really have something…"

Of course. Denida chuckled. "The Gate, Danyel has in the building, he came through it."

The Colonel's eyes widened. "Deal," he abruptly yelled and shook Denida's hand.

Great, she'll remain safe then! Time to see her…

Denida's drive back was a journey towards his worries. *What'll she say? Will she say anything? Does she remember me- No,*

279

these thoughts won't help. I have to talk to her, give or take, that'll fix my thoughts!

He parked, and again headed towards the building the girl was inside. With each passing step, it felt like his feet got heavier and heavier. The inside of his guts turned, but he had to, or else he would forever regret it.

When Denida stepped through the door, he locked eyes with Nina behind the desk.

"Hello, can I help?" Nina smiled at him.

Denida stood there, frozen, still grasping onto the door handle. "I…" Nothing more came out, heat traveled across his face. Any thoughts he had was gone. His hand sweated, he swallowed and let go of the door. He tried to return her smile.

God, her eyes. "I'm… Denida," he stuttered.

"Dan's friend," Nina asked.

Just as she said it, Dan came rushing through the door. He stopped at the sight and giggled. "I take it he hasn't said why he's here," Dan smirked.

Nina raised her hands and shook her head.

Dan glanced over at Denida with a smile. "Denny has something he wants to say."

Dan, no… Denida's face full of sweat, his eye widened.

Dan pulled Denida forward to where Nina was standing.

It's now or never. Denida took a heavy breath and moved forward, he grabbed hold of the counter in front of him and smiled back at Nina, this time, he succeeded.

"Dan's right. I saw you once, your presence could not escape me, I couldn't get you out of my head-" Denida breathed heavily. "-so I'm here to ask you out!"

She peered over at Dan. "If you're a friend of Dan's, I guess- yes, so you better think of something good." She winked at Denida. "-and not make me regret it."

"I won't." Denida chuckled back.

"Good." Dan applauded.

They both turned to Dan and grinned.

***

"That's how your parents met?" Dana viewed at Daniel with her old, tender eyes.

"Forget that," Arthur yelled. "That was how Denida got involved with Colonel?"

Calm down. "Yes- to both," Daniel said. "This was how it all began…"

"Then don't stop now, you felt something bad coming, didn't you?" Arthur locked eyes with Daniel.

Daniel glanced nervously at the window behind Arthur before he returned to Arthur. "All right. Dad informed the Colonel of some of Danyel's ways of control. His focus, however, wasn't on the Colonel, it was on planning his date with Mom…"

***

"Why already? The building's not even done yet," the builder insisted.

Just do it! Denida just raised his eyebrows, he wasn't going to budge. "Indulge me!"

The builder tramped away while he mumbled obscenities. *I always was good at persuading others for some reason.* Denida grinned a little to himself.

He went from Dynasty to his city office where he ran his legit operations. He went in, but didn't go to his office, he went to the division of purchases and acquisitions.

"Sir," the man asked him.

Sir? I like that! But anyway… "I need you to find me something. A horse, but a really *good* one, I wouldn't know a good from a bad one, myself."

"Want me to show you?" the man asked.

"I…" Denida was at a loss for words. "Why the heck not, I might learn something."

"Great." The man ran over to shake Denida's hand. "I'm Claus by the way, sir."

"OK? You were going to show me?" Denida held his hand upwards.

Claus led the way, they needed Denida's jet to get to where Claus wanted to go.

"How can you afford this," Claus suddenly asked on the plane. "The business is expanding, isn't it?"

Denida gave a faint chuckle. "I have other sources of income."

Claus wrinkled his forehead. "Which? The Dark Angels limit everyone…"

Denida shrugged. *Good point, why does he not want to hurt me?* "Well, not me…"

The plane set down on the other side of the world. As soon as they got off the plane, they were taken to a stud farm, as Claus had called ahead to arrange.

Denida walked behind Claus, trusting him to know where he was going.

Claus guided him towards the stables, stopping an employee to make sure they had the right one.

Inside was a horse huffing heavily, as it gave birth.

"Maybe, we should wait till they're done," Denida said behind Claus.

Claus peered back towards the horse. "You might be right…"

Denida sauntered out, there was a track next to the stables, a little fascinated, Denida went over to it. *Interesting, must be nice to have.*

"Why do you want a horse, anyway?" Claus went up to him.

Denida smiled. "I'm building my new estate." … *also Nina likes horses…*

A man came out and washed himself in the barrel of water next to Claus and Denida. "What can I help you gentlemen with?"

"Your famous stud," Claus said.

"Another one of you," the man mumbled.

"Hey," Claus yelled defensively. "Do you not know who this is?"

Denida stepped forward, pushing Claus behind him. "Please ignore my friend, he only meant, we came a long way just to see your horse."

The man dried his head with a towel. "You can see her, but she's not in her best position, she just gave birth."

The man led Denida back into the stables. Claus followed a little behind them. Inside, the horse was laying in the hay with her foal next to her.

"I couldn't take it even if you wanted to sell her." Denida shook his head a little.

"We have to separate them eventually," the man said.

"Not just them, you and them. *You* care, I can tell."

The man gave a smile. "I never met anyone who saw it like that..."

"I don't just see it like this; I want to take all three of you with me. Ask your boss his price!"

Denida kneeled and petted the foal, while the man went to see his boss.

"Hi, sweetie." Denida's eye almost glowed as he stood next to the little foal.

Claus cleared his throat.

"You were right Claus, do you know other things, other than where to find horses?" Denida tilted his head to look at Claus.

Claus smiled back. "Of course, sir."

After Denida talked to the owner, he flew back to see Nina. Denida felt ready for their date.

He smiled tenderly at her as she walked over to him when he pulled up in his car. He got out to greet her with a hug. He revealed a single red rose from behind his back.

She blushed slightly and smiled.

"One rose for one princess- to signify our first date." He handed her the rose. "-out of hopefully many!"

Denida hurried to the car door to hold it open for her. She smiled and got in. Denida climbed in on the other side.

"Where are you taking me?" Nina asked as Denida got back into the car.

Denida raised his eyebrows and smiled. "You'll like it." He set the car in motion and sped out of town, through the countryside to an airfield.

Nina craned her neck. "An airstrip?"

The door opened next to her and Claus smiled at her. "Miss?"

Denida came up behind Claus and took her hand and led her into the plane. Inside the plane, there were already treats laid out for them. He led her forward to her seat.

"This is too much," she said.

"It's only the beginning." Denida chuckled. "Enjoy!"

The flight went quickly as Denida enjoyed talking to her so much, they barely touched the food.

As soon as they left the plane, there was a car waiting for them. It took them to the Stud Farm.

Nina read the sign, as she passed it. "A stud farm?"

The car stopped, the door opened to let them out. Denida led her off.

"Denny," she yelled.

He grinned at her as two men came out with the mare and her foal behind him.

Nina lost interest in Denida as her eyes fell unto the horses.

"My god, such a big animal with so much power, yet-" She patted the foal tenderly. "-such a little angel."

Denida went towards her, the mare and he shared eye contact for a moment, he stopped dead in his tracks, for some reason he felt a deep connection.

"There's a connection," both Nina and Denida both muttered at the same time.

They looked at each other in surprise, then shared a tender gaze.

Chapter 26: Mara

"Lucifer..." Jack examined Claus' room as he muttered his Master's name.

Lucifer, Denida, Medusa- they're all connected. Jack was sure of it, he just didn't know how.

"The Darkness," Lucifer suddenly spoke behind him, as if he had been there the entire time.

Jack's eyes lit up from being surprised. "But where exactly does she come from? She not like anyone else, is she?"

"Perceptive," Lucifer grinned. "Of course, you're right..."

Jack's face got pale for agreeing with him.

"You know now, I was lured by the Darkness-" Lucifer stared so deep into Jack's eyes, he felt his soul get violated. "-Medusa wasn't, she was deep down bad to the bone..."

Lucifer went into the room with a pentagram in the center. He turned to glance at Jack with a wrinkled eyebrow. "Come."

What does he want?

When he stood next to him, Lucifer raised his hands and a Dark cloud started pulsating under his hands.

"I'm going to show you, what she was before..." The Dark cloud blended with the pentagram and an image formed. Within the image, a little girl could be seen.

She looks sweet.

"So you think." Lucifer smirked.

The girl walked into a room, where adults waited for her.

A man stood up. "Mara, we need to talk."

She grunted but sat down staring at them with eyes which could kill.

The man and his wife exchanged uneasy glances. "We have to, what you're doing is unholy!"

Mara grinned. "I'm only fulfilling my heritage."

The man ran his fingers through his hair and sighed. "As I told you time and time again, it's just an old tale..."

"Wrong," Mara yelled. "You'll see in time." She pointed at her Mom. "You all will!" She stormed out.

"I told you," her mother said.

"No," her father insisted. "God can bring her on the right path, the Father can help..."

On a starry night, Mara strolled into the house.

"Mara, come here for a second," her Dad yelled.

Mara came in, she stopped in the door when she saw them sitting there.

"We need you to stop what you're doing."

Mara shrugged and giggled. "I'm not doing anything-"

"Stop! We found Flour!" Her mother started sobbing.

The man held her close in his embrace. "You loved that cat!"

"He served his purpose," Mara chuckled.

"You do realize, summoning the Dark Arts can be dangerous!"

Mara snickered. "Only for you."

"You never get anything for free, the price for admittance is your soul," it sounded from behind the others.

Mara spun around to see who spoke.

"A priest." Mara rolled her eyes.

"I see disgust within your eyes, my child."

Mara gestured scornfully at the priest. "No." She turned and trudged back out.

The priest jumped up and stormed after her. "Mara."

She stopped annoyed it wasn't over.

"Your parents only want what's best."

Best? Mara gave an angelic smile. "You really want me to stop? Come with me then, only you- if you truly want to stop me…" She continued down the road.

The Priest ran back inside. "I got through to Mara, I'm going with her, I'll be back! Just wait here." He ran back outside after her.

She walked for a while into a desolate forest.

"You like to keep it private. Luckily the Lord is watching."

Mara rolled her eyes, she kept going but increased her pace. It was growing dark when they finally reached an opening in the forest, but she didn't stop. They came to a cave not far from there.

She smiled at the priest. "Follow me, come on in."

The Priest held up his Bible as he walked into the dark cave.

The night sky didn't shine much light inside the cave.

The Priest's eyes tried to adjust to the darkness as he stepped inside with his hand feeling at the wall. "You come here a lot?"

"Only when I try to use Dark Magic, but I couldn't, I kept running into an obstacle…"

He tried to find Mara, confused.

"My soul would not be enough, even Flour's sacrifice didn't do it…"

The room lit up like a switch was turned on.

"But a man of God might be." Mara grinned from the center of the room.

The Priest grasped at his Bible and held it up to her. "You're a child of God, not Satan!"

Mara giggled. "Am I really? Then why does no one see what I see, then?"

"You must seek the answer from the Lord. The salvation-" The Priest grunted, Mara whipped a knife she'd held behind her back across his throat. The Bible fell with a bump.

He stared in horror at Mara as he fell to his knees.

Mara stood behind him smiling. "Guess your God didn't come to save you."

She dragged the body to the middle of the room, where she positioned candles around it and marked the ground with the blood of the priest.

She sighed as she gazed at her bloody work within the cave. He's not gonna be enough; I need more- there's no going back now. I know where I can get more... Mara strolled out into the dark forest, she went back to her house in the lonely night, only lit by the moonlight.

It was late at night when Mara arrived back at the house, she stood outside and gazed in the window. Her parents were waiting. She chuckled deviously.

"The priest wants you to come," Mara said as soon as she entered the room.

Her mom shrugged. "Really?"

"Yea, he said he needs you for some reason..."

"All right then." Mara's dad stood up. "Let's go."

They followed Mara to her cave.

"Mom, I'll lead you in, Dad can follow us, don't worry it's not far."

"OK," Mara's mother reluctantly took her daughter's hand and Mara led her mother further into the pitch-black cave.

Her father followed behind in the darkness, he stumbled into a wall. "It's wet." He rubbed his fingers. "What is this," he muttered. He shrugged and rubbed his fingers dry in his clothes.

Deeper within the cave, Mara left her mother alone. "Wait here."

"Mara," her mom called as Mara lit the lamp, then walked carefully forward with the light, revealing the blood spattered about.

Mara's mom cringed back stopping when she stepped on something, she bent down and picked up a Bible all covered in blood.

"Father…" she screeched, the echoes sounded like demonic laughter.

Mara's father edged towards the light revealing a horrific scene. He moaned.

"Perfect." Mara grinned and smashed the oil lamp over her mother. The flaming oil lit her clothes on fire and lit up the macabre cave with the Priest's body lying in the middle.

Mara's father gazed in horror at the sight. Then Mara and her father locked eyes, the fear in his eyes clear, but so was the evil look in Mara's. He turned and ran as fast as he could, not looking back until he reached the town.

Mara glanced at her Mom's body, whose flames were dying down.

Oh well, she should be enough.

Mara cut her mom open to get to her heart. She needed the blood to finish her sacrifice.

***

"Like so many others, wanting the power of the Dark Arts," Jack smirked. "Where's the rest of your story?"

Lucifer glanced at him with eyes as red as fire. "You sure you want to hear it all?"

"Yes, she summoned you, and-"

Lucifer grinned and shook his head. "She didn't summon *me*..."

Jack wrinkled his forehead.

"She found a way to summon the Darkness itself."

"*Your*-"

"You don't want to finish that sentence..." Lucifer's red eyes pierced Jack.

Jack gulped.

"Anyway..." Lucifer turned away. "Mara sealed her destiny with the Darkness. A seal that nothing can break."

"The Darkness- you never saw this then," Jack smirked.

"*We* can then!"

The image in front of them shaped again, revealing Mara sitting deep in meditation in the middle of the cave, covered with nothing but blood.

***

Mara was chanting. *Come on, work!*

'...Mara...' a dark formation appeared above her head.

"It worked!" Mara jumped up ecstatically.

'You summoned us?'

"Definitely." She smirked. "I wish to serve you, which I why I brought these to you." She pointed at the bodies laying across the cave.

'I answered your call; what do you desire?'

Mara squeezed her hand which had blood dripping from it. "I want to bring forward the Darkness within me!"

The Darkness swirled around her, blocking out all the light in the cave. All Mara could see were those Dark eyes peering at her.

'Darkness has a price,' rung in Mara's head; she sat entranced by the Dark eyes.

"I've been waiting!"

'Your soul,' the Darkness said.

"I'm yours!" She got up and raised her arms out.

The Darkness enveloped her and flew into her, as she stood still with her arms raised. *At last!*

As morning broke, Mara lay in the blood. She wrinkled her face.

What's that racket, they're gonna get it! She stormed out, ready to kill whatever, or whoever made the noise.

She was grabbed as soon as she exited the cave. Mara tried to yank free from their grip, but it proved fruitless.

A man went up to her, with Mara's Dad walking behind him. Mara's father ran up to her and smacked her across the face. Blood spattered on the ground.

"Your Mom was right, you're *crazy!*"

Mara grinned and stuck out her tongue. "Think you can hurt me, *Daddy*? Want to try again?" Her eyes went flat and pale. "I never liked you, you were always stuck in *your own* ways."

Mara's dad shook his head as if he wanted to convince himself it couldn't be.

"This is who I always was," Mara chuckled.

Her father snatched her from the man holding her and dragged her while she laughed to a huge tree and threw her against the trunk.

"This world is mine, I belong here now, not you." Mara sneered, still as cold as ice.

"You never did," her dad screamed.

"The Darkness lies in our family." Mara smirked.

Her dad sighed heavily. "Not this again. You're such a screwed-up child, it was only an old myth. Not a gospel…"

Wrong. Mara's face turned red, she swung up her arm and her father was thrown across the forest.

She spun around to the other guys, who stood frozen by what they just witnessed.

Mara rubbed her hands. "Now I'm going to have fun with you."

292

The two men ran into the trees in opposite directions.

What a hassle, can't they just run the same way! She stood at the end of the trees looking in the two directions. *Which one should I take first?*

Mara spun around from the sounds of branches cracking. The man who came with her dad dashed towards her with a dagger. She held out her hands and a Dark Cone lifted around her, deflecting the man.

She picked up the dagger, grinned and jabbed it into the guy. *More to the Master!*

Mara sniffed, she searched for the two hiding in the forest.

One man ran further away, but he stumbled over a fallen tree. His foot wedged in the roots. "Help me," he yelled in terror.

The other man ran to him, trying to free him.

Mara sauntered after them whistling to herself. "Ready to die."

The other guy frantically ran away. The man left behind wept and hid his face.

"Guess he left you!" She grinned.

"Wrong," it sounded from behind her.

The other man jumped on her back and tightened his grip on her neck. She threw him off like a doll. Mara chuckled.

"You think you can beat *me*? A weakling such as you? I created- ugh." She grabbed her throat. Her battered and bruised dad held the blade she'd left stuck in the man by the cave.

"If you were destined for evil, your magic would have protected you from me cutting your throat!"

She fell to her knees. "You... ca..." She keeled over, next to the bruised two men.

***

Jack shook his head in disbelief. "But the Darkness, she summoned..."

Lucifer chuckled. "Darkness was within her, but she was too young, it was not strong enough yet. She still believes in her heritage, deep down to her core. The Darkness controls her with that!"

"So in a way, she's like you, lured by something; in her case the belief she's important..."

"Her belief is what makes her dangerous." Lucifer smirked. "Better be careful."

Lucifer turned and disappeared into a dark cloud.

Guess he left with his version of Astral projection... Jack hurried out to gather his demons, he was now sure this would only work if they *all* went.

They all set off towards Medusa, or more exactly, to the demon watching her. Jack's car slowed down as he approached the car of the other demon he told to watch her. *Something doesn't feel right.*

"Go check."

The demons in his car got out and walked towards the other car, they stopped suddenly halfway there. One of them scurried back to Jack. "Master, he's um-"

Jack growled impatiently. "What? Spit it out!"

"Dead," the demon said.

Jack pushed open the car door and ran to the other car, but he too stopped when he got halfway there. He saw something no demon wanted. The demon sat in the car, his heart ripped out. Red gore spattered the windows. Except for the windshield, it had a message written in blood – *Come for me, and you will face the same destiny.*

Jack glanced at the ripped-out heart on the hood of the car. His eyes wandered to the other demons, he knew what they all thought about, as even he thought it.

Is she really worth it? YES! "Let's go get her!"

The demons followed him, as Jack knew one other thing; *a demon always follows orders!* The sky was covered in a dark cloud as they approached Medusa's house. Jack craned his neck to see it. *Is this a warning, I wonder?*

The cars slid into the courtyard of her farm-house. The demons piled out and stormed through the building looking for Medusa, but after a few minutes, most of them came back out, looking lost.

"She's not here?" Jack asked.

The demons all shook their heads in despair and shrugged.

Where's she? Jack kicked a stone across the yard. *Is Daniel gone? The other house!*

He ran to the road and down it until he got to the house, the giant dark cone was still present.

"Looking for me?" a familiar voice asked.

Jack turned around.

Medusa stood in front of him grinning. "Still came after you saw my message?"

Jack shook his head. "I don't fear you, *Mara*!"

Medusa frowned. "You should. I take it Lucifer told you my story…"

"A little girl lost in her own world," Jack smirked.

The other demons came rushing out to them.

"But guess you're outnumbered, why don't you give us Daniel, then you can go." Jack gave a broad, gloating smile.

"Not yet." Medusa held up her hand and time froze the approaching demons.

How did she do that? Jack's eyes widened. "What are we waiting for?"

Medusa pointed towards the Dark Cone shielding the house.

Daniel came out with an old couple.

"Perfect." Medusa smiled. "I wanted him to see this too."

I've got a bad feeling...

Medusa flicked her fingers and went towards the demons, not fazed at all.

When she got near them, she grinned at Jack and Daniel. "This is what happens when you oppose *me*!"

The demons all ran towards her.

Jack glanced back at Daniel, who watched curiously. He turned back to the demons, to see a black cone, even bigger than the one over Daniel, appear above the demons. The demons banged into the wall of the cone.

Jack shook his head in disbelief, he felt no urge to run to them. *I think I know what's coming...* His eyes focused on Medusa and the cone that trapped the demons. Medusa stood grinning in front of the cone, she lifted her arms above her head and Darkness covered her.

She moved her hand outwards and her hand appeared inside the cone. Medusa ripped the hearts from the demons, ignoring their cries. All Jack could see was blood and Darkness in the air.

Screams like back in Hell...

Medusa suddenly appeared right in front of Jack with a smile.

"Jack! Lucifer's little errand boy- left all alone."

"I can help you," Jack whispered. "I wasn't originally involved, but you all suspected me, so I got to them, became the head of security. I handled everything with Daniel..."

Medusa grabbed Jack's head, he twitched his eyes seeking an escape. The magic hiding his true face vanished.

"Want to help me?" Mara's eyebrow raised.

Jack tried to nod, with her still holding his head. "I... I..." he stuttered. "I'll clean up this mess, get rid of the demons..."

She let go of his head, spun around and the demons vaporized in a Dark Cloud, similar to Lucifer's. But she didn't disappear into it, she changed her form into a sparrow and flew above the cone, where she circled around until she created a vortex, sucking up all the demons. The sparrow flew back to the ground, where she transformed back into her shape in the same Dark Cloud.

"No cleanup needed. Watch Daniel as you did before then." Mara walked close to Jack. "- if you fail me though, you'll earn a worse fate, than your demons. The real reason Lucifer *fears* me!"

Jack waved at the cone with Daniel. "I can't enter that."

Medusa patted Jack's cheek. "You can now…"

Chapter 27: The Story Continues

Crap. Daniel sighed and shook his head. *There's no way out of here after all, is there?*

Jack had come walking in through the cone. "Hello, Daniel." He gave the same fake smile he always did. "Long time, no see."

Not long enough… Daniel turned away from Jack.

Jack waved and walked over to Arthur and Dana. "Hello, I'm Jack. I'm here to keep you company."

"What are you," Dana said with a tremble in her voice.

"I'm a demon, my dear!"

"Let's go back inside." Daniel moved quickly to lead Arthur and Dana back inside the house where he poured Dana some tea. *Hope this can calm her.*

Behind them, Jack came in. He stood in the doorway watching them.

"What do you want?" Daniel huffed at Jack.

"To watch you. Mara's request."

Mara? Daniel scratched. "Medusa?"

"Michelle, Medusa, Mara; she has many names," Jack chuckled.

"Daniel, won't you continue your story?" Arthur came in from getting Daniel some tea and sat at the couch in the living room.

Must want to distract me...

"Oh, more of Denida, what fun!" Jack grinned.

"When he came to our world, the Dark Angels-" Daniel rubbed his hand. "-you may remember them Jack, weren't you a part of them?" Daniel gave Jack a smile.

"Gotten cocky, have we?" Jack hissed and bared his teeth.

"Always was." Daniel turned back to Arthur. "Dad was getting big in the business world, the more he did, the more he hid his other persona." He tilted his head with a smile to Jack. "He also gave more and more details on Danyel to the Colonel."

"Danyel," Jack murmured under his breath.

***

Denida sat in his office, looking out the window when Claus came in.

"Sir," Claus announced himself from the door.

Denida came back to focus and turned to face Claus. "Yes, Claus. Come on in."

Claus came closer and handed him a dossier. "The latest updates on your Dynasty project."

Denida grabbed it and nodded. He caught and held Claus' eye. *Maybe...*

Claus broke the contact and spun towards the door.

"Wait," Denida yelled. He got up and went out with Claus. "I won't be here for the remainder of the day, clear my schedule."

His secretary nodded.

Denida turned to Claus. "I need to see someone, why don't you come with me?"

Claus nodded in agreement and followed Denida out to his car.

Denida drove outside of town, into a remote laying forest, where he put his car to a halt.

"What are we doing here?" Claus turned with wide eyes.

"Meeting someone."

As soon as Denida uttered those words, another car pulled up behind them.

"They're here." Denida smiled and got out of the car.

Claus stayed in the car watching.

After a few minutes, Denida said bye to them, shook hands with one of the men and got handed a briefcase. The men got back into their car and drove off. Denida threw the briefcase in the back seat and sat in the driver's seat. Claus sat with a half-open mouth, but he closed it without uttering a word.

Denida buckled his seatbelt. "What do you think happened here?"

Claus shook his head and waved his hands defensively. "Not my place, I saw nothing!"

"You know about the *Lord of the Underworld*?"

"Sure, the mobster," Claus said. "The one-eyed kid."

Denida grinned. "That's the one, he wears a patch over one eye to differentiate himself."

"Differentiate himself, from what?" Claus gestured with his hand.

"Me, of course."

Claus stared at the briefcase, eyes filled with worry.

"It's money, a bribe to Danyel," Denida said when Claus didn't answer but stared at the suitcase like it might explode.

Claus ran his hand over his forehead. "What about all the other money from your illegal activities, they can't all go to Danyel?"

"I used it to build the business, but now it can run without it. I have it stashed away." Denida raised his eyebrows. "But we should deliver *this* to Danyel." He set the car back in motion and drove towards the Dark Angels headquarters.

Denida took the briefcase and marched towards the building with Claus following right behind him.

Claus shrugged how Denida got so easily let in, the guards all smiling at Denida.

When they got to Danyel's office the guard stopped them. "Sorry, you'll have to wait, he's inside the Gate."

Denida gave a fake smile back to the guard.

"You've come here a lot," Claus said after a few minutes of silence, sitting and waiting.

Denida nodded. "As long as I can remember. How the world is; you pay them to operate…"

"Denny." Danyel walked up behind them, startling them. "What brings you here and who's this?" He shook Claus' hand while gazing at him.

"I'm here with your payment, this is my assistant, Claus." Denida handed Danyel the briefcase.

Danyel pushed past them without taking the case. "Come," he yelled from inside his chamber.

They followed him, where Danyel grabbed the case.

"Claus, huh?" Danyel chuckled. "You remind me of someone from where I'm from…"

"…and where's that?"

Danyel glanced over at Denida. "Far from here!"

Why did Danyel look at me? Why's he so interested in Claus? Denida shook his head. "We're leaving!" He rushed out.

Claus shrugged at Danyel and followed Denida.

"He's nice," Claus said after a while, bringing Denida to a complete halt. Claus almost bumped into Denida.

Nice? Denida spun around, he could feel the anger in him about to burst.

301

"Denny, you're here," Nina came towards them waving.

The anger Denida felt subsided, he turned to embrace Nina. "We're just leaving though," he said with a smile.

"Who's this?" Nina shook Claus' hand. "I'm Nina, I'm this one's girlfriend." She smiled shyly.

Denida kissed Nina on the cheeks and hurried off.

They returned to Denida's car. Denida set the car in motion as soon as Claus got in, not even giving Claus time to tighten the seat belt. He sped down the road. After they drove for a few minutes, Denida suddenly halted the car and tightened his grip on the wheel.

"Before you call Danyel *nice*, you should remember what he is."

Claus shrugged "I-"

Denida put his finger on Claus' lips.

Claus watched Denida's hand which took out an eye patch from his pocket and tied it around Denida's head.

"Come. Follow me, but don't utter a word!" Denida got out of the car, Claus followed behind.

Everyone got out of the way as Denida and Claus walked forward, some even bowed as he passed them.

In front of the building two soldiers waited. They saluted Denida as soon as they noticed him. Their eyes fixed on Claus. One of them reached for his sidearm.

"He's with me." Denida raised his hand, stopping the guard in his tracks.

The guard nodded and opened the door. Denida and Claus continued through it, the door slammed shut behind them. Claus turned in a circle to take in the huge dark room.

"This is where the Dark Angels have their *fun*; we clear the area from any intruders."

"You-" Claus paused himself and rubbed his face, before turning to Denida. "-who's we?"

Denida grinned. "You'll see." He moved further into the building.

Screams could be heard from each room they passed. The further they went, the louder and more intense the screams got.

"Denny," a man greeted Denida from a security booth. The man waved his arms towards them.

It was one of the men Denida had been given the briefcase by earlier.

"Wait-" Claus grabbed Denida. "The mob's protecting the Dark Angels?"

"Go on." Denida waved his own hands towards the door.

"I… in… there," Claus stuttered.

Denida raised his eyebrows. "They're the *good* guys, you said."

"Danyel, I said!"

Denida raised his eyebrows. "Danyel's *their* leader…"

Claus stared at the door in terror and he shook his head hysterically.

***

"No… no… no…" Jack kept muttering.

They all focused on him.

Jack shook his head in disbelief. "That's not possible!"

"What isn't?" Arthur asked.

"Denida led the rebellion, he didn't work with the Dark Angels!"

Daniel giggled. "Eventually, Dad did, but he worked with Danyel until…"

"Mara." Jack spun around and stormed out. He ran back towards the farmhouse. *She has to know!*

"Mara, are you here?" Jack screamed at the top of his lungs after he searched the house. He found no sign of her, though. "Come on, Mara!" *Where is she?*

In a second Medusa appeared. "You have to love projections!" She grinned.

"Danyel!" Jack waved his arms wildly. "Denida worked with him?"

"I thought you already knew that? The legends say this much. I first discovered Denida here after the fall of the Dark Angels."

Jack shook his head in despair. *You've got to be kidding me!*
"How is this a problem?"

Jack spun around 360 degrees and he threw his hands in the air. "It changes everything!"

Medusa tightened her eyes. "How's that?"

"You betrayed them, he knows how the Dark Angels worked. If any of them are left…"

"Crap," Medusa muttered. "The one I left alive, of those working with the Dark Angels…"

"Left behind?" Jack asked with worry in his voice.

Medusa nodded. "Nina was getting suspicious, I've gotten all I needed from them; I had no other use for them."

This can't be good! "But one is left?"

"I left one alive, so my story would be corroborated…"

Jack walked closer to her. "Tell me you're using a different face now?"

Medusa chuckled. "Of course, Denny can't find us using that guy."

You think… Jack gave a half smile.

Medusa made a face. "I can read your minds, you know."

"Really," Jack said sarcastically. "Maybe you should listen then."

***

Denida paced back and forth in the Colonel's office.

The Colonel rolled his eyes. "It won't do you any good to pace aimlessly around!"

Denida stopped and glared back with a blood-shot eye.

The Colonel shrugged. "Nothing we can do, Michelle outsmarted us, even with the associates…"

She can't be smarter than us, I have to find a way! Denida spun back to face the Colonel.

"You're right; *the associate!*" Denida bolted out of the office, he sprinted past the elevator and down the staircase, so fast he almost fell. He didn't stop until he reached the basement, where the cells were located.

"Lord Denida?" The guard put a hand on his gun. *Is this real?'*

Denida ground his teeth. "Of course, I'm the real Denida," he yelled. "I'm here for the associate, who worked with the Dark Angels."

"You'll have to wait; he's seeing his lawyer in room five." The guard pointed at some chairs.

His lawyer? "He doesn't have a lawyer, everyone he knows is dead."

"Well she's in there," the guard said dismissively.

She… Denida glanced down the hallway. *It couldn't be…*

Denida sped down the hallway, past the guard, feeling uneasy. He started to walk slowly the closer he got, each passing step, growing more nervous, yet it didn't take long before he stood in front of room five. *Why didn't it take longer!*

Denida glared up the corridor at the guard and back to the door. He grabbed the handle, he stood there for a second before he threw it open, revealing a body in the center of the room in a bloody pool. The heart lay in the center of the room.

Michelle. Denida ran into the room, to look around, there was no sign of anyone else. He kneeled to examine the body.

"The name's Mara, actually," Medusa gloated, she appeared sitting hovering above the body. "I've been waiting, Denny. You shouldn't keep a girl waiting, you know."

The door slammed shut.

"Why are you here? What do you hope to gain?"

Medusa grinned and gestured at the body. "I came to clean up my mess, of course, but then I thought; *why not?*" She gave Denida a broad smile. "I have Daniel, you want him back, don't you?"

Denida rolled his eye. "You do? Claus could-"

Medusa shook her head. "Claus' back in Hell, Jack works for *me* now, his demons all dead."

Denida bit his upper lip. "What do you want in exchange for Daniel?"

Medusa sneered, she projected from where she was to right next to Denida, she smiled.

"Hi, Denny."

Denida jumped back, he turned to face her. "I could just kill you..."

"You would be leaving Daniel with Jack, is that such a good idea?"

Denida sighed. *That won't work.*

"Only way is to give me what I want, you know what it is!" Medusa smiled with a glee of red in her eyes.

No, I don't!

Medusa gave him a chortle. "What did I ask you once, before you came to this world?"

"How the hell would I know what-" Denida froze mid-sentence, his heart skipped a beat. "You wanted me to replace Lucifer..." His face turned cold as ice.

"Kill him, take his place in Hell, yes," Medusa smirked. "-with the Darkness."

Denida moved madly about the room. After a minute, he turned to Medusa. "You'll free Daniel then?"

Medusa nodded, she reached her one hand towards him with a broad smile. "Come with me."

"Last year, Daniel and I-" Denida grabbed her hand. "-went through the Gates, I remembered everything then..."

Medusa nodded. "I remember, Claus tried to stop you."

Denida raised his finger. "Which included something Lucifer taught me; *never trust a demon*." He tightened his grip on her hand. "Why don't you just tell me where Daniel is?"

"No," she smirked.

Medusa projected back to her hovering position above the body.

Denida charged her, she projected back again to the door.

"You can never win," she gloated.

"You think!"

Denida spun back to face her with his arms, sending a blast of air at her. The door flew off the hinges behind her and went flying into the wall.

Medusa waggled her finger at him. "Light magic won't work on me; you aren't ready yet. Why don't you talk it out with your Nina." She turned into a rat which scurried away down the hall and disappeared into a hole.

Denida ran after her, but as she vanished into the hole, he sighed. His eyes fell to his hand with the ring. *'Light magic won't work on me.' Can it be?* He turned his eye at the door, that lay broken on the floor. *It moved past her, as she was never even there...* The Colonel ran up to Denida with Nina.

Crap.

The Colonel watched the door with wide eyes. "What happened here?"

Nina moved Denida's face, he smiled reassuring at her and turned away.

"Oh... my... God," Nina yelled when she noticed the body in the room.

The Colonel ordered the Headquarters locked down.

Denida took hold of the Colonel's arm. "She's gone, don't bother!"

"Who?" the Colonel demanded to know.

307

"Michelle," Denida muttered. "She was here, killed him and-

"And?" The Colonel stared impatiently at him.

"She has Daniel-"

"And you didn't stop her?" Nina grabbed Denida and shook him.

Denida shrugged.

"We already knew she had Daniel, but you-" Nina pushed him off. "- you just let her go!"

"She wants to return him…"

Nina's face lit up with hope. "Great! When? How?" Her smile faded quickly though. "Wait- Why? What does she want in return?"

Denida licked his upper lip. "Me, in Hell."

"You're going?" The Colonel winkled his forehead.

Denida shuffled his feet. "I never wanted to- I swore to myself, but if it can save Daniel…"

Nina shook her head. "You once told me, you can *never* trust a demon."

Still, maybe she…

'No!' Nina said into Denida's thoughts. "John, get this crap cleaned up!" Nina stomped down the corridor.

The Colonel reached after Nina. "She never calls me 'John', did I miss something?"

Denida shrugged his shoulders.

As they cleaned up the cell, Denida leaned up against a wall and watched them carry off the body. *Do I really need to - Kill off the devil - become the Devil myself?* The Colonel followed the others out with the body.

Denida rushed after him. "Colonel, I wonder something; how did Michelle end up working for you, anyway?"

"I never checked at her history." The Colonel shrugged as if embarrassed by what he'd just said.

308

Interesting. Denida went to the room with all the records in. It was a giant room, it still had all physical papers there, even though everything was digital nowadays.

"Hello," the clerk greeted him.

Denida gave a soft smile and stepped up to the counter, he glanced around the room, unsure. "No chance you could find me something in all these files?"

"Sure, what are you searching for?"

Denida bit his lip. "Sgt. Michelle, she used to work with the Colonel, her personnel file."

"Easy." The clerk rubbed his hands, gloating. "Come with me." He led Denida to the back of the room, where old folders lay in boxes which were scattered about. "They're all here; she'll be under M." He pointed towards a row of boxes. "Everything's cataloged, it's easy to find!"

Denida nodded and went over to it and started scrolling through the boxes. He handled dozens, hundreds of yellowed files, sneezing at the dust on them, then suddenly his hand froze.

Denida checked and double checked the folder, his hand shaking. *I've gotta show Nina and the Colonel this!* He shut the folder and sprinted to the Colonel's office, ignoring something the clerk yelled at him.

He spurted up towards to the Colonel's office. In the office, Dan and Nina were talking, while the Colonel was doing paperwork.

The Colonel dropped his pen. "Denny? Why are you sweating?"

He threw the folder on the desk. "You've got no idea!"

The Colonel sighed as Dan and Nina came over to watch. He opened the folder and his face paled. "This can't be!" He scrolled through the pages of the folder.

"What is it?" Dan leaned over trying to see.

"Michelle didn't look like she does now when she first joined-" the Colonel began. "but exactly like the person Nina witnessed in the video."

Nina lit up at that remark, but only for a second. "...and you had this file all along?"

"Gathering dust in the records." Denida rubbed his eyes.

Nina growled, and the Colonel edged back as if her eyes could kill.

"Forget that!" Denida took Nina's hand and squeezed it tight. "We need her found now, any of those many faces she had, it has to be one of them..."

The Colonel leaned his head back and took a deep breath.

"We had this all along..." The Colonel slammed the folder shut.

Chapter 28: Birth of the Resistance

Back under Jack's control. Daniel sighed.

Arthur sat next to Dana, holding her hand tightly, caressing it.

"Isn't that adorable." Jack smirked at them from the door.

Arthur shifted to get up, but Dana squeezed his hand tight, stopping him.

"Why are you back, Jack?" Daniel walked over to Arthur and Dana.

Jack grinned. "The rest of your story, of course."

"Why do you care? It's the old days of the Dark Angels, after all…"

Jack swaggered over to Daniel, a dark glee in his eyes. "I'm just curious, how he became what he is now."

Something doesn't feel right… Daniel could see the Darkness within Jack. "I went to Hell with Dad. I can tell when something's up…"

Jack sneered. "Really? Are you sure about that?" He lifted an eyebrow. "Do you know why you were taken?" He stared into Daniel's eyes. "Since you can feel *something's* up!"

"The ring."

"But do you know *why*?"

Daniel frowned. *Why? What does he mean?*

"Your face hints no," Jack gloated.

"Like it matters," Daniel yelled. He clenched his fists.

"Lucifer," Jack whispered, his lips beside Daniel's ear.

Daniel stumbled back, his heart raced at the mere mention of the name. "No, not-" He fell into a chair.

"Your Dad's Master!" Jack leered cruelly.

No... Daniel fought back tears as he trembled.

"No one can enter here, where 'Michelle' has you. Why not tell me the rest of your story?" Jack handed him a tissue. "Don't you worry."

Daniel grabbed it and nodded. "All right." He crunched it into a ball and threw it to the floor. "One thing was clear for Dad, something had to change; the resistance was not a concern to the Dark Angels, up until now..."

***

Two men paced nervously around the dark room, Denida sat on a couch waiting.

"Why not just relax, John is just training, he'll be back." Denida watched Claus and the other man striding about the room. They didn't listen, they just went faster.

Oh, Jesus.

A car could be heard coming from outside. The guy next to Claus ran out. Denida and Claus followed casually behind. Outside, the Colonel climbed out of a car in jogging pants, all drenched in sweat.

"That look suits you." Denida grinned.

The other guards around the Colonel chuckled.

The Colonel glared at them, making them go silent. Denida grinned wider at the glare from the Colonel who threw his bag at Denida and rushed him.

Denida grabbed it and flung it back at the Colonel, who threw it aside. He held up his hands, as the Colonel reached him.

The Colonel gripped Denida's arms and slammed him up against the door. "You think you're something?"

Denida met the Colonel's gaze. "You're strong, but not enough…" He wrested himself loose from the Colonel's grip and spun around to slap the Colonel, only to be met by his fist.

"Clever, where did you learn that?"

Denida yanked his hand back. "I just *knew*. I always did, like how I overcame the soldier at the Gate."

"Interesting." A floorboard creaked, and the Colonel stepped back. Claus cowered to the side. The Colonel nodded. "Right, you're here for something?"

"We need to stop Danyel. Up until now, all our attempts have been fruitless-" Denida glanced at Claus. "-not anymore, not with *my* help! I know how to damage the Dark Angels."

The Colonel looked at Claus. "If you do this- if it goes bad I mean, he won't be enough to protect you…"

"I can protect myself," Claus insisted.

"You too." The Colonel moved lightning fast and threw Denida to the floor. "If Danyel realizes what you're doing, what you know, won't be enough. Even I can beat you in my sleep!"

Denida laughed. "Then why don't *you teach me, John.*"

The Colonel helped Denida up. "I might just do that."

Denida and the Colonel marched into his office, shutting the door behind them, leaving Claus outside.

Denida came out from the office after a few hours. "The Colonel wants to see you," he

told the guards waiting.

Claus stood up, as the guards ran into the office. "Are we leaving?"

Denida squeezed Claus' arm and strode past him out of the house. Claus hurried after him.

Denida stood with his head back, he could see stars as far as the eye could see, more than he could imagine counting. A shooting star flickered across the sky.

"Must be an omen," Denida said.

"What-"

"What we have set in motion tonight will change everything; maybe this is a sign." Denida lifted his hand across the sky. "A foreboding, if you will…"

***

"Melodrama," Jack interrupted.

Daniel shook his head at Jack "Think so?" He peered over at Dana and Arthur. "Either way, he wasn't wrong; The resistance *really* started that night!"

"So, their attacks worked?" Jack straightened his posture.

Daniel turned back to Jack, he shook his head. "It wasn't just an attack."

"But-"

"I said this was the night it began, not an attack but the resistance itself."

"You mean the *broadcast*," Dana suddenly said, making Jack scratch his head.

"Exactly," Daniel gloated. "Dad thought what they needed was to show they existed. The Colonel used the Dark Angels signal to declare the resistance to fight."

"Danyel must have been pissed!" Jack grinned loudly.

Daniel nodded solemnly. "The Colonel became the most hunted man overnight, with an unreal bounty on his head."

"But he vanished, didn't he? He became a myth?" Dana's voice interrupted Daniel.

"Dad now had a completed Dynasty, which had a hidden underground few people knew about. This is where the Colonel would lead the resistance from."

***

The Colonel sat watching a newsreel on a giant monitor inside a brightly lit room, wall covered with monitors, when Denida entered the secret chamber.

"Something intriguing?" Denida smiled.

The Colonel spun around with a broad smile. "They didn't care about us before; they *fear* us now!" His expression changed from smiling to worry. "But are you sure you're going to be okay? Danyel might suspect-"

Denida held up his hand to stop him. "Let me stop you there." He patted the Colonel's shoulder reassuringly. "I'm not stupid, they won't discover my double hand." He gave a cocky smile. "The guy you brought is Butler. No one else but us should able to enter the chamber- let alone know about this place…"

The Colonel spun back to his monitor.

Denida went back up to Dynasty.

"Sir," the butler met Denida as he came out of the doorway, hidden under a set of stairs.

"Denny," Denida insisted with a lifted finger.

"Sure, Denny." The butler wrung his hands. "There are soldiers here!"

"Really? This should be fun." Denida grinned. "Show me."

The butler led Denida to the soldiers, who were all waiting outside.

"Welcome to Dynasty!" Denida lifted his arms in a welcoming gesture.

"Thank you," Danyel yelled from the car behind the soldiers. He got out when Denida joined them.

"Danyel?" Denida's eye widened. "You're here?"

"Not a way to greet an old friend," Danyel chuckled. "Such a pretty estate you have; away from everything. I should have thought of this!" He looked Denida in the eyes. "Are you still my Denny, I wonder?"

Why would he ask that? Of course. Denida went over and hugged Danyel to welcome him.

"Why don't I show you the inside?"

Denida guided Danyel into Dynasty and gave him a tour of his new mansion. Danyel peered curiously around, as Denida explained with excitement every new place he showed him.

When they got back to the soldiers, they saluted Danyel.

"Nice place." Danyel turned to Denida.

"Glad you like it." Denida smiled smugly. "There's a great forest too, sure you don't want me to show you?"

Danyel shook his head. "Why so far out of the way though?"

"Illegal stuff needs a more desolate place."

Danyel lit up. "Where no one can see…" He turned back to his soldiers. "They're staying though, you can see it as an extra protection!"

Danyel got back into his car. "It's a dangerous time now."

Denida approached Danyel's car.

He leaned over the car. "I need to see Dan, won't you let me accompany you?"

Danyel slid over to let him in.

"Headquarters," Danyel commanded.

Danyel sat quietly peeking out at the countryside they passed.

"I really don't need the soldiers, I hired extra security for the new place."

Danyel sat silently for a minute. "As I told you once; this is my world, so not your call!" He turned to look out the window.

Denida sighed and ground his teeth. "Why did you take an interest in me, anyway?"

"I told you before; I saw something in you that reminded me of someone I once knew."

"What happened to him?"

Danyel's eyes darkened. "He changed…"

OK…

Danyel let Denida out in front of the building. Denida stood watching the car leave. *I'm sure now, I'm doing the right thing.* He turned and walked briskly towards the building, as soon as Danyel's car was out of sight. He didn't stop at the door which led into Dan's office, he continued towards where Nina was.

There were few others inside Nina's office. She smiled as she noticed Denida. He grabbed Nina's hand and kissed her tenderly before he led her outside, away from the building, into the street, where there were passing cars and soldiers.

"Denny, where are we going?"

Denida let go of her hand, he checked the road while he ground his teeth. "With the rebellion, you need to be careful."

Nina shook her head. "The soldiers will keep us safe. They'll be gone soon, anyway…" She smiled softly.

Denida bit his upper lip. *Only one way.* He hailed a taxi, he guided her in and climbed in after her. "I want to show you something. Dynasty!" He ordered the driver.

As the taxi drove toward Dynasty, Nina became more and more intrigued as they came closer to it. Nature was a clear change from the inner city. And the towering beauty of Dynasty really struck deep in her.

Nina got out of the cab still in awe at it. "What... is ...this place?" she muttered.

Denida paid the taxi and came over to her, he put his arms around her.

"My new home; it's called Dynasty."

He took her hand, he led her into Dynasty where several soldiers greeted them.

Nina frowned nervously at them. Denida guided her quickly past them and gave them a fake smile.

Nina tilted her head to glance back at them. *She worries about the soldiers.* Denida bit his upper lip. "Come, I want to show you something outside." He guided Nina away from the building, towards the stables.

"Angel!" Nina's eyes sparkled at the sight of the horse she had seen on their first date.

Nina ran over to Angel's stall, Angel rubbed up against her, clearly happy to see her again. She caressed the horse, who kept stroking her cheeks. "You wanted to show me him." She smiled.

Denida moseyed slowly over towards her with his head down on the ground. "Not exactly-" He took her hand. "that's just a plus. The Dark Angels are what I wanted to talk to you about..."

Nina wrinkled her forehead. "What about them? The soldiers in your house?"

Denida sighed deeply and lowered his head. "Come." He took Nina's hand and went back into the house.

He suddenly stopped, examined the surroundings carefully, before he moved a picture frame and entered his hand on a scanner. A secret door appeared next to him. He put the picture frame back in its place. Nina stared in disbelief at what she witnessed.

"Hurry." Denida grabbed her hand again and led her inside.

They climbed down the stairs, a big set of monitors sat in the middle of the room.

Nina turned slowly around in the room. "What's all this?"

The Colonel spun around startled by her voice. He reached for his gun, hidden under the table.

Denida ran in front of Nina and held up his arms. "Wait, this is Nina."

The Colonel froze for a second. "The informant?" He held onto his sidearm with a firm grip.

"Why's the guy from the resistance here?" Nina shook her head violently. "You didn't..."

"I'm merely helping-"

"With soldiers right above here," Nina yelled.

The Colonel hushed her.

"Don't worry," Denida chuckled. "I built this, so no sound can travel out."

Nina still shook her head looking at Denida.

"Hi, nice to finally meet you. We appreciate all your aid." The Colonel shook Nina's hand.

Nina greeted him, only to change her focus to Denida again. "Why would you show me this? Do you not realize how dangerous this is?"

Denida gave a broad smile and kissed her on the forehead. "Have I told you how beautiful, you are today?"

"What-"

"That's exactly why. You need to learn how to be careful, just in case. Only *John* would convince you why..."

"John?" She tilted her head.

"The Colonel." Denida pointed at the Colonel.

Denida started to show Nina tactics of self-defense, as well as how to sneak and detect anyone near her- a thing Denida always knew when there was someone near, for some odd reason. Like an innate ability.

She has to learn, it's now or never!

Denida drove Nina back to her work after he provided her with her instructions. *Maybe, I should take the chance to go see Dan.* He marched into the building towards Dan. It felt different somehow inside. There were more soldiers passing him by, than usual.

As Denida reached the door, several soldiers stormed out before he could knock at the door. He peeked inside, Dan was sitting all alone inside. "Dan?"

Dan slumped in despair. "It's not safe here. Danyel has declared war on anyone even having *anything* to do with this infamous Colonel!"

Denida bit his upper lip. "How-"

"All operations have been seized Denny, everybody's hunting them now…"

Denida nipped at his upper lip.

"I know that look, what is it?" Dan got up.

Denida sighed before he turned to Dan. "It's not going to get better, they won't find him…"

Dan shook his head. "Wrong! They'll hunt him until-"

Denida put his arms on Dan's shoulders. "Trust me!"

***

Daniel smiled smugly at Jack who shifted uneasily. "You must remember this time, no? Were you not working with the Dark Angels?"

Jack straightened himself. "I was working for them, yes. I worked on the Gate, with the Dark Magic, it connected straight to Hell, but only when we used strong Dark Magic on it."

"You were in the middle of all this," Arthur said.

"There were a lot of us, who went into hiding afterward…"

"Were?" Arthur asked, wrinkling his forehead.

"I don't… feel them… anymore," Jack muttered.

"You think Dad found them?" Daniel's eyes lit up.

Jack shook his head determined. "Never, they were too careful. Something else happened, I'm sure of it."

Chapter 29: The Compound

The Colonel had an idea. He had found Dan and taken him to a hidden room where no one would see them.

"Found it," Dan yelled.

The Colonel went to look over Dan's shoulder at the monitor. "I know this place," he muttered. "Follow anyone who leaves or enters there!" He ran to the records room.

"First Denida, now you, Colonel."

"Spare me." The Colonel ran to the back of the room, ignoring the clerk completely.

The clerk ran after the Colonel. "What can I help you with, sir?"

The Colonel pushed a box away from him and stood. "The Dark Angels?"

The clerk's hand shook as he pointed towards some old boxes in the back, behind an old dusty rack. "Everything we have is in there from back then…"

The Colonel opened one of the boxes ecstatically. He flipped through the papers. *Where is it?*

"Maybe I can help you? What are you looking for?" the clerk asked after watching him for a few minutes.

The Colonel sighed and stretched his back. "I'm not really sure what I'm looking for..." He flicked the box. "It's a place the Dark Angels had..."

"They had many." The clerk laughed.

The Colonel grunted. "A place where they conducted secret experiments."

"That sounds familiar," the clerk agreed. He came over and sat next to the Colonel and started searching another of the boxes.

The only sound in the room was the flip of papers and the occasional scrape of a box being moved.

"Wait! I think I found it." The clerk handed the Colonel an open folder.

The Colonel's eyes lit up, he threw his own papers back into the box. "God. You're right, this is it!" He stumbled up and headed for the door and hurried upstairs to his office, he looked frantically across the floor. *He's not here, where is he?*

He stopped a soldier who passed him by. "Lord Denida?"

"He went back to Dynasty, there's nothing more to do here," the soldier said.

The Colonel slapped the folder in his hand. "Wait! Dan is below us checking something for me, tell him where I went."

I've got a feeling we're going to need 'the unit.' He took his personal cell phone to call a number he rarely used. "It's the Colonel, meet me at Dynasty." He ended the call and went downstairs and commandeered a vehicle.

When he pulled into Dynasty a van was parked waiting. *They're here.* The Colonel got out to greet them. He smiled, enjoying seeing his old friends again.

The Commander saluted the Colonel. "Why are we here, don't you have the military?"

The Colonel wrinkled his forehead and shook his head. "They won't be sufficient."

He went with them up to the mansion.

The butler came out. "Johnny," he chuckled.

The Colonel smirked. "Long time, no see. I need to see Denida."

The butler tilted his head towards the mansion. "Inside the chamber."

"Wait here." The Colonel walked inside Dynasty. He went straight to the bookcase. He peeked around the room, unsure how he should enter it.

Ah, I know! The Colonel revealed the control panel, he put his hand on it, it beeped loudly; '*INTRUDER, INTRUDER.*' A camera above him turned to face him, while the alarm rung loud.

The Colonel looked up. "Denny? I know where their hideout is!" He held up the folder to the camera.

The alarm stopped ringing and the door behind him unlocked with a click. The Colonel went down the stairwell. *I haven't been here since the Gate incident...*

"That you haven't," Denida's voice echoed from the room under the staircase. "You found their hideout?"

The Colonel flickered his folder above his head, with a gleeful smile.

Denida went over and grabbed the folder. He examined it skeptically. "The old research center of the Dark Angels?"

"Dan tracked those from the exchange for Daniel to there..."

Denida glanced at the picture in the folder again. "Let's get the military there." He dashed towards the door.

The Colonel stepped over to block the stairwells. "Not the military. Michelle might know."

"Then-"

"My secret unit, I brought them," the Colonel smiled grimly.

Denida and the Colonel went to where the unit waited. Denida gave the same smile which the Colonel had.

"Where are we going?" the Commander asked.

Denida waved the folder. "The Dark Angels' research compound."

They drove off towards the compound.

Denida examined the folder again. "You really think this is where they're at?" He tried to contain his rising hope.

"Yes," the Colonel insisted. "There's no doubt they went here!"

Denida ground his teeth and crumpled the folder.

"Johnny, we haven't heard much from you lately, you been busy?" The commander peered back at the Colonel.

"Priority has been on Daniel," the Colonel said.

The Commander turned around. "But why did you call the unit then?"

Denida smoothed the folder and raised an eyebrow.

"We're going to where the Scientist worked, yet Claus should have been in charge-" The Colonel took a deep breath while looking at Denida. "- yet they went here. I've got a bad feeling Michelle could still have a connection with the military somehow."

"So, you need us." the Commander pointed at himself with his thumb.

When they arrived at the compound, two things were clear; it was humongous, and it was like a ghost town. They got out at the front entrance.

"Where's everyone?" the Commander asked.

"I don't like this. This is not a good sign." The Colonel wandered around the premises.

"Be ready," the Colonel insisted before he led them inside.

Denida followed the Colonel. The inside was as empty as the outside.

It was very advanced for an old research place. Not a soul appeared as they walked through each room with guns at the ready.

"My, my," Lucifer smirked as he appeared behind them. "You can drop the guns, Medusa killed all of them."

"You!" The Commander glowered at Lucifer. He drew his pistol and aimed it at Lucifer. "We gave you Claus, so we would never see you again."

"Oh well," Lucifer chuckled.

The Colonel put his hand on the Commander's gun, who reluctantly put the gun back in his holster.

"Why are you here? What's in it for you?" The Colonel stepped forward.

Lucifer placed his hands on his heart. "I just want to help you find Daniel, to prove I have nothing to do with it." He walked over to Denida. "Daniel's place is in the dungeon, Claus' office is in the center…"

The Colonel led the rush to the dungeon. Denida followed at a slower pace. In the dungeon, they found a cell, as barren and empty as everything else.

"I didn't say he was still here, did I?" Lucifer appeared in the doorway with his usual smile.

"Then where?" The Colonel was starting to lose his patience, Lucifer or not.

"I believe Medusa-" Lucifer's eyes glared red. "and Jack have him."

***

Something is not right. "Where are all Jack and Claus' demons-your demons?"

Everyone turned to look at Denida, who was inside the cell.

"Gone-" Lucifer shrugged.

"You mean Michelle usurped you, you no longer have him!" Denida charged Lucifer.

326

They glared at each other, eyes glowing red.

Denida projected in front of Lucifer. "You had Daniel! You better watch your steps…"

"Or what? You were my apprentice, no need to 'watch my steps.'" Lucifer smirked.

Denida peered back at the others, thumb rubbing his ring. The others had frozen while Lucifer and Denida talked.

"Back together again, how nice," Lucifer grinned.

Denida lifted his hand with the ring on. "Never forget what I have."

Lucifer's eyes wandered from Denida's finger to his hand. "I would never hurt you."

"Me," Denida muttered. "But you would Daniel! If anything happens to him…" He stroked his ring, everything returned to normal.

Denida trudged back into the room while Lucifer spun around and disappeared into a dark cloud.

"Daniel's not here, let's check this office of Claus.'" Denida sped out of the dungeon.

The Colonel had to run to keep up with Denida as he found Claus' office and pushed through the door.

"He always liked it big and fancy." The Colonel's lip curled in disgust.

Behind the desk was a camera monitoring the dungeon, they had just been in.

"John, get in here," Denida's yell sounded muffled.

The Colonel stopped shocked when he reached Denida. The room was all dark, the giant pentagram on the floor was unmistakable. "Must be to summon Lucifer."

Denida examined the pentagram. "You're right; He was Lucifer's pawn; meaning he failed him."

"Because of Michelle?"

Denida shook his head. "Not just Michelle, Jack too." He turned and walked past the Colonel.

"Where are you going?"

Denida stopped and sighed, he never bothered looking back, he just stood there for a minute.

"Are-"

"I need to go see someone in the darkest place there is!" Denida continued out the door.

A scream echoed throughout the darkness that raged in Hell as Denida appeared

next to the Gate, not from within the Gate but by traveling with the ring's power.

I never wanted to come back here, now I remember why... He twitched as the screams in Hell reached his ear.

As he started to walk away from the Gate, a demon approached him.

"I haven't seen you before, one eye," the demon grinned.

Denida sighed and looked down. "You sure about that?" He tore his eyepatch off. He lifted his head.

"What about my name? Remember perhaps; 'Little Evil'?" His bad eye flickered a dark red.

The demon's gaze turned from gloating to outright fear, then he fled as fast as he could. *Guess he remembers the name.* He passed by a spot where a lot of demons were gathered and headed down a path away from them until he arrived at an old building which stood in shambles.

Ignacio... Denida sighed.

"What brings you back here, Denny?" Gabriel appeared in a flash of light next to Denida.

Denida gazed at him. *Like he knew I'll be here.* He straightened himself up. "Claus, Lucifer used him."

"...and Claus failed him, bringing him back here, yes. Why do you care?"

"I never should have let Lucifer have him in the first place. I messed up, no one should have to go through what I did..." Denida shook his head. *My mistake then...*

Gabriel scanned the sky before turning his attention to the building. "You came back here, first?"

"Ignacio died here," Denida uttered in a weak voice.

"The seven of you..."

"Yes, Danyel used that. Lucifer used us all..." Denida went inside the ruin.

The memories stabbed at him with each passing step. "We stood together in all this Darkness. Ignacio always suspected there was something off with Danyel..." He kneeled and laid his palm on the ground, running his fingers over the floor. *I'm sorry Ignacio, my old friend.*

"Yes, that's-"

"Time for Lucifer!" Denida stood up and went past by Gabriel, completely ignoring him.

There were demons guarding the door to Lucifer's mansion. *Times have changed.* Denida stopped in front of the front entrance. He sized up the guards.

"No admittance," one of them said.

Denida charged the guards, who set a barrier of Darkness around them and the front door.

As he reached the barrier his ring flickered, and he burst through the shield as if it were a soap bubble.

One of the guards threw a ball of Darkness which devoured everything it touched. Denida ducked, Darkness enveloped his hand as he jabbed into the demon's body and tore out his heart. The other demon transformed into a crow and flew frantically away.

Lucifer won't like you running away. Denida shrugged and continued into Lucifer's mansion.

Back again. Denida stood in the hall of Lucifer's mansion. *I have not been here since...*

click.

Denida's eye lit up, he ran towards the sound, stopping suddenly in front of a heavy door.

It came from within here. This is Lucifer's… He pushed his hand with the ring forward. The door blew open.

Denida entered the Darkness which was Lucifer's throne room.

The demon who ran from the entrance stood next to Lucifer at the throne.

"See, he's here, Master."

Lucifer waved his hand; the demon morphed back into a crow and flew out a small window in the back.

"Welcome home, Denny. No eyepatch too, embracing your Darkness, I see." Lucifer smiled broadly.

Denida ground his teeth and sauntered closer to the throne. "Not here to stay."

"Then what?" Lucifer tilted his head.

"You've got Claus, I want him back."

Lucifer chuckled. "I do, but you gave him to me personally, remember? Why would I give him back?"

Lucifer got up from his throne. "What's in it for me, is it in exchange for *you*?" He smiled.

"I should never have given him to you, I made a mistake."

"You want to correct it." Lucifer smirked. "I still don't see where it benefits me."

Denida fiddled with his ring.

"Before you try, let me remind you, you're in Hell now," Lucifer spread his arms. "-where the Darkness is the strongest. Your ring won't be enough to hurt me!" Lucifer winked. "But you're welcome to try."

Fine. Denida stomped his foot. "I'll make you a deal."

"I'm intrigued," Lucifer checked his fingernails. "Do go on, but don't give me another *fake ring*."

The fake ring, he did have something to do with Daniel! "I need to correct my wrongs, you can see the logic in that, no?"

Lucifer shrugged dismissively. "I don't care."

"Heavani," Denida muttered.

Lucifer's eyes lit up with the mere mention of her name. "You want to do something for me, the Devil?"

"Yes," Denida blurted out before he could think of what he had just uttered, but it was too late. The words had already been spoken.

"Good, you can have Claus in exchange for you doing something for me."

"I'll not hurt anyone for evil-"

"A favor, Denny. It'll never involve anyone from your world or Earth. No one here in Hell either."

Denida frowned at Lucifer.

Lucifer held out his hand for him to shake. "Do we have a deal?" He smiled broadly.

He seems a little too confident with this, but how can it hurt? Denida grabbed Lucifer's hand and shook it.

Lucifer grinned and flicked his fingers. A demon appeared next to Denida. "Bring him to Claus, he's here to take him back home."

The demon led Denida out and closer to an area of Hell which was filled with agonizing screams- each one worse than the last. The demon stopped suddenly in front of the loudest, most agonizing scream.

"Claus," Denida asked the demon, who nodded in response.

Denida marched through the flame.

He entered a dark room resembling Claus' office within the Underworld when he was Denida's assistant. Claus sat behind a desk, folders higher than his head was all around him on the desk, Denida could barely see him sitting there.

He stretched his neck. "Hello, Claus."

Claus frantically shook his head as fast as he could. "No, not again, not more work."

Another stack of folders magically appeared.

"I promise I'll make it!" Claus grabbed a folder from the stack, which lit his finger ablaze. "Ouch," he yelled and threw it on the desk and blew on his fingers.

Denida walked over to him. *His own nightmare, Lucifer's not using torture...*

Claus went over to get more papers to fill out, he ran back to the desk with them, he blew on his hands.

Denida leaned over the desk. "Claus, I think it's time for a promotion. Come with me." He held out a hand to Claus. "- to take over for me." He smiled tenderly.

"Take... over," Claus carefully grabbed Denida's hand.

As soon as he did, the room changed from the office to nothing but flames all around them.

Claus shook hysterically. "What-"

"An illusion of Dark Magic created by Lucifer..."

"But you!" Claus pointed at Denida accusingly.

"I'm here to bring my friend back home." Denida raised a brow. "Unless you want to stay here, that is?"

"No, no, no," Claus insisted as fast as possible. He shook his hands, just to make sure.

"In that case-" Denida grabbed Claus' hand again and pulled him into the fire. They appeared in a flash next to the Colonel.

"Denny, you're-" The Colonel stopped, his eyes sprung open wide. "Claus!" He spoke the name with contempt. He threw Claus to the floor forcefully. "I've got you!"

"Denny," Claus desperately yelled.

Denida stepped over to Claus, now in handcuffs. "I want to help you, but on the other hand, you *kidnapped* Daniel." He sighed and turned away from Claus.

Chapter 30: The Choice

Jack paced aimlessly around in the garden, behind the house. He stared up at the cone, which surrounded the house. He peered back towards the house, where Daniel, Arthur, and Dana were inside.

What is this feeling I have? I feel 'bad', why now?

He noticed Dana watching out at him through the kitchen's window. He smiled and waved back at her. Dana reddened and vanished. Jack went back into the house, Dana stood in the kitchen, she worked harder as she saw him enter. She must be scared. He chuckled to himself.

Daniel came over to Dana to help her with her dishes, she smiled and stroked him on the cheek.

"Daniel," Jack yelled. "Is it not the time for you to continue your story?"

Dana grabbed Daniel's shoulder and stepped in front of him.

Daniel smiled at her reassuringly, so she released him. He turned to face Jack. "Why do you care? The story is for them, not you."

He's trying to distract them. "I like to hear how it happened, a different point of view."

Daniel gave Jack a faint smile, once he saw Dana was listening he started. "Danyel's hunt for the Colonel didn't lead anywhere, but the Colonel kept broadcasting stuff."

Jack narrowed his eyes. "The Colonel always was a hassle!"

Daniel cleared his throat. "He became a myth, a thing the demons feared. Dad played on both sides, he did well at it too, Danyel didn't suspect a thing…"

***

Denida strolled into a room, where seven men sat behind a large table. Danyel sat at the far end of it.

"Come on in." Danyel stood up and waved his hands in the direction of the other end of the table.

Denida sauntered cautiously over to the table, not taking his eye off the men sitting at the table, who watched him intently. After he sat down, he gave a cautious smile back.

"Denida leads the criminals in the Underworld," Danyel acclimated. "Have you found anything on the '*Colonel*'?"

"Are these your soldiers?" Denida frowned.

The room got very dark.

They all turned to Danyel.

Danyel chuckled as he raised himself up and lifted his arms. "These are all from back home; this is the Seven Dark Angels who lead this world- never forget that!" He dropped back down into his chair. "The Colonel?"

Denida shook his head. "Sorry, all we see is the myth of him is growing…"

"More and more are joining the resistance too, it's a real danger now," the Dark Angel next to Denida said. "If the Master-"

"Thank you Denida" Danyel smiled. "You'll inform us if you find out anything," He suddenly stood with Denida outside the door. He patted Denida on the shoulder before he went back inside.

What just happened? Master? What master? Danyel? Denida shook his head, there was no point worrying about it.

Denida went back to his car, as he always drove alone to see Danyel, so no one would suspect anything.

He got into his car, he put in his key and set it into the ignition, but before he could drive off, someone knocked on his window, startling him.

He rolled down the window. "Who are you? What can I do for you?"

"Denny." The man smiled warmly.

Denida narrowed his eyes. "I know you?"

The man suddenly vanished and reappeared in a flash of light in the seat next to him.

"What-"

"My name's Gabriel, I'm here to aid you."

Denida ground his teeth. "With?"

Gabriel glanced back at the building. "You shouldn't be working with Danyel, it's not going to end well."

Denida rolled his eyes. "Thanks for the wisdom, anything else?"

"*'John'* might be a better guess…"

"Out," Denida yelled. "I have no idea who you're talking about!" He pushed Gabriel out of the car and slammed the door shut. He sped off away from the Headquarters.

Denida drove back to his own office. He grabbed his eyepatch and threw it into the glove compartment, afterward he strolled back inside his office building.

When he got to his office, he was met by Claus.

Claus straightened himself nervously. "Sir."

Denida continued through the door to his office. "What do you want?" He brushed past Claus.

Claus followed Denida into his office. "There's an executive order- by the Dark Angels."

"Order?" Denida turned.

Claus handed a piece of paper to Denida, he opened it and stumbled into his chair.

"What's going on?" Dan came in the door. He saw Denida slumped down into his chair, rubbing his forehead. Dan pushed Claus and the secretary out.

"Why don't I talk to him with no interruptions, please." Dan closed the door shut, with them both outside, he turned the lock.

Dan kneeled next to Denida. "What's the matter, old friend?"

Denida handed Dan the paper he held.

"Jesus," Dan muttered under his breath. Dan and Denida stared at each other.

"It's over, all the data will be monitored. All businesses will have soldiers present now…" Denida sighed. "Danyel will know it's *me*!" He got up and leaned against the window. "Nothing can stop it now." He rested his head on the windowsill.

"There's a way though."

Denida shook his head dismissively.

Dan grabbed Denida by the shoulders. "I know *you know how*, you even wanted it deep down…"

Denida bit his upper lip. "I've got Nina now."

Dan grinned. "You kept the Colonel safe, no? Why not Nina, or more exactly, *for* her?"

Denida ran his fingers through his hair, his eye lit up. "We can't raise suspicion." He looked out the window. "You keep an eye on Nina." He stared into Dan's eyes. "I always had this strange sensation, Danyel was someone I should watch out for."

Dan nodded with a confident smile, he turned and walked out.

"Claus." Denida cleared his desk, then followed Dan out.

Claus half stood, then paused and almost stumbled.

"I want to show you something, come with me." Denida shook his head as he passed by his bodyguards.

Claus stumbled after him. "Where are we going?"

"North."

Denida led Claus up to the roof, where a chopper was waiting. Claus stopped for a moment then took a deep breath and followed Denida. The helicopter lifted off. Claus peered down as it flew over the buildings towards the airstrip.

Denida laughed. "Don't worry, we won't crash."

"You sure about that, it's far down after all." Claus shuddered.

"Yes. Remember this, I'm taking you somewhere to show *you* something, few even know exist."

Claus lifted his head. "Really?"

"Yes. Only you, but it brings with it responsibility too."

Claus nodded frantically. "I won't disappoint you!"

I hope I'm not wrong about Claus...

The chopper sat down on a private airstrip, where Denida had a plane ready to take them the rest of the way. Claus was reading a magazine during the flight when he glanced out of the airplane window. "Ice?" He raised his eyebrows. "Where exactly are we going?"

Denida shook his head. "All you need to know, it's in the north."

Claus peeked at the window. "No kidding, it's all ice! Will be a cold time seeing your thing..."

The plane sat down on an airstrip in the middle of a white expanse.

A machine which looked like a box on tank tracks stood in wait for their arrival. Denida let his pilot wait on the plane. He drove off with Claus out into the snow.

Denida drove towards some mountains in the distance, this was the closest the airplane could get.

He glanced over at Claus. "It's a long way, I really need to get roads to this place..."

"You know where we're going in all this snow? Going to tell me yet?"

Denida shook his head with a faint smile.

"So quiet out here, nothing as far as you can see," Claus said as he watched out the window, admiring the landscape they passed.

"No Dark Angels... out here." Denida ground his teeth so loud Claus turned his head at him. He gave a half smile to Claus.

Denida continued towards the mountains, they reached the site, where the first sign of life appeared. There were a lot of workers working at two old mines. Men and machines bustled in and out of the mines.

Denida stopped the mobile. "We're here."

Claus stared in disbelief at the mines. "Here? You want to show me a mine?"

"You better get dressed warm, this will be cold." Denida got out of the snowcat.

Claus hurried after him, while he struggled to pull on gloves and ear warmers. Denida turned into the mine, he suddenly took a turn away from the workers and kept going. Claus followed uncertainly. Denida took a flashlight and continued down a musty old corridor. It got more damp, the further they went, but somehow warmer too. Claus stopped to take off his gloves and ear warmers again.

"Claus, we're here," Denida yelled in front of Claus.

Claus ran towards the small beam of light. He stopped as he got closer. "There are bars here?"

"Security." Denida smiled, he turned back and unlocked the bars. "Come on." He went inside and opened a steel door which was behind the bars.

"What are the bars protecting?" Claus pointed back where they came from, they were so far in now, no light was shining from the rest of the mine. "- away from everyone?"

Denida raised his eyebrows with a smile.

Claus took a deep breath. "You're the boss." He continued inside the steel door, Denida gave him the flashlight.

Denida went in after Claus, closing the door behind him.

"Oh... my...God." Claus ran the flashlight through the room as he walked in. It was littered with stacks of money. Bills as high as it was physically possible. The room was almost full.

Claus gasped.

"Do you like my hidden stash?" Denida waved his hand at the money. "It's only one of them."

Claus gasped in shock. "One? You've got more of *this*?"

"I do. I'm showing you, cause I trust you, Claus. The Dark Angels can't know of this."

"But we can't get rid of them..." Claus sighed sorrowfully.

"Sure about that? There's a rebellion now..."

Claus spun around, aiming the flashlight into Denida's eyes, Denida narrowed his eyes from the light. "You can't!"

"But, I am." Denida grabbed the flashlight from Claus' hands. "If it fails and I die, this is to safeguard Nina- forever! Can I count on you?"

Claus still stood with wide eyes, trembling in shock.

"Claus," Denida yelled.

Claus snapped out of it and nodded frantically. "You can count on me. She'll be taken care of if it fails... so shall your secret!"

Denida smiled and hugged Claus.

**

"Are you nuts? Claus thought of himself first and foremost, always!" Jack grinned.

Daniel sighed. "My-"

"Wrong." Medusa appeared. "Denida informed his son well." She glared straight at Daniel. Her eyes wandered over to Jack. "I had a hunch I should check on you. Don't let me regret letting you live, little boy!" She scorned Jack.

"But Claus was-"

"He was hoping Denida would die, if he didn't, he had himself covered for influence." Medusa sneered. "You're really a disappointment if you can't guess that. Enough of this!" She transformed into a sparrow and flew out.

Jack felt a strange heat on his face. All eyes were fixed on him. "All right, Denida showed Claus, then what," he yelled.

Daniel cleared his throat and peeked at Dana and Arthur. "Dad showed Claus cause he had an intent with it. First to test Claus, if he would take the money when he showed him, also he gave him the key. Secondly; Mom."

**

Denida now had changed everything, he drove everywhere with a security detail. Starting with the most important place; to show Danyel he feared the evil *resistance* himself.

Danyel glared in disbelief at Denida. "*You're* scared?"

"Everyone needs to take precautions," Denida insisted.

Danyel grunted. "That sounds like the old Denida…"

What does he mean by that? Denida squinted his eyes.

"What brings you here Denida, if you're so worried," Danyel smirked.

"Nina and Dan."

"Who?" Danyel's eyes went blank.

"My fiancée and my best man." Denida raised his eyebrows.

"Your-"

"Nina's my bride to be. Dan works for you in ground planning."

Danyel giggled. "A boy in love, how far you've come!" He jabbed at Denida. "Sure, Nina can leave. Dan can be excused too, but only for a short time."

Denida nodded with a flicker in his eyes.

"Congratulations," Danyel yelled after Denida, as he rushed out.

Denida waved back with his arm, the bodyguard jogged to keep up. Dan's office was empty.

What! Where is- Oh yeah, I told him to keep an eye on Nina. He went towards Nina's office.

Dan sat on a bench peeking every few minutes towards the building. He concentrated on his newspaper when he wasn't looking.

"Boo!" Denida yelled from behind Dan, then sat down next him.

Dan took a deep breath.

"The plan we talked about is in motion."

Dan smiled. "You just need Nina to agree."

"Hopefully." Denida arched his neck, looking up at the clouds. "Stay here," he ordered his guard and marched towards the building.

"Good luck," Dan grinned.

Nina's office was hectic, people coming in and out to drop off papers or pick them up.

Denida stopped in the doorway, he lowered his head at the floor.

"Denny," Nina yelled and rushed over, she jumped and kissed him. "Why are you just standing here, why are you not coming over?"

Denida kissed her on the cheek. "We need to talk," he whispered into her ear.

Nina frowned and raised an eyebrow. She nodded and jumped down.

She led him out the door.

Denida waved at Dan. "Remember 'The Colonel'?" he whispered while looking cautiously around them.

"John, yes."

Denida kicked the dirt, he ground his teeth. He looked at Nina, while he bit his upper lip. "We have to make a move; now! I used a way to get you and Dan away from here."

Nina started to frown again. "A way? What way?"

Denida took a deep breath. "I told Danyel, I was in love with a girl. I'm getting married to her…"

Nina tickled Denida on the stomach. "Talking about me?"

Denida fiddled with her fingers, he was laughing from the tickling. He finally got hold of her hands. He held them for a second, to calm down. "I need you safe, first…"

"Then we must, mustn't we?" She gave a flirtatious smile.

"Why do you care?"

Nina's face went stone cold. "I've seen what they did. To my friends too; *Hell doesn't know fury like a scorned woman.*"

***

"That was a bold maneuver," Jack remarked.

"Dad's clever." Daniel smiled.

Jack nodded. "You sure about that?"

Daniel nodded. "How do you think he managed to beat you and Claus when we were stuck within the Gates?" Daniel crossed his arms.

Claus was sure he could stop Denida. Lucifer was sure he would catch him, just like now… He glanced at Daniel who was still smiling. "You *do* realize, Lucifer will never stop'"

"Eventually, Dad *will* stop him."

Denida truly did change since hell, maybe that's why- Jack stared at Daniel. *-he thinks so highly of his Dad. Denida is truly dangerous with his Dark magic, white, even the ring too...*

Chapter 31: Help from Claus

Denida stood peering at Claus sitting in an interrogation room.

Only a tiny bit of glass between us, it'll be easy... Denida could feel the rage burning within him.

The door in Claus' interrogation burst open and the Colonel and Susan entered.

The Colonel sat down, but Susan stood with her arms crossed at the door, only moving to lock the door.

"We meet again." Susan twisted her lips as if she smelled something rotten.

Claus gave her a cold pale stare. "Last I saw you, you handed me to the Colonel's unit, who delivered me to Lucifer." Claus tried to chuckle. "You must regret that, thinking back at it, huh?"

Susan glanced at the screen and cleared her throat.

"Is Denida behind there?" Claus lifted his chains, trying to wave. "Denny, are you in there?" he yelled mockingly.

"Claus," The Colonel slammed his fist on the table. "You're not here, because of Denida. You're here because of me!"

Claus turned back to the Colonel. "You," he said in a scornful tone.

The Colonel leaned in over the table. "I'll find Daniel, whatever it takes!"

Claus glared back at the mirror. "But Denida-"

"Denny lets me do what I want, he wants his son back, at whatever the cost…"

"Whatever… the cost," Claus muttered. He smiled deviously at the Colonel. "I might be able to help you then; in exchange for my freedom!"

The Colonel scratched his forehead. "How can you possibly help?"

Claus leaned over the table. "It's Jack and Michelle, who has Daniel, no?"

The Colonel and Susan shared a thoughtful look at each other.

"Denny, you bring me what I want and I'll tell you everything you want to know," Claus screamed, with his eyes fixed on the mirror.

Denida watched impassively from behind the mirror. Nina squeezed her eyes.

He put his hand on her shoulder. "What are you doing?"

Nina sighed. "I can't read his mind, however much I try!"

Denida chuckled. "Dark Magic- you can shield anyone from entering your thoughts…" He gazed back at Claus, he licked his lips.

"Don't!" Nina squeezed Denida's hand tight.

"What?" Denida half smiled at her then he dropped his head and sighed. "I've got to try if it saves Daniel." He turned and gave Nina a kiss, and walked out the room and into the next room, where the Colonel was still trying to persuade Claus.

Susan startled as the door opened.

Claus' eyes lit up. "You came."

"I came for you in Hell too, didn't I?" Denida sat down next to the Colonel, opposite Claus.

"That you did, 'Little Evil.'" Claus grinned.

Denida twitched. "You want your freedom, then tell me where Daniel is."

Claus gave a vicious smile and leaned over the table. "I heard some interesting stuff about you in Hell, Denny!" He smirked. "I heard about Ignacio too, sad what happened to him."

"Susan and John; leave us!" Denida clenched his fists. "Out," he repeated.

The Colonel and Susan left the room, still looking back at Denida doubtfully.

Denida pulled over a chair next to Claus. "Don't disrespect Ignacio, I won't warn you again!" He sat straight up. "Why did you take Daniel?"

"The Devil..."

Denida's eyes shut open. "Luci made you?"

Claus nodded. "He would grant me my freedom in exchange for your ring." He peeked at Denida's hand and the ring. "Lucifer wanted me to use your weakness, he thought Nina would be too headstrong..."

Lucifer... Denida's anger curled like a monster in him.

"Jack, I learned was the Scientist. He came to me with another face." Claus scrubbed at a spot on the table, embarrassed. "I should have realized. When you tricked me with the ring, Lucifer gave him my job, and sent me back to Hell..."

"How can you help me then?" Denida jumped up, smashed the chair against the wall. "We're done!" He stormed towards the door.

"Wait," Claus yelled. "I said in Hell, you hear things, didn't I?"

Denida turned back, frowning. "What things?"

"Sgt. Michelle is Medusa. The arch-demon, the devil himself fears her. She killed all the demons. Jack betrayed the Devil to work for her; she has Daniel."

Denida scratched his forehead. "All of which I know… Are you saying you can find her?"

Claus gave a gloating smile. "Yes."

Denida got up, he paced slowly around the room while he glanced into the mirror. *Wonder what Nina thinks?* He tilted his head towards Claus. "Don't you go anywhere." He grinned and left the room.

When he entered the room behind the mirror, everyone fixed their attention on him.

"Miss me?" Denida smiled to break the mood lingering in the room. "So, you heard; Lucifer was behind it the entire time!"

"Forget that." Nina rushed over to Denida. "We have to do what Claus wants. He knows where Medusa has Daniel!"

"I don't know about that…" Susan stood in front of the screen facing Claus. "He might just be playing us to get free; I don't trust Claus."

Nina frantically pointed at Susan. "… and you're bringing Susan too!"

Denida ground his teeth. "Colonel, prepare the unit."

"Unit? They're still at Claus' hideout."

"That's perfect, I want to take Claus there anyway." Denida stood next to Susan, peering through the mirror at Claus, just sitting there. "We need to be careful, he was in Hell. He knows Dark Arts." Denida fiddled with his ring with his thumb.

Denida, Nina, Susan and the Colonel went back into Claus' room.

"So many," Claus smirked. "I must be loved."

The Colonel went over and unlocked the chains then handcuffed him, then attached Claus to his wrist. He double checked the cuffs, making them tight enough for Claus to wince.

Denida led the way to the car, accompanied by a military escort. Denida smiled at Claus. "You'll remember the place."

Claus shook his head ruefully. "Jack found it, you know, after we were betrayed, the Devil helped us get away in the nick of time."

Luci sure did have a hand in this. I'm going to make him pay! "Get in," Denida yelled.

The cars drove off to the compound, they came to a halt at the entrance, where one of the soldiers from the unit stood guard.

The guard greeted them welcome, as he nodded in recognition and waved them through.

"Back again," Claus smirked at Denida.

"Only this time, all of your demons are gone!" Denida's expression wiped away Claus' smile.

"Colonel," the Commander came over to greet them. "What can I-" He froze in his tracks the minute his eyes fell on Claus. "My my, haven't seen you since we delivered you to the Devil." He grinned.

The Colonel led Claus forward. They walked into the cell, where Daniel was supposed to have been.

"Daniel's cell, why are you taking me here?" Claus hunched nervously.

"So, it was here." Luci was right…

"Yes, Edward took care of him, until he betrayed us…"

Denida narrowed his eyes. "Edward?"

Claus nodded. "The demon, I had-"

Denida shook his head. "Not possible! A demon never betrays his master, that's not possible for anyone but an arch-demon to do, low demons would never dare. They fear their masters…"

"We got sold out, we had to escape!"

"The call." Susan smacked her forehead.

"What call?" The Colonel scratched his head.

"Oliver Favier, the one who called to inform us."

"Ah, when we were looking for Jack…" The Colonel pulled Claus forward towards the cell, but Claus wouldn't move, he was standing still, spacing out. "Claus," he yelled.

Claus came back to himself. "Jack," he muttered. With a Darkness lingering within his eyes. "It was always him, wasn't it!" He turned to Denida. "Want to see Daniel, take me to my office. I'll show you the recordings of everything which happened in here."

They all went towards the Claus' office.

All the eyes turned to Claus inside the room, waiting.

Claus raised his eyebrows, smiled and raised his chained arm. "You'll need to release me if you want me to get the films."

Susan drew her gun and held it ready, as the Colonel unlocked his handcuffs.

Claus sauntered past his desk to the bookcase, where he revealed a hidden door.

The Colonel gasped. "Why didn't we find that?"

"Wait here," Denida ordered the others to stay, then entered the secret room.

Claus stood inside a room covered from wall to wall with monitors.

"They're all saved on the hard drives," Claus raised his eyebrows. "I had a screen behind my desk for a live feed, but I had a hunch I might need this…" Claus plopped down in a chair and typed something into the computer in front of him.

"Wait, what are you doing?" The Colonel walked over to Claus.

"Something I should have checked when it happened." A video loaded on the screen. Claus could be seen hovering over a man in chains. Claus left the room with another demon, leaving two men all alone in the room.

"This is?" Denida tapped his finger on the screen.

"The man in chains was who 'allegedly' betrayed us; Edward. The other one's Jack, the Scientist..."

"Someone has to take the fall and you're getting too close to Daniel. It makes you the prime suspect." Jack giggled.

"God," Claus muttered.

But before he could think of anything else, Jack ripped out Edward's still beating heart.

The Colonel gasped in shock at what he witnessed.

"He set... him up," Claus muttered. "We were always just his pawns." He shook his head in despair.

"How does it feel being played?" Denida gloated.

Claus glanced at Denida then dashed for the door.

Susan swept Claus' legs from under him and put her gun to his face.

"Susan," Denida yelled from the entry of the secret room. "You stopped him, don't shoot."

"Denny." the Colonel came out of the room with a thoughtful expression.

"You've got an idea," Denida raised his eyebrows with a smile.

The Colonel nodded. "Our secret unit lacks a place to be, why not use this place?"

Denida bit his lip. "Interesting, we don't need it anymore, so why not!"

Susan put the handcuffs back on Claus, cuffed him to herself and escorted him back out to the car.

The Colonel and Denida told the Commander their idea for the place. His eyes lit up at the idea.

"We need the unit first though," Denida said.

"Claus." The Commander nodded.

Denida trudged back to the cars where Susan stood with Claus. "Where are we going, Claus? Where's Daniel?"

Claus sniffed his nose and scratched it. "Medusa's got him."

"Yes, but where," Denida asked with an impatient voice.

"Only she knows-"

"Then you're going back to Hell!"

Nina came rushing forward and grabbed Susan's sidearm. "I knew it, he's wasting our time!" She grabbed her gun and pointed it towards Claus.

Claus frantically ran behind Susan. "Wait! There's a way to find her."

"How?" Nina shot at the dirt next to Claus.

"She uses Dark Magic- High Dark Arts, she can be tracked with that. As she's the only one within this world."

Nina glanced puzzled at Denida. "Can we, really?"

Denida sighed at the faces of the people watching him "If she uses Dark, yes." He rubbed his forehead. "I really should have sooner, but I really wanted to stay away from Darkness..." Denida shrugged.

Claus chuckled. "Yea well... I have a room-"

"The pentagram, yes." Denida sped back to the room he'd found on the first visit.

Denida flung his hand across the room, lighting up all the candles in the room. He gave a faint chuckle and sighed as he knelt in the center of the room.

"The Darkness," he muttered and twisted his hands together.

A Dark Cone appeared around him, enveloping him and the room in a thick mist.

Denida's eyes turned red inside the mist as he cast his awareness out into the world.

Denida came back out, walking calmly and casually. "I found the Darkness."

"Daniel!" Nina rushed over with hopeful eyes.

"Soon." Denida smiled and hugged her.

Denida, the Colonel, and the special task force drove towards the spot of the Darkness Denida had discovered.

Nobody spoke on the trip, or at least not that Denida heard until the Colonel ran his hand through his hair. "Are you sure, no one other than Medusa could be using the Darkness?"

Who? No… There's no one else- Me maybe. Denida shook his head. "Only an arch-demon can gather this much!"

"So, it's a lot?"

Denida shook his head. "It's a high concentration."

The cars drove on, following Denida's direction, he felt towards the Darkness.

As they got further out of town, the more rural it became.

"It's here," Denida suddenly said.

He could feel the tension from the others.

"Don't worry, I'll lead…" Denida jumped as the car parked in a yard.

Men piled out of the cars and the soldiers readied their guns.

They stormed towards the building's front door, led by Denida.

I feel the Darkness is strong behind this door. It has to be here! He grabbed the handle, but it was locked from within. He stepped back moved his arm in a pushing motion, the door flew off its hinges.

Denida continued into the house, the soldiers followed behind him.

Demons came rushing in their directions shooting Balls of Darkness, hitting several soldiers. They jumped into cover and started returning fire. Denida threw up a shield and watched the demons get gunned down.

But more and more demons came in a seemingly endless flow.

"Cease fire," Denida yelled. "Withdraw, I'll handle it with magic."

"But-"

Denida grabbed the Colonel's hand. "Trust me, old friend."

The Colonel nodded. "Withdraw!" He ran outside with the rest of the soldiers.

Denida closed his hand, sending the door shut with Dark energy.

The demons kept pouring out and they shot more towards him.

Denida lifted his arms around him, creating a Cone of Darkness, which deflected the shots the demons kept sending.

They kept bashing spells at him until the room filled with darkness.

Denida smiled bitterly and his eye burned red as a wave of his hand sent the demons crashing into the walls.

The Demons got back up growling in fury.

Denida held his hand up covered in Dark Power. "I'm here to see your master, won't you tell him; 'Little Evil' is here!"

All the demons knelt with their heads down, as a large doorway opened.

"The... Master's... waiting," a short demon next to the newly opened door stuttered.

That was easy... Denida trudged past the demons to the giant doors.

He stopped and glanced back at the demons. "You know who I am?"

"Little Evil, Lucifer's apprentice. We know," the short man said.

Denida nodded and continued through the doors.

He tried to adjust to the blackness in the room.

"Welcome."

No! It can't be! Denida's eye shot open. Not that voice, it can only be… "Lucifer!"

Lucifer appeared in a dusty cloud in front of him.

"Why are you here. The Darkness, it was you!" Denida bit his lip.

Lucifer broadly smiled. "We can no longer track Medusa, since Jack did. She's able to conceal it now…"

Denida ground his teeth. "Still doesn't answer why you're in my world?"

"I don't need to. It was mine! I took control after the leader of the Underworlds perished."

Denida raised his voice. "By your hand!"

"You think I would ever give it up?" Lucifer smirked.

Denida held up his hand. "You might not, but by force, you will!" He let his hand fall. "-and you might want to."

The Darkness stirred in the room. "Never!"

"I hear Daniel being taken is your doing…"

Lucifer smirked as the Darkness in the room got heavier.

Denida shook his head. "I'll find Daniel, afterward you'll pay!"

He turned and walked away.

"Darkness lingers in your soul!" Lucifer grinned.

Denida ignored Lucifer, he disappeared into the air, he re-appeared outside with the soldiers.

"Medusa isn't here, Lucifer is. Stay here and make sure they leave!" Denida ordered the Commander.

"Us?" The Commander said wearily.

Denida turned back to the Commander with red eyes. "Yes, you!"

The Colonel wrinkled his forehead. "How are we going to find Daniel then?"

"The videos, Claus mentioned. There has to be something on Jack in there..." Denida sighed.

Chapter 32: Plan of Dark Angels

Medusa stood on a hilltop watching Denida leaving.

Guess Lucifer won't be here much longer. She transformed into a sparrow and flew down and into the house through the basement. The soldiers there were too occupied guarding the front door, in case any of the demons came out again.

She flew up from the basement as the demons were preparing their departure. A huge door stood behind them, but it was closed and none of the demons seemed to be doing anything near it.

'He' must be in there. She flew towards the door. When she neared it, she changed form and flew through it.

Inside it, Lucifer stood in the center of the dark room.

She changed herself again into her demonic state, one she had not used since she was in Hell.

"Mara," Lucifer muttered. "What brings you here? Can't be a desire. You dislike me- as much as I dislike you..."

"So true, but I have to, I have what you want," she grinned.

"Really," Lucifer smirked. "And what would you want for it?"

"Nothing from you," Medusa sneered.

356

Lucifer frowned at Medusa. "Then why are you here?"

Medusa appeared right in front of Lucifer. "Your 'Little Evil'."

Lucifer and Medusa had identical expressions of contempt.

"What do you want with Denida?"

"Not just me, the Darkness is ready to replace you too. When Denny sees the right path, you'll be removed. Last chance to leave by yourself..." Medusa gave Lucifer a gleeful grin.

"Denny will never take my place willingly!"

"Not up to him." Medusa transformed back into a sparrow and flitted away leaving a cloud behind.

She flew straight back to where the cone was, now concealed from the outside, so normal bypassers would not see it. She had used the "Spell of Concealment" on the magic itself, so she couldn't be tracked with the Dark Magic.

She transformed back to her human form and sauntered through the cone.

Jack saw her entering from the garden. "Mara!" He waved his arms in the air.

Medusa turned from the house to the back of the Garden, where Jack was.

"What brings you here?" Jack asked.

"I'm your Master now, what I do doesn't concern you!" Medusa leered down at Jack. "How's the son of Denida?"

Jack gave a shrug, his eyes shifted away from Medusa for a second. "He's his father's son. He's distracting the others with how Denida fought the Dark Angels."

Medusa raised her brow. "How?"

Jack shook his head. "He didn't get to that, only how he got involved in the resistance. How he started helping the Colonel through Dynasty..."

357

Medusa sat down on the bench. "Tell me he what told you!"

Jack nodded and started to tell her the stories Daniel had told so far...

***

Daniel stood at a window, glaring out at the garden, where he could see Jack sitting on a bench next to Medusa.

This can't be a good sign. He glanced back at Arthur and Dana, who were playing cards together, to pass the time. They just need the distraction; they don't know the Darkness in the same way...

"Daniel," Jack's voice yelled from the doorway to the garden.

Daniel turned to face Jack, who was accompanied by Medusa.

Medusa smiled. "I heard a lot about you, Daniel." She glanced at Jack. "Jack told me you're telling how your Dad handled the Dark Angels?"

Daniel sighed. "You want to know too..." Maybe...

"Curiosity," Medusa winked.

Daniel swallowed deeply. "Okay. Dad had everything prepared-" He sighed, as he peered over at Jack. "-the Colonel had discovered everything the Angels did was connected to a place very well guarded, a place of research on how to get stronger. That was where they had to strike first..."

***

Denida and the Colonel stood looking at a well-guarded structure.

The Colonel was in a disguise since he was still the most hunted person in the Underworlds.

"Are you certain of the info?" Denida peeked over at the Colonel.

"Look at all this security, they wouldn't guard it this much, if there was nothing behind those doors," the Colonel insisted.

Denida stared at the compound in front of him. *He's right, there's A LOT of security.* "What's the plan, how do we get in?"

The Colonel smiled in a way which worried Denida to his core.

"Simple!" The Colonel took off his mask. "You bring in the most heinous and wanted man in all the Underworld." He handed Denida a soldier's uniform he had folded together. "I've got everything prepared, why it's only you and me."

Denida changed into the uniform.

"You do look nicely demonic." The Colonel grinned.

Smartypants. Denida grabbed the Colonel and escorted him to the entry of the compound.

The guard saw them approaching, he first didn't pay them much attention, until he noticed the Colonel's face. He ran out to the road with his gun drawn.

Denida stepped in front of the Colonel and raised his own gun. "No, you don't! He's my catch, let me in, so I can turn him over to your boss."

Denida and the guard held a staring contest for what seemed like forever.

The guard broke it by lowering his gun. "You win, I guess," he said. "I'll let you in."

The guard marched back to the front gate. Denida followed, dragging the Colonel behind him with the help of a chain tied around his hands.

The guard guided them inside then he stopped and looked around. "You," he yelled to a man in a lab coat.

"I'm called 'the Scientist," the man yelled. He went up to the guard. "The ones you should be protecting!"

The guard dismissed what he said, he just pointed towards Denida and the Colonel. "They need to see the boss, bring them to him, I need to watch the entrance." He watched the Scientist, who reluctantly nodded. The guard ran back to his post.

"This way." The Scientist led them the rest of the way to the boss of the compound.

This plan has better work. Denida glanced around as they were led towards the boss.

The Scientist stopped in front of another set of guards, protecting a wooden door. "They need to see the boss."

"Says who," one of the guards moved his hand towards his gun.

"Take a look. This is the Colonel from the resistance." Denida pushed the Colonel forward.

Both the guards and the Scientist scanned the Colonel's face.

"I didn't even-" the Scientist began.

The guard moved forward. "We'll take it from here."

Denida jerked the Colonel back and shook his head. "He's still my catch!"

"Let them through," the other guard knocked on the door and opened it in response to a muffled command from within.

Denida and the Colonel stepped into the dimly lit room with a man sitting in the center.

Crap. Denida pulled the Colonel in front of him. "I brought in the Colonel," he spoke in a deep voice.

The Colonel paused briefly.

"It's one of the Dark Angels, he knows me," Denida whispered.

The Colonel deliberately stood in front of Denida, so the Dark Angel couldn't get a good view at Denida.

The Dark Angel tried to see around the Colonel, but the Colonel just mimicked the Dark Angel's moves.

The Angel snarled and stalked towards the Colonel. "I can see why Danyel wants you gone. Unfortunately, Danyel wants you himself, so I can't kill you…" He stopped right in front of the Colonel, baring his teeth.

The Colonel raised his eyebrows. "You won't have me just yet." He grinned and headbutted the Angel, making him drop to the floor with a bloody nose.

The Colonel took off the handcuffs and cuffed the Angel instead.

The Dark Angel shook with rage. "How did you get in?"

"I helped him." Denida came out from behind the Colonel.

"Denny, *again*?"

The Colonel sat the angel down into a chair. The angel's mouth moved, but no words came out.

Denida kneeled next to the Dark Angel. "You all use this here. How do I destroy it?"

The Dark Angel took a deep breath. "But, you don't remember!"

Denida narrowed his eyes, then slammed his fist into the angel's stomach. "Remember? What I do remember is waking up, next to the Gate Danyel uses." He fixed his gaze on the angel's eyes. "I've helped the resistance now, I like it; killing *you* people!"

The Dark Angel struggled to get free.

The Colonel grabbed him and held him down tight. "There's no escape!"

The angel's eyes wandered to Denida, the fear in them couldn't be mistaken. "I know… Little Evil."

The Colonel yanked his head backward. "How!"

"Dark Magic, we can't use it in full if this place doesn't work," he said, while the Colonel squeezed his head so much his face turned red.

The Colonel let go of the angel's face and stepped back. "Dark Magic?"

Denida shrugged. "If we destroy this place, you all will be weaker, do I understand correct?"

The angel nodded hysterically.

"You've yet to tell me how." Denida grabbed the angel's throat.

"Please don't!" His eyes rolled frantically around. "Our scientist team extracts it. Destroy their reactor," he croaked.

"They'll just rebuild it…" The Colonel shook his head in despair.

"If we destroy it-" Denida smiled at the Colonel. "we can hit the rest of them at once, never giving them a chance. I have been there with Danyel several times, I know this place…"

The Colonel paced across the room. "No, we need them all together, for this to work."

Denida grinned at the Dark Angel in the chair. "I've got an idea on how." Denida pulled the angel to his feet and back over to his desk. "Call a meeting; say you've discovered something they all need to hear!"

The Dark Angel shook his head rapidly. "I'll die if I do it."

Denida kneeled. "What do you think will happen, if you don't?" He winked at the angel.

The Dark Angel breathed heavily as he wrote Danyel and the rest of the Dark Angels. "They won't come though, after what happens here."

"Done?" Denida inquired.

The angel nodded in response.

Denida smiled. "Good!" He got back up and stood behind the angel and put his hands on his shoulders. "You were right to fear us, we're stopping you, after all!" He grabbed the Dark Angel's head tight. "Sorry." He broke his neck in one fell swoop.

The Dark Angel's head slumped to the table.

Denida and the Colonel carried him over to his bed and covered him as if he was only napping.

Denida nodded to the Colonel. "Next step of the plan."

He locked the Colonel back in the handcuffs and led him back out to the guards. "The boss wanted me to take him to Danyel, as a reward for catching him."

The guards patted Denida on his back.

"He said he wanted me to tell you, he doesn't want to be disturbed. He needs to see the other Dark Angels tomorrow, he needs to prepare..." Denida poked the guards to make sure they heard him.

The guards solemnly nodded.

"He told me you have a reactor which extracts Dark Magic, where's that, can I see?"

"Sure, I'll show you." One of the guards started to walk forward. "Keep an eye on 'the Colonel', while we're gone, it'll only take a few minutes."

Denida followed the guard, leaving the Colonel behind with the other guard.

The guard led Denida to a huge room, which had an immense machine in the center of it. A giant pentagram was drawn on the floor.

"Awesome, isn't it?" The guard puffed with pride.

Denida smiled and nodded, while he examined the room. *How do I distract him?*

"Well, you saw it. Let's go back." The guard turned back towards the door.

I can't leave without-

Energy poured out of the pentagram and into the machine.

"Wow, let me check that out." Denida ran on the other side of the machine, where he was sure, the guard couldn't see him.

The guard shook his head and rolled his eyes. "Just make it fast."

"I am," Denida yelled. He steeled himself to do what he needed and set the bomb to explode during the Dark Angel's meeting. He pushed it down under the machine and hid it in a crevice.

Denida got up and started to walk back to the guard.

The guard bumped into Denida as he rounded the corner.

Denida widened his eyes. "I'm coming, it's awesome."

The guard frowned suspiciously. "You sure took a long time."

"It's some fascinating machinery." Denida smiled.

"Yeah well…" The guard led Denida back to the Colonel.

The other guard had his eyes fixed on the Colonel, with his gun pointed at him.

"Thanks, I'll take him to Danyel now." Denida escorted the Colonel out.

When they had gotten a good distance from the compound, the Colonel glanced back to be sure no one was following them. "Did you get it set?"

"Of course, everything is set for tomorrow, where we'll kill off the rest of the Dark Angels…"

Chapter 33: End of Dark Angels

Denida drove up to Danyel's headquarters with the Colonel. The Colonel wore a disguise to make him look like Denida's usual bodyguard.

When Denida stepped inside, none of the guards paid them any attention.

Denida and his 'bodyguard' were guided into the room Denida had been in before.

The room with the big desk was still filled with a thick dark mist when they entered.

Six men sat around the table, missing only the Dark Angel Denida had killed the day before.

"Sit down, Denny." Danyel tapped the table. "Why isn't he here? How dare he be late after calling the meeting," Danyel yelled and snatched up a glass of water and swallowed it in one swoop.

The Colonel tilted his head, so he could whisper into Denida's ear. "When-"

Dennis Scheel

"Not now," Denida said under his breath and pushed the Colonel away. "Danyel," he rubbed his face. "What are we waiting for?"

Danyel glared at the empty chair. He picked up the phone. "They'll know at the compound when he left." He dialed the number and waited.

The Colonel glanced nervously at Denida, he grabbed his arm.

"Yes, it's Danyel. Has the Dark Angel left?" Danyel spoke into the phone. "He's not come out of his room today? Go get him already!" Danyel shook his head and rolled his eyes. "He's gonna get it!"

He already did. Denida observed Danyel while inside he counted down the seconds.

Danyel's eyes were filled with a red glow and his hand had white knuckles clutching the phone. His attention came back to the phone. His eyes went wide. "Dead? How?" Danyel put the phone down and put it on the speaker, he raked his gaze across the other Dark Angels.

The Colonel got up and scoped worried around the room. Denida, however, just sat leaned back.

"Sir? He has gotten-"

A painful screech came from the phone then the feed went silent.

"Hello? Anyone there?" Danyel picked up the phone, taking it off the speaker. "It's dead..." He slammed it down.

The room's thick dark mist thinned.

Denida got up from his seat and tapped the Colonel's shoulder. "It's time."

Danyel wrinkled his forehead. "Time?"

The Colonel and Denida drew their guns and shot the closest of the Dark Angels, at the opposite of the table the furthest of the Dark Angels slumped down over the table in a bloody pool.

366

Danyel opened his mouth in shock as the Colonel directed his gun towards the next of the Dark Angels and fired.

The Dark Angel eluded the Colonel's bullet, then straightened and lifted his hand muttering something. Only a small flicker came from his hand. As he stared in disbelief, the Colonel shot him.

Danyel spun around in a circle and raised his arms above his head, but nothing happened, he just stood still there.

He looked at the dead Angel, then at Denida with eyes wide in terror. Denida met his gaze coolly. Danyel swallowed hard.

"Not again," Danyel muttered. He slammed the doors open, ordered the guards to attack as he sprinted away.

As the guards came in with their guns blazing, the remaining Dark Angels tried to follow Danyel, but the Colonel and Denida shot them before they reached the guards.

Denida pursued the last living Dark Angel in the room.

The Angel ripped out a dagger from under his shirt and slashed at Denida.

Denida's gun fell across the floor; he scrambled after it, by the time he grabbed it and spun to shoot, the angel was gone.

The alarm sounded loudly.

Denida hid behind a cabinet and glared at the Colonel, he could see him hiding from behind a corner of the room.

He made moves with his hands and tilted his head towards the guards.

The Colonel shook his head, he ripped off his mask, pointed at himself then up, then he pointed at Denida and he made a gun with his fingers.

The Colonel jumped up close to the guards who aimed their guns at him.

Denida rose from behind the cupboard, he shot one guard before they noticed him, but the other one turned his machine gun towards him. Denida dove behind the cabinet as bullets tore through where he'd been standing.

The Colonel pulled his trigger, ending the carnage in the room.

Denida came back out from behind the cabinet. "Danyel, we've got to go after him."

"What about the other Angel?"

Denida ground his teeth. He shook his head. "Danyel first, he's the boss!"

Denida and the Colonel ran towards Danyel, the Dark Angel's office. Several guards had positioned themselves outside of Danyel's office, as soon as they reached the office, the guards opened fire.

Denida and the Colonel hid behind the corner where the guards couldn't reach them.

"We have to get Danyel before the generator works again. We can't wait until the rest of the resistance reach us!" Denida tried to look forward, but as soon as he tried, the bullets started flying. "Go, bring backup!" Denida steeled himself.

"You going to be OK here?" The Colonel frowned.

"We can't let Danyel get away, be quick!" Denida started shooting towards the guards, giving the Colonel the chance to run away.

As soon as Denida stopped shooting, the guards returned fire.

How do I get through them? Denida stood fiddling with his gun, checking to see how many bullets he had left, there were only a few. *They'll start moving in if I don't fire back, I need another way...* Denida bit his upper lip. "The rest of the resistance will be here soon," he yelled. "It's not like before, this time we've killed all of the Dark Angels-" He squeezed his gun and fired towards the guards. "Danyel's the last one!"

"Wrong," a guard yelled. "We have two here!"

So, the other Angel is here? Perfect! Denida sighed. *I'm out...*

Denida's eye widened. "Dark magic- they can't use it now; we disabled it!"

The silence filled the air. There was no response, no bullets flying either, just silence.

Should I try to peek?

"We give up," a guard yelled back.

The bump of metal being thrown on the floor could be heard.

Denida peeked towards the guards, all their guns were thrown into a pile in front of them.

The Colonel and his resistance fighters came running in with guns at the ready, they stopped a few steps from Denida.

"They surrendered?"

"With no Dark Magic, we can stop them," a guard waved his hands.

Denida grabbed a gun from the pile on the ground. "Time for Danyel!"

Denida, the Colonel, and several resistance members rushed into Danyel's private chambers, guns blazing. There was no sign of Danyel or the other angel.

Is he hiding?

"Find them," the Colonel yelled to the others.

Everyone spread out and started searching.

The Colonel investigated the rooms, as everyone else. He entered Danyel's private chamber.

"Hold it!" The other Angel put his dagger to the Colonel's throat. "Get me out of here- past your resistance!"

The Colonel threw down his handgun. "Sure, don't hurt me!" He looked frantically around the room, but no one had noticed them yet. The Angel forced him out into the main room.

The resistance fighters saw them and aimed their guns in his direction.

The Angel pushed his blade unto the Colonel's neck. "Drop them!"

What's that noise? Denida was in another of Danyel's rooms when he heard it. *The Angel, he wants out without Danyel? Why?* Denida bit his lip. He examined the room. *Knives?* Old knives and daggers hung on the wall in front of him, he took one down.

He inhaled deeply then flung the dagger at the Angel; it stuck into the Angel's back.

The Colonel grabbed his throat in shock as the Angel collapsed behind him. A small cut bled on his neck. He turned.

"You're welcome," Denida smirked, as the Colonel gasped.

What's that? Denida narrowed his eyes. *That looks off...* He walked over to a bookcase, which had a small flicker of light. He checked the light to reveal a door hidden behind, he readied his gun and opened the door. It revealed a hidden room.

"Danyel?" Denida had raised his gun as he examined the room, the floor was covered with a giant pentagram, candles burned throughout the room.

"No Danyel." The Colonel came into the room. "It's like he just disappeared." He scratched his forehead. "What's this place?"

"I've never seen it before..." Denida strolled out.

The Colonel followed him. "It sure went easy."

"... but Danyel..." Denida sighed.

"We'll find him, count on it!" The Colonel held open the door to the outside. "You ought to go see Nina."

Claus is watching her... "Maybe I should." Denida stopped as soon as he got outside. The sight before him shocked him.

The yard in front of the building crowded with people, more and more kept coming.

"Is it over?" someone from the crowd yelled.

The Colonel nodded, he grabbed and raised his arms with Denida's. "We're free from the Dark oppression at last!"

The crowd cheered after the Colonel's proclamation. Denida glanced back at the building which until today was the Dark Angels' Headquarters. "What are we going to do now?"

"The Colonel can lead us," a man standing near them in the crow started yelling, getting everyone in frenzy.

The Colonel shook his head and tried calming the crowd's loud screams with his arms, but it was pointless, they just got louder and louder. "I'm not... the hero," he yelled to get through the crowds' roars.

The crowd died down.

"Who then?" someone yelled.

The Colonel turned and grinned at Denida. "You; you thought of the plan, we never would've beaten them without you." He turned to the crowd. "Denida!" He pointed to Denida with the roar of the crowd.

"Denida, Denida, Denida," the crowd started chanting.

Denida ground his teeth while gazing at the Colonel.

"We need someone to lead or it will be chaos. Just until we find someone..." The Colonel tilted his head towards the crowd. "They like you too, plus you know a little about leading."

He has a point. Denida stepped forward, he raised his hands to quiet the crowd.

The chanting of his name died down.

"This'll be a new beginning for all of us..."

***

Medusa chuckled. "So, that's how he got away to the next world, where he continued in the service of the Dark Angels- just only him, one Dark Angel."

Jack bit his lip. "He used the last of his Dark Magic to escape. So, he was in another of the Underworlds, continuing the Dark Angels path." He turned to Daniel. "You must remember him. Lucifer was so disappointed, he was happy to use him."

"Doing Lucifer's work," Medusa smirked.

"Use, how?" Dana asked.

"He wants Denida, he allowed Denida to have his vengeance within Hell." Jack smiled. "Didn't work, Denida outsmarted him- again…"

Medusa rolled her eyes and turned to Daniel. "You had more?"

Daniel nodded. "Dad never went back to Dynasty to see Mom, he went straight to leading the government. The Colonel was busy hunting Danyel. Dad called Dan to have him bring Mom…"

***

It was hectic in the former Headquarters of the Dark Angels. The resistance had made it their headquarters, led by Denida.

Denida didn't have a second to himself since he had taken on the role of leading. He was inside Danyel's chamber when the Colonel came to him. He saw him approaching. "John."

The Colonel nodded to him. "I think it's best to just call me *Colonel* when we're around others." He scratched his forehead and glanced at them. "More and more are joining us, including the former guards of the Dark Angels."

Denida bit his upper lip and nodded. "I see what you're getting at." He grabbed a folder one of the aides brought. He looked up after signing it. "Why don't we make a secret unit from a select trusted few of the resistance- only you and I will know of it - have them track Danyel."

Dan stepped in with Nina and Claus.

Denida jumped over the desk and swept Nina into an embrace. "Claus, Dan, we need all the help we can get!" He brushed his thumb across her cheek and gave her a tender kiss. "I'm so happy, you're safe. Claus watched over you the whole time?"

Nina nodded.

Guess Claus really can be trusted.

Over the next few days, everything started to calm down again, Danyel, however, remained missing. As if he'd vanished out of existence. The former guards, who now were the normal military worked to remove any reminder of the Dark Angels, they either disposed of it or locked it away in the old compound Denida and the Colonel had been to.

A few loyal servants of the Dark Angels hid, evading both the military and the Colonel's special force.

Claus remained close to Denida to serve him. "Denny, you wanted to see me?"

Denida waved his hand for him to come closer. "Yes, I wanted to talk to you. Now that everything has settled down."

"Yes, we didn't expect any of this." Claus sat down in a chair in front of the desk.

"You did well at protecting Nina-"

"I forgot!" Claus got up and fiddled in his pocket and put down a key on Denida's desk. "Your key!"

Denida smiled and grabbed the key. *As I expected.* "I want to show you something..."

"Again? Is it in the north, again?

Denida chuckled and shook his head. "We won't be going alone either. It's a dangerous time now, we'll need protection at all times."

Denida sauntered out, followed by a security detail. Claus followed.

They followed Denida in a separate car, leaving Claus and Denida alone.

The cars drove to the outskirts of a forest, Denida got out.

"Wait here," Denida ordered his guards, then tilted his head at the forest, turned towards it.

Claus scurried to catch up. "Is it another deposit, you want to show me?"

Denida ignored Claus and continued further. After twenty minutes of walking, he stopped and spun around to face Claus. "I don't remember anything from before waking up here."

"Here?" Claus turned a circle and scratched his head.

Denida chuckled and went a few steps further, to reveal a giant Gate.

Claus gasped at the sight of it.

"Danyel used another of them. I had Dan start to investigate that one…"

Claus was still shocked when he turned to Denida. "Why show me, then?"

"Don't you want to help me lead the Underworlds? I need someone to do it with me. one I can trust!" Denida smirked.

Claus smiled and peeked at the giant gate, standing in front of him.

"We need to build a new tomorrow now." Denida circled around the gate. *Wonder if the Dark Angels made this?* Denida examined the gate. *Peculiar.*

***

Medusa gave a harsh laugh. "The Gates existed before Lucifer, even *he* uses them. The Dark Angels could never have made them."

"Dad learned that, eventually," Daniel said. *Not soon enough though.*

Medusa leaned close to Daniel. "Anything else?"

I wish- it never convinced neither you or Jack... Daniel glanced at Dana and Arthur. "I finished my story."

"Not yet, but I'll write you the final chapter." Medusa chuckled and walked out.

I have a bad feeling about what she meant...

Daniel caught a strange look on Jack's face, almost sympathy.

Chapter 34: Finding Daniel

The Colonel had instructed his task force to investigate the videos Claus showed them. The videos contained a lot of material so Nina and Susan were helping to go through them too.

Denida sat in Claus' former office, opposite from Claus. He was tapping his fingers impatiently on the desk. *This is agonizing!*

Claus watched at Denida's fingers but said nothing.

"Enough of this; I can't just sit here doing nothing!" Denida jumped to his feet.

"But what can you do?"

I can go see the one place, I haven't yet… Denida gazed deep into Claus' empty stare. "To see an old friend." He leaned down to Claus, he grabbed his arm and cuffed him to the radiator.

"Hey, I won't go anywhere," Claus yelled.

Denida shook his head and smiled. He stroked his ring and started to become less visible until he suddenly vanished in front of Claus.

Denida appeared outside of Heaven's Pearly Gate.

"No way, you're not coming back in!" Peter positioned himself in a defensive position.

This won't work, he never liked me. Denida held up his hands. "I'll leave with the Gate." He spun towards the Gate but stopped when Peter no longer could see him. *Wonder if there's another way in...* Denida examined his surroundings and shook his head. *It has to be through Saint Peter, there's no other way. Maybe...* He nipped his upper lip and stared down at his ring and glanced back towards the pearly gate.

Denida clenched and concentrated until his hand and the rest of him was invisible. He sauntered towards Peter. It didn't take long before he could see Peter in the distance. Denida stopped, nervously. *There he is, I'm back again, but can he see me?* Forcing himself to walk closer, getting more anxious with each passing step.

Peter kept his watching. Denida stopped in front of him, but Peter stared right through him.

"Stop!" Peter held up his arms, he ran towards Denida.

Denida came to a complete halt, there was nowhere to hide, nothing but cloud between him and the Pearly Gate.

Peter didn't stop but ran through him, stopping a row of people who were behind Denida from walking further.

Denida glanced back, he ran towards the Pearly Gates and inside without looking back.

Wow, Heaven. I haven't been here since- Daniel... He unclenched his fist, revealing himself.

He stepped further into Heaven, scoping around everywhere he went, he was looking for someone.

Where's Gabriel at?

"Denny, you're back?"

Denida froze in spot when he heard those words spoken. *I've been spotted, but by whom?* He turned slowly around cautiously. "Jesus?"

"Hello, I thought you'd be back."

377

Denida didn't know what he should think seeing Jesus again. "I'm just here to see Gabriel."

"Forgot?" Gabriel appeared in a flash of light right next to Jesus. "All you need to do is call."

Gabriel gave the same tender smile Denida remembered.

Denida patted Jesus and went with Gabriel.

He turned to him when they were away from prying eyes. "I'm lost Gabriel, you always were able to set me on the right path."

"Daniel, I take it?"

Denida sighed and nodded in response. "Claus showed us tons of videos from when they had him, but that'll take time. I have a bad feeling we don't have that time."

"So, you came here?" Gabriel held up his arms in an embrace sort of gesture.

Denida paced around, he kept on sighing. "I don't know what to do…"

"The answer lies in front of-"

"I don't need a riddle; I need an answer!" Denida shouted at Gabriel.

"Shame I can't help you." Gabriel strode over and hugged Denida. "God's listening, riddles are the only way I can aid you," he whispered in Denida's ear. He turned away, waving his arm. "Godspeed. Remember, the answer is within you and all around you!"

Within me and around me, what did he mean by that? Denida rolled his eyes. *This was useless!*

Denida used his ring to go back to his own world. He appeared at the Headquarters, on the same floor as the Colonel's office.

He was trudged towards the office when Dan burst through the door to the stairs.

He crashed into Denida, dropping the papers in his hand.

"Denny, you got rid of the eye patch again, it suits you." He picked up his papers. "We've got to see the Colonel!" He ran to the Colonel's office clutching the mess.

Has he found something? Denida sped after Dan.

Dan stopped in the doorway, his eyes scattered across the room. "Nina's not here?"

The Colonel shook his head. "She and Susan are examing the videos Claus found, guess you wouldn't know…"

"I found some-"

The Colonel blew him off with his hand. "You already showed me, we're past that now."

Dan rushed to the Colonel's desk. "No, we're not," he yelled. "I found something else!"

"What?" Denida came in behind Dan.

Dan handed Denida the folder he held.

Denida opened the folder and scrolled through it. *Interesting.* "We do need to see Nina." He closed the folder and tilted his head backward and turned to the elevator.

The Colonel rushed after Denida and Dan, and they went to the compound to see Nina.

"Bring the Commander to Claus' office," Denida instructed the Colonel. "-Nina and Susan too."

Denida grabbed the folder and marched, accompanied by Dan to Claus' office, where Claus himself was still sitting.

Dan glared at Claus, his fists clenched.

Denida noticed Dan's look. "Oh yeah, Claus had you prisoner, forgot about that…"

Dan didn't move and Claus shifted uncomfortably. Denida threw down the folder and sat down behind the desk.

"Why's he here?" Claus pointed at Dan.

Denida got up and went around to show him a piece from Dan's folder.

Dennis Scheel

Claus' eyes turned back to Denida. "Guess this means you know the time to check in *my* videos." He turned to Dan, grinning.

The door swung open, Nina, Susan, the Commander, and the Colonel came in.

Nina's eyes widened as she saw Dan.

Denida handed the Commander the folder. "Check those times. The videos may have a hint where all those demons went..."

"I knew leaving you to examine the rest, was a good idea," the Colonel chuckled at Dan.

"We wait, yet again." Nina sighed in despair.

"Not long," Denida hurried to say. "We know where to look now." Denida bit his lip. *Wonder if that's what Gabriel meant?*

"Denny?" Nina stroked Denida's forehead. "Something the matter?"

Denida shook his head, he grabbed her hand and caressed it. "Just something Gabriel said."

Nina withdrew her hand, she turned to face Denida. "Gabriel, the Archangel?"

Denida nodded.

"Seen him too. Where I got Michelle's other face from..."

He's always aiding us...

Nina leaned against the desk. "So-"

The door swung open, everyone turned to look. "Lord Denida, Lady Nina, the Commander told you to come," the soldier in the doorway said.

The Colonel got up.

"No." The soldier held up his hand. "Only Nina and Denida."

The Colonel sat back down, baffled. The soldier steered Denida and Nina out.

The Commander stood awaiting for them outside of the room, where they were investigating the videos.

The soldier stopped and saluted the Commander.

"Why are you out here?" Nina glanced at the soldier walking away.

"We found out where Michelle- Medusa, as they called her went."

"Where's that?" Nina stepped closer to the Commander

The Commander tilted his head backward and continued into the room behind him.

Nina hurried after the Commander.

I've got a bad feeling about this. Denida followed them into the room.

On the screen in front of them, hordes of demons ran out to their cars. They were clearly getting ready for something big.

"They went to Michelle, they never returned." The Commander sounded thoughtful.

Denida just looked back at the monitor. "You know where they went?"

The Commander sighed heavily before he turned to Denida. "Jack wasn't quiet about it, he had a demon watching her since he found out where she was…"

"Let's go then," Nina yelled.

The Commander sighed.

"What," Denida asked.

"Hundreds of demons, not one returned…" The Commander's voice was scratchy with worry.

"We've got the military," Nina insisted defiantly.

"Is that better than hundreds of demons?" The Commander clenched his jaw.

Nina clutched Denida's hand. "Denny, you've got your ring!"

Denida stroked Nina's chin. "Yes, it's the only way. Get ready, *all* of the military is coming too!"

He got everyone ready for the confrontation.

"Isn't this a little much?" Dan got out of the way of a soldier carrying a box.

Denida glanced at Dan.

"Doubt your ring can do it?" Dan asked as if afraid of the answer.

Denida checked at Nina to be sure she was out of hearing distance. "I saw Medusa at the Headquarters. Like Luci, she wants me by her side with the Darkness- within Hell!"

"But the Dark-"

"Lucifer fears *her*," Denida grabbed Dan's shoulders and shook him. "He fears no one, but he does her. I fear what she may do to Daniel."

"All these soldiers are-"

"She had a force of hundreds of demons after her- she lived! We need them." Denida took a heavy breath.

"Let's go, time's wasting," Nina yelled.

Denida rushed over to Nina, shaking his head. "You're-"

Nina hushed Denida. "Don't start with me! Remember, behind every bitch is a nice girl who got pushed, don't push me."

She has always been headstrong. "So true!" He hugged her and entered the car with her.

They all got into the trucks and drove off to where Michelle, Daniel, and Jack were supposed to be.

***

Jack sighed, looking out towards the Dark Cone, sweat beaded on his forehead. He slapped himself. *Jack, don't even think it!* Jack turned back to the house when he'd calmed himself.

Dana came over to the table, bringing Daniel some food then sat at the table herself.

"You came from your parents love after the war?" Dana poured tea.

"After the war, Dad felt he was sure of what he wanted; he wanted to be married to Mom! He felt it was time." Daniel smiled.

"It was a new start for us all," Dana said, squeezing Daniel's hand.

"...and forgetting the past," Jack smirked from behind. "Not his fault!"

Jack sauntered over to Daniel and Dana. "I know, Lucifer..." He made a face. "-but your Dad found happiness, together with Nina, they had you."

Daniel licked his lips. "I-" He sighed and stared into Jack's eyes. "I'm not from Earth. Dad and Mom are both children on Earth, still. I only-"

"You're just an Underworld child," Medusa interrupted.

Daniel nodded. "*'Just'* an Underworld soul..."

Dana grabbed Daniel's hand and squeezed it tight. "That's enough too!"

Never a human existence, yet he has been through so much. "Maybe we should-"

Medusa held up her hand, stopping Jack in his tracks. She opened her mouth, but a word never came. "Not... possible," she went to look out the window. She spun and transformed into a sparrow and flew off.

"What was that about?" Jack glared out the window but didn't see anything.

"Maybe she wants to let us free," Arthur went over to the table.

Never- maybe I ought to... Jack glanced at Daniel.

A ruckus from outside the Cone caught Jack's attention. He rushed towards the side of the Cone which faced out towards the road. He couldn't see what the noise was, so he continued to the edge of the Cone.

Near the other house, the farmhouse where he had first found Michelle, there were tanks and dozens of military vehicles.

It can't- Jack was startled by the sight of Denida, who came towards the house with the Colonel.

There's so many; this could be the chance for Daniel; I have to free him! He ran back inside the Cone.

A sparrow squeaked at the ground in front of Jack. He stopped and paled as Arthur and Dana came out to check what the noise was. The sparrow transformed into Medusa. She glowered at him with bloody eyes.

"I told you never to betray me!"

Jack turned to speed away.

Medusa pushed her arm forward and a dark cloud grabbed Jack and pinned him up against the door.

Jack shot Darkness filled balls towards her. The balls just deflected.

"You need stronger magic," Medusa smirked. She took her other hand and held it up for him to see. "I told you, you would meet your end the same way as your demon friends!" Her hand had Darkness circling it as she rubbed her fingers, getting ready to tear his heart out.

Jack couldn't fight it, he tried desperately to wrestle loose, but couldn't. *Must be how Edward felt, guess I was always destined to join him...* He faded into darkness.

***

Medusa chuckled. *Serves him right.* She clenched her fist.

Arthur smashed a chair over Medusa's head and she fell to the ground.

Jack dropped as the magic ceased, then grabbed his throat as he coughed, trying to grasp for air.

Medusa spat out blood, she stumbled back to her feet. "Big mistake," she said, red-eyed, and lunged at Arthur stabbing her hand into his guts and ripping out his heart.

She dropped his lifeless body.

Medusa spun around to face Jack, but he was nowhere to be seen.

Where is he? Medusa searched around the house, but there was no sign of him.

"Arthur," Dana screamed and rushed to Arthur side. "Please wake up!" She tried to rub his head, which was now a pale white.

"Oh, shut up!" Medusa rolled her eyes, she flicked her fingers and set Dana on fire. "Now you have a reason to scream." *That never gets old.*

Daniel watched in terror from the door. He ran back inside the house.

"Aw, don't run; I've only started." She followed casually after him, grinning.

Daniel ran panicked from room to room, checking frantically for a place to hide.

Medusa caught up with him in the garden. "Going somewhere?" She gave a devious smile.

"You killed them all," Daniel screamed.

"Only the old couple, they would be dead soon anyway." Medusa chuckled. "Plus Arthur stopped me from killing *Jack*!" Her eyes filled with Darkness.

Daniel held up his hands. "Wait! You need me, you can't get my Dad's ring without me!"

Medusa's eyes glowed as she giggled, then projected next to Daniel and grabbed his throat. "That's Claus, I have something very different in mind."

"What?" Daniel tried to pull loose.

"Bring Denida back to his rightful place- in Hell," she raised her eyebrows with a smirk.

"Medusa, stop!" Denida held up both his arms to calm her. "Let him go, it's over!"

Medusa tightened her grip on Daniel. "Figures. You can enter here, being 'Little Evil.' I should have remembered!" She shook her head. "No matter, it works in my favor."

"As I said-"

"Hush," Medusa said, she tightened her grip on Daniel's throat. "The demons couldn't beat me, you think soldiers can?"

"Little Evil, you called me. Then you should know what I can do, even without the ring…"

Medusa nodded. "I couldn't get how to free you, but Daniel's story made me realize."

"Free?" Denida shrugged.

Medusa caught Denida's eyes, they were locked for a few seconds. Medusa slashed her other hand and Denida flinched, the spear of Darkness impaled Daniel. He screamed in agony, then she plunged her hand into his chest and ripped out his heart.

"Dad… help… me," Daniel stuttered as he tried to reach towards Denida.

Medusa crushed Daniel's heart.

Daniel's arm fell limp next to his impaled body.

Denida transported to Medusa, where he grabbed at her throat, but she transformed into her sparrow. Denida flung his arms in succession upwards to shoot spears of both light and Darkness after her, but it was no avail, as a Dark cloud appeared to protect her, she flew into it and vanished with the cloud.

Denida screamed at the top of his lungs, lighting the sky on fire, but she was already gone. He fell to his knees gasping for air, he turned to his son, Daniel.

"I would have gone to Hell to save you." Denida's eyes were filled with tears, his head fell between his legs, as the Cone which had sealed the house vaporized around it.

"Daniel!" he moaned.

Chapter 35: Searching for a Way

Denida couldn't move, a hole in him as if his own heart had been ripped out sucked all his energy. *God…* Tears ran down his face, the ones from his bad eye burned like acid. *What if I could have avoided this if I just took Hell with her!*

Nina wailed, the soldiers walked around Daniel silently removing the old couple, but none of it mattered.

Denida pulled Daniel into his arms and rocked him like he'd done when Daniel was little. All the times he could have spent with Daniel flashed through his mind. *What is running the country worth if I can't spend time with my son?* Sobs wrenched his body.

A hand on his shoulder made Denida look up to see the Colonel with a face which could have been carved from stone but for the sorrow in his eyes.

"We must find Michelle, she can't get away with this." He ran his fingers over Daniel's eyelids to close his eyes.

"Jesus." Dan choked out. "It really is true." He glanced over to where Nina lay crumpled on the ground sobbing. "Shame we don't have a time machine, like the other Underworld did…"

Hope slammed into Denida like a bullet. *If I had a time machine, I could undo everything that has happened here.*

Denida jumped to his feet and shook Dan. "The time machine!"

Dan shut his eyes. "I'm sorry, I shouldn't-"

"You should," Denida insisted. "Can you?"

"It took them too long- even for us it would take-"

Of course! Denida ran away from the house leaving Dan and the Colonel watching.

When he was far enough away he rubbed his ring and projected to another world, next to a gate and one of Dan's many robots.

The Warlock's aide squeaked and scuttled away from Denida.

"Hello?" The aide trembled in the corner of the room.

I don't have time for this. "The Warlock, where's she?" Denida stepped forward.

The aide frantically pointed. "She's at the Holy Grounds."

Denida rubbed his ring and projected there.

He scanned the surroundings. He saw her talking to the High Sorcerer, he ran over.

The High Sorcerer smiled and greeted him.

The Warlock took him to the side, away from the rest. "Why are you here? Were you not looking for Daniel?"

Denida sighed heavily and ran his hands through his hair and down his face. "Medusa killed... Daniel," he muttered.

The Warlock gasped and moved in to hug Denida.

Denida stepped back with his hands out. "I need your help!"

The Warlock let her arms fall to her sides. "How can I help?"

"The time machine."

The Warlock's face turned from full of concern to a face of no emotions, she shrugged. "Magic can't transform time…"

"Darkness can!"

The Warlock raised her eyebrows. "You would be doing what Lucifer and Medusa want…"

OK… "What if you shield my team while I invent it!"

The Warlock grabbed Denida by the shoulders. She stared into his eyes and it was as if she looked into his soul.

Denida shook himself free.

"You can't," the Warlock yelled. "It's still Dark- you need to let Daniel go…"

"Never," Denida wailed. He sighed. "You really won't help me."

The Warlock shook her head. "It's not possible, haven't you learned it will always turn out badly?"

I don't have time! Denida grunted in response.

"Didn't it take them 30 years or something?"

"What else am I supposed to do? Go to Hell with Medusa? Lucifer?" Denida ground his teeth and paced around in a circle.

The Warlock sighed. "Of course not, but you know you can't build the time machine!"

"Why not? Claus did it in their world!"

The Warlock shook her head. "…And how did that go?"

Denida exhaled heavily. He nodded. "You're right…" The wild hope which brought him here withered and died. He closed his eyes. "Forget I came." He faded back into the air.

***

The Colonel scrolled through his reports about the place where Daniel had been found.

'The magic shielded normal people from seeing the barrier…'

390

The Colonel grunted. *If we had only known, it could've ended differently!* He slammed his papers down on his desk.

All the soldiers on the floor startled and turned to the Colonel. He stood up and shrugged.

"Sorry, I-"

Nina pushed through the soldiers, then slammed the door to his office.

The Colonel twitched at the sound as loud as a gunshot. Nina stood in front of him. He thanked the heavens she didn't have much magic, or he might be ash on the floor.

Susan cowered behind Nina. "I tried to stop her, she insisted."

Nina slammed the Colonel's chest with her fists. "Tell me you found them!"

"Them?"

Nina grabbed the papers from the Colonel's desk and threw them in his face. "Jack and Michelle!"

"Oh!" The Colonel straightened up. "- but we have no-"

Nina raised her hand to hit the Colonel again. "Daniel's... gone! She better not escape as Danyel did."

"No, she won't, she wanted to enrage Denny."

"She got me mad too, do I need to show you how mad?" Nina moved until standing on her toes, her nose almost touched his.

I might still end up as ash.

Someone knocked on the door.

"We found him," a soldier came rushing in with a broad smile. "The Scientist?"

"Show me!" Nina pushed the soldier out of the room, Susan and the Colonel followed.

The soldier led them to a set of monitors which showed the search for Jack's face across all the Underworlds.

"Dynasty?" The Colonel's head swam in confusion.

The soldier nodded. "The cottage actually, deep in the forest of Dynasty, the one Claus was captured at."

The Colonel raised his eyebrows. "How then?"

The soldier nodded and went over to the Colonel. "The video's-"

"I think I get it," Nina interrupted. "Denny has video cameras all over Dynasty. He must have connected them to the server." She touched the image of Jack on the screen. "Jack's there by himself? No Michelle there?"

"As far as we know, ma'am," the soldier nodded.

"Then we can't waste this chance." Nina shook her head.

The Colonel shook his head. *If Michelle's there…*

Nina stomped her foot. "We have a perfect opportunity! He knows where she is…"

The Colonel pinched his nose. "We do need to capture him, so we can get him to talk."

"Exactly, we need to trick Jack into telling us where Michelle is-" Nina poked the Colonel in the chest. "-your military can't do that!"

His stomach sank. "I have a feeling, you've got an idea how!"

"I do," Nina bared her teeth.

At least she will focus her anger on Jack. The Colonel suppressed his sigh of relief.

***

The morning sun stood high in the sky when Jack went out collecting wood to use for the fireplace.

This ought to be enough. Jack stacked it up and carried it back to the cottage, hidden amongst the trees.

He pushed the door open with his foot, then let the wood fall to the floor, next to the fireplace.

"You should be more careful, it's an old house."

Jack spun around, his hands up to defend himself.

Nina, here? Jack checked the windows. *I don't see anyone.*

Nina's giggle sent chills down his spine. "No one's here, relax! It's just me. I noticed you on the camera Denny set up." She pointed to the bookcase.

Jack grunted. "Why are you here?"

"Michelle!" Nina's eyes were stone cold.

Jack gulped and ran his hand through his hair. "Medusa was going to kill me- when I wanted to free Daniel-"

"Lies," Nina yelled.

Jack shook his head and sighed. "The old man saved me."

Nina rolled her eyes and swept his legs. She grabbed his head.

Jack felt his memories flashing by. "See? I remember Claus escaped here after he had been surrounded."

"Just tell me where she is now." Nina clenched her fists.

Jack fought back the tears that wanted to pour from his eyes. "I would tell you if I knew. I'm sorry."

Nina wavered then shook her head.

"He's right, Lady Nina," Gabriel said, startling both Nina and Jack.

Nina glared at Gabriel who stood by the fireplace. "Why are you here?"

"I wanted to see if you were okay…"

"Daniel died, of course not!" Nina shrieked at Gabriel. She took a slow breath. "I don't need your help!" Nina tied a rope around Jack's hands and yanked him out of the cottage, then dragged him through the forest towards Dynasty.

Gabriel appeared surrounded by light in front of her.

She pushed past him.

Gabriel sauntered along beside her as if they were friends out for a stroll.

Nina glanced over at him, where Gabriel returned with a smile. She grunted and increased her pace.

"Medusa never would tell him, even if she didn't try to kill him. Don't do something you'll regret."

Nina stopped, yanked Jack off his feet. "Really? What makes you so sure of that?"

"She would consider him, beneath her..."

Jack's eyes opened wide. "What!"

"She's always felt she's in the right, I remember that since I met her on Earth watching Denny..."

Nina dropped the rope to face Gabriel. "Watching... Denny?"

"Luci wanted someone to watch Denny, protect him from God's attempts on his life..."

Nina held up her hands like she wanted to cover her ears. "Why are you telling me this?"

"Medusa has to be dealt with- only Denny can..."

"You're here to convince me to let Denny take care of this?" Nina clenched her fists as if to hit the Angel. "Never!"

Jack rolled to his feet and ran a little way. Something in him forced him to turn and watch Nina.

Nina quivered glancing between Jack and Gabriel.

Gabriel put his hand on Nina's shoulder. "She's an arch-demon, who Lucifer fears- the Devil himself."

"Still," Nina ground her teeth.

"Do you know how strong Medusa's magic is?"

Jack ran without looking back, he didn't care what Gabriel wanted. But Gabriel was right. *Even Denida might not be able to...* He ducked down behind a fallen tree. He risked a tiny bit of magic to burn off the rope. No one seemed to be following after him.

Have I gotten away from them? He slowly turned 360 degrees to be sure none was there.

A branch cracked, and he ducked behind the log, but a squirrel came scurried into sight. He could hear nothing but birds chirping. *I've got to get out of here!* Jack ran into the trees and away from Dynasty.

Chapter 36: Revenge

Denida stomped through Headquarters paying no attention to the people around him, who jumped out of his way.

The Colonel was meeting with the Commander in the control room when Denida busted in.

"Medusa," Denida demanded.

The Colonel couldn't meet Denida's eyes as he marched over. "I'm sorry, we don't-"

Don't start. "Use the machines, find me her face! She has to be somewhere in the Underworlds!"

The Colonel wrinkled his forehead. "We're trying, but apparently not yet…"

Nina crashed through the door, her expression not much different than Denida's.

Denida opened his arms in an embrace. "Nina, how are you-"

Nina swung her fist and punched Denida in the face. He staggered back.

Denida let the blood drip from his nose as he tried to understand. "Why?"

"You knew," Nina yelled hysterically. "Medusa was watching you. You lowered our son's protection and let Michelle- a demon Lucifer sent to watch you- kill him!"

Denida pinched his nose and opened his mind to Nina, not hiding a single thing. *If I'd only known.*

He took her in his arms and she sobbed into his embrace. He lifted her head and kissed it. "Don't worry, she'll pay!"

"How?" Nina's voice cracked, tears still pouring down her cheeks.

"Lucifer- Medusa double-crossed him, he'll want her just as bad!" Denida took Nina over to the Colonel. "Watch over her."

The Colonel nodded.

Denida appeared in Hell next to the Gate which led back to Underworld 8, where Jack's other self, the *Gatekeeper* was. *Now or never.*

Denida set off towards Lucifer's mansion, where there were two guards again. He let the fire burn in his eyes. The one guard he saw last time froze on the spot, then took a few steps back.

"What's wrong?"

"Little... Evil," the guard muttered and pointed at Denida, he spun around and ran into the mansion.

Denida stalked towards the door. The second guard intercepted him.

Lucifer's magic was stronger around his mansion. *Is this guard part of the extra security?*

The Guard's fists flared. "Hello, Little Evil. I've been waiting."

"Waiting for what?"

"After you were here last time, the Darkness wanted extra precautions..."

"You don't-"

The Guard flung arrows of Dark Spears toward Denida, the guard charged Denida while flinging more spears.

Denida deflected them, still trying to understand what was going on. The guard lunged at Denida with a hand surrounded by Darkness, he jabbed his hand at Denida's stomach.

Denida grabbed hold of the guard's hand, but the guard kept pushing forward, leaving a red mark on Denida's stomach. The pain became agonizing as Denida tried to concentrate enough to stop the guard.

Suddenly the guard grew weak.

The guard slumped to the ground revealing Lucifer standing holding the demon's heart in his hand.

Lucifer and Denida's eyes met.

Denida ground his teeth. "Thank you, but I'm here for Medusa!"

Lucifer tilted his head back towards his mansion, he turned and walked back inside it.

Denida bit his lip as he followed him into Lucifer's chamber.

Lucifer gave broad smile and embraced Denida. "So nice to see you again!"

Denida growled at Lucifer impatiently.

Lucifer nodded. "Medusa, yes…" Lucifer waved his hand to dismiss the other guard. He shook his head while looking at the floor, then dropped onto his throne. "She was the Darkness' choice. It wanted her sent to watch you on Earth."

"You don't like her?" Denida licked his lips.

Lucifer shook his head. "I don't like her; she doesn't like me…"

That sounds intriguing. "Why is that?"

Lucifer stared into Denida's eye. "If you wish, I'll tell you; the Darkness insisted I teach this girl, she was known by her human name, Mara then…"

Lucifer flickered his fingers and a Dark Cloud formed before them, a picture started to form of Lucifer's throne room, just more rustic in its appearance.

***

Two demons led Mara into a room, where Lucifer sat on his throne, the room was so dimly lit it was hard to see anything. The two demons bowed and chanted 'Master' before they both left the room.

Lucifer tilted his head and studied this child who dared to stare at him.

"Are you going to talk?" Mara stomped her foot.

"You've been chosen," Lucifer said. "We see great potential-"

Mara waved her hands dismissively. "Of course you do, I'm destined for greatness! I was born into a-"

Lucifer couldn't help but laugh hysterically. "No one in your family were anyone. True Darkness does not belong to a mere human..." Lucifer tried to control his laughter.

Mara's eyes went black with rage.

"- however, you should use that anger, it'll help you." Lucifer walked over to her, smiled reassuringly and put his hand on her shoulder.

Mara pushed him off. "You know... nothing!" She grinned deviously. "You're only here 'cause *Gabriel* protected his little pansy!"

Lucifer growled as his eyes burned red.

Mara crossed her arms and turned to Lucifer.

"Allow me to show you true Darkness." Lucifer smirked.

"About time." Mara grinned.

***

Denida wrinkled his forehead. "You showed her Darkness? I don't get it."

Lucifer glared at Denida. "I always knew she would be bad news, she still believes the myth of her family to her core- she'll never forgive what I said, or did."

"Did?"

"I took out my anger on her…"

Oh well… Denida shrugged.

"Not oh well! The Darkness got her and believes it can use her!"

"She wants me to take *your* place," Denida smirked.

"But *you* want revenge- we can help each other!" Lucifer smiled broadly.

Denida shook his head. "I'm not making a deal with the Devil!" He stroked his ring and appeared back in Dynasty. He chewed his lip as he sauntered towards Dynasty.

Lucifer appeared in front of him.

Denida sighed. "We're done!"

"Wrong; you owe me! I gave you Claus, remember," Lucifer gloated with his face predatory. "Break it and your soul belongs to me; you won't be able to escape this time, even with *Gabriel's* help!"

Denida stood in silence grinding his teeth. "You know where she is?"

"Always; you can have your vengeance and you can fulfill my wish; *kill* her!"

"We're done then?"

Lucifer nodded with a wicked grin.

Lucifer and Denida appeared in a forest, it opened up just in front of them.

Denida faced Lucifer.

Lucifer pointed his finger towards a cave which stood on the other side of the opening. "She's in there."

Denida studied the cave. He turned back to Lucifer, but the devil had already gone. *He must really dread her…*

Denida clenched his fists. *Medusa, time to meet your end!* Denida went forward towards it, being careful not to make any noise.

The minute Denida stepped into the clearing the world became black.

"Welcome, Denny." A sparrow flew down and Medusa appeared in her demonic form.

The red fire flared in his eyes. *Time to die.*

"Such anger!" Medusa grinned. "Daniel was only a soul of the Underworld. Not a *real* child of yours."

"I traveled into the Gates to save him!" His hand tightened until the bones creaked. "Lucifer was right, you have a twisted sense of reality. You're *bad* news to your core!" He snarled. "Still, I'm guessing you think you can get me to come to Hell with you!"

"You will," Medusa spoke with absolute certainty.

Denida bared his teeth and shook his head.

"How did you even find me?"

"Lucifer…"

"Lucifer led you to me? Interesting… This is where everything began for me, my home!" Medusa lifted her arms and swirled around, turning to Denida with a smile. "I was merely removing what made you want to stay where you don't belong!"

It is my fault, she killed Daniel, Nina was right. Denida clenched his hand so hard it hurt from his ring.

"Never will I return to Hell- for either you- nor Lucifer!" Denida huffed and ran his hand over his face. He shook his head in despair. "Good thing you need to die here!" Denida banged his fist to the ground, making a cone appear around them. "No escape."

"I've no desire to leave!" Medusa spread her arms. "The Darkness is with me, I can *never* lose."

"We'll see about that." Denida shot a Spear of Light towards her.

Medusa lifted her hand to deflect it with dark magic. "You really want to do this?"

"You killed Daniel!" Denida glared at her with hate-filled eyes. "Yea, I'm going to do this, alright!"

"Your loss." Medusa vanished and re-appeared behind Denida with a sword of Darkness, she swung it at Denida.

Denida spun around and grabbed her arm before she could move it forward, he pushed it back towards her. Medusa struggled to keep the blade away.

The Darkness closed around Denida, bringing an evil joy to Medusa's eyes.

"Get ready to join Daniel."

Darkness filled Denida's eyes and the cloud vanished. Medusa projected to the other side of the Cone.

"No way," she muttered. "So the Darkness *is* within you!"

Dark figures appeared in the Darkness and charged at Denida.

Denida sent Spears of Light through them.

One grabbed Denida from behind, stopping his Spears of Light. They surrounded him trying to devour him. Pain shot through him.

Denida squeezed his hand and a flash of brilliant light filled the Cone and vaporized the figures.

Medusa's skin blistered in the light. She formed a Dark Beam but lost control of it and it shattered against the cone. Then Medusa transformed into a sparrow and flew to the top of the cone.

Denida lifted the ring which glowed brightly.

He breathed heavily in then released a scream of rage he hadn't felt since his days in Hell. Fire streamed from his hand struck the sparrow. Medusa screamed in agony, transforming into her true form and fell, still burning, to the ground.

She desperately slapped at the flames.

Denida transported from where he was to right up in her face. He jabbed his hand into her, the fire and anger still in his eyes and burning from his hand.

Medusa snatched at his hand, but she could not reach it through the light covering his arm.

"We can... rule Hell... together," Medusa stammered.

"Never." Denida exploded with light which caused more pain to Medusa than the hand around her heart. "You die now- *for Daniel*." *No not just for Daniel, for the old couple, for her parents, the priest, everyone she's tortured and killed.*

Denida ripped out her heart and it burst into flame. He took one last look at Mara, a child warped by the Darkness into this thing. *Even for you, now you're free.*

"Den... ny," Medusa turned to ashes, the breeze scattered them across the clearing.

The light faded from Denida's eyes. *Never again...* He stroked his ring once more and traveled to Dynasty.

He went upstairs to Daniel's room. Susan stood watch in the hall. "I'll take it from here."

Susan nodded and went downstairs.

Denida ground his teeth and went into the room. Nina lay sobbing, holding a shirt of Daniel's tight in her grip. Denida knelt and kissed her.

Nina glared up with her sorrowful eyes. "Denny?"

Denida nodded and helped her up from the bed. "I've got something to show you!" He took the shirt she clenched on to.

Nina was reluctant to let it go. "But Daniel..."

Denida took her tight into his embrace and transported them to the clearing where he'd fought Medusa. He knelt and scooped up a little ash and poured it into Nina's hand.

"It's over, she's gone forever!" Denny closed her hand around the ash.

Nina screamed and threw the ash at him, then snatched his gun from his waist.

"You let him die! You could have killed her any time."

Denida spread his hands and didn't look away from her.

"If it will heal your heart…"

Nina's hands shook as tears cascaded from her. With a sob she spun and emptied the gun into the trees, then she sighed.

"What do we do now? Daniel's still gone…"

Denida stroked her hair. "We fight through it, together!" He kneeled and kissed her.

Epilogue

On Earth Denida went to see his human form, the same young boy, still playing and sneaking peeks at Nina running giggling with her friend. He sat down looking at himself. *So innocent, just like Daniel.* He sighed.

"Denny? You told me to meet you here?" The Colonel sat beside him.

Denida half smiled. "Medusa watched over me, you know, we never can trust neither Lucifer or God ever again!"

"I'm not sure I understand?" The Colonel wrinkled.

"John," Denida said. "I have realized we need to change. Everyone I know needs to be protected from now on- their human and soul counterparts!" He glanced at his human self. "The task force is to watch my other self at all times; I leave it to you!"

Denida stood then held out a hand pull the Colonel up.

"Going back to see Nina?"

Denida shook his head. "Not yet. I need to make sure we won't see Lucifer again!"

"Free us from him menacing..."

Denida shook his head. "Not just me-" He waved at the world around them. "The Darkness has to stop- Medusa- Lucifer- even God!" He fiddled with his ring and projected into Lucifer's throne room.

Lucifer startled and smiled broadly. "Denny, you're here! Medusa's gone then?"

"She's gone, but I'm not!" Denida lifted his ring covered in light.

"What do you mean by that," Lucifer took a few steps back.

Denida walked closer to Lucifer and let the light go. "We made a deal. I want to make another one!"

"Intriguing," Lucifer gloated. "What about?"

"You'll never touch anyone on Earth or in my Underworld ever again!"

"Aren't you determined! You think you can get me to do that?" Lucifer grinned and paced around the room laughing loudly. "What'll you give me for that?"

"I killed who the Darkness chose," Denida raised his eyebrow. "You know what I can do."

Lucifer winced. "True, that I do." He sat on his throne. "Alright, let's make a deal."

"So?" Denida waited for the Devil to speak.

"Heavani." Pain and despair flashed across Lucifer's face before he covered them with his smile.

"Let's." Denida and Lucifer shook hands.

www.ingramcontent.com/pod-product-compliance
Lightning Source LLC
Chambersburg PA
CBHW070015140726
47908CB00021B/1605